Blackout

THE LIFE AND SORDID TIMES OF BOBBY TRAVIS

Edgar Swamp

ISBN: 0692832440

ISBN 13: 9780692832448

Library of Congress Control Number: 2017900492

Edgar Swamp, Carlsbad, CA

Special thanks to my sister Gina Kelliher for reading an early draft of this novel and giving me valuable feedback. To show my appreciation, I named one of my characters after her, a dubious honor indeed!

This book is dedicated to the loving memory of Ms. Ruby, who unfortunately passed before I finished the book. I love you, honey. RIP, 2006–2016.

Foreword

This book is not autobiographical; all of the characters are figments of my imagination and are in no way meant to be construed as real people (see disclaimer on the previous page). And by way of explanation, I'd like to offer here a brief story that inspired this novel, at least the crux of it anyway, involving a person who blacks out repeatedly hence making anything in life possible at any time.

The year was 1993, and I was working at a bar and grill called Rosie's Water Works in Milwaukee, Wisconsin. I was on my two weeks' notice, planning to leave the city for Raleigh, North Carolina, in pursuit of my musical ambitions. At the time, Raleigh was being touted by *Rolling Stone* magazine as the next Seattle. Um, they were wrong, although Superchunk came from that scene. Super-who? Yeah, that's what I mean. Anyhow, I was nearing the end of my day shift, reading the newspaper and watching the clock, when I noticed a woman who was obviously checking me out. Ah, to be in my twenties again! I don't get that kind of interest from the opposite sex that much anymore, and it's a shame. But I digress. So, I wandered over and started flirting. In all honesty, I'm not that great with the ladies. I get nervous and awkward and sweaty in the presence of pretty women, but in this case, I'd had a few beers, so courage was on my side. One thing led to another, and she asked me if I wanted to get out of there and go somewhere else. Of course I did. She then asked me if I had a car. "Yes!" I nearly cried. I owned a piece of crap that was going to drive me to Raleigh only a few short weeks later. So we left Rosie's, located my wreck, and pulled out of the lot whereupon she began flirting with me to the point of almost steering us into oncoming traffic. Not that I minded her attention; I just didn't want to kill anyone, ourselves included. We successfully arrived at another bar, had more drinks (one of which she spilled on me), and then went back to my place. I'll spare you the lurid details, but she stayed the night. I was a gentleman, I assure you. Everything was consensual. Here is where the idea for *Blackout* arrived:

I awoke first, was gazing longingly at this lovely beauty, wondering how the hell she wound up with me. I'm certainly no Clooney, neither am I Mo Szylak, but this woman was smokin'. The explanation...drum roll please...She woke up, and the look she gave me was one of confusion and fear.

"Where am I?" was her first question, quickly followed by "Who are you?" I'd like to tell you that I was crushed, my feelings hurt, yada, yada, yada, but I was a young man in his twenties. How a woman ended up in my bed (without the use of a date rape drug or handcuffs) did not matter to me. What did was that I got some lovin', and it only cost me a few drinks. However, she was serious. I'd picked her up while she was in a blackout. Apparently, she'd been drinking all day before she entered Rosie's, and then I sauntered over with a grin and a semi-chub. Her drink of choice was whiskey and Diet Coke. After about seven or eight of those, she didn't know much more than her name, probably. I should have known there was a reason she went home with me so easily! Turned out, she told me while I was driving her home, that this was a regular occurrence for her. Because of this, she was trying to quit drinking. I believe I recommended she switch to beer, but that was me back then. Now I would suggest AA. Turned out I'd never find out how she fared; I was gone two weeks later, as planned.

Many years later, when I was thinking of ideas to write about, I recalled that incidence and it got me to thinking: what if someone did that all the time? What kind of life would they have? In a blackout, anything and everything is possible. I took that premise and went way overboard, of course, because that is what fiction does—takes an idea and exaggerates the heck out of it. I'd be a liar if I said I'd never blacked out myself. Regrettably, binge drinking will do that to you from time to time. Yet the idea for this novel was based on a one-night stand I had with a woman I'd probably have never slept with had she not been so inebriated that she got a good look at my ugly mug. Score one for me, right? And wherever

you are Cassandra (not her real name), I hope you got your drinking problem under control. Maybe you took my advice and switched to beer? I
hope so. Peace.

Edgar Swamp, 2017

Chapter One

"Hi, my name is Bobby Travis, and I'm an alcoholic."

It was Monday at three thirty in the afternoon. Bobby Travis stood before the group of nine other people (plus the moderator), wringing his baseball cap in his hands, feeling the same guilt he felt every Monday because, well, he'd gone and screwed up again.

"Hi, Bobby," the group intoned.

"Now, I know this ain't gonna come as a surprise..." he began, and when he looked up, he could see the looks of anticipation in his fellow alcoholics' eyes. These folks, these other rummies who'd finally had enough and wanted to pick themselves up, dust off the grime, and get out of the gutter, the majority of them had earned their sixty, ninety and three hundred and sixty day chips. Bobby? Well, let's just say if there was a chip for making it four days, he would have earned a year-and-half's worth by now. Instead he hadn't earned a single one, yet he kept coming back because by God it would eventually stick. He was certain of that. In the meantime, his stories were of great amusement to the others so that they might live through him vicariously. His exploits were nearly legendary.

"I blacked out again," he confessed, and there was an almost audible sigh among the people gathered. Yes, this was what they had come here for every Monday since Bobby had joined AA—to find out how he had spent his weekend, well, what he (barely) remembered of it anyway. What was most interesting was where he wound up, because that was the part he *did* remember, and it rarely failed to disappoint.

"I finished my last swimming pool around four thirty, and I had my mind set that this was gonna be the week that I wouldn't do it, that I was just gonna go home and call my daughter and find out what time her soccer game was on Saturday. But, like always, I got kinda sidetracked..."

This was Bobby's standard line, one everyone gathered knew by heart. The moderator felt a tug of pity for the desperate man, but also felt an overwhelming curiosity as to what happened next. He couldn't help it; he was a sucker for a train wreck just like everyone else in the room.

Bobby glanced around at the others, briefly caught the eye of the man in the crowd whom he'd been sidetracked by, and knew it was best to leave him out of it. Tommy had recently earned his ninety-day chip, and there was no reason to spill the beans on the poor guy. His family was really counting on him to get his shit together, whether it was for real or not. Mostly not. He and Bobby had been tying one on together on and off over the last several months, respectively. The only difference was that Tommy stuck to the booze and never got caught. Bobby wished he could say the same.

"So I wound up at Hooligans again, right around Happy Hour." At the mention of "Happy Hour," several mouths in the room went dry, hearts started pumping faster than usual. *Oh yeah, a cold beer would taste great right now, maybe paired with a shot of whisky or tequila. Or maybe a martini with extra olives, hold the vermouth, thank you very much. I prefer them neat, bartender, and keep them coming until I am no longer able to sit on this bar stool. And that's an order.*

"After about four or five drafts I began to think maybe I needed a bump..."

This was all in standard order for Bobby's stories. They always started with beer and then segued to drugs. This was also when Tommy departed and some of Bobby's seedier friends oozed out of the woodwork.

"I know a guy who could get me a teener, and so I gave him a call."

The "guy" was actually the Mexican American bartender at Hooligans, and instead of giving him a call, Bobby merely leaned over the bar and asked if Tony was holding. He was. He always was. A handshake followed. One hand had a clump of sweaty, crumpled bills, the other a small bag of crystal meth. This then led to a trip to the bathroom, where a bump was snorted in his favorite nostril, the one without the inflamed tissue a doctor had previously warned him about. Shortly after he returned to the bar and resumed his beer drinking, the speed kicked in. This was always where Bobby's stories got interesting, or where they became the most mysterious. It simply depended upon how much Xanax Bobby took.

"Pretty soon my heart was beating pretty fast, and I started getting nervous…"

Bobby had once overdosed on methamphetamine. He'd collapsed outside his trailer (the dump he lived in before he'd inherited his father's house) following a minor heart attack, and a Hispanic gardener saw him and called nine one one. An ambulance deposited him at Scripps hospital in Encinitas, where he then spent eight hours in the emergency room, getting lectured by everyone who came through his door. From the nurse, who placed his catheter to run a bag of IV fluids, to the technician, who took x-rays of his chest, everyone took a turn. The only one who hadn't given him a speech was the doctor, who made jokes, told him he probably hadn't done any 'permanent damage,' and left the room saying, "See you soon." The rest had all made it their official duty to let him know what a loser he was, and he took it to heart, literally, and ever since, whenever he took the drug, he always felt as if his heart was beating too fast. This never failed to prompt another meeting with the bartender who, besides selling meth, cocaine and various "research chemical" stimulants (synthetic cathinone's, ethylphenidate, and pyrovalerones), also sold standard benzodiazepines (alprazolam, clonazepam, lorazepam, diazepam, etc.) as well as analogues of the compounds, procured via the World Wide Web. Clonazalam, flubromazalam, diclazapam, etizolam, whatever you wanted, Tony the bartender at Hooligans could get it. Bobby preferred Xanax because it worked fast; he chewed three or four .5-mg tablets, and soon his beating heart was no longer an issue. Another two or three of these coupled with more meth and whole lot more alcohol and…surprise! Instant blackout. This, as previously mentioned, was where it always got interesting. Or murky, depending.

"The last thing I remember I was talking to this woman, well, girl really. She couldn't have been more than twenty-one or twenty-two…"

Another thing about Bobby: despite being a chemically dependent screw-up, he was exceptionally good looking (the ravages of drug use making his rugged good looks more...rugged), and had no problem making time with members of the opposite sex, even when his speech was slurred and his vision doubled. Not only were his drunken antics entertaining, but the exploits regarding his sex life were also endlessly amusing/titillating. Presently, the people gathered around unconsciously leaned forward on their chairs a little more, as if this would help them to better hear his story.

"I can't remember what we were talking about," Bobby continued, "maybe my pool cleaning business, because I figure chicks want to know how I make a living..."

Bobby was totally making this up. He actually had no idea what he talked about with the woman. All he knew was that he went to the bar to order a few more beers and the next thing he remembered was waking up on a floor smelling of urine and dirty socks, his pants around his ankles. Propitiously, his butthole didn't hurt, but a quick check revealed his wallet was missing. *Again.* Crap. And not only did this mean that his last fifty bucks in cash was gone, but also a bunch of uncashed checks, payments received from his pool-cleaning clients. There was no way he could tell any of them that he lost their checks; he was simply going to have to go without being paid this week. This also meant he couldn't buy food, pay his electric bill, put gas in his truck...all in lieu of giving money to the mother of his daughter for child support.

Yet this was only the beginning of the story, and the others listened rabidly, although it meant they wouldn't get a chance to share this week. But that didn't matter. None of them, not even Frank (who was constantly getting into fights with strangers after one too many Jack and Cokes) could top him. Nor Sasha (the one-breasted cancer survivor who had accepted Jesus as her personal savior only after she drove her car through a crowded school playground and miraculously missed every single kid while trying to aim *for* them) had anything more than "I caved and drank a whole bottle of peach schnapps while watching *The Voice* over and over on my DVR—I'm better than all those cheesedick bastards!"

And no one cared. They came here, after all, to listen to Bobby. He was like a real-life soap opera. You could just imagine the narrator's voice in your head.

"Will the drug-addled, booze-soaked, sex fiend, gambling addict Bobby Travis find out who took his (fill in the blank: wallet, pants, shoes, kidney) or will he be forced to eat ketchup packets from McDonalds again this week? Tune in and find out!"

His fellow addicts gladly tuned in, and they loved this program. Every week they were all ears, ready for more. They even made bets before he arrived—wagers that involved him siring more children, crashing his truck, or winding up in jail. He rarely disappointed.

But for Bobby it was a nightmare, a vicious cycle that he was doomed to repeat over and over ad nauseum until he at last took the program seriously and accepted his various responsibilities. Luckily for the group, this was unlikely to ever happen. Unfortunately for Bobby, it would seem.

Chapter Two

"Hi, my name is Bobby Travis, and I'm a sex addict."

It was Tuesday, seven-fifteen in the evening. Bobby stood with his baseball cap in his hands, wringing it as he prepared to share with the group. Before arriving, he'd finished work early so he could phone his daughter. Sometimes she took his calls, sometimes she didn't. Today, miraculously, she had, and it went something like this:

"Hey, Gina, it's Daddy…" he began, only to receive icy silence. "Did you win your game?"

"What do you care?" she groused. "You said you were going to be there and you weren't."

"Well, here's the thing, honey," he started, before realizing he had no idea what he was going to tell her. What? That he'd been mugged in a seedy rent-by-the-hour motel room, and from there scored more meth on credit and smoked it all day while watching a *Dog the Bounty Hunter* marathon on TV? Even if that was what really happened (lamentably that wasn't it, not by a long shot) he couldn't tell her that. "I had to work over the weekend," he finished lamely, and could tell by her refusal to comment that she didn't buy it for a second. And not that she should. This had been his usual lie for the last, oh hell, who knew how long? Not him. He generally couldn't remember where he'd been, much less what he was doing. How was he supposed to recall his lies and how often he used them?

Her continued silence confirmed this belief, and he couldn't blame her. He'd lied to her so much that even if he did start telling the truth, she wouldn't believe that either. He was pretty much screwed, just like with every other aspect of his sordid existence.

Although she was upset, and it was a facet of his life he considered deplorable, Bobby was a perpetual optimist. She'd come around, would forgive him eventually. She'd hold a grudge, but his endearing personality would ultimately win her over. This held true for every other stupid thing he did. Because, no matter what debauched action he perpetrated, he could always figure out a way to win people over, even if they were pissed off at him. *Especially* if they were pissed off at him. It was a gift he had.

As an optimist, he could always look at the glass as half-full. Making lemonade, he called it, as in: when life hands you lemons…He'd mutter this sometimes in the throes of his drunken misery, and his drinking or drug buddies would think he meant he'd just soiled himself.

"Bobby's makin' lemonade again!" one of them would cry merrily, and maybe some other goofball would add: "Make us some fudge while yer at it, Bobby!"

"Hi, Bobby," the group intoned.

"Now, I know this ain't gonna come as a surprise…"

Everyone leaned forward on their chairs, especially Melissa, a woman whom he'd been sleeping with on and off since his first meeting over a year ago. Another member of the group was especially curious as well, a guy named Lance whom Bobby (thankfully during a blackout) had also had a tryst with, fortuitously only one. Bobby had no memory of it (honestly, not even any bits and pieces), but he didn't doubt Lance's sincerity about the fact that it happened. Ever since their liaison, Lance had been so nice, opening doors for him, bringing him coffee from Starbucks. If Bobby were gay, Lance would probably make a nice wife. At least, he guessed Lance was the woman in the situation. For all he knew it could have been the other way around, and he wasn't about to ask. He was afraid to.

Say, when we…you know…um, did it, um…who was on the receiving end?

Bobby did not want to go there now, nor did he hope to go there ever again. And not because he was homophobic, it was simply another problem he didn't need. He was truly impressed with Lance's affection toward him, nevertheless he didn't desire to rekindle the romance any time within the next century.

Yet to say he was surprised that it happened? No, nothing surprised him; not anymore. The fact that he blacked out on a regular basis made anything in his life possible. After all, it was how he had a daughter. Hell, he didn't even remember sleeping with the girl's mother, but it was a fact, made reality by the physical presence of the girl in this world, and not only her, but her monetary needs, which Bobby did his best to keep up with. If he didn't his daughter's mother (Carolyn) threatened him that she'd take him to court and have his wages garnished, as well as promised him that he'd never see Gina again. But the truth was she was such a lush that she actually liked the fact that Bobby wanted to take custody of her because it got the kid off her hands for a couple of days every other week or so. It allowed Carolyn to spend time indulging in her hobbies, such as hard drinking and chain smoking, but could also include boning a twerp named Barry, whom she'd married shortly after Gina had been born.

Another item of special note regarding his SA meeting presence: Bobby wasn't truly a "sex addict" in the general terms of what is construed for someone to deserve such a nefarious title. He did have a lot of sex, mostly one night stands with women he picked up at Hooligans, but none of it was deviant (child porn, barnyard animals, unusual devices, feces, urine, etc.), and it wasn't done because he hated women, or required it to boost his self-esteem. He just liked having sex, but he was very bad at relationships because he could never remember anything, like the woman's name, phone number, etc. This never went over very well. The reason for his presence at this group was court mandated, following an incident in which he was deemed abnormal. He knew it wasn't true, but he had to do what the court said or face other consequences, like not being able to see his daughter. Hence, his continued attendance.

At the moment, Bobby told his SA group the story about being at Hooligans, and how he met the young woman, blacked out, and then woke up with his pants around his ankles and his wallet gone. The group listened intently, their ears pricking up when he got to the part about the man in the black shawl and executioner's hood.

"This guy," Bobby said, gulping so ferociously his Adam's apple bobbed up and down comically, "he was scary as hell. He grabbed me by my hair and hauled me to my feet. That's when I knew I was in real trouble." He paused for a moment, catching his breath. He looked around him at the curious faces, their eyebrows arched expectantly.

"Do go on," the moderator begged.

"Well, this guy dragged me down a flight of stairs into a filthy room, and there was a chick there, probably the girl I picked up at the bar. She was wearing one of them, what do ya call it? Some super tight leather outfit complete with a mask—"

"A full-body, leather bondage suit," Melissa supplied casually, owing to the fact that she was in the know about anything and everything that was sexually aberrant. She was familiar with bondage, torture, sado-masochism, water sports, anal play, girl on girl, and assorted other odds and (heh-heh) ends, but she'd never revealed this to Bobby because she didn't want to scare him off. He was simply so innocent in myriad ways sexually. Even though he was such a chemically dependent screwball, he still held on to old-fashioned ideas about sex, as demonstrated by his affair with her. He was so polite, so caring. Sometimes she wished he would just shut up and slap her in the goddamn face...

"Yeah, one of those. Like Forrest Gump wore in *Pulp Fiction*."

At this ostensibly casual reference, everyone laughed.

"That was the gimp," Albert, the chronic masturbator said, and Bobby nodded.

"Yeah, right, I mean him. Anyway, they made me strip down to nothing and then they chained me to this rack...a torture rack, they called it..."

Everyone in the room was practically holding their breath. This was good, really good. How Bobby managed to find himself in these situations every week was anyone's best guess; nonetheless, they were entertaining as hell. His fellow sex addicts couldn't help but be jealous of him and his exploits, if only for the material they could be sharing at the meetings.

"What happened next?" they pleaded.

"Well, the lady in the suit—"

"The dominatrix," Melissa again explained, and Bobby nodded.

"Yeah, her. She told me I was a worthless piece of crap and that I should take my punishment like a man or else the executioner guy would have his way with me. And, hell, I wasn't sure if he already had!"

Except for Lance, nobody would have a story this exciting. Melissa could talk about having sex with a stranger she met at a peepshow booth in a sex shop downtown, and Albert could lay out a lurid tale involving his dick, his hand, and a bottle of lotion while standing buck naked in his living room window as school kids passed by, but none of them could top one of Bobby's stories, not now, probably not ever. If Lance was given the chance (and this week he wasn't, simply because Bobby's story went on for so long), he would have told a loopy tale that involved five young men, a lot of whipped topping, and enough semen to impregnate a sorority house, regrettably gone to waste up the young men's anuses or down their throats. Lance never spared any details.

"The next thing I knew, she was flogging me with this whip that had a bunch of leather tassels on it—"

"A cat-o'-nine tails," Melissa said.

"Yeah! One of those. And it hurt like a mother! And then the executioner guy set up a camera, and he was filming everything while he took off his robe—"

"Was he hung?" Lance asked, and Bobby cast a quick glance in his direction before looking away, blushing slightly.

"Um, yeah, I guess, and it was rock hard and all red, and he started pinching his own nipples, and then he spit into his hand and started, um, well, he began to—"

"Beat his meat!" Albert cried merrily, tugging at his trousers as if they had suddenly become too tight.

"Uh-huh. And then she lit a candle, and she let the wax drip onto my nipples and balls, and I was freaking out, thinking, 'How do I get the hell out of here?' And then it came to me, what I needed to do if I wanted to get out of this alive…"

He had the crowd eating out of his hands, pretty much had as soon as he said his name and told them he was a sex addict, but what he was about to say sealed the deal on his notoriety, absolutely sold the bill of sale that he was the undisputed master and champion of sex addicts all over the world…at least this week, in this group.

"Have you guys ever heard of felching?"

Multiple gasps where loudly emitted around the room, but not out of astonishment; it was more like an expulsion of pent-up sexual energy.

"It's when a man places his mouth over the anus of a sex partner and sucks vigorously."

"Let Bobby tell the damn story!" the moderator reprimanded Melissa, and she nodded sheepishly.

"OK," she cheeped.

And as he continued his shocking tale, the room remained silent, save for the occasional outcry of "holy balls!" or "oh my!"

Melissa and Lance glanced at him with hungry looks, both of them wanting something from him that only one of them was likely to get. And sure enough, when the meeting was over, one of them got their wish.

◆ ◆ ◆

Bobby and Melissa lay in the bed of Bobby's pickup truck, a dilapidated piece of crap that was falling apart one bolt and two screws at a time. It was a 2002 Toyota Tacoma that had seen better days back in 2003, and it was probably a sure bet that if he hit a big enough pothole, the front end would become misaligned or the engine would fall out. It was the vehicle he used for his pool cleaning business, so it stank of chlorine and various other pool cleaning chemicals. Every Tuesday, after work, Bobby took everything out and replaced it with a worn and soiled mattress just in case Melissa wanted to hook up. He was certain no self-respecting woman would accept such a lousy arrangement, but you can never say "never" with a sex addict. Hell, they'd screw just about anywhere; it didn't have to be fancy. And it seemed as if Melissa had very little self-respect; he believed it was safe to say that she had close to none when it came to screwing, but he could be wrong.

For Bobby, the afterglow of sex was always marred by the fact that they had just left a meeting. This never failed to inspire guilt in him. Bobby felt remorseful after every destructive thing he did, more than ever since his daughter had turned ten, which was five years ago. Basically, what made him feel so low was her dawning awareness of the fact that he was a lying, whoring, drug addict, alcoholic piece of garbage. Once the cork was out of the bottle, there was no turning back. She knew him for what he was. It was akin to a child finding out there was no Santa Claus or Easter Bunny or Tooth Fairy, except in this case it was a whole lot worse because this was her father, a man she had once looked up to, no matter how many birthdays he forgot, or how cheap and plain and downright awful some of his presents at Christmas were.

What compounded his guilt regarding her birthday or Christmas gifts was the fact that they were so crappy because he was forever losing what little money he had while blacked out, or spending it on the agents that caused the blackouts. He thoughtlessly bought her presents at convenience marts where, for a while back in 2009 and 2010, you could buy a product called "bath salts," a synthetic drug that contained MDPV (methylenedioxypyrovalerone), a chemical invented in the '60s as a weight-loss remedy, or to relieve symptoms of narcolepsy, but was later abandoned because of its addictive potential and overly euphoric high. It was rediscovered by basement chemists in the 2000s, and was soon for sale at smoke shops and convenience marts, as well as over the Internet (where Tony the bartender procured some of his more dubious wares). Bobby would be standing at the counter, clutching the cheap teddy bear and even cheaper card in his sweaty, chlorine stained hands, when he'd spy the little foil packages. Soon the gift was just a card, the teddy bear stowed next to the gum and the mints as he purchased the drug instead, doing a bump after he got in the car, his heart revving along with the motor, Bobby doing his best to drive as slowly and cautiously as one could while tweaked out on speed. Once he arrived he put a pinch in his "oil burner" (meth pipe) and smoked before going in. That was back in the days when his drug and alcohol use had been twenty-four seven. He used to black out maybe two to three times a week. Thankfully he now only blacked out on the weekends, and for the most part just once. Sometimes he went for two though; it all depended on where he ended up and if he had any money left after the first go around. All that being said, he still managed to save enough money to give to Carolyn for child support; he simply wasn't convinced she was spending it on Gina. Whenever he'd go to pick her up to take her to the park or the dollar matinee, he'd notice some new piece of clothing or jewelry ornamenting Carolyn's svelte frame or bony fingers and wrists. Meanwhile Gina was wearing the same clothes from last year, the pants riding high up the ankles, the shirtsleeves looking ¾ lengths. Often times she also needed a bath, and when she was little (and he was in the proper state of mind i.e. sober) he'd bathe her, and when she got older he'd wait while she took a shower and then they would go out. The poor kid had been vain from an awfully early age; she didn't like walking around stinking any more than he did.

Why he felt guilty about screwing Melissa after the SA meetings was simplicity in itself: if his daughter ever found out, he wondered how he would explain it. Not that he couldn't come up with something plausible; he mostly didn't want to lie…well, lie more than he already had. He hoped it would never come to that.

"That was some story you told tonight," Melissa said, running a hand through Bobby's hair while she smoked a cigarette with the other. At least that was one vice Bobby couldn't own up to. He'd never been an addicted tobacco smoker, had only dabbled in it when he was a kid. As far as he was concerned, if he was going to smoke something, it had better get him high. "I think you finally topped yourself."

"You know I don't go out looking for things like that baby," he said, turning his head toward her and gazing at her amenably. Not that it mattered. As far as Bobby knew, she'd lay *anybody* if they appeared to be a willing candidate. It wouldn't matter if the likely beau wore pants with the pockets cut out with his dick hanging ten in the breeze, she'd go home (or somewhere) with him.

"Yes, Bobby, I know," she sighed, and for a minute this really pissed him off, that she could be so hypocritical, but then it passed. Another good thing about Bobby was that he didn't have much of a temper; it was for this reason that the majority of his crimes were misdemeanors. He never committed any violent acts, and when he was arrested, he always went peacefully. This was a good thing too. Bobby had a cousin who was an Escondido cop. If Bobby were a violent drug addict or drunk-driving loser, he'd probably have to disown him. And that would be a shame because they had been friends since they were little kids. Bobby even babysat for him when he was a toddler, being five years his senior. Why anyone trusted seven-year-old Bobby to sit for his two-year-old cousin is beyond a doubt a mystery; nonetheless, it happened. Suffice to say young Bobby only almost burned the house down *once*, and for that he got a serious talking to.

In point of fact, his cousin had been the one to arrest him on several occasions, and even though the arrests spurred heated exchanges between the two, Bobby was always glad it was Teddy. At least that way Bobby got preferential treatment. Some of the other guys on the force weren't so cool, owing to the fact that Bobby was a general nuisance they could do without. Now, Bobby had only been arrested once for drunk driving, and under California law he had done his time (six months in the county jail plus a six-month license suspension) and paid a hefty fine. Fortunately, no matter how wasted he was, he knew not to get behind the wheel of a car again while in a blackout. The time he got caught, he was lucky that no one had gotten hurt (as well as all the other times when he *didn't* get caught). A CHP pulled him over for weaving back and forth and a Breathalyzer revealed he was more than two sheets to the wind. He was promptly arrested, and even though he was guilty as charged, his cousin stood by him.

"Everybody makes mistakes," Teddy told his fellow officers. To Bobby he said, "You do that again and I'll let the drunks in the bullpen sodomize you."

And he hadn't ever done it again, yet certain members of California's finest still took it upon themselves to bash his head against the doorframe of the car when they put him in the backseat, muttering "sorry" under their breath as if they hadn't meant to do it. Even in a stupor Bobby always knew they'd done it deliberately. In a blackout, however, he simply came to with a large goose egg on his forehead and had to make the conclusion for himself. It wasn't hard to do. A+B=C. Drunken insubordination + getting busted= getting your head bashed against the doorframe of a police car. It wasn't freakin' rocket science.

"Did *you* have sex with a stranger this week?" Bobby asked, offering a wry smile. Every other week she had a story about some guy she met on line at the grocery store, some young kid in a fast car in the lane next to hers, or some chick (she was bisexual) she met at the "gym," a euphemism he took to mean the titty bar by the airport.

She turned her head away for a moment and dragged silently on her cigarette. After a minute or so she turned back, looked at him thoughtfully.

"Would it matter if I did?" she said softly. "Would you stop screwing me?"

Bobby gave it about two seconds thought before replying "No." After all, she was beautiful, in a wrecked, disaster movie kind of way. She looked like she could play the leading lady in a feature film, if the movie was about a woman down on her luck, or a drug-addled prostitute (not that she took drugs; in fact, to the best of Bobby's knowledge she didn't). What Bobby found sexy about her was that her dress always looked wrinkled (from taking it off and tossing it carelessly on the ground when she boned a stranger), her nylons always had runs in them, and her makeup was constantly smeared. She worked as a cashier at a Goodwill store on El Norte, so she took home any merchandise she could, most of it hidden in her overlarge purse, buried under packs of Virginia Slims, maxi pads, and her battered and worn diaphragm, a gadget that had seen a lot of use it in its day. It was because of her occupation that she was forever wearing a dress that had gone out of style two decades ago, accompanied by a pair of high-heeled pumps that made her five six stature five nine. He was always surprised at how short she was once she kicked them off. Her physique and occupation aside, she was smart as hell; this was what really turned Bobby on. She could have been anything she wanted, and yet she seemed content with her lot in life. He supposed that was the biggest thing they had in common, the fact that they could both do better yet had chosen to wallow in the mire of mediocrity. It was safe, maybe, to not hold yourself to too high of expectations. That way you rarely let yourself down.

"Will this ever get old, I wonder?" she mused aloud, and Bobby found himself asking the same question, but its application revolved around a lot more than having sex with Melissa in the back of his pickup truck. It held deeper meaning to him, beyond their relationship.

Will I ever get sick of blacking out and decide I need to change my life for good?

The thought wasn't a new one; it was the driving force behind his decision to go to the meetings. Well, that and his daughter.

"Not with you baby," he answered after a few moments of silence, said in a voice fairly reeking with sincerity. He kissed her softly on the mouth, tenderly, and this made her smile.

"Bobby the hopeless romantic," she joked, and he had to smile with her. That's not what the mother of his child would say, but then again she never had anything kind to say about him. When she spoke of him, it was always in adjectives: frickin' lazy, frickin' stupid, frickin' jag-off, and so on.

"You bring it out of me."

"Oh, I bring something out of you, all right," she breathed, and it was with these words that he felt himself stirring. She felt it too and pressed closer against him. They made love again, this time slower, the two of them clutching one another desperately, as if the act could stave off the demons that swirled in their heads like acrid smoke. When they were finished, they lay there silently while Melissa smoked another cigarette and Bobby thought about his missing wallet. Because of his tendency to lose it, he'd taken to keeping important things like his Social Security card, essential phone numbers, and his one, nearly maxed out credit card at home in his chest of drawers. He'd had that card canceled and replaced more times than he could count on two hands.

She stubbed out her cigarette and Bobby reached for her, caressing her shoulders gently. It was a gesture he'd taken to doing over the last couple of weeks. He actually thought he might be falling for her, even though they both had sex with other people on a regular basis. She'd noticed this display of affection, and for the most part had ignored it, but tonight was different. She gave him a half smile, something more than lust smoldering in her gaze.

"Are you trying to tell me something?"

"I don't know," he answered honestly, and he could swear he saw her flinch slightly, but it passed quickly and was gone. It was like the tremor that passed through her if he ever mentioned her father, a man who had done unspeakable things to her when she was a child. These things were not a secret; she'd shared them with the group in past sessions. No one knew if she did this to shock everyone, or if she simply couldn't afford a therapist and just wanted to air them out. Whatever the case, no one could walk away (not even her fellow sex addicts) without feeling touched, perhaps a little sickened. And that was something, considering that the people who populated sex addict groups tended to wind up in the emergency room after putting absurd things up their butts, and screwed anyone who smiled politely at them at the car wash.

"You don't know," she mimicked. "So Bobby, what do you know?"

"I know that you're pretty in this light," he said before he could stop himself, and again the quick flicker of pain in her eyes and it was gone.

"In this light?"

"That came out wrong," he said weakly, and she smiled.

"Everything you say comes out wrong Bobby. Maybe that's why I like you."

He smiled, a slight flush on his cheeks. "I like you too."

"You trying to go for three?"

"Just being honest."

"Honesty will get you everywhere," she whispered, and they went for three.

Chapter Three

"Hi, my name is Bobby Travis, and I'm a gambling addict."

It was eleven thirty on a Wednesday morning. Light trickled through a dusty window pane from the far corner of the room in the basement of St. Elmo's Methodist church. Bobby was wearing the same clothes from the night before because he'd skipped doing his laundry after staying out too late with Melissa. He was also unshowered and un-shaved, and he knew this was going to haunt him all day on the job whenever he had to deal with a client. Most of them didn't care, but some did. Like older women in nice neighborhoods who didn't appre-ciate it when disheveled people showed up at their house to perform some service akin to unclogging a toilet, as if these casual workmen should be wearing a tux and tails.

Yet in the fluorescent light of the Methodist church, he looked more the part of the seedy gambler he was. Perhaps this was to his advantage, if only for the tale he was about to impart.

"Hi, Bobby," the group intoned.

"Um, I know this ain't gonna come as a surprise…" he began, and everyone leaned forward on their chairs to better hear how much money Bobby lost this week, and what other trouble he got himself into. It was amazing how stupid Bobby could be when he really set his mind to it. Especially when he was wasted, which was every weekend. "But not only did I bet on the Milwaukee Brewers to sweep the Padres at home—"

"Freakin' sucker bet!" Clay exclaimed. Clay was a small, mousy fellow with a receding hairline and a large, red, bulbous nose. He was an easy mark for Texas Hold 'Em, or any other game of chance involving cards, but poker was his specialty, even though he couldn't play it for sour ap-ples. "What were the odds?"

"Ten to one," Bobby said quietly, and everyone in the room (including the moderator) shook their heads dejectedly.

"Wow, that's just plain stupid," another gambler muttered, even though he'd just lost five hundred dollars to his brother-in-law betting who could hold their breath underwater the longest. Much to his chagrin his brother-in-law was a lifeguard and he, in turn, was a heavy smoker. Why he took the bet he'd never know, except that he wanted to shut the smug SOB up. Mission failed.

"How much did you lose Bobby?" the moderator asked.

"Well, plus the money I lost because my wallet was stolen, about sixteen hundred dollars. But that isn't even the worst part…"

Sighs all around. Someone let out a low whistle.

"Jesus," Larry lamented. "You just never know when to quit."

Not that Larry could talk. If he got a turn to share (and this week he wouldn't, thanks to Bobby's lengthy tale), they'd find out he was taken to the cleaners by a bunch of old ladies at a bingo hall playing, of course, bingo.

"I really don't," Bobby agreed.

Bobby had been coming to St. Elmo's Methodist Church for the last year and a half, the same timeline as his other assemblies. His presence, like the other meetings he attended (except for the sex addicts meeting), was for his daughter's sake. If he couldn't do this for himself, he had to do it for someone. Hell, for all he knew he was one drink/drug binge/wager away from death on any given day. Best to nip it in the bud before it got too out of hand, as if it wasn't already.

"So what all did you get yourself into this weekend, Bobby?" the moderator asked, not because his heart overflowed with the milk of human compassion, but because he, like everyone else in the room, was entertained by Bobby's stories. All things considered, Bobby was a natural born storyteller, and the content of his tales never failed to amuse. Sometimes Bobby's delivery was rife with contrary statements, as well as confusing elements that the listeners struggled to make sense of, but one could certainly extol his adeptness at build up, and his ability to drop subtle hints until the all-important plot reveal. There were also engaging key words that peppered his adventures, such as: "underage girl," "sucker bet," "methamphetamine," "cocaine," "Xanax," "unprotected sex," "soiled underwear," "casino guards ejecting him from the premise," "mugged," "blackout," "cops," "arrested," "jail," etc. etc. etc. There was never a dull moment when Bobby was at the helm, sharing his latest tomfoolery. Sometimes the others made up stories simply to compete. If they'd lost five hundred dollars, they'd say it was two thousand. Some would claim that they bet on the Chicago Bears to beat the Green Bay Packers by two scores at Lambeau Field in December; others said they bet on the San Diego Chargers to trounce the New England Patriots at Foxborough and beat the spread...foolish bets all.

On cue Bobby's tale unfolded before them, and it was just what everyone needed, just what the black jack dealer dealt, no less.

"What's felching?" Clay asked. He was, after all, a gambler, not a sex addict. He hadn't had sex since Bill Clinton admitted he'd been fellated in the Oval Office while security personal guarded the door, keeping an eye out for Hilary. "Is that some kinda bondage term?"

"I think he's talking about making arrows with turkey feathers," someone said.

"That's fletching," another said.

"I think it means—"

"Let Bobby tell it!" the moderator interjected, silencing the room.

"I'm almost embarrassed to admit this," Bobby said, flushing slightly (as Melissa was well aware, Bobby was somewhat shy when it came to talking about matters of a sexual nature, although he indulged in it so much), "but it's a term to describe when a person puts their mouth on another person's um, well, they...um, they uh, they, uh, put their mouth..."

"It's when someone eats out someone else's ass," a fellow attendee and acquaintance of Bobby's named Terry finished for him, and the moderator frowned. "Sorry, I couldn't just leave him hanging there." Terry should have kept his head down, maybe try to blend in with the scenery, but he couldn't help it, he was a bigmouth. Truth was he trolled the GA groups, looking for fresh blood. He wasn't a gambling addict; he was a bookie. He got all the action he could handle from these rubes and then some. He'd been Bobby's bookie since either of them could remember, and had followed Bobby to the meetings to drum up a few more suckers and to keep an eye on Bobby. The last thing he wanted was for him to go straight, not with how much money he made off of him.

"It's not that," the moderator said, looking openly at Bobby. "Did the man rape you?"

"Um…no…"

"Then it wouldn't have been felching."

"Huh?"

"Felching is the act of sucking out one's ejaculate from another's rectum after having anal sex."

"For Christ's sake!" a woman cried, echoed by several others, and for a moment the room was in pandemonium, everyone expressing, to varying degrees, their utter disgust. Except for Clay. He was eerily silent.

"Quiet!" the moderator shouted. "Everybody be quiet!"

At length, everyone settled down, all eyes upon Bobby fairly suspicious now.

"There something you want to tell us Bobby?" Terry said, narrowing his eyes.

"Yes Bobby," a woman named Karen (who'd been subtly hitting on him for the last three months) echoed. *No wonder he's been turning me down!* "Is there something else you'd like to share?"

"No one ever put their, um…thing in my, uh…you know…" Bobby stuttered over the last part. He was an honest man by nature (only lying when he had to, to save his own skin), and quite truthfully he wasn't sure if that was correct or not after his experience with Lance. He very well might have had someone's thing in his yoo-hoo chute and he didn't even *know* it. Not wanting to fib, he finished: "That dude didn't do anything to me."

"Then what happened?" Terry demanded.

"Yes," said Karen. "What exactly *did* happen?"

Bobby looked around at his audience; saw the confusion and hostility in their eyes. He knew that when he explained they would fully understand, would actually appreciate his story.

"I asked the guy in the executioner's hood if he was a betting man," Bobby said, and he was correct in assuming that he clipped the red wire instead of the green; the bomb had been partially defused. After a moment of silence, the moderator queried:

"Was he?"

"Oh yeah," Bobby said, nodding.

"What could you possibly bet them?" Terry wanted to know.

"I bet them that I could get out of the straps."

"What were the terms of the wager?" Clay asked.

"The terms were if I got free, they had to let me go."

"What did they say?"

"They accepted the bet."

"So," Terry said, his eyes still betraying his skepticisms regarding Bobby's supposed heterosexuality, "tell us what happened."

◆ ◆ ◆

"That's it?" Terry said when Bobby finished, and the other nodded. For a moment Bobby couldn't tell if he was pleased or let down, not that it mattered all that much which it was. Terry was, of course, the guy who arranged his bet on the Brewers. He placed bets for a lot of them, including the moderator, who had an unhealthy fixation with Mexican wrestlers. In all actuality, everyone in the room should have hated Terry because he didn't have a gambling problem himself and was furthering their own addiction, but they let it slide. They needed him.

The moderator glanced at his watch, saw that their time was almost up for the week. Once again Bobby told such a whopper of a tale that no one else got a chance to share. Not that anyone cared. Now they'd have something to talk about with their spouses instead of their own lousy problems for a change, and that was just the way they liked it.

◆ ◆ ◆

"That was a messed-up story you told in there." Terry was picking at his fruit salad, a clump of decidedly unhealthy-looking fruit stuck together with whipped cream that was neither whipped nor cream. Bobby looked at it with a mixture of disgust and awe. He had ordered the safest thing on the menu at the greasy spoon: cheeseburger and french fries. Even though the burger was probably a mix of beef from seven different countries (half of which may or may not have been on steroids, antibiotics and contained traces of feces and mad cow disease) and the french fries were deep-fried in oil as old as Methuselah, containing enough trans fat to kill every healthy cell in his body, it was still the safest bet. The soup de jour looked like dirty dishwater and the "special" looked like a conglomeration of the week's previous specials, after the cook jerked off on it. Not a great place for eating quality food, but an excellent location for Terry to do business because the grub was so cheap. The restaurant had a sign that boasted "Lousy food, terrible service." The dump lived up to its claim.

"You saying I'm full of shit?"

"Oh no, I believe your story," Terry said, turning his chair to face away from the windows. He wasn't a fan of natural light, as his pale countenance attested. "You can't make up stuff like that." He took a bite of his fruit salad then frowned. Apparently, it tasted as good as it looked. "So what kind of action you looking for this week?"

"What looks good to you?" Bobby asked, and this was just the answer Terry was looking for. Now, Terry wasn't a bad man, and he actually liked Bobby a lot. In fact, they were friends. That said, he also didn't mind that Bobby lost as much as he did. For Terry, this meant the money kept rolling in. If Bobby won (which Terry allowed him from time to time, just enough to keep him betting) he had to pay him, and that money (not all, but some) came out of Terry's pocket. He protected himself against any major windfalls, but winners were bad for business. Just ask a Las Vegas craps dealer. If the chips weren't so stacked against the bettors, so to speak, the casinos would go out of business. That's why it's called "gambling." You were taking the chance that you might lose your money. Winners weren't the norm; they were the exception.

In light of this, when Bobby asked what he should bet on, it was in Terry's best interest to suggest something that had a slim chance (like 100–1 odds) of winning. To keep him coming back, Terry suggested a tried and true winner every five or six failed bets. It gave a gambling addict exactly what they needed: hope. One win every four to six weeks gave the problem gambler the confidence to keep trying, which was win/win for bookies everywhere.

Occasionally Bobby came up with his own bets. These were always sure-fire busts, as Bobby had about as much sense for gambling as he did for picking women. Like, take the horses for example. Every summer the Del Mar Racetrack opened in July for two months, right after the County Fair had passed through and right before the start of the "fests" (craft beer fest, Indian summer fest, wine tasting fest, etc.), and for those two months Bobby lost his ass daily not only on the horses but his whimsical baseball bets as well. Every now and then, though, Bobby got lucky at the track and he'd win big, to the tune of a couple G's. When he did it made him feel as if he was invulnerable, like he had a system. Terry knew it for what it was, though; a fluke and nothing more. He ought to know; it was his business to know. But that was all in the past since he started going to the meetings, since he decided he wanted to change his life. Now it was strictly baseball wagers. Not that it mattered to Terry; with the track no longer taking Bobby's money, Terry got all the spoils. And then he could take that money to the track and make himself a little dough. It was how the world went 'round.

"The Cubs are due for a win any day now," Terry suggested cautiously, wondering how much Bobby followed the team, and to his delight the other accepted the proposition without hesitation.

"Put me down for two hundred," Bobby said, stuffing the last of the cheeseburger in his mouth and chewing noisily.

Terry smiled. He wasn't foolish enough to be more specific with the bet, like, two hundred to win, or two hundred if he beat the spread. The vaguer he was, the more likely Bobby was to lose. He pulled out a battered notebook from his back pocket.

"Two hundred it is," he said, writing it down, then casually held out his hand. Bobby saw this, and colored slightly.

"I'm good for it. I lost all my money last weekend, but it's been a busy week. I can pay you on Friday."

Terry played as if this put him out, but only for a couple of seconds before he grinned, shrugged, and said OK. Hell, he knew Bobby was good for it. He always was, except for when he lost really big, and to avoid that Terry never took any bets from Bobby that he knew the other couldn't repay. If Bobby wanted to make a big time wager, he needed to take his business elsewhere, something Bobby had done from time to time. There were loan sharks and mob-connected bookies that could handle any size stake. Bobby had been in trouble with some of these guys before, and was lucky he never got in too far over his head. Those bastards didn't play around. If you lost and you couldn't pay, they took it out of your ass and then some. Terry shivered just thinking about the tactics they resorted to, none of them pretty. They involved torture and broken bones, sometimes beatings that necessitated facial reconstructive surgery. That was way out of Terry's league. He liked to keep it small-time.

Terry continued to pick at his fruit salad as Bobby ate the last of his fries and sipped his milkshake. Did he ever feel bad that he took Bobby's crummy bets? Maybe, in passing, but he never lost sleep over it. Somebody had to take Bobby's money, and if Terry didn't, somebody else would. At least Bobby was losing it to a friend. And to make up for it, he sometimes paid for meals. As a matter of fact...

"Hey man," Terry said nonchalantly, pulling out a roll (not his real one, but the thinner one that he showed to all of his "clients") "Since you're a little light, lunch is on me."

"Aw, you don't have to do that," Bobby said, but inside he'd been hoping the other would offer. He currently didn't have two nickels to rub together, and he knew the pattern. He wasn't, like, totally stupid. Every month or so (sometimes as much as six weeks) Terry would feel guilty about taking all of Bobby's hard-earned money and would offer to buy lunch. Shortly thereafter (as if the act of good karma somehow aligned the stars) Bobby would win a bet. It was a pattern that repeated itself over and over, much to Bobby's delight. And not for a second did he ever think it was anything else but "luck."

"Thanks buddy, I owe you."

"Yes you do," Terry replied, knowing it worked in more ways than one. "Yes indeed you do."

Chapter Four

"Hi, my name is Bobby Travis, and I'm a drug addict."

It was six o'clock on a Thursday evening. He always attended this meeting wearing clean clothes, freshly showered and shaved. He knew it was wise to look his best, if only for the reason that cops occasionally patrolled the parking lot, looking to bust junkies who only showed up so they could score. Any dealer worth their salt knew that a good place to do business was recovery meetings. Anyone going to meetings for their problem with narcotics was most likely to fall off the wagon with only the slightest provocation. Actually, getting a drug addict to buy drugs (even when they were trying to quit) was easier than shooting an elk in a pen tied to a post. They tended to fold faster than Superman on laundry day.

Bobby looked around, saw the same faces he saw every Thursday. Some of them looked good, happy, healthy. Others, like him, wore their shame like a halo, as their resolve had been broken by something or other (most likely "other"), and they had relapsed. For some it was a matter of enduring excruciating withdrawals, their habit so out of control that physical pain called them back time and again. For others, it was simply because they couldn't stand dealing with life without being high. Either way, falling down was still falling down, no matter how you got there.

Lily sat in the corner, staring at him as she always did. Her eyes shifted back and forth fearfully, her slouched posture revealing more than her "sharing" ever did. This woman was in pain, real pain, from abuse, neglect…whatever. She was the unwanted dog, hunkered in her kennel at the shelter, just waiting for the lethal injection to take her away.

Opposite her was Ricky, looking rather beat-up for a Thursday. Bobby would swear that if the other belched, meth smoke would pour out of his mouth. Like or not, Ricky and Bobby had a casual, drug buddy relationship outside of the group, forged shortly after Bobby's second meeting when he scored a teener of meth from Ricky in the parking lot when the meeting was done. The two then proceeded to smoke it off of tin foil in Bobby's truck until it was gone, at which point Ricky suggested they should do more.

"I'm out of money," Bobby told him.

"I got this one." And Ricky busted out an eight ball (unpaid for; he would later face the wrath of Ricardo when he came up short at the end of the week) and over the course of six or seven hours the two got to know one another. For Ricky, there wasn't much to tell. Bad family upbringing, low IQ, socioeconomic problems, crappy job, house repossessed by the bank, ex-wife, kids that hated his guts...hell, anyone would find solace in crystal meth if they had his lousy lot in life.

"Uh, I know this isn't gonna come as a surprise..."

Everyone leaned forward on his or her chair, anxious to hear what Bobby had got himself into this week. Within this crowd it was hard to be the most exciting character, but somehow Bobby generally beat out the others, with the exception of two kids who never failed to entertain with their stories because of the severity of their addiction to oxycontin. They were, like Bobby, forever getting arrested for possession and passing out in public, but they took it a step further into the realm of breaking and entering, purse snatching, and armed robbery. That they weren't in prison was nothing short of amazing. This was the only group Bobby went to each week where he actually had some competition.

"Um, I blacked out again..."

As Bobby had surmised, not a single eyebrow was raised, not even by the moderator. This woman, through her many years of drug counseling, had heard it all. She'd listened to tales of addicts overdosing on heroin while their baby slept in the backseat of their car. Stories of people passing out behind the wheel and crashing through a fence and into someone's living room and then trying to order a drink from the bartender when in fact it was the home owner. She'd heard of relapse after relapse after relapse until the addict was sent into treatment where they somehow found drugs, relapsed yet again and fatally overdosed. Nothing could shock this woman, and yet somehow, from time to time, Bobby Travis did. It was his incessant blacking out that made her cringe, and every week she was afraid that he wouldn't be at the meeting, and not because he'd finally quit for good, but because he was dead, lying in the city morgue with a tag on his toe and a dirty glass pipe clutched in one rigor mortis stiff fist. When he showed up, she was momentarily relieved...until he got up to speak, that is. Then malaise blossomed within her like black smoke from a poorly made Chinese firecracker.

Bobby proceeded to tell them his tale (with genuine panache, since he'd been telling the story all week and he had it down pat), arriving eventually to the point where he'd been shocking his audience all week. No one in this group needed an explanation; every single one of them had, at one point or another, performed various sex acts for drugs. Also, having learned the true meaning of "felching," he modified the term to "rimjob," if only to preserve his standing as "heterosexual."

"You asked her to give you a rimjob?" the moderator asked, an unpleasant look on her face. "What for?"

Bobby smiled. This was surely the best part of the story. He'd been having a ball with it all week.

The rimjob was necessary, he explained to his audience, so that he could "gather his strength." The dominatrix was hesitant but, after some cajoling by the man in the executioner's hood (not to mention some barely concealed threats), she agreed and proceeded to affix her mouth upon Bobby's puckered starfish and began the act of rimming, to which he replied in kind by twisting and moaning, begging her to go deeper. The dominatrix made good on this request, snaking her tongue around inside until it caught on something. Bobby felt the item loosen, could sense that she'd snagged it and quickly begged her to (at this plot point everyone in the room groaned) kiss him.

"Gross!" one of the teenage oxycontin addicts exclaimed.

However, the urgency in his voice spurred her on, and she lifted her head from between his spread buttocks and placed her mouth over his, unwittingly transferring the payload that Bobby had planted in there earlier in the evening. At this part of the story he elucidated:

"I always keep a teener crammed up my ass in case I get arrested. That way, if I go to jail, at least I have some dope."

"Makes sense," Ricky said.

"Yeah, good idea," Lily agreed.

Bobby nodded, pleased at their acceptance. The group in the Gamblers Anonymous meeting didn't understand, but these guys got it: survival was survival. You just never knew when you were going to need a bump to get you through...well...whatever it was you needed to get through. Bullpen, arraignment, or court mandated counseling...some things just sailed along smoother when you were high.

So he went on to explain how he tore the baggy open with his teeth and quickly swallowed its contents.

"What the hell was that?" the dominatrix asked.

"My spinach," Bobby claimed to have replied.

"What?" the moderator interjected, shaking her head. "What the hell does methamphetamine have to do with spinach?"

"It's a Popeye reference," Bobby said with a slight grin, and slowly, as it sunk into his audience's drug-shriveled brains, they guffawed.

"Good one," Ricky admitted.

He continued to explain how the man in the executioner's hood almost choked on his gorge.

"Did you just eat your own shit?" he gasped incredulously, a hand placed over his mouth, his hairy paw barely restraining a riotous cavalcade of vomit.

"Maybe..."

It took twenty minutes, possibly more, before the drug kicked in and Bobby felt the strength of ten men within him.

"How many men did you have in you?" Lily quipped and Bobby ignored her, although he was genuinely amused by her wit. He'd come to expect comments like that from Karen (the woman in his GA meeting), but

Lily…all he expected of her was longing stares that scarcely obscured her outright pining for something she couldn't have.

Meanwhile, in the sex dungeon, Bobby had struggled against his bonds, found he had the strength to break free and, striking while the other was in shock, delivered a left hook across the executioner's chops that sent him sprawling on the cracked, oil stained concrete. He then turned on the dominatrix, a smile crossing his face as his hands grasped her cowhide clad arms, pulling her toward him roughly and yanking the zippered mask from off her head.

"Kiss me you bastard," Bobby claimed she'd said, when the moderator cleared her throat loudly, stopping him.

"We don't want to hear that part," she said (with much protesting from the others who in turn *wanted* to hear that part), and Bobby nodded at everyone in the circle and sat down. That was the part his SA group had wanted him to tell twice, but he understood. Different meeting, different vibe. "Would anybody else like to share with us this week?" she asked, and Lily raised her hand and nodded.

"I do," she said, shooting another hungry glance at Bobby before settling her gaze on her dry, wind-chafed hands. Poor, poor Lily, with the needle tracks up and down her arms blue in the cold light of the weak fluorescents, the cold sores circling her mouth like a parade of diabolical circus clowns. His heart went out to her; it truly did. One of these days she wouldn't show up and they'd all know she went tits up in her shithole apartment, dead and cold with the needle still stuck in her arm…

While Lily told a tale involving forced oral copulation upon her bull-dyke heroin dealer to secure her fix for the weekend (somewhat like bobbing for apples except smellier and less access to fresh air), Bobby reflected on what had to be the most ridiculous story he'd ever told in this group, preposterous not only because it was such a tale of human stupidity, but also because somehow he'd made it through unscathed. Truth be told he'd done stupider things, but this one was a bamboozler simply because it had taken him completely by surprise. He could barely remember the majority of it, but here's what he did recall:

It was a typical Friday, and he was on his fourth or fifth beer at Hooligans, looking to score. This was usually when Tommy ducked out. He didn't use drugs, so at this point he generally went home. Bobby approached Tony, and the bartender had taken him aside (the crowd was light, Happy Hour still twenty minutes away until kicking into full swing) and said he didn't have meth or coke, but he did have something called alpha-php, or a-php for short.

"What is it?" Bobby had asked.

"You ever try bath salts?"

"Yeah."

"Same thing, just a variation of it. It's sorta like meth, but you'll want a couple extra Xanax. It can make you pretty jumpy."

"But it gets you high?" Bobby remembered being skeptical. His experiments with bath salts had varied. The results were sometimes good, sometimes bad, but always...*unusual.* He couldn't think of a better way to put it. He'd only continued to use them because they were so cheap and easy to procure. Once they were banned, he went back to meth and coke without a second thought. The only thing he missed about them was the price.

But, there in the dim light of Hooligans, having nothing else available, he took what he could get. Tony sold him an eight ball for the low, low price of fifty dollars, cheap compared to everything else. An eight ball of blow was at least $150-$200, and an eight ball of meth was about $180. Usually Bobby couldn't afford more than a gram of the Peruvian marching powder or a teener of crystal. For fifty bucks you couldn't go wrong, at least, that was what he thought at the time.

The drug was a tan color, sold to him as one big crystal. He had to crush it with his lighter. He then took a piece and put it in his oil burner. He took a hit, held it as long as he could, and then blew it out. Nothing. He took another, held it again, then blew out the rank smoke. The rush eventually came, after a slight delay. Normally, with crack or meth, the second you blew the smoke out the effects were felt. With this drug, however, there was a good minute or so and then the buzz descended, but it came on sort of *creepy*. He couldn't think of a better way to describe it. And it was somewhat malicious too, like his experiments with salvia divinorum A (another experience that could elicit a story, best saved for another time). This drug didn't just stimulate your central nervous system, it attacked you. It was as if the substance wasn't merely getting him high, it was *coming after him*. His heart started beating raucously, and he quickly popped two Xanax. Twenty minutes later he still felt wonky; he popped (actually, chewed) another Xanax. Next thing he knew, (a segue he didn't recall, a mini-blackout) he was in the bathroom hitting the pipe again, and then his heart was at it once more, beating so fast and hard he could see purple lightning bolts flash behind his closed eyelids. Then he was popping another Xanax and then...nothing. Last memory: putting the pipe down on the top of the toilet tank as he exhaled, hand shaky, reaching to feel for his pulse...and then a dark void in which all remained a mystery until... he was waking up on a soiled couch, a ratty, reeking blanket draped over him. He had no idea where he was, how he got there, what time it was, or (most importantly) what day it was. He only recalled his last memory, and that didn't really serve to offer up a clue, only that the a-php had genuinely made him feel as if he was going to have a heart attack and so he popped too much Xanax on top of however many beers he'd drank (he was never sure of the tally, but he guessed anywhere between eight and ten, possibly more) and this combo had been the one-two punch that took it over the top.

He remembered lying there on the fetid couch, feeling suicidal. Thoughts of killing himself were commonplace after many of his off-the-rails benders, but were more likely to occur if he woke up in jail, or suddenly remembered he'd missed an important event of his daughter's. This time, however, there was nothing like that, yet all he could think of was how soothing it would be to slit his wrists in a nice warm bath and watch as his life swirled down the drain. The idea of dying actually comforted him. It was, seemingly, the only thing that made him feel better. Sometimes the thought of doing more drugs brought peace to his troubled mind, but not this time. The idea of taking a-php again made him feel sick to his stomach.

And then Ricky entered the room, and Bobby gathered he must be at his apartment. He wondered if he'd ever been here before, and quietly assumed he had, only he didn't remember it. *Good thing.* The place gave the word "dump" a whole new meaning. It probably made Lily's studio apartment on Martin Luther King Dr. look like a Brownstone in Manhattan. Glancing around, he saw wallpaper peeling from the walls like giant pieces of shredded skin. Mold stood out in places along the baseboards, large, unhealthy patches that promised cancer or any other number of carcinogenic contagions. Shit, maybe even the plague, perhaps leprosy.

Ricky's hair was sticking up every which way, his face looking like a piece of bruised and rotten fruit, all swelled up and discolored. He yawned loudly and Bobby swore he could smell his sour breath from across the room. In his mouth, yellow, crooked teeth leaned like tombstones in a long-forgotten graveyard full of unknown soldiers, men who had given their lives so their betters could live in bigger homes and have more children. And these children? Why, they would be the noble sons and daughters of the fortunate, none of them a bastard but children of a higher God, children entitled in every way…ready to live lives full of hope and promise, ready for others to step in front of bullets and die for them…

Bobby blinked once then twice. Were these thoughts actually going through his head? Had he gone crazy?

"What the hell was that shit we smoked?" Ricky asked, lighting a cigarette, a cheap one with a name like "Maverick" or "Cyclone" that stank to high heaven. He plopped down into a chair that looked as if it was salvaged from a hobo tent village, the cloth tattered, the seat threadbare and ass-juice stained.

"Alpha-php."

"Alpha what?"

"You heard me."

"Ya got any more?"

"Christ," Bobby muttered, trying to sit up. "I hope not."

"Check your pockets."

Bobby honored the other's request, and found an almost empty bag with a few shards left in it. He tossed it to Ricky.

"Knock yourself out."

"Ya sure ya don't want it?

Bobby said something that surprised him more than it did Ricky: "*Hell no.*"

"Well, thanks." Ricky got up and went into the kitchen, came back with a square of tinfoil. He picked up the bag and dumped the contents onto it. "This shit is weird," he said as he extracted a lighter from his pants pocket and heated the crystal until it melted into a yellow pool. He then grabbed a rolled bill off the coffee table, stuck it between his lips, and lit the liquid. A cloud of thick, noxious smoke plumed up and Ricky chased it with the bill. When he got all he could handle, he gently set the foil down and held in the hit as long as he could. When he exhaled, a familiar scent wafted Bobby's way, and at once memories came to him, albeit fractured ones with no clear meaning. Reality dawned on him in a serious way, fear making his heart race as fast as it had when he was smoking the foul drug.

"How long have we been smoking that crap?"

Ricky shrugged, picked up the foil and placed the bill between his lips. After he hit it again (holding the smoke as long as he could before blowing it out) he set the foil down once more and looked at Bobby slightly cross-eyed.

"I don't know. Six, maybe seven days?"

"Seven days?" Bobby got up quickly, went to the window and lifted the shade.

"What the hell man!" Ricky cried. "Don't do that!"

"That eight-ball couldn't have lasted seven days!"

"You bought more when it ran out, another ten grams I think."

"Ten grams?"

"Man," Ricky said wistfully, "you were on a total bender dude. I remember you calling some of your clients, telling them you were sick and you couldn't make it to clean their swimming pools." Ricky laughed until he started coughing, a deep wretched hack that promised a closed casket funeral. When it subsided he continued, "Dude, they had to hear the jukebox in the background. You kept playing Metallica and Slayer songs until everyone wanted to kick us out of Hooligans."

"What day is it today?"

"Thursday, I think."

"Jesus Christ..." Bobby moaned, unable to believe it. Everything was a total blur. How could six days go by (seven, counting today) and he couldn't remember? The fact that he missed work was devastating. Who knew how many clients he lost? And what the hell had he told them, if he'd told them anything? What kind of sick? Diarrhea? The flu?

"What did I tell them?"

"Tell who?"

"The people I called when I called in sick!" This said as if he were speaking to someone with the intellect of a three-year-old or a man with Down Syndrome. Looking at Ricky, either was possible. No offense to anyone with Down Syndrome (or three-year-olds), of course.

"Shoot, I don't know. I couldn't hear ya over the music." And he proceeded to hit the foil again, the smell making Bobby nauseous.

"I gotta go," he said, and he left the filthy apartment in a hurry, rushing home to the solace of his own distressed thoughts. When he got there, he looked at himself in the mirror, saw there was black gunk in the corners of his mouth, his tongue was white and scorched, his nostrils red-rimmed and sore, and every time he swallowed, he felt a lump in his throat the size of a golf ball. "Oh my God..." He could only wonder what kind of crap was in that poison; shit, he felt better after a meth binge, and he knew from his amateur attempts at cooking it that it contained butane, Drano, match heads, lithium battery strips, and all kinds of other toxic garbage one wasn't supposed to put in their body. This stuff had that beat by a mile.

He lay on his couch, eyes closed, and tried to piece everything together. Here and there were brief fragments of memory, but he couldn't put them into any chronological order. He remembered it was raining at one point, but he had no idea when. He recalled driving his car, but to where was anybody's best guess. Most of all, he remembered smoking the drug, taking great big hits and following them with another. This was usually trailed by a panic attack that led to him popping another Xanax. And then nothing but darkness. His moments of clarity within his blackouts always surrounded his use of the stimulant; they brought him back from oblivion until the Xanax spread its wings and enveloped him once again.

In an inspired fit of ingenuity, he grabbed his phone from where it lay on the coffee table. In the past, during blackouts, he'd been able to piece some of the events together by the calls, texts and emails he'd sent. Sometimes they led to dim recollections; other times they were met with nothing but a total blank. Scrolling through, he was hoping to figure out where he might have been (other than Hooligans or Ricky's) and what he may have said to some of his clients. Christ, he'd be lucky if he had any left.

He started with the phone calls, saw that he'd responsibly called every one of his Monday and Tuesday clients, but Wednesday and Thursday were unaccounted for (as Friday would be if he didn't get on it). He saw that one of the calls from Tuesday was only thirty seconds so, figuring he'd left a message, he checked under "Missed Calls" and sure enough, there was a voice mail from the client. There were others, and he would eventually get to those, but for right now he hoped this would shed a little light on things.

"Hi, Bobby. It's Chuck Redland, getting back to you. You all right, buddy? You don't sound so good. And I don't know what kind of emergency room cranks heavy metal, but I'm assuming you meant you *were* at the hospital and are now recovering at home. I hope you didn't lose your entire hand; be hard to clean pools with only one. Give me a call back when you can. Thanks. Bye."

Bobby listened to the message again, and then another time for good measure. He tried to detect the disbelief in Chuck's voice, thought he heard it, but then was unsure of himself. He told him he'd almost lost his hand? What the hell was he thinking? But Bobby knew the answer to that rhetoric question: obviously he wasn't. Otherwise he would have come up with a better lie. He then went on to look at the texts, and what he saw there dismayed him even more. Some of them were nothing but symbols and random letters: &#%#*#_JLDMA.....................?*@*W&%$^_++.

Good God! Whoever got those had to think he was out of his mind. Actually, there were quite a few like that. As he scrolled through and read their replies his face turned a violent shade of crimson.

"What?" Charlene Vanderbilt had texted back, to which he answered:

"Cabt mak it ovr todat...& ({_$# am verby unner th whether)(**U&)(&*"

"Are you OK?" she then replied and, fortunately for Bobby, he'd kept it simple:

"OK."

There were several more like that, but the message to Charlene was by and far the worst of the bunch. She must have thought he'd completely lost it!

Because the thing was, despite everyone at AA, NA, GA, and SA knowing what a deviant he was, his customers had no idea, at least, the clients he now catered to. In the bad old days when he partied all the time, he was often late, unwashed, sometimes incoherent, and most of his clientele dropped him in favor of a more reliable service after seeing him in that condition more than once. He couldn't say he blamed them. After he began his self-improvement regimen, he always showed up for his assignments on time, showered, shaved, and dressed in clean clothes. He was sober and articulate, knew what he was doing, could answer any questions asked about their swim-ming pool, as well as others regarding sports, politics, religion, etc. He was, after all, a high school graduate (albeit a college dropout) who had learned a few things along the way. His regulars didn't hold him in as high of regard as they would a school teacher or some other educated professional, but they did think he was exceptionally bright for a guy who cleaned swimming pools for a living. To those who had cared to ask, he'd told them honestly that he'd gone to college but had dropped out in his third semester because he wasn't sure what he wanted to be and didn't want to rack up any more debt until he figured it out. Unfortunately, he never did figure it out. He didn't tell his clients the sordid details, but he ended up in his current occupation after several years of eking out a living working physically demanding jobs that offered crappy pay, lousy hours, and no benefits. He'd done the rounds of house painting, line cooking, hosing out dog runs at a kennel, Sandblasting pavement, pressure washing windows, factory work, etc., when he'd met a fellow barfly who told him all about the benefits of going into business for himself. Over countless drinks he told Bobby that in California (southern California) it could be virtually anything. He could do a door-to-door car detailing business; a dog walking/pet sitting enterprise; he could do gardening/landscaping; or (the one that really grabbed him) he could clean swimming pools. He could work for himself, and the best thing about it was that he was his own boss. No fat ass, smug bastard leaning over his shoulder telling him what to do and how to do it faster. He'd worked for plenty of pricks like those, and he'd had it up to here with their kind. He'd walked out on those assholes when the abuse got too much to take (which was often), so Bobby didn't have a lot of references he could use.

And now here he was, throwing it all away because he lost his mind on some drug with a name that was seemingly a bunch of random letters (like the texts he'd sent). Jesus, was he completely crazy?

He then went through his phone some more, saw that he'd sent Facebook Messenger emails to a couple of his buddies, some of which were accompanied by photos. In one he was standing in dim lighting, shirt off, eyes wild, his hair in disarray. He didn't know where the photo was taken; he didn't recognize the background. In yet another he'd sent an animated text—a character from a popular cartoon about life in the future, and the character was saying, "I don't know if I have free time or I'm just forgetting everything that I have to do!" This message was also accompanied by a photograph, one in which he and Ricky were hitting the glass pipe as smoke swirled about their heads. The friend he'd sent it to? One of his sponsors from NA. One of? you might ask. Yes, Bobby was so deplorable that he didn't have one, he had two. He couldn't remember who the other one was, but apparently in a stupor he'd thought of this guy. The sponsor had not replied to the text, but when he saw him the next week at NA he had a few choice words for him. In fact, that entire next week, a lot of people had choice words for Bobby. His sponsor dumped his sorry ass; he was so frustrated at what a mess Bobby was. I mean, come on, really? Sending him a photo of him and his drug buddy hitting the goddamn glass dick? He had to be a complete freakin' idiot. Bobby couldn't recall if he'd ever replaced him with someone else or not. It had yet to come up. He supposed one sponsor was probably enough, if he could ever remember who it was.

All in all, he lost about eight clients; these were mostly folks he hadn't contacted on Wednesday and Thursday (he'd managed to salvage Friday). One was Charlene Vanderbilt, the receiver of the confusing texts. Over the phone she insisted that he seek professional help, and that if she ever saw him anywhere near her house she would call the police. He was smart enough not to argue with her. He simply thanked her and hung up the phone.

The surprise save was Chuck Redland, especially when Bobby showed up the following week with both hands.

"They reattached it?" Chuck joked, and Bobby did his best to make himself look guilty, which wasn't hard because a) he did feel guilty, and b) he'd been practicing his story all weekend (along with all the emotions he was supposed to display to accentuate each plot point) and figured he had it all down pat by now.

"I didn't cut off my hand, Chuck." This said as self-effacingly as possible.

"No kidding?" Chuck replied, a small smile playing along his lips. "So what really happened?"

This was the story that Bobby had concocted over the weekend, a weekend, it might be added, that he spent uncharacteristically sober. Christ, he'd done so much damage during the week there was simply no need to further destroy himself. Besides, his own culpability kept him from wanting so much as a light beer.

"I'm sorry I missed coming by, I was really sick," he began, wondering if the BS he was about to spew would be believed. Chuck cocked an eyebrow that said, "Do continue…"

"I ate some chicken from my fridge that must have gone bad, and I got a bad case of food poisoning. I found some loperamide in the medicine cabinet. It's an anti-diarrhea medication—"

"I know what loperamide is."

Bobby laughed (fake laughed, as was part of his script). "Yeah, I guess I didn't. I didn't know it was an opiate, and when one tablet didn't work, I took another couple of 'em. And when I couldn't sleep because I kept getting up to go to the bathroom, I drank a bunch of Nyquil."

This was the part where he hoped Chuck would put two and two together and commiserate, and here was why: after an extensive Google search (keywords: "over the counter medications not to combine") he found that if you mixed loperamide with antihistamines, it could cause symptoms of an overdose, which manifested as dizziness, nausea and…drum roll, please…excessive sleepiness and loss of consciousness. If anyone looked it up, it was practically airtight. The only flaw in it, the part Bobby hoped no one would investigate, was that loperamide and diphenhydramine were not to be combined, not doxylamine. The active ingredient in Nyquil was doxylamine succinate, not diphenhydramine. If any of his clients believed he was lying and they felt it was worth investigating, they would certainly discover this. Bobby hoped like hell none of them would. He needed the business. If this went sour, he'd be lucky to get a job at Ralph's grocery store, stacking cans of creamed corn and wishing he could bang the little girls who worked the registers. The thought made him apprehensive and horny simultaneously.

Chuck laughed at this admission. "You didn't know you shouldn't combine those?" he said jovially. "Haven't you ever had diarrhea before?"

"Of course," Bobby said, allowing a tiny smile. "But I'd never taken loperamide before. I didn't have any Pepto, so I took the pills from my roommate. I didn't know they were so strong."

Another lie Bobby hoped not to get caught in; he didn't have a room-mate. And as he told the lie, he wondered if he'd ever told Chuck that or not. Fact was, he couldn't remember what he told anyone on a day-to-day basis because his memory was so bad.

"If your roommate was responsible, he would have told you."

"He wasn't home," Bobby said. "I found them in his medicine cabinet." He licked his lips, swallowed a couple of times. "I was looking for Pepto."

"So what was all that about not losing your whole hand?"

Bobby took a deep breath. He liked Chuck, really liked him. If there was one client he respected (and actually thought might have a bit of respect for him), it was Chuck. And now here he was shoveling a truckload of BS and laying it on so thick roses would be sprouting up any time, and he was doing it to someone he wished he'd never have to be dishonest with…ever. Jesus, if he made it through this he promised he would…he promised he'd…oh the hell with it. He couldn't promise anything.

"I didn't know what I was saying Chuck," he said, knowing this part of the story was 100 percent true. It was easier to lie when the story was somewhat based on fact. "I was whacked out of my mind." He nodded meekly, and Chuck's smile beamed back that he believed him. For what reason one could only guess, but Chuck had no doubts that Bobby had no idea (at the time of the phone call) what the hell he was saying or doing, and his smile seemed to put everything back in place. Where the world was once suspended on an invisible string, dangling and spinning precariously, it was now firmly attached again.

"You feeling better now?" he asked, instead of questioning his story.

"You bet!"

"Well, I suppose you learned a lesson, huh?"

"I sure did!"

"OK," Chuck said, and Bobby knew the discussion was over. His story was accepted. Whether or not Chuck really believed him was another matter entirely, but who cared as long as he got away with it? "I'll let you get to work. Thanks for calling that day though. I would have been worried if you hadn't."

"Thanks," Bobby said, touched that one of his customers (one he respected) actually gave a tin fart in a strong breeze whether he was OK or not. "Sorry about the stupid message," he finished lamely. "I wasn't in my right mind."

"Obviously," Chuck laughed, and that had been the end of it.

So Bobby told that yarn to his clients over and over during the course of the next week, adjusting the time frame for it to make sense (for each day he'd missed, that was the day he said it happened; fortuitously, none of his regulars were friends and could check out that part of his story). And as for the clients he'd failed to call (as well as Charlene Vanderbilt), they were history. He could have been mad about it, but he knew he only had himself to blame.

But that damn drug could be blamed too, right? How could something like that happen to him? It had never happened before on any other substance. It was as if it had taken his brain hostage, had compelled him to continue using it until either his body couldn't take it anymore or he'd run out. And, judging by the fact that there was some left, his body must have given out, most likely his heart had started hurting. Through all of his hard-drug using years, he'd never gone on a bender of that length; he'd always had the sense to stop at some point (even in a blackout). But this crap, this alpha-php, had taken him for a ride he hadn't been prepared for, had stolen his free will and left him nothing but a hollow, drug-crazed shell. He'd read trip reports on Erowid (a website dedicated to all drugs, both recreational and non) where users reported what they took, how much of it they ingested, height and weight, level of familiarity with such compounds and, finally, their experience, be it good or bad. MDPV and other synthetic cathinones had this effect on many users, but this had never happened to Bobby. Maybe it was the drug, or maybe it was the point in his life he was at. Either way it spelled big problems in the long run if this were to happen again. He couldn't afford it. More so, he couldn't afford to lose his business.

Over the course of weeks, bits and pieces of memory came to him, fragments that he couldn't place as Monday or Thursday or Tuesday; all sense of time had escaped him. The more he thought about it, the more it seemed to him that that must be what it was like to have multiple person- alities. To be walking and talking and doing things he wouldn't normally do, but had no control over whatsoever. And he did this *all the time*. It wasn't like this was anything new, for Christ's sake. But this time it had really gotten away from him.

With that story in mind, echoing in his head as a reminder of how quickly he could lose control at any given time no matter how much he thought he had it together, Bobby listened as other members of the group shared for the week. Given the depravity of this crowd, the meetings went on longer than the others. It was enormously cathartic to share such di- sastrous tales, and none of them could afford a shrink, so the meetings tended to go over two hours some times. No one cared. Where else did they have to be? On the street, offering hand jobs to frat boys in exchange for drug money? They were safer here.

Ricky stood up and spewed some bullshit about being sober for an entire week, but no one believed him. He might as well have told everyone he got blown by a Nigerian Prince after he'd paid for the bank transfer fee and the million dollars had been deposited into his bank account.

When the meeting wrapped up, Bobby and Ricky met outside by the big metal ashtray. Ricky fired up a generic smoke and coughed into one gnarly, nicotine stained hand.

"So what are you up to tonight?" Ricky asked. He was totally unfazed by Bobby's story, or maybe he'd heard so many they didn't even register any more. It was hard to tell.

"I'm going home," Bobby replied honestly. Tomorrow, however, was another story, a tale he'd be telling at each of his meetings next week, no doubt.

"So...tomorrow night at Hooligan's?" Ricky said, and Bobby felt something inside him snap and break loose, a little piece of him that he knew he couldn't control if he wanted to. His second personality, his Tyler Durden, his Sybil.

"Probably," he replied, and Ricky nodded, put out his cigarette, and walked to his shitty Ford Focus and drove away while Bobby watched him silently, wishing he were someone else.

Chapter Five

One thing Bobby knew for sure was that he had a mother; this he had photographic proof of—a single Polaroid, faded and worn with time. In the picture, she was young and pretty, laughing and carefree. She was standing on a beach, wind blowing her hair, a secret Mona Lisa smile adorning a tanned face with eyes that fairly gleamed. Unfortunately, he was only familiar with her in that single moment because she'd abandoned him at birth; he'd never met her. Therefore, he knew he *had* a mother, but he didn't know if she ever loved him, or even if she had the capacity for love to give him. Sometimes, when he couldn't sleep, that missing detail bothered him, a whole lot more than he ever would have believed. She'd left him with his dad, a decent man who'd raised him and clothed him and kept him safe, but he didn't like to talk about the woman who had brought Bobby into this world. When Bobby got old enough to be curious about why she'd left and asked the inevitable questions, his old man clammed up.

"I don't want to talk about it, son," Andrew would say. "Now go get your daddy a beer."

He knew he should hate this woman for leaving them (whoever and wherever she was), but it simply wasn't in him. Bobby wasn't a natural born hater, nor was his father. Between the two of them, they couldn't muster up enough hate to condemn her. This was a good thing, and it would carry the two of them through their lives, keeping things uncomplicated. Hate is a nasty thing; makes more work for you in the long run. On the contrary indifference was much easier, one simply had to just let go and not care.

The two of them got on well, living in the house that Bobby would later inherit when his father passed away. He was a good man, his father, so when a heart attack claimed him at the age of sixty-three Bobby took it hard. Andrew was known for speaking his mind, but he wasn't harsh about it; hearing the truth from him was like getting hit with a whiffle bat. It stung, but it didn't hurt *that* bad. His father could tell him things that others couldn't, truths that were too painful to hear from folks not as linguistically savvy. Andrew could make criticism sound like a compliment, could pour on enough sugar to make the foul medicine go down nice and smooth.

Despite their mutual amicability, Bobby never expected to get the house; he'd figured his father would sell it and the land to square away any debt he'd accrued. But Andrew was shrewd; there was no debt, and he even left enough behind to pay for his funeral, casket, plot, and tombstone with a little left over for Bobby to blow on drugs and booze. Therefore, when Bobby was informed by the lawyer who handled the will that it was now his property, he was surprised, and wasn't sure if he wanted it or not. There were too many memories. In the end, he moved back in because he didn't want to sell it; it was too much of a hassle, and maybe it would be worth some money someday. As the weeks turned into years, he made his peace with the ghosts of recollections past, savoring the sound of a creaking floorboard as if it were his old man entering the room. He got solace from this.

As a child, Bobby hadn't been a troublemaker; he was a good boy who did what he was asked or told. Andrew wasn't a strict man, nor was he lax enough that Bobby could do whatever he wanted. Whenever he reflected upon it later in life, he was always of the opinion that his dad had done him right. The two lived together mostly in harmony, although they did have the occasional row over the common things family members fought over. Still, the demands made of Bobby weren't outrageous. His dad believed in hard work, but he didn't overdo it. He made him earn his keep by mowing the grass and tending to the many plants in the backyard and, later, on his own accord, Bobby got a paper route. His dad thought this was a good way for him to learn the value of a dollar, and how to successfully manage money. Regrettably, Bobby was terrible at financial administration and most often either broke even or lost money. As he grew up, he realized he didn't have a knack for economic expansion. Neither, for that matter, did his father. He worked in the warehouse of a musical instrument supply company, barely moving up the ladder over his many years of service and dying before he could retire.

His dad never married, so it was just the two of them while Bobby grew up. Andrew devoted his life to his son, eschewing dates and unnecessary fraternizing with buddies from the factory and instead choosing to be a homebody. His hobby was his enormous garden, a well-tilled five square acreages that was the envy of many of their neighbors.

Contrary to what one might suspect, this easy-going existence was not the reason for Bobby's later delinquency. He wasn't a "rebel without a cause"; he didn't strive to get into trouble unless there was an ulterior motive attached. He was an intelligent boy, given every chance to excel at the public schools he attended, if only (and he heard this a *lot*) he applied himself.

Bobby worked his way in and out of many social orders over the course of his school years, but would mainly find a home with the "heads," those social misfits who traversed all walks of life, sharing numerous personality traits, but mainly those of a chemical nature. With them he discovered escape from the traditional values and morals within the succor of inebriation. Their fellow students called them many names: "freaks" was one, "stoners" another. Whatever the moniker, a cloud of pot smoke followed Bobby and his buddies around, and within it they laughed and caroused and snorted speed and engaged in a variety of activities, such as petty theft and vandalism, that ultimately had a negative impact on the others around them. Bobby was called before the vice principal many times during his high school years for his frequent transgressions, but he was slippery as an eel coated in Teflon; somehow he always snuck by. He had an aptitude for making up plausible excuses, and this would follow him well into his adult years.

It was for this reason that his father didn't know he was already a habitual pot smoker by the age of fifteen, and his sexual awareness was well beyond what was appropriate for his age. He'd innocently lost his virginity when he was thirteen to a friend's mother, a woman of questionable (obviously) virtue, who had no idea she was awakening a hunger within him that would follow him for years to come. His good looks easily lured the girls in, young ladies whom he had casual affairs with that never lasted more than a couple of weeks. In hindsight, one could call it fitting that it was one of these young women who turned him onto alcohol, and then cocaine in turn. Also, it was a young woman who would later introduce him to the horse track. Vice upon vice upon vice, and he loved them all.

In his senior year of high school, his grades were at the lowest they'd ever been; however, he was still eligible to get into a state college because Bobby's intellect was such that his worst performance academically was many others' best. Unbeknownst to his stoner pals, he was actually smart. He made no point to hide this from anyone, yet his outward apathy steered everyone in the opposite direction, save for baffled teachers and a guidance counselor who couldn't believe he didn't have a college and a career picked out already.

His father, knowing his son possessed above average intelligence, very much wanted for him what he could never have, a chance at respectability. All his adult life what he dearly desired for Bobby was what he thought he deserved: veneration for a mind that was clearly head and shoulders above the rest. This young Bobby could attain by enrolling in a decent state university and graduating with honors. Andrew was certain Bobby could do this if he just buckled down and studied. Bobby in turn eschewed such a possibility as if it were a disease. Honor, decorum, and all that nonsense were for people who actually gave a crap about maintaining the status quo. Bobby couldn't care less what anyone thought of him; despite getting good grades he was, for all practical purposes, an idiot. When he rebelled against personal growth, he was campaigning against the probability of a decent future, but he didn't know that because he was a kid, and as his addictions grew, so did his hair, and his outlook of the world became one based upon daily gratification instead of seeing the big picture. Bobby was smart, but he lacked foresight—the ability to predict where he'd be in five years if he continued to live as he did. Each day existed for him to get high, which he did with great aplomb.

Owing to his financial liability, Bobby stayed at home for nearly two years after high school. He stayed on until after his failed attempt at college, and then finally found new digs at the age of twenty when he rented a place with a friend, a small trailer that was better suited for a couple than two buddies. This lasted until his father passed away, roughly eighteen months after Bobby had moved out, and then he moved back into the house, pursuing womanizing, drugs, booze, and the horse track full-time. Several years and over half a dozen crummy jobs later he started cleaning pools.

It was this profession that kept him content while he drank and drugged and screwed and gambled himself into oblivion, until the day when Carolyn (a chick he'd been banging on and off for about five months) told him she was pregnant, the child was his, and she was going to have it. The party certainly didn't stop, but it slowed down for a little while as he processed this information, trying to decide what he was going to do about it. In the immediate future, he did nothing; simply resumed doing what he did best. It was only later, much later, that he began to understand another human being's life was at stake, and that was when he started to question his beliefs. He decided to do the proper thing, and on a whim bought a cheap ring and proposed to her, only to be rebuffed by a woman who probably had more notches on her belt than he had, which was saying a *lot*.

After his daughter was born, and he hadn't been there, Bobby had an attack of his conscience; he felt like a complete fool. While Carolyn was in labor, he'd been smoking meth with some "friends" under a pier in Ocean Beach. He'd never once considered offering her support in the delivery room, maybe being there when the kid popped out. How was that for irresponsible?

When she got out of the hospital, she only returned to his house once, to tell him he was a father and that she'd be expecting money from him on a monthly basis. He never even saw his daughter until several months later when he tried to visit her, but Carolyn wouldn't let him through the front door.

"Until you're ready to take some responsibility you have no right to see her," she said plaintively, holding the infant in her arms as she suckled her breast.

"But she's my daughter!"

"Then act like it." And the door was slammed in his face.

This left Bobby to ponder some of his life choices in a serious way. Could it be possible that the way he was living was no longer in his best interest, what with having fathered a child? Could it be he needed to straighten up? Was he doing to his daughter what his own mother had done to him? After much thought, an internal debate that raged like a mighty wildfire, stoked by various chemical stimuli, he decided he should continue doing what he did best: getting wasted, screwing any willing participant, and pissing his money away on sucker bets. After all, it was what he knew. Besides, Carolyn appeared to be doing fine; she had a new beau all lined up and he'd moved in with her and was taking care of the fathering responsibilities. Everything had sorted itself out.

So for ten years this was what he did, as his hair grew thinner and grayer and his gut more pronounced. He made it a point to show up for birthdays when he was invited, presenting cheap cards and (sometimes) gifts, if he hadn't blown the money on drugs, and he did his best to contribute with child support payments (always late, mostly the full amount). And he watched as his kid grew up, although generally from a distance, through a haze of crack and meth smoke, and it was only when she became increasingly aware and her once innocent gaze turned jaundiced and wary, that he had to step back, take a long look at himself, to try and see himself through her eyes. What he saw dismayed him significantly; it was the great, eventual truth that spoke to him in a voice as icy as a January wind.

I'm a loser…

This voice spoke to him in no uncertain terms. It was as unequivocal as a cold rain that battered the roof of his father's old house in the midst of a winter day.

I'm a total fucking loser...

And this was when he at last took the steps to stop slowly killing himself, to try and salvage what he had left. This was the point in his life when he decided to start attending the meetings, if only to try and win his daughter's approval. It was hard at first, putting down the pipe, the bottle, the race track tickets, the lace panties he found in the bed of his truck left there from some unnamed stranger, but he found that if he only indulged on the weekends then things were easier. His memory functioned better, he lost less money, which meant he could buy her presents. But to win her love and respect?

Well...he eventually found that after so many broken promises, forgotten birthdays, lies, and half-assed attempts at fathering, that was going to be a lot harder than he thought.

Chapter Six

"Bartender! Gimmie another pitcher of Pabst!"

Tony worked the taps with feverish intensity as Friday's Happy Hour kicked in full throttle. And not only was he doing great business selling suds, the blow, meth, ecstasy, weed, and benzos were selling like hotcakes too. Fat wads of cash bulged in his pockets as he went up and down the bar, filling and refilling pint glasses and pitchers, making the occasional fruity cocktail, pouring rotgut shots for the financially disadvantaged who considered sobriety a demon that needed slaying.

Among this throng was Bobby, standing at the bar with his money in hand, a sheen of sweat, shiny and repugnant, drenching his forehead. His daughter had a soccer game the next day, and here he was, on his fifth beer and looking to score some ice or powder for the long night ahead. How was it that he could be so stupid? Didn't he ever learn? The answer dear friends, came in the form of a well-meant adios from his drinking buddy Tommy. Once Bobby was ready to hit the hard drugs, Tommy split.

"Hey, buddy," Tony said, sauntering up with a grin as sleazy as a politician's. His Snidely Whiplash mustache didn't help to dissuade anyone of this comparison. "What can I do for you?"

"You holding?"

"Of course."

"Not that alpha shit…"

"Coke or meth, amigo," Tony said amiably. "With the Xanax chaser I presume?"

"Please."

"So?"

"I'll take a gram of meth and six…make that eight Xanax."

"I hope you're not driving," Tony muttered, reaching beneath the counter and into his stash, grabbing the requested items and passing them over the bar in exchange for the crumpled wad of bills. "Have fun."

"Thanks."

Bobby backed away from the bar and was halfway to the bathroom when he realized he forgot to get another beer. Oh well. He'd get one after he popped a Xanax and powdered his nose. He was two steps to salvation when Ricky popped out from seemingly nowhere.

"You holding, bro?"

"I only got a gram, dude," Bobby answered reproachfully, in a tone that insinuated "get your own drugs." Ricky caught on fast, one of the only things he apparently did understand without hesitation. Everything else (sports, women, politics etc. etc.) went right over his head.

"OK, OK, relax man, I get it." He stepped closer. "Maybe you could just hook me up with a bump..."

"You got any money?" Bobby was getting impatient; had Ricky not showed up he'd be rinsing his nostrils with water right now, wincing with pleasure as the chemicals slid down the back of his throat.

"Yeah, I got a couple of bucks."

"How much?"

"Why?"

Bobby considered for a moment, thought about his daughter's soccer game, but then thought about how solid it would be to keep the party going a few more hours than planned. Besides, if he had some weight he could probably get Ricky laid by one of the many sluts lining the bar like so much window dressing, and Christ knew the sorry son of a bitch needed it.

"I haven't opened the bindle yet. You got enough to go half on an eight ball?"

"How much?"

"$175, maybe $200."

"Let me see." Ricky took out his battered wallet, a piece of vinyl masquerading as leather he bought at Wal-Mart for twelve bucks and some change back when Bush Jr. was doing his best to screw up the free world. He ruffled the bills, his lips moving as he counted, and then a large smile spread across his face.

"Is it good?"

Bobby smiled in return. "It's always good."

"OK." He handed Bobby five twenty-dollar bills. "Hook it up."

"Ten-four."

And Bobby turned around and headed back to the bar.

♦ ♦ ♦

The sound of sirens was what brought him around; that and something wet splashing him in the face. It was oddly warm, thick, quickly growing tacky, and as some semblance of sobriety crept into Bobby's drug addled brain, he had a brief flash of memory.

(Uncle Bill…something about my uncle Bill working on the killing floor at the Mission Road slaughter house.) Then he was dragged back into reality by the dawning horror that what was gushing into his face, hot and sticky, was blood from Ricky's right carotid artery.

"Jesus Christ!" he exclaimed, turning his head and retching, and that's when the light shined in his eyes, bright and blinding.

"Keep your hands where I can see them!" a voice ordered, but Bobby was so confused he continued struggling with his gorge as his shaking hands fought with the seat-belt clasp which, for some reason, wouldn't open and set him free.

"I said 'keep your hands where I can see them.' Are you deaf?"

The cop was only twenty-two years old, just out of the academy. He obviously didn't recognize shock when he saw it, but thankfully for Bobby (just as the young punk was reaching for the Taser on his holster) the older and much wiser officer did, and he reached out and stayed the others hand.

"You keep that where it is, son," he muttered, shaking his head sadly as he watched his cousin fumble with the seatbelt. At least Bobby wasn't behind the wheel; the guy who was wasn't going home tonight, that was for sure. He wasn't going anywhere but the county morgue where (Teddy was sure) an autopsy would reveal the presence of alcohol and drugs in his bloodstream that was *way* beyond the legal limit for someone operating a motor vehicle. "Go back to the car and shut off the siren but leave on the flashers. I'll take it from here." He considered the victim for a moment. "And call an ambulance. You can tell them they don't need to hurry."

"But I was here first!"

Teddy eyed his new partner speculatively, gathering everything he needed to know in a glance: young, cocky, headstrong, ready to rush in, shoot first, ask questions later.

"Go," he said firmly, and the conviction in his voice was compelling enough for the other to obey.

"Fine!" He stalked off in a huff, his stride indicating the anger which seethed inside. And to think he'd been *this close* to tasering that wasted bastard.

"Bobby," Teddy said, reaching into the car and taking hold of his cousin's hands. "You OK?"

"I can't get this seatbelt to open…"

"You know where you are?"

"In a car?"

"Let me help you with that." Teddy reached inside and easily unclasped the seatbelt that his older relative had found so hard to open. Bobby's hands were shaking, and Teddy could tell by the (passably) coherent look in his eyes that he wasn't in a blackout; this was all registering and he was having a hell of a time processing it. He didn't blame him. It wasn't every day your drug-buddy squirted their life's blood into your face as they died behind the wheel of a beat to shit Ford Focus.

Teddy opened the door, took Bobby by one arm and helped him out. Fortuitously, Ricky hit the empty parked car on the driver's side. Bobby was completely untouched except for a scrape on his forehead. A small trickle of blood oozed from the wound, but it was nothing a bandage wouldn't fix. He wouldn't even need stitches.

"Come on." He took Bobby to the cruiser, opened the back door and gently helped his cousin in. At times like this, he often wondered what Bobby's dad would think if he knew this was how his son turned out, that he was an absentee father and a drug addict. Teddy's father, Bill, had been a proud, hard-working everyday Joe who raised a family he could be proud of. He and Andrew had been brothers, and Bill never understood why the other never remarried. He'd thought that maybe some of Bobby's delinquency was due to him not having a mother. Despite this notion, the two had been good friends, and the boys had each other as companions growing up. They were still buddies, but they tended to travel in different circles, seeing as they were essentially polar opposites. Notwithstanding, Bobby was always invited to his house for holidays and barbecues, but Bobby often didn't show up. Teddy knew why.

Like Bobby's dad, Teddy's father was deceased as well. When Teddy was seventeen, Bill left home for work and never came back. Doctor Taylor (with the assistance of the coroner at the county morgue) surmised his passing was due to all the eggs and bacon and sausage Billy consumed by the truckload, for it was a stroke and three consecutive heart attacks that put him down for good at the tender young age of forty-eight. That and genetics. Andrew had died of multiple heart attacks too; they'd both been hard drinking, smoking, meat eating laborers who ground out their sixty-hour work weeks with sweat, blood and piss. Never did they complain, nor did they miss work. It was as ingrained as the hereditary factors that gave them leaky heart valves and induced the plaque-filled arteries that hardened like freshly poured concrete in an August sun. Hell, Teddy himself was pushing thirty-four; he supposed if he was going to break the curse it was his wife Maggie that would be his saving grace, for she had him eating more vegetables than meat these days, and a lot of fish. Not to mention soy…lots and lots of soy. And he didn't tip except maybe the occasional beer. He didn't smoke, and he certainly didn't use any drugs, although he had done his share (sometimes with Bobby) when they were kids. Mostly grass, but sometimes LSD and magic mushrooms, but not much, and once he decided to become a cop, he put those activities behind him. He supposed, in light of his own experience, that was how he was able to commiserate with his cousin and bail him out whenever the poor bastard really needed his help, which was more often than he cared to mention. Still, Bobby was on the fast track to Heart Attack City if he didn't lay off the cocaine and speed.

"Where we goin'?"

"Someplace safe."

Another police car pulled up behind Teddy's cruiser. It was Adam's. He gave Teddy a curt nod that said he could take off; he'd handle the situation from here. Teddy nodded in return and then shut the door and walked around to the driver's side. His partner, the young, cocky, insolent son of a bitch who would have tasered Bobby had he not intervened, sat there with a smug look on his face.

"I called it in."

"Thanks."

"The ambulance is on the way."

"Good." Teddy opened the door. "Move over."

"But I'm driving—"

"Move or I'll move you myself."

Teddy stood six foot three with muscles that bulged and rippled beneath his uniform like coiled snakes. He got up every afternoon at five o'clock to work out with free weights and a medicine ball. He still had a gut though, a present from his favorite vice: sugar. It pressed urgently against his tucked-in shirt, threatening to pop the button opposite his navel. His new partner, Kirk, was tall but lanky, and Teddy knew that if he were pushed to fight, he'd eventually back down if he thought he was going to lose. Now was no different.

"I'm goin'!" Kirk sulked. He would have simply slid over, but the twelve-gauge, pump-action shotgun was in the way. He had to get out of the car to move over to the passenger side. When he passed Bobby, he tapped the glass with his giant class ring (a reminder that his high school days weren't long behind him), but Bobby barely glanced at him. Apparently he'd passed out again, which was just fine with Teddy; at least that way he wouldn't have to put up with any of Kirk's badgering.

"Leave him alone," he said anyway, just so his new partner knew who was boss. Teddy had been in law enforcement for over fourteen years. There was no way he was going to let some hotshot punk intimidate him, or his alcoholic, druggy relative.

"Why do you care?"

Teddy looked at the other before putting the car into gear. Hadn't he told him? He supposed maybe he hadn't.

"He's my cousin."

"Your cousin?"

"Did I stutter?"

Kirk turned around and looked at Bobby, whose face was covered in blood, the skin slack and wrinkled, a five o'clock shadow that had hit the twenty-four-hour point obscuring his face in the semi-darkness.

"I don't see any resemblance," he said, and Teddy gave a begrudging laugh.

"That's what they all say," he retorted, then put the car in drive and left the scene before the ambulance arrived.

◆ ◆ ◆

"You still going to those meetings?" Teddy asked Bobby. It was nine hours later, after Bobby had slept it off in the drunk tank. How his cousin could sleep on those metal benches was beyond him, but he supposed as wrecked as he was, he could probably sleep on a bed of nails. Teddy's shift had ended at 7:00 a.m., so he went home and got a few hours of shut-eye in his large, comfy king-sized bed before coming back to the station to check in on Bobby. He had the day off, but since this was a family matter, he felt so inclined to do his familial duty.

"Monday through Thursday."

"Probably would help if you went Friday through Sunday too." He sipped his coffee and set it down on his desk. Bobby was working on the short stack Teddy had brought him from Denny's, slouched in a chair across from him. It was lucky for Bobby that he had an in at the police department because of his cousin. Otherwise he wouldn't be enjoying any privileges except the right to remain silent and the right to an attorney.

Teddy had to decide if there was anything he could do for Bobby. Should he offer to help pay for rehab, maybe find a state-run program? Bobby wasn't a total loss per say; he wasn't a criminal or a bad guy; he simply had dependency issues. Over the years, the criminal justice system had adapted and changed, trying to go after the dealers and not the users. Like alcoholism, they were recognizing that drug use was a disease, one that needed to be treated with therapy rather than jail time. Not that it always worked; the system still had a ton of bugs in it and people had a way of slipping through the cracks. Innocent men still rode the lightning every year, and faced life sentences for crimes they didn't commit. No industry was perfect.

But Teddy was damned if he was going to watch his cousin destroy himself if he had any say over it, and the fact that Bobby was going to the meetings showed he was at least taking an active role in his own rehabilitation. He simply couldn't do it on his own; this was made painfully apparent by his weekend binges. He needed some help.

"Yeah," Bobby agreed, forking another bite of pancake in his mouth. "Probably would help if I went on the weekends."

"Do you want to quit?" There, the question was out there. He watched Bobby carefully, looking for the telltale sign of a lie.

But Bobby remained passive. He looked Teddy in the eyes, and what the other saw there was genuine remorse.

"Hell yeah," he said. "It's why I go to the damn meetings."

"Yet you always wind up in the same place. It's a miracle that you don't hurt yourself or someone else during your blackouts."

Bobby's face flushed. Even though he was able to talk about his blackouts with the people at his weekly meetings, talking about them with Teddy made him feel uncomfortable. He was, in fact, dreadfully embarrassed about them; he put his life and everybody else's around him in jeopardy by doing so, especially when he got behind the wheel of a car which, thankfully, was rare at this point. As far as he knew, he supposed.

"I'm damn glad you weren't driving last night. That might have been you the ambulance drivers put in a body bag."

"I don't drive when I'm blacked out anymore—"

"How the hell would *you* know?" Teddy snapped, more out of exasperation than real anger. His cousin could be so damn dense sometimes.

Bobby opened his mouth to say something and then closed it. He didn't know, not really. The only time he did was when...when...

When I wake up somewhere I don't recognize and I wonder how I got there. Then I find my car parked outside, the keys sometimes left in the ignition, but most times in my pocket. The car might be parked a little crooked, but that's all...

"Don't give me some bullshit answer," Teddy warned. "I don't want to hear it."

A moment of silence passed. From the jail they heard a guy singing in an off-key voice, some song about a woman named Charlotte the harlot and activities she engaged in with a donkey. After thirty seconds or so Landon Williams, one of the senior guards, yelled at him to shut up. The voice cut off, but not after a hearty gust of laughter and one final verse:

"She straddles him like a pro! Now that's my kind of ho! Up and down and all around that's all the donkey knows!"

Suddenly Teddy and Bobby burst out laughing, and this made Teddy remember all the trouble the two used to get into when they were kids. They were no strangers to the long arm of the law, damn tootin' on that count, but it was mostly harmless fun. A little graffiti here, a little vandalism there. They never hurt anybody, not deliberately anyway. Not to mention all the beers they drank by the railroad tracks out by Valley Center Park, all the doobies Bobby bought for a dollar and they smoked outside Aunt Jenny's house after Thanksgiving or Christmas dinner. They'd come back in reeking of weed, eyes red and radiating paranoia, then eat everything they could stuff down their gullets and then go back for seconds and thirds. Yes, Teddy could not claim to be a saint, but once Maggie came into his life and then they had Emily and he was working full time for the force, he'd left it all behind. Now Bobby, on the other hand...he'd confessed to him that he didn't even remember sleeping with his daughter's mother, Carolyn, and when he'd told of his half-assed attempt at a marriage proposal (for the unborn baby's sake) and how the woman had laughed it off, it just sounded so *Jerry Springer* to him. He hated that he felt that way, but he did. And he and Bobby had come from a good upbringing of middle-class hardworking values. That Bobby had taken the turn he had, well, it was a damn shame. That's what it was, a damn shame.

"That guy certainly sounds like he knows what he's talking about," Teddy said between laughs, and this got Bobby going even harder.

"He does," Bobby admitted, wiping tears from his eyes. "He really does."

After the laughter passed, Teddy fiddled around with some papers on his desk for a moment as the two sobered, and when it seemed as if the tension couldn't get any thicker, Teddy finally spoke. His voice was earnest, his tone sincere. He wanted the old Bobby back maybe, or possibly he just didn't want to be writing the report about Bobby's early demise anytime soon, not before he had a chance to get his life turned around while there was still time.

"What are we going to do with you, Bobby?" he asked, almost so quiet that Bobby couldn't hear him. But he did; he heard every word. He looked into his cousin's eyes, licked his lips nervously, thought of what he should say, but nothing came to mind so that's all he could come up with:

"I don't know Teddy," he said softly in return. "I just don't know."

Chapter Seven

Bobby hadn't seen Teddy's wife since last year at the Fourth of July. Every year like clockwork, Teddy threw a Fourth of July celebration, inviting friends, coworkers, family and neighbors. Bobby hadn't gone for several years running, so he at last decided to make an appearance. The reason he was able to attend was the holiday fell on a Thursday, and the party was shortly after his NA meeting. Freshly sober and looking to repent, he decided to show off his newfound clarity. It didn't last long though; Friday kicked off a long holiday weekend. Even though he'd managed to stay sober in front of his cousin, his family and his cop buddies, the very next day he was in rare form, drinking, scoring meth, popping Xanax, and blacking out. If he remembered correctly (what little he could recall), he awoke on a cement floor in a seedy warehouse with rats sniffing at him, trying to determine if he was edible or not. When it turned out he wasn't, the rats were awfully disappointed.

"Bobby," Maggie said pleasantly (maybe too pleasantly; she did, after all, know him well). "We haven't seen you in forever! How are you?"

"Fine." Bobby looked her in the eyes briefly before quickly averting his gaze. Maggie had a way of looking right into you. She seemed to know everything and it was mildly disturbing. "Doing just fine." By all rights, seeing as it was a Saturday evening, Bobby should have been two sheets to the wind by now, on his fifth going on who-knows-how-many beers, snorting and popping his way to oblivion, then nursing a hangover the size of the Grand Canyon the next day, wherever it was he should wake up. As it stood, he'd gotten through the worst of his pain by about three o'clock that afternoon, and if he didn't get drunk on Sunday he could look forward to greeting the new week clear headed. Or whatever passed for clear headed, Bobby Travis style.

"You missed our Fourth of July party this year."

"Yeah, um, I couldn't make it. I had to work." He shot her another quick glance before looking away to spare himself the inevitable skeptical stare. She knew he was lying, but what else was new? On the evening in question he'd been at Hooligans, up to his usual shenanigans, no doubt. "Those swimming pools can't clean themselves."

"I'm sure they can't," she said. "You're quite the workaholic." He was an "aholic" all right, but she doubted "work" was the proper prefix. Bobby chose not to reply.

Maggie held her tongue about the accident. Best not to discuss it in front of Emily. She didn't need to know her second cousin had been up to no good...*again*. If it made it on the news or in the papers and she saw it like that, well, it couldn't be helped. But she wasn't going to unnecessarily facilitate her knowledge of his indiscretion if she could help it.

"Hey Bobby!" Emily cried, running into his outstretched arms, and Maggie had to smile. He may be an alcoholic drug addict, but kids sure liked him.

Other people's kids anyway, she thought, and then mentally chastised herself. She was a good Christian woman. Surely there was no call for being so judgmental. That said, she couldn't speak on his daughter's behalf, she of the missed birthdays and soccer games. She did know, however, how Gina's mother felt about Bobby, and it wasn't good. And not that she could blame her. Bobby barely managed to pay his child support payments on time each month, and he couldn't be counted on to care for the girl at his house because he simply couldn't stay sober. It was appalling was what it was.

"It's nice to have you over for dinner," Maggie said when the hug between him and her daughter ended. Teddy entered the room, a plastic cup of root beer in his hand, which he handed to Bobby when he straightened up.

"Mug Root beer, just like you like it...cold." Teddy smiled, his grin casual but his eyes slightly nervous. Did he smell a hint of booze on Bobby or was it his imagination? And why wasn't Gina with him? He'd told him she could come along if she liked.

"Thanks," Bobby said, accepting the cup, noting to himself that it was plastic and not glass.

Can't trust an alcoholic with glass; I might break it.

He took a sip. "Ummm, good." He smiled at his cousin, dismissing his thought. He knew Teddy meant well. "Thank you," he said again, this time meaning it. Teddy had driven him home after he'd been released from jail that afternoon, then invited him and Gina over for supper that evening. Maybe he just wanted Bobby to stay out of trouble, or maybe he really cared. Bobby chose to think it was the latter of the two.

"Come on in and take a load off." Teddy directed him into the living room and pointed at his recliner, meanwhile taking a seat on the sofa. "And where's that daughter of yours? You forget to ask her if she wanted to come?"

"No," Bobby said, sitting down. "I didn't forget." He took another sip of his root beer, then set the cup on a coaster on the end table beside him. "Carolyn said yes at first, and then she turned around and changed her mind."

"Is that so?"

"Yes, sir."

"I wish I could see her," Emily pouted, and Bobby gave her a small, sad smile.

"I wish you could too, honey," he said wistfully. "I wish you could too."

"Well," Teddy said, "We'll see her next time. In the meantime, Maggie has prepared a sumptuous feast. Haven't you, honey?"

"My famous homemade vegetarian lasagna is in the oven baking as we speak," she said, smiling.

"I appreciate it," Bobby said, really meaning it. As a confirmed bachelor, he either ate most of his meals out of takeout bags (crap like McDonald's or Burger King) or cheap frozen dinners full of enough preservatives to give him colon cancer several times over. "I like eating real food."

"It's as real as it gets, I suppose," Maggie said. "I also made a salad with real greens and tomatoes, celery in it too. You look like you need to eat more vegetables."

"That I do," Bobby agreed.

They made small talk for ten or fifteen minutes while the TV played silently before them, broadcasting the local news, then Maggie got up to check on the lasagna in the oven. She declared it was done and called them to the dinner table.

They ate the meal mostly in silence; every now and then Emily told them about something one of her friends said, maybe a scrap here or there about a TV show she watched, but that was about it. The elephant in the room, of course, was the accident Bobby had just been in and what, if any, the impending ramifications were. Teddy had done his best at the station to simmer things down, arguing that Bobby had merely been a passenger and that the driver of the vehicle (now deceased) was the one to blame on all counts. It hadn't gone as smoothly as he liked, but fortunately the evidence spoke for itself. It was Bobby's bad reputation that kept some of the other sheriff's deputies interested but, all things considered, it was starting to die down.

When dinner was finished, Teddy asked Maggie if it was OK if he and Bobby retired to the porch to talk about "men stuff." She knew exactly what he meant, and nodded casually.

"Of course, honey. Emily and I will clean up."

"But, Mom," the girl whined, "April's expecting me to call. We have to pick a new title for our book club."

Maggie knew this was teenage code for talking about boys, maybe even the new One Direction album (or so she thought; little did she know they had broken up about a year ago and her daughter was now into Adele and K-Pop).

"Now, honey," she said with no hint of reproach. "We all have to pull our weight around here."

"Fi-ii-ne," Emily retorted, making Bobby chuckle. Kids always thought the smallest tasks were such a hardship. Just wait until they got older and saw how much the world gave a crap then. Teenagers always thought it was bordering upon Armageddon when they couldn't talk on their cell phone with their friends or play endless video games. They had so much to learn. Christ, his daughter didn't even *have* a cell phone, thanks to his and her parents' cheapness. The poor kid had to talk to her friends on the landline at home. He sort of felt like a prick, but he couldn't afford the monthly plan. In his opinion that was Carolyn and Barry's department.

On the porch, sitting in the waning light of a warm July evening, Teddy leaned back and crossed his legs, enjoying the feel of the setting sun on his skin. A light breeze picked up, and this too felt good.

"So…am I going to get charged with anything?" Bobby asked at last, after the sun had gone down, the streaks of orange and pink lingering long after the brilliant flash of green on the horizon had passed. Teddy watched the dazzling hues and pondered the question.

"Depends on who you ask." Teddy had processed Bobby himself, fingerprinting him before Al took his picture for, like, the hundredth time. He'd left the "Criminal Complaint" line blank; for the time being he wasn't sure what he should write there, and the captain wasn't sweating him on it. Come Monday morning he'd need to handle it, but for now Bobby was a free man, and without any help from Gary's Bail Bonds to boot.

"I shouldn't be in trouble," Bobby said defensively. "I wasn't behind the wheel."

"That's what I told everyone."

"Is it a crime to be the passenger in a car crash?"

"No Bobby, it isn't, but this obviously isn't your first rodeo."

What he meant, of course, was that Bobby was no stranger to the Escondido jailhouse. If he spent any more time there, they might feel obliged to get him his own honorary cell.

"So what's the problem?"

"Some of the boys at the precinct want to know where you've been getting the drugs."

Bobby looked at his cousin sharply, holding his tongue. There was no way he was going to give up his source, as Tony had been responsible for nothing but providing a service. How people chose to interpret that service, well, that was their problem.

"I'm not going to say where I…um, I mean, Ricky got the drugs. I can't. I don't know."

Teddy eyed the other thoughtfully. "Bullshit."

"Well, *duh!*" Bobby said, and this made them both laugh.

"I'd have to be an idiot not to know you get them at that bar you hang out at," Teddy said, uncrossing his legs and leaning forward. "That's where all your trouble starts every weekend."

Bobby knew this was as obvious as the botched plastic surgery on the Desperate Housewife's faces. He shrugged. "Can't prove anything," he said. "It could be anyone."

Teddy sighed. "This problem of yours isn't going to go away unless you get help—"

"I go to the meetings!"

"And they obviously aren't working! Otherwise you'd have your shit together!"

This brought their conversation to a halt for a few minutes while instead they listened to the tree frogs burble and babble among themselves while the grasshoppers created a symphony possibly only Jiminy Cricket could appreciate. Bobby stubbornly kept his mouth shut because, dammit, it was nobody's business but his own. He knew his cousin was only telling him this because he loved him and wanted the best for him, and he'd be a liar if he said that Ricky's death hadn't scared the crap out of him. It could have easily been Bobby who'd gone balls-up if Ricky had steered the car the other way and Bobby's side had crashed into a parked car (or tree, or whatever), or Bobby could have been holding the meth pipe that impaled Ricky's jugular upon impact. It wasn't as if the whole thing hadn't given him food for thought, but there was no way he was physically capable of just kicking everything cold turkey. He was proud of himself that he'd made the progress he had.

As if reading his thoughts, Teddy nodded solemnly. "I know you've been trying Bobby, and you know damn well I cut you all kinds of slack for that. I'm constantly defending you at the station, even when you make piss-poor decisions that could follow you for life. Hell, it could be worse. If it weren't for me, you'd have had to go around the neighborhood telling everyone you were sorry but it was court mandated that you inform them you're a registered sex offender, and it was in their best interest to keep to their side of the fence."

"You know as well as I do that wasn't fair! I didn't intentionally flash those school kids!"

"I know Bobby, I know, but you try telling the court that it wasn't your desire to whip it out, so much as you just needed to relieve yourself in broad daylight on the side of an elementary school."

This shut Bobby up. It was something he'd done (*no shit*) in a blackout. If he'd simply been wasted, there was no way he'd make the poor choice of pissing on the side of an elementary school while the kids were outside at recess. It wasn't in his DNA to be that stupid. In his blackouts, however, Dr. Dumbass was in control.

"It took a lot of convincing to get you out of that one," Teddy said. "I don't know how much longer I'm going to be able to keep bailing you out." He looked at his cousin imploringly. "This one really takes the cake man, seriously. You have to give me something or I'm not sure how much I can help you anymore."

Bobby swallowed, hard. The thought of turning in Tony hurt him in two very pertinent ways. One was that he wasn't a narc, and Tony would most certainly know it was Bobby who'd spilled the beans, seeing as it was his ass that was so consistently in hot water. Secondly, if he did turn him in, where was he going to get his drugs? Because, let's face it kids, there was no way in hell that Bobby was going to quit, not at this juncture, unless something extremely serious came up. Not that a crap-ton of serious things hadn't come to pass (like Ricky practically drowning in his own blood with a meth pipe sticking out of his neck for instance), but you know…something *really* serious. Something in which Bobby personally jeopardized someone's life and he was in real danger of spending the rest of his days using his mouth to suck his way out of beatings from either the Aryan Brotherhood or black and Mexican gangbangers who knew he was completely inept at turning his toothbrush into a shiv.

After a long moment, he turned to his cousin, looked at him with eyes that could barely contain the guilt and indecision that raged within. At long last he said:

"Let me think about it Teddy, OK? Really, let me give it some thought. I can't just decide to do something like that unless I can sleep on it. OK?"

Teddy sighed, a truly profound sigh that came from the deepest recesses of his ample belly.

"You know I'm just trying to help you Bobby, right? You know that's all I'm trying to do."

"I know," Bobby said, sighing in return. "I know. And I appreciate it man. You gotta know I do."

"Do you?" Teddy mused. "Sometimes I wonder."

But he let it go at that and, about thirty minutes later, Bobby went home.

Chapter Eight

The doorbell hadn't worked in, like, forever, yet Bobby tried it anyway. As a warm breeze kicked up around him, he waited, knowing that no one was coming to the door. Finally, he knocked, three solid raps, and then he heard the footsteps approaching on the hardwood floor, the clomp-clomp-clomp of steel-toed boots, which was funny, because the owner of the boots was unemployed. All he really needed was a pair of slippers.

The door opened and there stood Barry, his thinning hair greasy, his unshaven face as vacant as a mannequin's.

"Yeah?" he said, like he didn't know Bobby, as if he were some solicitor that wanted to sell him a timeshare in Siberia or something equally unpleasant and/or useless. For a moment (only the briefest of moments) Bobby wanted to punch him in the face, but it quickly passed. He wasn't, after all, a violent man. Although Barry's callous demeanor screamed "unrepentant butthole" he could turn the other cheek. He was used to playing this game.

"Hi Barry," Bobby said, attempting a tone that suggested amiability, however was more akin to exasperation. He didn't like to (how the moderators at his meetings liked to call it) *explore his feelings*, but if he did he'd realize that he hated the other's guts with a passion that bordered on psychotic, despite his pacifist leanings. Bobby was forever offering the olive branch of peace, and Barry continued to piss on it time and time again. The ship had long sailed on Bobby's attraction to Carolyn (if it had ever existed at all beyond banging her), yet Barry continued to act as if he was his replacement and liked to think Bobby resented him for it. Bobby couldn't care less where the other man's penis called home, but what he did dislike was that he was the one who got to live with his daughter, even though he was almost as big of a screw-up as Bobby. The only difference was that he didn't have to go to meetings; he got to drink cold Coors Light by the case during lulls in the afternoon while Carolyn worked her ass off and no one gave a crap because he didn't black out *(how could you on light beer?)* and never did much more than munch himself into a coma on the living room couch.

"Is Gina here?"

"You mean Carolyn?"

Now Bobby genuinely wanted to punch the other in the face.

"No, I mean Gina."

"Now," Barry began, as if he were lecturing a child. "You know you can't see Gina unless Carolyn knows about it first." He belched, then looked at Bobby solemnly. "Did you call first?"

"You know I didn't, or you would have known I was coming over."

"That answers your question then." He attempted to shut the door but Bobby (who was taller than the other by several inches and broader in the shoulders) stepped forward and put up a hand, easily holding it open. Barry was probably ninety pounds soaking wet; he was a skinny little puke who amazingly didn't gain any weight no matter that his diet consisted mainly of beer and pork rinds. Because of his physical stature, he didn't intimidate Bobby in the slightest. "Now, you take your hand off this door Bobby Travis," he said in a schoolmaster's tone, and for second Bobby almost obeyed. Almost, until he realized the importance of his visit and decided to carry out his plan.

"No can do, Barry," he countered. "I'm coming in."

"No...you're...not..." Barry wheezed, struggling against the door, but Bobby was stronger, and he won out, crossing the threshold. "I can call the cops, you know."

"Impressive," Bobby said, walking past him to the staircase in the hall. "Takes a lot of skill to dial those three digits. You sure you're up to it?" He planted his foot on the first step, leaned back, and called out, "Gina! You home?"

A moment of silence ensued, and then the clomp-clomp-clomp as Captain Dipshit of the No Balls Brigade staggered to the archaic trim line telephone on the wall. The entirety of the twenty-first century had been tailored toward advanced human communication technology and this jackwad didn't even own a cell phone, not even one of those old flip phones that only had a calculator and a calendar as "extra features."

"You brought this on yourself, Bobby," Barry announced just as Gina appeared at the head of the stairs, her bulldog, Ruby, trailing behind her.

"Hi, Dad," she called down, not too unkindly. In all honesty, she loved her father dearly and always enjoyed his visits, but because Bobby was constantly in the doghouse for one thing or another she couldn't simply forgive him his numerous transgressions. She wanted him to feel as if he was perpetually trying to win her love. Mission accomplished. "What are you doing here?"

"I had to see you, honey," Bobby said, trying to keep his voice from wavering tremulously with emotion. Maybe it was the dinner over at Teddy's and Maggie's that had sparked within him a desire to try harder, seeing how they were so in tune with their daughter Emily's life, or maybe it was the fact that he'd been sober long enough (one day, going on two) to think clearly; whatever the case he had to start making amends, and what better time than now?

You're here because if you were at home you'd be drunk by now. You can lie to Gina, but you can't lie to yourself...

"I think Barry's calling the cops on you," she said, but there was a small grin on her face. Ruby seemed to be smiling too, her large tongue hanging out of her mouth and dripping saliva on the shag.

"I called the cops onnnnn...you," Bobby sang in an out of key voice, one more adept at yelling over loud music when totally wasted than actually carrying a tune, but this brought out his daughter's grin a little more, like he hoped it would. It was an old Johnny Vegas song, popular when Bobby was in his teens. "There's nothing you can do! You know that you're through, 'cuz I called the cops onnnnn...you!"

"That song is stupid," Gina giggled, and Bobby knew he had her. He'd been singing it to her since she was a baby, always with his own sorry ass in mind.

"You think you're tough," he continued, this verse for Barry's benefit. "A real ladies' man. Well, let's see how much trim you get when you're sitting in the can. You like it rough, so let's do it again. 'Cuz killers, rapists, and convicts are your only friends...so..."

"I called the cops on you!" Gina joined in, coming down the stairs. "There's nothing you can do!"

Ruby stayed at the top for a moment, then issued a bark and came barreling down.

Barry came back from the kitchen, his face flushed. "You two go on and quiet down!" he scolded. "'Cuz—"

"I called the cops on you!" Bobby and Gina directed at him, and he gulped so severely his Adam's apple bobbed hilariously. "There's nothing you can do! You know that you're through. 'Cuz I called the cops...I called the cops...I called the cops on you!"

"Let's see how much you're laughing when they get here," Barry said, eyeing Gina reproachfully. After all, he thought she liked him, and that she was just as disgusted with Bobby as her mother and he. What he didn't know was she harbored a soft spot in her heart for Bobby because he was, for Pete's sake, her *dad*. She could run him through the dirt any old time she wanted, but she didn't like it when other people did.

"So," Bobby said cheerfully. "Would you two like to go for a ride?"

"Where?"

"Does it matter?"

"You ain't goin' nowheres, honey," Barry warned. "You walk out that door and you're grounded for a month."

"You can't punish me, Barry," Gina said, walking toward her father. "Only Mom can, and she isn't here."

"You don't have permission to go anywhere with him. The court said—"

"What the court said is bullshit!" she hollered, her voice strident, bandy as a buzz saw. The two men were astonished at her use of profanity. "And you're not my dad!"

An awkward hush followed, lasting roughly thirty ticks of the small hand until Bobby spoke.

"Come on, honey," he said quietly. "Let's just go."

The two of them left, driving away just in time as the police cruiser pulled up to the dilapidated old house, only to find a ninety-pound weakling standing on the porch, looking as hangdog as a mutt that's gotten into the chicken coop and killed every last chicken. Teddy got out of the car, having been tipped off by one of the deputies at the station. He was in street clothes, as he wasn't presently on duty.

"He gone?" he asked, and Barry nodded halfheartedly. "Carolyn's gonna kill me when she finds out I let him get away."

"It isn't as if she was abducted, Barry," Teddy said. "He is her daddy."

"Some daddy he is," Barry complained, as if someone was going to show up any minute and pin a medal on his chest for Father of the Year. "He can't stay sober more than a couple of days."

"Why don't you go inside and have a beer, and I'll go look for them."

"I think I will," Barry said, unaware of the other's ironic grin. He spun around and went back in the house, popped a Coors Light, and turned on the *Montel Williams Show* as Teddy got behind the wheel of the cruiser and drove away. Barry hoped Teddy would have Gina back before Carolyn got home from work because if not, well, he could kiss any nookie goodbye for what very well might be the next couple of days, give or take. With that thought in mind, he turned his attention to the high school kids who liked to dress up as Goth rockers and have sex with each other while listening to Lady Gaga and Marilyn Manson. These freaks really had problems. He belched and took another slug of his beer. What a buncha weirdos.

◆ ◆ ◆

Bobby and Gina sat at a patio table outside of the Baskin Robbins ice cream shop, licking their cones. Bobby had opted for his favorite, Moose Tracks, while Gina had gone with her old standby, rainbow sherbet. Ruby sat on the ground between them, hoping for them to drip some of their frozen treats her way.

"How can you eat that crap?" Bobby kidded her. "It isn't even ice cream."

"This way I don't get fat," she said, and Bobby held back a laugh.

Ever since her thirteenth birthday, she'd been consumed with such things as her skin, her weight and her clothes. Overnight she'd gone from being his little girl to a teenager, and when he pondered this eventuality, it scared the crap out of him. It not only meant she was no longer "daddy's little girl," but that he was getting old as well. His life was disappearing before his eyes, and he couldn't remember over half of it. At the ripe old age of thirty-seven, that was considerably alarming.

Bobby ate his ice cream, thinking about things to talk about. A topic he'd avoid was making any mention of what had just transpired between him and Barry. It was a waste of his breath. Any time he spent with his daughter, in his opinion, shouldn't be squandered talking about Sir Dickhead of Nuttingham Forest.

"How's your summer going?" he asked instead.

"If you came to some of my soccer games you'd know, wouldn't you?" she said, only half joking, and this silenced Bobby for a moment. He honestly didn't know what to say.

"I'm sorry—" he started, before she gave him the wicked grin she'd inherited from him.

"Cripes, I'm kidding; relax!"

"I can do better, honey," he said quietly, his eyes shining sincerely, and this wiped the grin off her face.

"If you did," she said casually, licking her cone, "Bare-assed Barry wouldn't be such a jerk." She looked at him earnestly. "Nor would Mom."

"I've been going to the meetings—"

"And they aren't really helping, are they?" This she said defiantly because, what the hell, despite his participation, he was still a screw-up.

"They're helping more than you know," he replied, in his head knowing what a lie this was, and hating that he had to hear the truth from both

Teddy and Gina in the span of two days. For God's sake, he was banging a woman in his sex addict meeting, getting drunk with a buddy at his AA meetings, placing bets with a bookie in his gambling addicts meeting, and if Ricky hadn't died two nights ago, he'd be getting high with him this Friday when he cashed his checks. And, for that matter, how did he feel about good old Ricky's demise? To be honest—to be really, frankly honest with no bullshit spread around for good measure—he didn't give a flying hump through a rolling donut; that's how he felt about it. Sure, he'd felt guilty at first, and scared as hell that it could have been him, but Ricky was trash, pure and simple, someone who holds out a cup when you pass him on the street, hoping to make enough meth money to stave off his addiction for a while. He was a joke, a loser. As big a loser as Bobby himself.

Gina saw all this on his face, the raw emotion, the desperation in his eyes. She knew she had touched a nerve, and she was glad, but not so glad that she wanted him to wallow in it.

"It's OK Dad, really," she said, finishing her cone and wiping her hands with the tiny napkin that accompanied it. "I know you can do better; I really do. And I know you've been going to those meetings for me."

Bobby almost choked, and when he blinked he felt a single tear slide down his cheek.

"You…you do?" He'd thought she had no idea, as if he'd been going to them all along because he truly wanted to quit.

"I know you're not suffering for your own sake, Dad," she said, the wisdom in her words well beyond her years. Man, he didn't give her enough credit sometimes.

"I started going to them because I wanted you to be proud of me," he said, his voice a papery thin whisper. "I just wanted to…to…to do better… you know?"

She looked at him solemnly, her large blue eyes starting to water too. Man, she hated crying; it must have been something she inherited from her mother because her dad, well, he was never afraid to cry. In fact, he did it so much it was almost unnerving. She thought grown men weren't supposed to cry, but her dad did it almost every time he saw her. Not, like, pulling his hair out and beating his chest sobbing, but somehow he always managed a few tears without any trouble, and she knew it wasn't contrived. He was probably holding back too; if he started wailing piteously he probably thought he'd scare her away.

"From what I hear, you are doing better," she said, reaching out and taking his hand. "You don't get trashed every day anymore," she observed. "That's good."

"I got it down to weekends," he said, and another couple of tears streaked down his cheeks. He swiped at them absently, not caring who saw him. When he was with his daughter, the rest of the world just disappeared, its importance greatly reduced in significance compared to her physical presence. She was the only female he felt he could be real with, that he could be entirely honest around. Because she was his daughter he didn't look at her like he did at other women; he viewed her as another species altogether, one that was an advanced life form that he had the pleasure of knowing and spending time with, when he was lucky enough to spend time with her. Because of his current standing as "unreliable dad," he didn't get to see her as much as he would have liked to, and that broke his heart more than anyone would ever know. What he'd done today was going to have serious repercussions, of that he was sure, and sooner than later, but he needed this, really, truly needed this. He required her strength to embolden and empower him. With her love, there was no telling what he could do.

"That's good, real good."

"Not as good as it could be," he admitted, and she nodded.

"Everything happens in time, doesn't it?"

He looked at her forlornly. "I want you to know that if I'm ever able to do it…to sober up…it's because of you."

"Don't say that."

"I mean it! I'm not doing this for me, although I should be. And I'm certainly not doing it for your mother. The only reason any of this matters is because of you. Hell, if you hadn't been born, I'd probably be dead by now."

This statement stopped her cold. Any remark she may have had in return was frozen on her tongue. The brutality of such candor had her momentarily paralyzed.

"Don't say that, Dad," she said softly, clutching his hand even tighter. "I don't like to even think of stuff like that."

Bobby wiped away another tear with his free hand and gave her paw a squeeze.

"Sorry hon, I don't mean to be a downer."

"I just don't like to think about that," she said, a tear trickling down her own face. As a girl, she knew she had the right to cry as much as she wanted; society deemed it an acceptable thing to do. But still, she hated crying because to her it showed weakness, and one thing her mother had taught her was how to be strong. Carolyn was a ball-busting, tough-as-nails, evil bitch who was probably incapable of showing any emotions other than anger, spite, jealousy, hatred, and good old-fashioned bitchiness, but maybe that was beside the point. Gina had seen her cry a few times, so she knew she was human, but it wasn't something she made a habit of. Not like her father. Maybe he had issues with depression; she'd read somewhere that a lot of chemically dependent people did. It was how the cycle worked: when they felt great they binged, and then they felt bad so they kept using drugs to ward of the inevitable come down. Once they ran out of money or drugs, the depression finally got a chance to sink its claws in. Her father, it seemed, was in a perpetual state of withdrawal.

When Bobby had himself back under control, he shot her a smile, one that dispelled the gloom and reestablished a light, whimsical tilt to their chat. In his grin there was a playfulness that reminded her of some of her teenage friends. It was the kind of smile an adult wasn't supposed to have, in her opinion, and it made her love him even more.

"So what do you want to do now?" she asked, and his grin deepened.

"I figured we could drive to a nice park and take you and your dog for a walk, then we could go and get something to eat—"

"Like Jack-In-The-Box?"

"Crap-In-The-Box?" he laughed. "Sure, sure, anything you like."

A police car pulled up along the sidewalk next to the Baskin Robbins, flashers lit up, and a man stepped out. The look on Gina's face fairly told him everything he needed to know.

"I'm about to get arrested, aren't I?"

"Well," a deep voice said, "that all depends."

Bobby swiveled around, saw his cousin Teddy standing there with a smile canted on his tan face. He didn't look as official in his jeans and t-shirt, and this made him smile.

"On what officer?" he asked.

"On whether or not you're going to buy me an ice cream cone."

Bobby got up from his chair, opened the door of the ice cream shop. "Um, Ms. ice cream scooper? This man needs a..." Bobby turned to his cousin. "What's your poison, sir?"

"Mint chocolate chip."

"This officer of the law needs a double scoop of mint chocolate chip in a waffle cone, stat!"

"Coming right up," she replied, grinning. The place was presently empty; she'd been sweeping the floor for the fifth time when he made the request. She set it down and started making his cone.

"One ought to be fine," Teddy said, rubbing his generous gut.

"Make that a triple scoop," Bobby said and winked. "This man looks dangerously underweight."

"Maybe compared to somebody from Milwaukee," Teddy joked amiably, taking a seat next to them and leaning back in his chair. "Now don't go telling the missus about this."

"What?" Bobby asked. "You busting me for snatching my daughter, or me buying you an ice cream cone?"

Teddy considered this for a moment before offering an even bigger smile.

"Both," he said, reaching out to take the proffered cone from the young lady when she presented it. "We better make it both."

Chapter Nine

When Gina got home, Barry and her mother were waiting for her on the porch, sitting in the love swing, both of them looking about as pissed off as if they'd just found out the house had been repossessed. Barry was drinking a can of Coors Light and, from the looks of it, Carolyn was drinking her favorite, a whisky and Coke. When she finished her shift at Wal-Mart, she generally spent the rest of the evening belting cheap booze until her voice started sounding more and more Norwegian (a heritage to a great extent she tried to conceal) and her face took on a ruddy hue. Barry, despite how many Coors Lights he drank, always looked the same: like an idiot deep-fried in sewage water and glazed with powdered pork rinds. This was an analogy that Gina had come up with herself, and it never failed to make her giggle.

"How come the cops didn't bring you home?" Carolyn asked, her voice betraying her dwindling sobriety.

Geez, for how bad they talk about Daddy, you'd think the two of them would have a sense of irony, she thought, and she giggled again.

"What's so damn funny?"

"Nothing," she said, stopping just short of the porch stairs.

"Is Bobby in jail?" Barry asked, sipping his beer.

"Nope."

"Why the hell not?"

Judging by Barry's exclamation, you'd have thought poor Bobby had killed someone.

"Because he didn't do anything."

"That damn cousin of his was the one who found him, wasn't he?" Carolyn said, slurring, and Gina almost wanted to scream "hypocrite" in her red, drunken face but refrained, albeit barely. Sometimes their ignorance just about killed her.

"No..."

"Don't you lie to me," Carolyn snapped. "Barry told me he was the one who showed up here after he made the call."

"Why did you have to call the cops, Barry? Too big of a pussy to fight your own battles?"

"Language!" Carolyn scolded, but she didn't further defend her hubby. She damn tootin' knew he was a freakin' pansy. If it weren't for her, Bobby would have kicked the crap out of him long ago, and Bobby was a goddamn *pacifist*. He avoided fights at all costs if he could.

"Now, you know the rules," Barry said, ignoring the fact that he'd just been emasculated not only by his stepdaughter, but by his wife as well by not standing up for him. "He ain't allowed to see you 'cept on the days the court ruled on, and if he has permission from your mother in advance." He nodded at her sagely. "What he done was *illegal*." This he said as if Bobby had been caught with a sniper rifle, ready to take a shot at the president which, judging by the idiot who was in charge, nobody would have cared about anyway.

"You're full of it Barry," Gina said, making a move to ascend the stairs and go to her room, when suddenly her mother was on her feet, her drink hitting the deck like a wounded soldier, ice cubes flying from the plastic cup every which way. Her cold hands were like talons, her Lee Press On nails sinking into the flesh on Gina's arms, her palms abrasive from hard-earned calluses. For a split second she wondered how Barry liked getting hand jobs from such coarse mitts, and she almost giggled again but it caught in her throat when Carolyn launched into a tirade.

"You-don't-talk-to-your-dad-like-that!" She shook Gina as she said each word, as if to further emphasize the point, and the young girl's head rocked back and forth on her shoulders. At times like these, Gina wasn't merely scared of her mother, she was terrified. However, the talk she'd had with her daddy today had changed something within her; maybe it had been his bluntness, or maybe it was because he was the only grown-up who didn't talk down to her, like she was still a little kid. She was *fifteen*, for cripes' sakes, almost sixteen, and these two acted as if they still had to change her diapers or wipe her snot-crusted nose. Where she might have once cowered, she felt a strong reserve shoot through her, and she raised her arms and shook off her mother as if she'd barely been hanging on.

"That asshole isn't my dad!" she shrieked boldly, backing away. She took one step down, then two.

Carolyn was stunned silent. In all her years, the girl had never talked to her like that, had never so much as raised her voice to her. She wouldn't; she was petrified of her. But now...this insubordination was confusing.

"What?"

"You heard me! That asshole isn't my dad; Bobby is! And if I want to spend time with him, I will!"

"Not while you live under my roof! The court says—"

"*Fuck* the court!" she thundered, and Barry gasped. Not her mother, though; when angered she had a mouth on her that would make a sailor blush. But not with her daughter though, oh no. When she was really, truly pissed, her voice got quieter, like that guy who always played a gangster in the movies. When next she spoke, her voice was calm, almost a whisper.

"I suppose you think you'd be better off if he raised you, hmm?"

"I'm not saying that." Another one of her mother's tricks was turning everything around, saying things that she knew weren't true, but saying them anyway just to get a rise out of her.

"I suppose he's a better parent than I'll ever be, what with his arrest record and ability to remember all of your important events."

"That's not what I'm saying!"

"OK then." Her mother's eyes focused on her like laser beams, her voice getting even softer still. "What *are* you saying?"

Gina's mouth moved but nothing came out. For a moment, she didn't know what to say, how to defend herself. Her mother was so good at this; Gina had too much of her father's conciliatory leanings in her to know how to properly wage war against a woman by whom she was so dreadfully outmatched. And if she did know what to say, did it matter? Would it change anything? The answer, ladies and gentlemen, friends and neigh-boreeno's, was no, N-freakin'-O. There was absolutely no way she could go toe to toe with her mother and come out the other side intact. Not now, maybe not ever. And the sad thing was that both of them knew it. Why her mother even toyed with her was beyond a doubt a mystery, except to flex her muscle, to show what a god-awful bitch she was.

"Nothing," Gina answered lamely, knowing when she was beat.

"That's what I thought," Carolyn said, her voice still soft, her demeanor like that of a coiled snake. "Now go to your room while your stepdad and I think of your punishment."

"That's not fair!" She couldn't help herself; honestly, it wasn't her fault.

"You didn't have to go with him, yet you did. I think you should learn a lesson in accepting some of the blame."

"And you laughed at me," Barry added. "You ought not to laugh at your dad."

"*Stepdad*," Gina corrected, and Carolyn shrugged.

"Whatever." She eyed her daughter a moment, reading within the girl a petulance that wasn't over, not by a long shot. She was only giving up because Carolyn had her on the ropes; if she had any ammo she'd use it, that was for damn sure, but the kid had nothing. "Now go."

Gina dropped her eyes and walked slowly up the stairs and through the screen door, being careful not to slam it because displaying anger would give her mother satisfaction, and that was the last thing she wanted. She may have lost the battle but damn straight she hadn't lost the war.

When Carolyn heard the distant click of her daughter's door latching, she sat down next to Barry, lit a smoke.

"How come you let him in?"

"I told you, he barged in! I didn't just let him."

"You ought to be more of a man than that."

"He's bigger than me! What the hell do ya want?" Barry lit a cigarette of his own and smoked in silence for a bit, fuming. The goddamn woman had a tongue made out of sandpaper, and she always knew how to use the rough side of it on him.

"I suppose," she said after a bit, "we should do something about it."

"Like what? We tried to get a restraining order against him, but his damn cousin persuaded the judge it wouldn't be (and I quote) 'in Gina's best interest.' How the hell are we going to use the law for any more than getting him arrested when he's got them in his pocket? We're screwed!"

Carolyn smoked her cigarette, considering this. Barry was a complete imbecile (an idiot savant minus the savant), but he was right, and it was really hard to admit that such a feeble brained twerp was *ever* right. It made the whole world seem as if it were as real as the moon landing, which everybody knew was fake. But what the hell could they do if they couldn't keep Bobby from showing up whenever he wanted to? If the law wouldn't help them, who would? She needed something she could use against him, something to get him to toe the line, but she was damned if she had any ideas.

"I suppose he has us over a barrel," she said, and Barry grunted in reply.

"That's what I keep tellin' ya," he said, and snubbed his smoke out in a tinfoil ashtray he'd stolen from a Pizza Shack in the good old days when it was legal to smoke inside. "It's the same song I been singin' for years."

"You need to learn a new song," she muttered and he looked at her sharply.

"What?"

"Nothing." She stood. "I'm going inside to make some supper. Sloppy Joe's OK with you?"

"Sure," he said, his mind already turning to other things, but not hers, and she continued to think about it for the rest of the night, but no easy answer came to her.

Chapter Ten

Bobby was just getting out of the shower when he heard someone pounding on his door. And pounding was the right word too; this wasn't just knocking. No, whoever was out there wanted to get inside, like, yesterday.

"Coming!" he hollered, putting on a pair of ripped, dirty jeans. "Hold your horses!"

Buttoning his worn flannel shirt, he squinted his eyes as the early morning sun blinded him while he eased the door open. Thanks to this disadvantage, he didn't see who was crossing the threshold into his humble abode until it was entirely too late.

"Why, Bobby," a voice as sincere sounding as a used car salesman's said, "long time no see."

"Huh?" he said, allowing the other to come in. "Sure, I suppose so." He vaguely recognized the voice, tinged with an accent, the tone smooth and calm, however laced with an undercurrent of violence. It was only when his early-morning visitor took a seat in his ragged seen-better-days Lazy-Boy did he realize he'd been foolish not to have inquired who it was before he'd opened the door. I mean, who did he expect was going to visit him at seven fifteen on a Monday morning? If it wasn't the cops, his bookie, or drinking buddy, there was no one else it could be, except...

"You owe me some money."

Gulp, aw, *shit...*

"Hey, Simon, long time no see."

It wasn't every day that the boss of the local British Mafia showed up at your door, rolling a Cuban cigar between pudgy fingers while his two favorite henchmen, Slugger and Rocko, loitered behind him, cracking their respective knuckles and doing their best to look menacing. As it was, they didn't have to try that hard. Both were born into their careers based simply upon what they looked like: tall, broad in the shoulders and chest, butt-ugly, with slightly crossed eyes, and brains that affirmed their lack of conceptual understanding regarding anything that didn't involve broken bones and two shots to the head, execution style. It looked like Bobby had picked a lousy day to stop drinking. If he smoked, this would be the proper time to light up.

"How much?" was all Bobby could think to ask, and all things considered, this was probably the best thing he *could* say. Eventually he'd ask for what, but now wasn't the time.

"I didn't bring an itemized receipt," Simon said in an accent so thick Bobby could scarcely discern what he was saying. He did, however, recognize that the other was making a joke and he chuckled politely. "But I believe it comes to fifteen thousand dollars and some change."

"Can I write you a two-party out-of-state bad check?" Bobby ventured, attempting a joke of his own. The material wasn't original; he'd stolen it from Homer Simpson. Simon, conversely, didn't like it.

"Come again?"

"I was just kidding," Bobby said dispiritedly, wondering if this was Rocko and Slugger's cue to proceed bashing his brains out, but instead Simon smiled.

"An attempt at humor at my expense? You really do have a pair on you, don't you?"

Bobby somehow managed a grin. "Yes?"

"Bollocks to that horse crap, mate." He waved a hand, and suddenly his henchmen removed their pistols from the waistbands of their trousers. "Would you care to make another joke?"

"No?"

"I didn't think so." Another wave of his hand and the pistols disappeared. "So I ask you: What are we going to do about this situation?"

"I'm going to pay you?" Bobby couldn't help it; like a college coed, everything he said was coming out as a question.

"You bet your sorry arse you're going to pay me, or these two cheeky gents are going to play tug-of-war with your dangly bits. Are we clear?"

"You know me, Simon; I'm good for it. Surely such a savvy business-man as yourself can understand when one of his clients is temporarily down on their luck."

"Get your tongue out of my arsehole, Bobby. I don't particularly like it in there."

"Um, sorry?"

"That's a good lad. Now, about my money. When can I expect it?"

"I don't know."

"That's not the answer I was looking for." He waved his pudgy fist, the one not clutching the unlit (thankfully) Cuban, and Slugger and Rocko stepped forward, taking Bobby's puny arms in their beefy hands. "I think these two are going to perform a little unnecessary surgery on you, Bobby. How does that sound?"

"Um...bad?"

"It certainly won't be a day at the circus, now, will it?" He nodded his giant head. "Tune him up, boys."

That was the last thing Bobby heard before a fist connected with his face, and he was aware of a loud snapping sound that was probably his nose breaking.

I don't have health insurance, he thought, before his legs went all rubbery and the carpet came up to meet him as the early-morning light was dimmed by a midnight sun.

◆ ◆ ◆

The waiting room at the urgent care center wasn't extremely full, yet for some reason Bobby waited over an hour and a half before a nurse came out and called his name.

"Bobby Travis?"

Bobby raised a hand holding a blood-soaked hanky.

"Here," he answered, as if it was high-school rollcall, and the young man rolled his eyes.

"This way, please."

Bobby got up and followed him, wondering if the phone calls he'd just made were evidence that he most likely had a concussion. For starters, he had called his daughter, trying his best to sound strong, yet asking her if she had any money he could borrow. When she asked why, he'd evaded the truth until finally he'd admitted that if he didn't pay off a certain local mobster, he'd most likely disappear one day only to reappear many weeks later at the bottom of the ocean in the backseat of a stolen car wearing nothing but a bucket filled with cement. This, of course, led to her putting her mother on the phone, which then led to many questions, some of which he answered, many of which he didn't. At some point she started yelling at him so he hung up. She hadn't called him back. The next call he placed was to Terry, his bookie. After a bit of hemming and hawing, Bobby burst out with a request for the money to place a bet that would earn him a lot of cash fast, something high-risk with a big payout.

"But you owe me money already, Bobby," Terry reminded him. "You haven't paid me from the last time."

"I know, Terry, um, but, here's the thing: I really need the money."

"Hell, Bobby, we all 'really need the money.' What, you gonna get your legs broken or something?"

"Probably 'or something.'"

"What does that mean?"

"I don't know, maybe just a couple months in traction, or maybe a one-way drive down homicide lane. I guess it depends on what kind of mood Simon is in…"

There was silence on the other end of the line for a long moment before Terry said, "Simon Blackwell?"

"Uh, yeah, that's the guy—"

"You owe money to *Simon freakin' Blackwell*?"

"Um, yeah, that's what I've been telling you—"

"Are you nuts or just stupid?"

"Probably a little bit of both—"

"That guy is going to *kill* you!"

"I believe that's the message I've been trying to convey—"

"Jesus hopped up Christ in a sidecar!"

"What?"

"You're fucked!"

"Again, none of this is new information to me." Bobby was starting to get a little frustrated. "Can you help me or what?"

"What, you wanna go shopping for tombstones?"

"No, I was thinking more about cremation...can you please just lend me some money, dude?"

"So you can dig yourself a bigger hole? I don't think so."

"Rocko and Slugger are already digging a hole, and if I don't throw some cash at them pretty quick their going to toss me in it."

Terry took a deep breath, sighed. "How much you owe them?"

"Fifteen grand."

"Holy balls!"

"Yes, and my balls. Simon indicated my 'dangly bits' might be in danger as well." Bobby drew a panicky breath. "So, can you back me on a bet?"

"It would have to be a long shot sucker bet...and what the hell am I going to get out of it if you lose and they kill you? I get nothing!"

He's got a heart as big as Santa's...

"I got collateral."

"Like what?"

"Um, my truck. That's gotta be worth something."

"It ain't worth no fifteen large!"

"I don't need that from you, I just need enough to make a bet."

"So where you thinking? At the casino, on blackjack?"

"You know where I'm thinking."

Another long pause. At once Terry knew exactly what was on Bobby's mind, and his silence told him everything he needed to know: he was genuinely as desperate as his voice sounded. Bobby was terrible at the horses; that it was a consideration at all confirmed he was truly at the end of his rope.

"You gotta be kidding."

"I'm not."

"You realize if you lose, your kid is gonna be without a father."

"She's going to be without a father anyway if I don't try."

"Fair enough," Terry conceded. "OK, I'll meet you there, but you bring the title of your truck with you, and a working ballpoint pen."

"Done."

"You've really gone and screwed yourself good this time, haven't you?"

"Yeah," Bobby agreed. "I think I did."

"You mind if I ask?"

Bobby groaned. The answer to Terry's question had been plaguing him ever since Simon's visit. While he was lying on the floor, barely conscious, he'd asked him what he borrowed the money for, and the answer had astounded him. How could he have been so stupid? The answer: there wasn't one. When it came to Bobby, when there was a bet to be made and he was in a blackout (no pun intended) all bets were off.

"Yes," Bobby said. "I do mind."

"Even if I threaten you with not giving you the money?"

Bobby sighed. "Fine. I'll tell you when I see you."

It was shortly after this phone call that his name was called and he was weighed, his blood pressure taken, and he was then asked to have a seat on a paper-covered table. Subsequently he told the nurse his "history" (short story: he was mugged by some kids, he was perfectly healthy otherwise, he didn't drink or use drugs, and he wasn't on any prescription medications). The nurse took his temperature, assessed his wounds, told him his nose didn't look too bad, and the doctor would see him shortly. He then left the room, but not before giving him a look that said he didn't believe anything he'd just said. What the hell, Bobby was used to such treatment. In the meantime, he cooled his heels and collected his thoughts, wishing he wasn't such a goddamn chump...

Chapter Eleven

"I'm really worried about Dad!"

"He was wasted, trust me." Carolyn took a long drag on her cigarette and then tossed it out of the car window. "There's no way he'd be so stupid that he'd call his own daughter to ask for money because some gangster was going to rub him out." After she said that, she thought about it for a moment. *Or would he?* One never knew when it came to Bobby. Maybe he was suffering from a head injury...

"He didn't sound drunk. He sounded scared."

"He was slurring his words."

"I guess, sort of..."

"I talked to him too. He was a mess."

"I don't know." Gina shook her head. "He really sounded sincere."

"I'm sure he did to you. To me he sounded like he always does when he's on a bender."

Carolyn took a left, then a right, then a left. In short order, she was parked at the curb opposite the park where Gina's soccer team practiced. "All ashore that's going ashore."

"So?"

"So what?"

"Are you going to do something?"

"About what?"

"Ahhggg! About Dad, duh!"

"What's to do? He'll sober up and sleep it off, and then he'll call and apologize." She shrugged. "It's what he always does."

"I told you; I don't think he was drunk."

"And I'm telling you, he was. Who are you going to believe?"

Gina looked at her mother in exasperation, but the coach was just arriving, and if she didn't fall in with the others she'd get yelled at for being late. Thanks to Bobby's call she'd had to get a ride from her mom, which was rare indeed. Also, they were still at odds with one another from their spat the day previous. Now wasn't a good time to continue this argument.

"Fine," she said, opening her door. "But if the police call—"

"I'll tell them what I always do: 'Book him, Danno.'"

"Not funny."

"Get out, I gotta go."

"I love you too." And she got out of the car and hurried to join the others as they were performing their warm-up calisthenics.

Thanks a lot, Daddy. The mob better be out to get you…

♦ ♦ ♦

Bobby saw Terry by the betting windows, studying a program. He walked up to him, clapped him on the back.

"Thanks for meeting me here."

"Yeah, I don't know who's dumber: me or you."

"Let's assume for the sake of the argument that it's me."

"I think we're running a close tie."

"So who looks good?"

Terry shook his head. "None of them." Truth be told, Terry knew how to pick horses based on a system he devised. But if he let on and Bobby figured it out he'd wonder why he'd never told him before and he'd want a piece of the action. With the cat out of the bag it would be hard to take advantage of him in the future because it would appear, dear friendereeno's, as if Terry was a liar. Heaven forfend! However, the way it looked, if he didn't help him out, there would be no future. He either tried to save Bobby's skinny ass today or he lost his business. He just had to make sure it looked like a lucky guess. And, besides, even though he had a system it didn't mean the horse he chose was going to win; there was still a lot of luck involved. That being said, the uptick to his success was that his scheme was based almost entirely on logic with very little guesswork. It was called handicapping, and he went about it like this:

First, he studied the racing form and discarded all noncontenders (the surefire losers), then decided which of the surviving runners merited a bet. He didn't bother with maiden-claimers, claimers, starter allowances, and other confusing, low-level crap. He only considered the following for wagers: Maiden-special-weight events, allowances, allowances/optional-claimers, and stakes. This exclusion against betting on the cheaper races and betting only on the better class of horses was because they tended to be the most consistent. If he was gonna shell it out, he wanted the best odds at reeling it back in.

With this system, he considered three horses in each race, and these were entrants that made the Daily Racing Form consensus. Basically, he tried to reduce his handicapping to its barest essentials and speed up the overall process of finding a pick and a bet. By restricting himself to consideration of just three horses, he skipped past the most painstaking stage of handicapping (weeding out the probable losers) and pinpointed the most likely contenders. If he found three exceptional horses, he could consider betting a Quinella, an Exacta, or a Trifecta. The payouts for these types of bets were huge, but the probability of winning was near nil. If he wanted to have the best chance at getting paid, he knew he should pick just one horse, and bet to win, not to place or show. Betting to win paid more than placing or showing.

After eliminating all but three, he could do one of two things. First, disregard the likeliest two winners, cross his fingers, and pick the third because the payout was bigger the greater the odds. Possibly that horse had been closing third or fourth in its last five or six races and was due for a win based on various factors too numerous to go into. It was that, or he could pick the favorite. The first option was a stretch because sys-tematically it was illogical. As previously noted it was typically based on luck because the issues regarding its success were far too many (track conditions, weather, the jockey's win/lose record, was the horse better suited to turf or dirt, etc.), and the stars had to be aligned just right to pull it off. The second option had a better shot, as it was a known fact that 33 percent of all horse races were won by the favorite. They weren't called the "favorite" for nothing; these were the horses that stood the best chance of winning. That said, he would only bet on the favorite horse if the odds were 11/8 or better. To arrive at these odds, he divided the first figure by the second. So, 11/8 is 11 divided by 8, which is 1.375 the horse's win/lose record. If he liked the odds, he'd bet on it. Yet he also looked at six other things that augmented his handicap: if the horse dropped in class off its last race, which he preferred to have been in the past forty-five days; if the horse had won 20 percent or better of at least five starts that year, or that year *and* last; if the horse posted a big win (by three lengths or more) in its last out in the past forty-five days; the horse posted a bullet five or six-furlong workout in the past fourteen days; the horse's trainer had won at least 20 percent of his starts that year; and last but not least the horse's jockey had won at least 20 percent of his starts that year. If he could find a contender with all of these things going for it, he could bet big (he had to, because bets paid out higher on longshots; betting the favorite wasn't as risky because it was more of a sure thing) and figure *that* horse stood the best chance of crossing the finish line first. In all actuality, his system wasn't even 50/50 but it was surely better than guessing, and it had served him well many times over. Gambling was still gambling, after all, and no matter what your system, providential fortune always played a big part.

So all this he debated, and when he found a horse that had all but two of his odds makers present (in a race that was worth betting on), he decided, somewhat against his better judgement, to place a large bet on it to win. He did this because he wanted the chance to see Bobby win to lose money another day, preferably to him and not some avaricious loan shark. Especially Simon Blackwell, the greedy son of a bitch. That guy had been extorting money out of his clients for years, especially those (like Bobby) who were prone to lose big. Some of them never lived to tell the tale. Terry had lost many of them to various accidents, a lot of them not so accidental, like gunshot wounds to the head and car crashes involving severed brake lines.

Still, for Terry to pick the winning horse he'd need Lady Luck to smile down upon him today, maybe take pity on worthless ole Bobby Travis and his sorry ass.

"You got any ideas?"

Terry nodded. "I do." He looked at the other with what he hoped was a dubious expression. When it came to acting, it was safe to say he wouldn't be thanking the Academy any time soon. "This is just a guess, mind you, but it's all I can think of."

"Your opinion is better than mine any day so cough it up."

"We have to bet the favorite to win, and the only way we can come up with fifteen large is by betting big."

"How much?" Bobby had no head for percentages and figures. As smart as he was, fractions and formulas were beyond him. Besides the simple arithmetic of adding up his weekly checks to deposit them in the bank, he was mathematically a dummy.

"Don't worry about it, you'll owe me. Now let's make the bet."

"You're the boss."

"One would think so." And he approached the counter, pulling out his roll (the one he let his clients see) and winking at the dour-looking woman behind the bulletproof glass. "Hello, honey," he said cheerily, and made his bet.

◆ ◆ ◆

Bobby had to reschedule two of his late morning clients, but he got back on track (ha!) by late afternoon. He had to skip his AA meeting to do so, but he figured it was worth it. He could make it up later in the week if he wanted, if he felt the need arise. Survival had become priority numero uno.

As he checked the chlorine levels in the Williamses' family pool, he reflected upon the time he'd hid drugs here, just so that he couldn't use them. It was something he'd done before with varying success, whenever he had drugs left over from the previous weekend and he wanted to try and stay sober for his daughter's sake. In this case, he'd failed miserably. He purposefully did their house last that day because they had the best setup for what he needed to do. They had a yard that was enclosed by a six-foot-high brick barrier, with guard dogs that circled the perimeter at night. What he did was wrap the gram of meth tightly in Saran Wrap, then he put it in a brown paper bag. This he then put in a small wooden box (he didn't want the dogs to dig it up and eat it, for their sake and his) and, when he was nearing the completion of his job for the day, he quickly buried it along the fence line, behind a large potted succulent where he knew no one could see him from the house. If someone wandered out to ask him a question, he'd be totally busted. As it was, luck was on his side; no one was around and he quickly hid his treasure, marking it with some strategically placed twigs so that he knew where to find it next week. Why would he go to all this trouble? Simply put, he couldn't trust himself to hold any product because invariably he would wind up doing it, no matter how badly he wanted not to. Regardless that he was going to the meetings, despite the fact that he was trying to be a better father, notwithstanding that he would almost certainly screw something up, he'd end up doing it because that was what drug addicts did. The only thing he could do was hide the drugs from himself in a place where he was almost certain he couldn't get at them no matter what.

This wasn't a new activity, Christ no, it was something he'd done many times before. In the past, he'd left drugs at Carolyn's because the chances of him going there to retrieve them were slight indeed. If he did risk it, it was almost a sure bet that Carolyn would be home, blocking the way, or Gina would be there and he'd feel guilty as hell. The main reason he didn't use her house anymore was that Barry had found his stash on more than one occasion, and when Bobby came back to retrieve it and found his drugs missing, there was nothing he could do about it. What was he going to do, complain to Carolyn that her husband was stealing from him? Even though it would get Barry in trouble (and this was pure speculation; she might have been indulging with him), this act would announce that Bobby was failing at his sobriety, and she could use this against him when it came to his visitation rights, despite the strings Teddy pulled for him. No, he had to find someplace else to hide it from himself.

He'd tried having Ricky hold on to it for him, but after one attempt (one he'd been dubious of in the first place) he found that was the equivalent of throwing it away. Probably the second Bobby left his house Ricky grabbed his glass pipe and had himself a party. When he'd gone over to claim his drugs, Ricky had worn a look of shame on his face like a patchy, pubescent beard. His apologies were profuse, but that didn't get him his ice back. Besides, he couldn't be an accessory any longer anyway, seeing as Ricky had gone to the great meth lab in the sky.

He also knew no one who was sober that he could trust. If they were drug-free they would most likely flush his stash, knowing how it was killing him. Melissa wouldn't be an accomplice; he was sure of that. There was simply no one he could trust to hold them who wouldn't toss or consume them.

His only option was to find someplace he had limited access to, a location that was off-limits to him 99 percent of the time. This got him to thinking, and he realized that hiding them at a client's house (on their property) was his best bet. He only had permission to be there once a week, so he carefully selected a client whose weekly cleaning could be repositioned to suit his needs (rescheduling them from Monday to Thursday), arranging their service for late in the day, and said client having a large yard that was practically impossible to gain entrance to unless he was expected to be there. Hence, the Williamses' house.

There was one flaw to his plan though, a fly in the ointment so to speak: all bets were off when he was in a blackout. And that was precisely what happened.

He'd stashed the drugs because his daughter had a soccer game on Saturday, and he desperately wanted to be there. If he was holding he'd never show up; hell, it was a miracle that he'd made it from Sunday to Thursday holding the drugs and he somehow managed to hold off doing them during the week. He remembered clearly that it had taken every ounce of his will power to have them under the same roof with him during that tortuously long stretch of time without busting them out. He'd gone to extra NA meetings that week every time he found himself removing a mirror from his wall and walking to the drawer where he kept them, almost totally unable to stop himself, their pull was that strong. He'd slept like crap all week, and dragged himself through every day with the promise of how wasted he'd get when all this was over.

He'd decided upon the Williamses' house because of all the previously mentioned criteria and, developing his system, stashed them. Hell, the fence alone was a major detractor, but throw in the dogs and he had himself a guaranteed Fort Knox.

Again, all of this was true until the inevitable blackout. It was a plan that by all means should have worked...until his conscious mind took a leave of absence and then his alter ego took over, the one that could never say no to a good time, no matter what the circumstances or the stakes. Dr. Jekyll and Mr. Jack-Off.

As one would expect, he wound up at Hooligans, and after six or seven beers (against his better judgement) he procured a gram from Tony. He wanted to keep himself in some semblance of control, keep the party short and sweet so he could still attend his daughter's game. When his heart started beating too fast, he popped some Xanax, a couple of two-milligram bars that had him blacked out within the hour on top of all the booze he'd consumed. He didn't remember what happened next; the story he'd pieced together through an assortment of clues he'd ascertained by looking at his clothing and various bodily wounds, drug buddy hearsay, his client's testimony, and the local evening news. All together it went something like this:

He'd used the gram of meth and wanted more, but he was out of money. When he was wasted, it was certain that he couldn't process information in a normal fashion. As usual, he was too fucked up to remember his PIN numbers, from either his measly bank account or from the one credit card he barely paid the minimum balance on. He tried to get money from the overpriced ATM in Hooligans, and after three incorrect tries on both cards he was shut out of his accounts. So the solution to his problem, it would seem, was to get his stash from the William's yard. Ricky had been with him at the time, so he was the one who recounted how Bobby had driven there and parked his truck a couple of blocks away. He then surreptitiously (or so he thought) crossed from yard to yard until he was at their property line, standing before the enormous stone fence. Ricky's testimony had been pretty spotty, so he also determined by his ripped shirt and pants (not to mention scratched and gouged hands, arms, and legs) that he'd climbed the fence and fallen from the top to the ground below.

According to his client, someone had scaled their fence and had a run-in with their dogs. Apparently, the dogs had managed to scare the intruder off, but not before he'd dug a large hole in their yard, the purpose of this crime unapparent. The Williamses didn't, to the best of their knowledge, have anything of value buried on their property. It did lead the man of the house to investigate over the following weeks; perhaps the previous owner had secreted some valuables when he was going through his divorce. Obviously, Mr. Williams never found anything.

The Channel Ten news team reported that two men were in a high-speed chase with the police after a seemingly failed break-in on an unnamed victim's residential property. The cops never got the license plate number nor the exact make of the vehicle; all they knew was it was a black pickup truck, maybe a Ford or a Toyota, but they never got close enough to be sure. Bobby always wondered if his cousin had something to do with this or if it was just dumb luck. As it stood, he'd never asked, and Teddy never told. There are some things you just don't want to know.

Because, when all was said and done, Bobby had jeopardized everything he had for that gram...*everything*. He'd driven while in a blackout for one thing, endangering not only his and Ricky's lives, but also everyone else on the road. It was fortunate he hadn't killed anyone. He'd also been guilty of trespassing (which was a misdemeanor, a felony if he'd been caught with the methamphetamine) and not only that but at a *client's* house. He could have easily lost his business in one fell swoop once that got around town.

Yet the real kicker was that *Bobby remembered almost none of it*. He'd gone to all that trouble, had risked his neck, his freedom, and his business, and at the end of the day he had nothing to show for it...nothing. Barely a vague memory of enjoying the drugs, just brief moments of clarity shortly after each bump before the Xanax took the remote control from his hand and tuned him back into channel Zero. He'd awoken on the floor at his house, face down, his pants around his ankles. Beside him was a bottle of lotion, explaining why his pants were down. He didn't even know if he'd successfully rubbed one out or not, but the lack of a semen-stained Kleenex pointed in the direction of "or not." Until, that was, he realized he had a turkey baster wedged painfully in his butt. Initially he didn't understand why he had a cooking implement crammed in his fudge tunnel, until later that day when he found a shot glass containing cloudy liquid and the crushed remains of what appeared to be several Xanax on his bathroom counter. Then it came to him: he'd plugged the Xanax. Plugging was something a woman had taught him once, a way to take drugs so they would hit you almost as hard as if you shot them intravenously. Bobby had rarely been brave enough to put a needle in his arm, and during those rare occasions, he had to have someone else do it for him, but apparently a turkey baster up the ass wasn't out of the question.

The guilt from that binge was so extreme that Bobby was able to remain sober for a whole week after, and when he'd told the story in his meetings the silence was so loud you could almost hear a syringe hit the floor on a shag rug. When it came to Bobby and his drug use, there was nothing that could stop him. His legendary status at his NA meetings grew. Even the oxycontin kids began to look up to him. Nevertheless, it wasn't the kind of notoriety he enjoyed; the only reason he told the others of his exploits was to make them real to him, as if by speaking of them aloud he'd better understand the ramifications of his deeds and try to put an end to them. Unfortunately, this tactic didn't work. All it succeeded in doing was cementing his reputation as one hell of a basket case. The moderator could have (maybe *should* have) called the cops and reported him, if only for his own safety. Why she didn't was a mystery to him, and yet again his cousin Teddy came to mind, and he thought his relative might have intervened. Unless he asked him, however, he'd never know. It remained a secret, and to this day he never stashed drugs at his client's houses anymore. It simply wasn't worth it. If he had drugs left over, he had to either do them or toss them, which was another source of wasted money besides losing his paychecks, or Carolyn spending Gina's money on herself.

Bobby finished checking the chlorine levels and retrieved his net, scooping the leaves out. He then ran the vacuum, dismissing his past catastrophe and reflecting on his big win at the track that day. How Terry picked a winning horse was beyond him. If Terry was that good at picking horses on a regular basis he'd use him all the time. As it stood, Terry placed a couple of bets after that one (for himself, using his own money and not Bobby's winnings that were meant for Simon) and both of them were duds.

"Guess I just got really lucky," Terry had lamented, possibly a tad too wistfully, but Bobby hadn't noticed. He was too busy being relieved that his "dangly bits" were no longer in danger of being manhandled by Slugger and Rocko. The thought of those mangy paws grappling his delicate privates sent shivers down his spine. "And keep your truck title for now. I'll let you know if I change my mind."

"Thanks for helping me."

"Hey, what's a friend for?" Terry had said, before breaking the news to him that the bet he'd placed last week was a loser. "You owe me another $500 on top of the five grand."

"Can we let the bet ride?" Bobby had asked, and Terry smiled wide.

"Of course we can, good buddy," he answered sincerely. "But you have to tell me how you lost fifteen large to Blackwell."

"Man, I don't want to talk about it..."

"If you want me to take your action in the future you have to spill the beans." This was a lie. Terry was all too glad to take Bobby's action in the future, regardless. Nonetheless, his ploy worked.

"It was a really stupid bet."

"They're all stupid bets when you think about it. That's why it's called 'gambling.'"

"On a keno wheel..." Bobby muttered.

"What?"

"I guess I was so wasted that I thought for sure my numbers would eventually come up."

"So you borrowed money from a mob loan shark?" Terry was practically in shock. This was idiotic by anybody's standards.

"I suppose I hadn't really thought the whole thing through," Bobby admitted.

"How did you think you were going to pay him back if you lost?"

"I didn't. I was in a blackout. I don't remember any of it."

This admission was a terrible temptation for Terry. If he could get Bobby to make some bets while he was blacked out he could tell him almost anything, but he dispelled the notion. Christ, Bobby lost enough money on bets he was aware of. There was no reason to skin him even more than he already had, even though it was enticing.

"You and those damn blackouts," Terry said instead. "One day you're really going to get in trouble and I won't be able to bail you out."

"Tell me about it," Bobby agreed. "Tell me about it…"

Chapter Twelve

Melissa couldn't believe the story as it unfurled, but it wasn't because she thought it wasn't true; it was because of Bobby's unaffected recanting, as if it wasn't a big deal. He owed a mob boss money and he couldn't remember it? That was like saying you had sex with an entire football team (plus the cheerleaders) and your recollection of the event was limited to the taste of semen (and vaginal secretions) in your mouth every time you belched. Un-freakin'-heard-of! Yet the more Bobby said, the further it seemingly proved how blissfully unaware he was of how close to death he'd come. It made her wonder if (when) he was going to simply start forgetting about her.

"Thank you for sharing that with us Bobby," the moderator said. "Even though it had nothing to do with your sex addiction, it certainly was interesting. Would anybody else like to share?"

Melissa raised her hand, glaring at Bobby.

It takes two to tango baby.

And she proceeded to tell a tale so lurid that only the staunchest of sex addicts could look her in the eyes when it was over. Suffice to say it involved a half dozen volunteer firemen, a couple of senior citizens from her macramé class, an escaped monkey from the local zoo, three nineteen-year-old rugby players who were looking to score some weed and got *way* more than they bargained for, and a large-bosomed, African American prostitute named Blondie who could crush beer cans between her aforementioned enormous breasts. Was the story true? Parts of it... OK, most of it (she made up the part about the monkey), but that was beside the point. The desired effect was that Bobby get jealous, and by the way he was looking at her when she finished, she'd achieved her goal. *That ought to serve the bastard right.*

"Um, thank you, uh…for, um, *sharing* with us today Melissa," the moderator gulped, his hands shaking ever so slightly, his erection hidden beneath a large sweater he wore for just such purposes. "Would anybody else like to share?"

And on it went until the hour was up.

♦ ♦ ♦

"What the hell are you doing, borrowing money from a mob guy?" Melissa scolded him while they were lying in the bed of his pickup. "You must have a death wish!"

"I thought that was obvious by now," he said, his immediate wish being that he could have just one drink but knowing exactly where that would lead. As it was, Simon was paid off and he was in the clear. It was best to keep his head above water while he could.

"Yeah, you'd think, judging by your crazy stories, but that one takes the cake!"

"I thought last week's was more exciting."

"That's not the point! Some guy in an executioner's hood isn't going to shoot you. But a mob guy? Without thinking twice, Bobby, without effin' thinking twice!"

"You're not exactly an angel yourself."

"What's that supposed to mean?"

"Well, judging by the story you told—"

"I made that up. I just wanted to make you jealous."

"All of it?"

"Um…that's not important right now. We're talking about you, and I think this has got to stop."

"What?" Bobby gulped. "*This*?"

"Not this, you idiot, the blackouts! What am I going to do if something happens to you?" This she said with genuine emotion. Why, if Bobby didn't know better, he'd think Melissa was falling for him.

"Have sex with a basketball team?" he quipped, only half joking, and she slugged him on the arm. "Ouch!"

"Not funny, you asshole." She lit a cigarette, blew smoke in his face. "I wish you'd start taking an interest in something other than getting wasted. You're scaring everyone around you who cares about you, Bobby."

"Are you saying you're one of them?" His voice sounded hopeful, as if her answer could unlock the door to a million undreamed of possibilities.

She dragged on her smoke and looked at him for a moment, taking in the scar on his lip (he'd been bitten on the face by a dog, funny enough, when he'd leaned down and tried to kiss it), the dark spots on his cheeks from not wearing sunscreen outside like, ever, and his liquid blue eyes that always looked like they were on the verge of laughing at some joke no one but he knew, some inner merriment that he couldn't tell anyone because to share it would be to ruin it. Her heart lurched in her chest for a moment, and it pained her because it wasn't something she was used to. She'd had sex with hundreds of people—men and women, and she'd walked away without so much as a venereal disease or any lasting emotion, yet she'd be damned because this guy was growing on her in a way that was downright distressing. She actually cared about his well-being, and that was unusual for a woman, a person, like her. She'd always thought sexual predators didn't characteristically get attached to anyone. Maybe this was a turning point for her. She sighed, took one last drag and crushed the cigarette out in a soda can.

"What if I was, Bobby, what would you do about it?" Now it was her turn to sound earnest. Her voice was low, almost a whisper.

"I think I'd really like that," he said, and for the first time that he could remember (ha! Good one!) it tickled something within him that wasn't just his nuts; it was something deeper, something more profound.

"Are you just saying that Bobby, or do you really mean it?"

"I really mean it, honey." He heard himself saying it, but he didn't know where it was coming from. Wherever it was, it was truly heartfelt.

"This isn't supposed to happen to people like us."

"People like what?"

"You know, people like *us*."

"Just because I joined the Mile-High Club when I was thirteen doesn't mean I'm incapable of love."

"You...*what?*"

"Just kidding babe," Bobby said, chuckling. Sometimes it was so easy to mess with her. "You know what I mean."

"If this means what I think it does," she said, her voice airy, light, yet something inside of her was twisting and turning tumultuously, "then we've got problems buddy."

"Don't I know it," he agreed, and he got punched again. "Ouch! What the hell was that for?"

"Never agree with a woman when she's trying to be romantic, you moron! It kills the mood."

"If that's romance—" he began, when his phone rang. It was a special ringtone so he'd know who was calling, but it was somewhat ironic. It was "Song 2," by the band Blur, commonly known as "The Woohoo song." It boasted a down-tuned, crunchy guitar while the singer sang "Woohoo!" among other throwaway rock lyrics, most of them ostensibly incoherent ramblings. It was a tribute to rock and roll happiness the world 'round, or, at least that was what Bobby made of it. The irony was that it was the ringtone he'd assigned to Carolyn. When she called, it wasn't exactly a "woohoo" moment, but it suited his sense of humor.

"I like that song," Melissa said as Bobby retrieved the phone from his pants.

"Me too," he agreed, then put a finger to his lips. "Let me take this." He punched the button. "Hello?" He knew who it was, but he always acted as if he didn't.

"She's gone!" the voice on the other end cried.

"What?"

"She's gone! They kidnapped her!"

"Who's gone?" he demanded, but in the back of his mind, Bobby knew who "she" was.

"You and your lousy goddamn bets, Bobby! I knew you were going to get us in trouble some day! I knew it!"

"Whoa, whoa, whoa! Slow down. You're not making any sense!"

"She was kidnapped right from the house while I was at work! They beat up Barry and took her!"

"Barry got beat up?" he said wistfully, and was shouted down.

"Yes Bobby, I don't know how else some mob guys could just come into my house and take my daughter! Obviously, they had to do it forcefully!"

"They took Gina? Oh my God!"

"Yes Bobby! They took Gina!" A long pause, then: "And the damn dog!"

"How do you know it was mob guys?" Bobby asked stupidly, trying to process what she was saying.

"Because they were quoting lines from The Godfather...how the hell do you think I know it was mob guys? They told Barry!"

Bobby was stunned into silence. He'd paid off Blackwell...it didn't make sense...unless he owed some other mob guys money, but how likely was it that he owed *two* mob guys at the same time? He wanted to posit this question, but what stopped him was the reality of his ill-spent weekends. In all honesty, he wasn't sure what he got up to unless someone told him, there was video footage, or an arrest record to document his time. For a guy like Bobby, it was possible that he owed several mob loan sharks without knowing it. Hell, he hadn't been aware of his debt to Simon; who was to say he didn't owe the Italian, Irish, or Russian mob a few frogs too?

"Are you there, Bobby? Earth to Bobby! Earth to Bobby!"

"I'm here Carolyn," he said weakly, his voice in his ears sounding as if it were coming from a thousand miles away. "I'm here."

"This is all your fault Bobby!" she shrieked. "You hear me? This is *all your fault*! You have to find her!"

"I'll find her, don't worry," he said, his lips moving without him even being aware. How the hell was he going to find her? Where was he even going to start looking? And then it occurred to him: if this was indeed a kidnapping, they'd find him. It was how kidnappings worked.

"Did you call the cops?" he asked.

"Of course I didn't call the cops! They told Barry "no cops." If we call the cops, they're going to kill her, you dipshit!"

"There's no reason to call me names."

"Shut it, dill hole! You got us into this; you have to get us out!"

"I...I'll do everything I can..." Bobby couldn't believe this was happening. Only a moment ago everything looked as if it was changing for the better, but now, this was the worst possible thing he could imagine. Oh Gina, poor, poor Gina.

"You better, you asshole!" Carolyn said, and then she hung up.

Chapter Thirteen

Bobby pocketed the phone and looked at Melissa. Although she hadn't heard what Carolyn was saying, she got the gist of the conversation from what Bobby said. Something was up and it wasn't good. Bobby brought her up to speed quickly, and the two of them sat in silence for several minutes, their individual wheels turning.

"Is it possible that you owe some other mob guys money?"

"With the way I black out?" he said grimly, "*everything* is possible."

"So what are you going to do? You going to call your cousin?"

Bobby had shared a lot of things with Melissa over the course of the last year and a half, and one of them had been his relationship with Teddy. Bobby had confided in her that it was his opinion that on more than one occasion Teddy had kept Carolyn from taking out a restraining order on him, and was also why he never got more than a slap on the wrist, or did more than a couple of weeks in the county slammer when he really screwed up.

He shook his head. "I can't. Carolyn said they told her no cops."

"But he's your cousin. You can tell him as a friend."

He looked at her thoughtfully. "I suppose I could, but I don't want to endanger Gina's life."

She let out a shaky laugh. "This is totally surreal. Like, it's a movie or something."

"It is weird," he agreed, but when it came to his life, everything was like a movie and, as much as he hated to admit it, his entire existence was full of wonky shit like this. To say he wasn't surprised would be a touch too severe, but to think that this wouldn't eventually happen to him? With the way he lived, *anything* was possible at all times.

"What are you going to do?"

"I don't know," he said. "What *should* I do…?" His voice trailed off, and suddenly his chest hitched. *Goddamn me!* He thought despairingly. *I knew I'd eventually endanger that poor girl's life! I knew it!*

Bobby tried to choke back a sob, but it was much too powerful, and he couldn't hold it in. Tears welled up in his eyes simply thinking of poor Gina in the clutches of some serious mob players, guys who made a living out of hurting people. The idea of her tied to a chair, blindfolded, scared, wondering what the hell these guys wanted with her and who was to blame.

But she'd know who was to blame, wouldn't she? I mean, who else did she know that could mess things up so righteously that she would wind up in the clutches of men who spoke in broken sentence and re-ferred to themselves in the third person. Also, he'd told her about his debt to Simon and how he'd taken care of it. She'd know all right, no question about it.

"Shit!" he cried, banging his fist on the bed of the truck. "Shit, shit, shit!" Each "shit" was punctuated by his fist hitting the truck.

"Come on, Bobby," Melissa soothed. "It'll be OK. We just have to ride it out. If this is a real kidnapping, they'll call us, trust me." She took his chin firmly and swiveled his head so he was looking at her. "So call your cousin, right now."

"Jesus, I should at least wait until I have some details."

"Call your damn cousin right now, or I'll do it for you!"

Bobby swallowed, snot running down the back of his throat, slimy and disagreeable, but he nodded, knowing she was right. It was the best thing to do.

"OK," he said at last. "I'll call him, but I should talk to him in person, I can't do it on the phone." He paused for a moment as another thought hit him. "And I have to be sneaky about it. For all I know they have some-one watching me, to make sure I don't go to the cops. 'Cuz if they saw me…"

"You're right," she nodded. "We have to have a plan. We have to as-sume the worst on all counts."

This made Bobby smile. "You're taking to this really well. You must have a knack for this kind of thing."

She laughed in return. "I watch a lot of television, Bobby. Crime shows are my favorite."

"Really? I would have taken you for a Kardashian fan all the way."

This elicited another punch, one that he knew very well he deserved.

"Point taken."

"You can't use your phone to call him...in fact, you can't call him. I will."

"Why?"

"If they know you even a little, they know you have a cousin who's a cop. They could have his phone tapped."

"His cell phone?"

She shrugged. "I don't know! But I watch a lot of shows and as far as I know anything is possible."

Again, Bobby had to smile. He was really glad she was with him when he got the call. He wasn't sure he'd have thought of these things had he been on his own.

And then another thought struck, one so random it came from seemingly out of the blue, but it was extremely pertinent nonetheless. What if he'd been wasted when this occurred and he'd been in a blackout? He'd never remember he received the call in the first place, and who knows what would have happened.

On the heels of this came a realization that plowed over him like an SUV driven by an elderly person going through heart attack death throes: *I have to stop drinking as of right now until all of this is over and I find my little girl. I can't trust myself if I drink because it will lead to...everything else...*

"Bobby? You all right?"

"What?" His eyes regained their focus and he trained them on her, bringing himself out of his reverie.

"You zoned out there for a second."

"Yeah, I guess I did."

"Anything you want to tell me?"

He shook his head, then changed his mind and nodded.

"I have to stop drinking," he said.

"And using drugs?"

"Yes…and using drugs."

"Good," she said, then looked at him sharply. "But you don't have to give up having sex, do you?"

He giggled, and again he was so glad she was with him. Christ, he really, truly needed her.

"Are you kidding? If anything, I need to have *more* sex! Preferably unprotected, and by all means kinky!"

"That's what I want to hear." She grinned, taking her phone from her purse. "Now let's make that phone call."

◆ ◆ ◆

Bobby and Melissa met Teddy at a diner in Temecula, a greasy spoon so greasy it was a wonder they were able to sit upright in their seats. Bobby nursed a decaf while Teddy gulped copious amounts of regular as strong as diesel fuel; his shift was just starting and he needed it for the long night ahead. Melissa worked her way through a stack of pancakes the size of manhole covers as Bobby told Teddy all the details.

"Wow," Teddy mused. "You just never know when to quit, do you Bobby?"

"No," he said. "I guess I don't."

"So that's why this is so cloak and dagger."

"That's why," Bobby agreed.

"Great." Teddy finished his coffee and signaled the waitress for more.

"You want me to leave the pot?" she asked.

"You mind?"

She rolled her eyes and set it on the table. "Enjoy." She moved on to another table where a teenage couple was probably planning a rendez-vous that involved marijuana and underage sex.

"Use protection," she advised as she slapped their check on the table, and the girl and boy looked at her oddly.

"So the question is: what do we do about it?"

"Are you sure this is the real deal?" Teddy said, blowing on his coffee. "I mean, Carolyn isn't exactly the most reliable source."

"I don't know why she'd lie." Actually, Carolyn's word wasn't the most ironclad (to put it kindly; honestly the bitch was full of shit), but he couldn't think of a reason (a good reason) why she would call him and make up something like this. It didn't make any sense, unless it was real. "She sure sounded convincing on the phone."

"OK, let's say for the sake of the matter that this is really happening," Teddy said congenially. "What we do is wait for them to call you."

"That's what I told him," Melissa concurred.

"So...we wait."

"Yep."

"What do we do until then?" Bobby asked.

"Go about your normal life," Teddy said. "Do what you normally do... uh, scratch that. Don't do what you normally do, you hear me?"

"Way ahead of you," Bobby said, hanging his head. "No drinking, no drugs."

"Maybe this fine young lady can help you think of other ways to pass the time."

Melissa set down her fork and linked her arm around Bobby's.

"I'm pretty sure I can, Mr. Officer, sir."

Teddy smiled. "So where did you two meet?"

The two looked at one another and shared a brief moment of hilarity before Bobby replied, "Our SA meetings."

"SA?"

"Sex addicts," Bobby clarified.

"Hell, Bobby," Teddy said, not without a hint of joviality. "Are you sure those meetings are helping?"

"Yes?" Bobby replied with a smile, and the three of them shared a laugh.

"I'll drink to that," Teddy said, and he downed the rest of his coffee.

Chapter Fourteen

The next morning Bobby got the phone call. It happened when he was at the Mclearys', talking to the missus while he let the chlorine work its magic. Bobby knew that she and the mister liked to throw "pool parties" (their euphemism for orgies), and Bobby had to work overtime to get rid of all the bodily fluids that built up in the pool each week. If he didn't, an ovulating woman could possibly get pregnant simply taking a dip.

Bobby looked at his phone, saw that it wasn't a recognizable number, and decided he should take it.

"I'm sorry, Mrs. Mcleary," he said politely. "I have to take this."

"Why certainly, son." Another detail about the Mclearys: they were in their seventies. The pool parties? Let's just say Bobby had to get creative with his excuses for not attending when the offer was made because he didn't want to offend them. Even though Bobby loved a rousing game of hide the sausage, he wasn't so desperate that he'd bone a woman older than he was. He preferred his women younger than him, but would settle for someone around his age if they looked young. That's why Melissa was perfect for Bobby. She was nine years his junior.

"Hello?"

"We have your daughter, Bobby Travis," a deep voice said, and the first thing Bobby took stock of was the lack of an accent. He wasn't British, so that ruled out Simon and his gang of thugs.

"Is she OK?" he asked urgently, and the voice on the other end was silent for a moment.

"She's fine," he said at length.

"Let me talk to her."

"That's not possible."

"Why?"

"Um, because she isn't here. But she's safe, trust me."

"What?" Bobby said, looking up to see if Mrs. Mcleary was within earshot. Fortunately, she was running a garden hose, and that and the gurgling of the pool most likely kept what he was saying indistinct. "That's extremely unprofessional!"

"You trying to tell me how to do my job?"

"Really?" Bobby snapped. "You call that a job? Where did you apply, and who the hell hired you? I want to speak to your manager!"

"Not funny, wise guy. You keep up those cracks and you'll get to hear what it sounds like when your daughter is having her fingernails ripped out one by one with a pliers."

This sobered Bobby immediately. "Please don't hurt her!" he begged. "What do you want from me?"

"What does any kidnapper want? Money!"

"How much?"

"How much is she worth to you?"

"She's worth everything I have!" he blurted before realizing that wasn't the right thing to say. He should have thought of a dollar amount instead.

"So it's safe to assume she's worth fifty large?"

"You want me to pay $50,000?" Bobby gasped, his mind unable to grasp the figure. "Who the hell are you, and how much do I owe you?"

Again, a pregnant pause, as if the man on the other end was thinking things over. "None of that is important. You just get us the money."

"Wait, wait," Bobby said, dispelling the cobwebs to some degree. The guy said "us," so he wasn't working alone. So far he had that to go on. "You have to tell me who you are, that's only fair. If I borrowed money to make a bet and I owe you, I can understand that. Seriously, I seem to do this all the time. I also understand it's just business. But you can't withhold information from me. Are you the Italian mob? The Russians? I just paid off the British mob, and I can tell by your accent you're not them—"

"Shut the hell up! We want fifty large, and you can have your daughter back! End of story!"

"How am I going to come up with that kind of money?"

"Not my problem," the other said. "You got thirty-six hours. If you don't have it by then, we start getting nasty."

"Thirty-six hours? That's impossible!"

"You better get on it then."

"I need to know that my daughter is safe," Bobby said. "You have to call me back and let me speak to her."

"Fine, fine! I'll call you back and you can talk to her. But you better get a move on partner and get us our money or we might do something we can't undo." He coughed, then added, "And no cops! We got your phones tapped."

"I still don't know how you think I'm going to be able to come up with that kind of cash."

"Do what you did last time," the voice said cryptically. "Remember: thirty-six hours."

And the phone went dead in his ear.

"Everything all right, dear?" Mrs. Mcleary asked, turning off the hose and shading her eyes with one hand to look at him across the pool. Bobby looked down, saw a used condom floating in the water, glanced up, saw a sparkle in Mrs. Mcleary's eyes, then turned away to get his net.

"Yes, ma'am," he said, trying (but possibly failing) to keep a note of despair out of his voice. "Everything is fine."

◆ ◆ ◆

"I can't believe they want fifty thousand dollars!"

"That is a lot of money," Teddy said, agreeing with his cousin for the second time. Bobby was so unraveled he was beginning to repeat himself. "How much did you owe the last loan shark?"

"Only fifteen thousand."

"You say that like it's chump change."

"Comparatively, it is."

The two were sitting at a picnic table at a wayside stop off of Highway 15 just north of San Marcos. Owing to what the kidnapper said, they had to continue to keep things covert if they didn't want to be discovered. The man hadn't mentioned Teddy by name, but his order of "no cops" and the declaration that the phones were tapped made a good case for their discretion.

"You want a soda?" Teddy asked, standing up and fishing a couple of bucks out of his pants pocket.

"No, thanks," Bobby replied, and Teddy walked over to one of the machines and got a Pepsi. When he came back and sat down, he sipped his soda contemplatively. "I'm supposed to be at my GA meeting right now," Bobby added forlornly. "Man, they'd love to hear about this."

"You'll make it up," Teddy said, mulling things over, cataloging the details of what Bobby had told him. "I'm still muddy on the fact that they won't tell you who they are, or how much you owe them."

"Me too."

"And how would they know how you got the money last time? Did you tell anyone?"

"Only you and Melissa." Bobby thought about it for a second, remembering he told Gina, but was slightly embarrassed about that. The call hadn't gone very well, and it wasn't important anyway. She sure as hell didn't kidnap herself. "I might have told Simon," he added.

"The British loan shark?"

"Yeah."

Teddy considered this piece of information, sipping the soda and issuing an "ahhh" every so often. Finally, he looked up at his cousin. "You think maybe they heard it from Simon, and just want to extort you?"

"What do you mean?"

"Well, you were able to pay off Simon; why wouldn't someone else think that, with a little motivation, you could pay off more than that. It isn't exactly rocket science."

"But how I got the money last time was totally by luck! If the horse had lost I would have been in even more debt."

Teddy set down his can and smoothed a wrinkle on his cotton khaki's. When Bobby thought about it, he realized that he seldom saw Teddy out of uniform. Almost every time they were together, Teddy was on duty, arresting his stupid ass or bailing him out. Seeing him in civilian clothes was rare indeed.

"How *did* you win that bet?"

"Hell if I know. Terry made it. The fact that it worked at all was a mathematical impossibility made possible by dumb luck!"

"OK…" Teddy didn't want to say it, but Bobby's bookie probably knew a lot more about betting the horses than he let on.

Bobby shook his head. "This is ridiculous! Isn't there something we can do?"

Teddy shrugged, thought about it, then shook his head as well. "Right now we have nothing to go on, and that's a really tight timeline. Our best bet is to try and raise the money."

"The only way, and I mean *only*, is if Terry helps me again. And I don't know how likely that is unless he gets a taste, and he's gonna want an awfully big taste because he'd have to finance the whole thing too."

Teddy knocked back the last of the soda and set the can on the picnic table. For a moment he studied the other, noted the lines etched deeply in his cousin's face. Probably from the all the drugs. Hell, they were only born five years apart, but Bobby looked like he was fast tracking his aging tenfold by all the crazy chemicals he consumed. And it was a damn shame too, because he was a handsome guy. If Teddy had his looks, he'd want to do everything he could to make sure they served him well into the twilight of his life. Of course, he had Maggie, so it wasn't truly a concern, but just the same.

"He doesn't have to finance all of it," Teddy said at last.

"What?"

"You heard me," he said, wondering if he was crazy or just stupid. Maggie was going to kill him when he told her, *if* he told her. He had to have some secrets. "I have some money saved. How much would you need to repeat what you did last time to get the dough?"

"I...I don't know..." Bobby looked off-kilter, and for a moment Teddy thought there was something wrong with him until he realized that the other was struggling not to cry. "Jesus, this is all so, so weird..."

"You OK, man? You don't look so hot."

"This is just throwing me for a loop, you know? I mean, just when I thought I was gaining some traction it feels as if it's slipping away from me, and I don't know what to do." He hitched a heavy sigh, got himself under some semblance of control.

"Hey, it's all right man, really," Teddy said, but he knew it was anything but. It wasn't every day your daughter got kidnapped. And since Bobby hadn't been able to talk to her when the perp called, for all Teddy knew Bobby was being taken for a ride. But then where was Gina? What had become of the poor girl?

"I can't take your money, Teddy," Bobby said plaintively. "You already do too much for me." He looked at his cousin through melancholy eyes, then gave voice to something he'd believed for a long time. "It's because of you she can't get a restraining order against me, right?"

Teddy held Bobby's gaze for a second before looking away. "Let's just say I know a certain judge who owes me some favors."

"And the fact that I never do more than a couple of weeks in the county slammer when I screw up? That you too?"

Now Teddy looked slightly uncomfortable. "Somebody's got to look after you Bobby..."

"Hell, if Carolyn wasn't so damn lazy she'd take me to court every time I can't come up with all the child support money, and I'd either have my wages garnished or I'd need you to sneak me beers in the pokey." He looked away, his face flushed. Since he'd been sober, it seemed he wore his emotions on his sleeve. They were harder to stave off. "Thanks," he said at last. "Thanks for keeping an eye on me. And you know why I don't think she deserves the money, right?"

"Yeah," Teddy nodded. "I know."

"It's like she thinks that she *earned* it. The hell she did! I don't remember her saying no."

"Bobby," Teddy said softly, bringing his cousin's tirade to an end, "You don't remember *anything*. You told me yourself; you have no recollection of the weekend you spent with Carolyn that produced Gina, am I right?"

Bobby stared at the other, swallowed, then slowly bobbed his head up and down. "Yeah," he admitted, "I don't remember anything about it. And that's a bitch, ya know? I love Gina, man I really love that kid, but the fact that I don't know if her mother's a decent lay or not…well, it kind of (if you'll excuse my language) fucking sucks."

"Shoot Bobby, I'm sure it *totally* fucking sucks," Teddy said, and this got the two of them laughing, just like when they were kids and they'd be talking seriously about something, and then one of them would inject some levity into the conversation, taking the other off guard, and they were reduced to gales of laughter. "I mean," Teddy continued, trying to keep a straight face, "if I had to pay for a kid, I'd at least like to remember the night I spent that brought her into this world."

"You and me both," Bobby guffawed.

"Do you want to talk about it?" Teddy kidded. "Maybe get a few things off your chest?"

"I'm going to meetings for it, so I'm OK," Bobby said, and this got them laughing harder.

"And Melissa is living proof that you're working through this terrible handicap."

"Yes indeedy, she certainly is."

They laughed a little more as cars pulled in and out of the large parking lot, semi drivers and travelers shuffling quickly into the bathroom to relieve themselves. When the two had themselves under control, they stood, shook hands.

"You get on back to work, Bobby, and I'll look into securing some funds. Wouldn't hurt if you talked to your bookie buddy, see if he has any ideas he's willing to bankroll."

"All right," Bobby said. "Maybe he can pick another horse for me. If I do it's a surefire loser."

"Well, get on it. You don't have much time."

"I know." Bobby looked at his cousin with eyes so earnest it was like looking at a dog that urgently wanted something from you, but you had no idea what it was. It was a heartbreaking expression, one that made Teddy uneasy. They'd been laughing and joking and out of the blue Bobby was deathly serious again. It was unsettling how quickly he could switch from one mood to another without a hitch. "I got the reverse Midas touch, bro," Bobby said. "Everything I touch turns into shit."

"Quit being so hard on yourself."

"You know it's true, man," Bobby said, turning away and walking slowly to his truck. "Tell me you don't know it's true."

For the life of him, Teddy didn't have a suitable answer to that, so he simply nodded and then headed back to his car.

Chapter Fifteen

As Teddy had suspected it wasn't rocket science, and Bobby had told more than just Melissa and Simon about how he earned the money that made his debt go away. He'd also told Gina (a detail he'd later omitted when telling Teddy because he didn't think it was important; turned out it was). He'd called her after he finished work on Monday evening in an attempt to apologize after scaring her so badly. He wanted to reassure Gina that he was all right, but the call had been awkward, his daughter not knowing what to say. What could she say? "Good going, Dad"? She certainly didn't want to encourage him to continue his vices. She in turn had told Carolyn and her mother, of course, had then taken the ball and run with it. In fact, Carolyn was so ruthless and conniving that she put the whole plan together and enacted it within less than twenty-four hours.

"You sure this is going to work?" Barry had asked Carolyn as she laid out the details. "I seen the movie *Fargo* and *the Big Lebowski*. Stuff like this doesn't work out as planned."

"You just shut up; I got this," Carolyn snapped. "I know what I'm doing."

"So did Steve Buscemi and that big blond dude, until poor little Stevie wound up in the wood chipper."

"Look," Carolyn said, trying her best to keep her voice civil. "He makes more money than he's letting on. He only claims what he makes from the pool cleaning business. I'll bet he makes a lot more from gambling."

"Doesn't he lose his ass gambling?"

"It's what he wants us to think! I told you what he told Gina: he bet on a horse and made fifteen grand to pay off a mob guy. For all we know he does that all the time. Don't you want us to get that money?"

"Us?"

"Yes, *us*, you imbecile! I'm going to share!"

"But isn't that technically Gina's money? You know, for clothes and books and stuff?"

"Technically," Carolyn had admitted, "but we provide her with all that. We take the money and we give her a roof over her head, clothes, food... do I really have to spell this out for you? That money is ours, and I intend to squeeze every dime I can out of him!"

During this conversation, Carolyn was able to speak as loud as she wanted because Gina was walking her stupid dog, Queen Drool from the Planet Buttwipe. There was no worrying that her daughter would over-hear them and become suspicious. For the plan to work, however, it was imperative that she hide for a few days, maybe even a week until Bobby got the money, so Carolyn figured she could put her up in a motel, an ex-pense she'd condone seeing as it would pay out and then some. It really was too bad her grandparents (Carolyn's parents) were dead. She could shack up there until it was over, and it would save her a few bucks. Her mother would have loved a hustle like this.

"So who's going to kidnap her?" Barry had persisted. "I mean, Bobby's got to meet someone and hand over the cash. And who says he ain't gonna call the cops? He might be a screw up, but he's got an ace in the hole with that cousin of his."

This crucial detail had eluded her. Barry was right; they needed some-one to help them. A lightbulb went on in her brain, albeit a dim one.

"I got someone in mind, this guy I work with. He's been around the block a few times, looks the part. The kicker is he's gentle as a pussy cat."

"Cats got claws," Barry pointed out.

"Not this one," she'd assured him, and that was that. He was on-board. Getting Gina to agree was another matter entirely, and as Carolyn was putting out her feelers later that day when Gina returned from her walk, trying to get a read on if her daughter would comply with such an escapade by ridiculing Bobby and his innate cheapness, she quickly came to the conclusion that she'd have to do what she'd figured all along: lie through her teeth. Gina could never be swayed to take sides against her father, so the problem with her non-compliance was that this ruled out the motel. She was going to have to stay with her coworker at his house, and he'd have to agree to that. He'd also have to agree to be her accomplice, which he hadn't yet because she'd failed to ask; she'd been too busy with the other particulars of her scheme. This led to a clandestine phone call to the man in question, the aforementioned coworker, a dimwitted but likable guy named Greg Hanson. He was a two-time loser who'd cooled his heels in the county jail more than a few times, had even done a three-year hitch in a state prison for armed robbery. But other than his penchant for guns and cheap liquor, he was a teddy bear if you got to know him. Carolyn was pretty sure of that. She also believed that he was presently retired from the crime game (meaning he may require some extra income), so she proposed they get together and talk, preferably during happy hour at his saloon of choice.

When she'd outlined her proposal to him over drinks at his local watering hole, a dump named Harry's that made Hooligans look high class in comparison, he didn't seem too enthused, especially when she got to the part about her daughter staying with him.

"Come on, Carolyn," he grumbled. "I ain't no babysitter."

"It'll only be for a few days, and besides, she's fifteen. She can take care of herself."

"I don't know. Isn't this whole thing kinda…illegal?"

She looked at him blankly for a second before rolling her eyes. "What the hell do you care?"

He shrugged. "I guess I don't."

"Then what's the problem?"

"I seen *Fargo*."

"What, you got somebody in mind you want to put in a wood chipper?"

"No…"

"Then cool it! This is easy as hell. You make a few of phone calls, let my daughter and her dog stay with you for a couple of days—three tops—and Bobby does all the work."

"Wait! She's got a dog, too?"

"She's a sweet little bulldog. She isn't any trouble."

He thought about it for a minute, then said "How much do I get?"

"I don't know...fifteen percent?"

"Fifteen percent of what?"

"Of what he pays, *duh!*"

Greg did some mental math, a feat that was quite a bit out of his grasp, and after a moment of staring into space over her shoulder he focused back on her.

"Um, OK..." But he still had some doubts. "Will I have to be the one that meets him, you know, to do the exchange?"

"Of course! Someone has to do it, and it can't be me."

"But what if he brings the cops?"

"He won't, trust me. He loves Gina and will do anything I...um, I mean, *you* say to get her back."

"Are you sure this will work?"

"Yes, how many times do I have to tell you that? As long as we keep it simple there won't be any problems."

"I also saw *A Simple Plan*. It didn't work out for them, you know, keeping it simple."

"Will you quit referring to movies you've seen? Geez! This isn't a movie, this is real life! In real life things are much easier."

"You think so?"

"I know so!"

"All right..."

"Great!" she exclaimed, finished with that bit of business. Now it was time to prep her daughter for her role, but she knew it was going to be a bit tricky, so she had to get Gina to drop her guard. To do this, she took her out for her favorite food, New York style pizza. Barry was mysteriously absent during this rendezvous (he was such a lousy liar, it was imperative he not be present), but one word explained it all without having to go into further detail: diarrhea.

"Barry and I have to go away for a few days, so I want you to stay with a friend of mine..."

"Where are you going?"

A straightforward question, really, but somehow Carolyn hadn't thought that far ahead.

"Um," she stalled, her brain working furiously. "It's a surprise," she answered at last.

"For who?"

Again, a blank. Carolyn, for all her bluff and bluster wasn't as smart as, say, your average fifth grader. If she ever appeared on the show of the same name, she'd make them all look like future Einstein's.

"For me," she said eventually, while Gina continued to pick at her slice of pepperoni. The girl, knowing her mother's characteristic stinginess, had been instantly wary when she was, out of the blue, asked if she wanted to go out for pizza. If a comfort food meal was being offered, there was most certainly a catch. Carolyn never did anything without there being an ulterior motive, and she was too stupid (or blind to her daughter's intelligence) to recognize that Gina saw through her shenanigans. "Barry wants to take me someplace special to celebrate our, um…uh, anniversary."

"Isn't that in August?"

"Um, yes, yes, it is, but this is the only time he can get off of work."

"Isn't he on unemployment?" Gina took a bite of her slice, keeping the expression on her face neutral. Something was going on, that much was for certain, but she was darned if she could figure it out.

"He, um, does receive a little assistance every month for being wrongfully terminated, but he also has his obligations…"

If by wrongfully terminated you mean fired, then guilty as charged.

"And this is the first time I'm hearing about it?"

"You think you know everything, don't you Ms. Smarty Pants?" When Carolyn was confronted by her own stupidity (or lack of imagination), she almost always resorted to name-calling. It was how she was wired. "So I suppose you keep tabs on Barry? You know what he's doing at all times?"

"I know he sits on the couch a lot," Gina said, sprinkling Parmesan cheese on her pizza and taking another bite. "He drinks a lot of beer too…

in his underwear." She considered this for a moment. "I really wish he'd put on some pants."

"He does a lot more than just sit on the couch!"

Gina waited expectantly, eager to hear just what types of activities Barry engaged in when he wasn't drinking beer and sitting on the couch, watching NASCAR or something equally stupid. I mean, seriously, cars going around in a circle? The only exciting thing was when they crashed. Fans went away disappointed if no one got hurt.

"Like...what?"

"I don't have to explain this to you!" Carolyn exploded. "You're going to stay with a coworker of mine."

"Why can't I stay with Dad?" This question was asked innocently enough, but Gina already knew the answer. Despite the fact that the court wouldn't allow Carolyn to file a restraining order against him, she understood that she couldn't stay with her dad because he couldn't be trusted to stay sober. It just wasn't in his DNA. And if she was in his care and he blacked out? He could kiss all of his perks goodbye. Even his cousin couldn't get him off the hook if Bobby was caught endangering her life because he was endangering his own. At the tender age of fifteen, this was all very black and white.

"You know damn well why you can't stay with Bobby! He'd most likely wind up in jail, or he'd drive drunk or black out. He can't be trusted! He can never be trusted!"

As much as Gina didn't want to admit this, she knew it to be partially (OK, totally) true, that was, until he got his life together. She had faith in him that he would sooner or later, but at present he was still at the mercy of his addictions. Someday he would kick it all, of this she was certain. He couldn't crash through the rest of his life being so reckless, not when he knew what was at stake. Her love, for one thing. Also, her undying support. That had to be worth *something*.

"This sounds kind of hokey," she said, taking another bite of her slice, and Carolyn frowned at her, well, frowned more.

"I'm your mother," Carolyn said with an air of finality, "and you'll do as I say."

The girl nodded, wiping her hands on a napkin. She had her there. But she still had more questions.

"Who's this coworker? Have I ever met her?"

"It's a "he," and no, you've never met him. You're just lucky he's being kind enough to take you in."

"Can't I stay with Emily? I'm sure Maggie and Teddy wouldn't mind."

"Hell no!" Carolyn thundered, startling the poor kid before composing herself, running a hand through her hair and smiling an insincere smile. "I…I don't want to impose on them is all," she finished lamely. "Greg is a nice guy. You'll have a good time."

"It's only for a few days?"

"Yes."

"He won't touch me, will he?"

"God no!" *Because if he did…*

"And Ruby can come too?"

"Of course."

"And I *have* to?"

"Yes!"

"OK…I guess…"

And that was that; Gina was onboard too. The next day her daughter packed her bag, and she and the dog were shuffled off to Greg's house, who fortunately lived all the way over on the other side of town. With all of this completed, all Carolyn had to do to launch her plan was make a very emotional phone call to one deadbeat dad named Bobby Travis and they'd be on their way to Easy Street.

"I honestly don't believe you're thinking this through," Barry complained after Carolyn had made all the arrangements. "No matter what you have the "kidnapper" tell Bobby, he's going to get his cousin involved, trust me."

"Not if I have Greg threaten him that Gina's safety is at risk if he does."

"I don't know…"

"I'll have him threaten Bobby that his phone...all the damn phones... are tapped. There! Happy?"

That Barry was the voice of reason was a very rare thing indeed, yet Carolyn still didn't want to listen. To her, the money was practically hers. "This whole thing," he said, "it could really get us in a lot of hot water. You really think Bobby is that stupid that he'd fall for it?"

"He's a damn drug addict! And he's owed mob guys before! I've told him lots of things that aren't true, and he doesn't know any better because he can't remember anything. Why, if I told you some of the things I've hid from him—"

She cut herself off, knowing that there were some things she should keep to herself.

"Like what?"

"Like nothing," she said. "Never mind."

"No, really," he continued. "Like what?"

"Barry," she sighed, resigned to living with such a dimwit. "Just let me do all the thinking and you go and get yourself a beer and watch some football."

"Football season don't start till August."

"Then watch...I don't know, whatever the hell it is you watch! Just get out of here!"

And that was it. Gina was kidnapped.

Chapter Sixteen

"Did you call your bookie friend to ask him to place a bet for you?" Teddy said. He was wearing a Hawaiian shirt and an ostentatious pair of shades, trying to look inconspicuous. They spoke to one another out of the corners of their mouths, standing about three feet apart in a large truck stop off Highway 15 near Rancho Bernardo. It was four hours after their first meeting at the way stop, and even though Teddy had only two hours of sleep under his belt, he was completely in command of the situation. In contrast, Bobby was muddled, pretending to look at road maps, whereas Teddy pretended he was interested in oversized coffee mugs bearing slogans like "World's Best Grandpa" and "I Can't Believe I Ate the Whole Thing." Given a choice, he'd gladly take the latter of the two.

"I called him but I got his voice mail," Bobby said, grabbing a map of the state of Wisconsin and unfolding it gingerly. He'd never been there, but he heard they made really good cheese. He wasn't a big football fan, but he knew they were also known for their team. "As soon as he calls me back I'll ask him."

"Will he do it?"

"I don't know. It's going to be a lot more money than I asked for last time."

"I told you I can loan you some money. He doesn't have to front the whole thing." Teddy examined another mug with a cartoon cat on it. He couldn't agree more; he didn't like Mondays either.

"How much can you kick in?" Bobby tried to fold the map, but this was the part that always confounded him. Unfolding them was the easy part, while folding them was often tricky. It was like trying to remove a smoke detector from a wall mount to change the battery. Every time he did, he broke something. "That way I'll know how much I need to ask him for."

"I have seven grand I can loan you. If he can put up the rest, you'll be fine." Teddy glanced over at him as he selected another mug. "And the sooner the better. Given the timeline, I'm sure the kidnapper is going to call anytime and ask for the money."

"I know, I know," Bobby said, putting the unfolded map back and grabbing one for the state of Idaho. He'd never been there before, but he knew they were known for their potatoes.

"Seriously Bobby, you call him on the hour every hour until you talk to him. Gina's life depends on it."

"I said I know!" Bobby said, louder than he intended, and a couple passing by looked at them oddly before continuing toward the chip aisle. "I mean," Bobby corrected, his voice softer, "I know. I love that kid and I'll do anything to get her back."

Teddy nodded. "That's the spirit." He set down the mug he was holding and grabbed the mug with the cartoon cat and headed for the cashier. "Let me pay for this and then you meet me at my car and I'll give you the money."

◆ ◆ ◆

After several more tries, Bobby finally got Terry on the phone. Contrary to what he may have thought, Terry wasn't avoiding him; he'd simply been busy fleecing marks out of their hard-earned dough.

"Bobby!" he said heartily. "What can I do for you?"

"Did you listen to my voicemail?"

"Nope, been busy. What's up?"

"It's kind of a long story…"

"Lay it on me, I'm just sitting down to a late lunch."

"It's four in the afternoon."

"Don't tell me when to eat, Bobby. Now spill it."

So Bobby told him everything (even though he wasn't supposed to; one weakness that Carolyn hadn't accounted for was Bobby's inability to lie in certain situations. This was just that situation). In the meantime Terry slurped soup and chewed crackers noisily on the other end. When Bobby was finished, he waited for the other to take a drink of his beverage, belch, and then ponder the matter.

"Wow," Terry said. "That's quite an earful. You sure she's really kidnapped, nobody's putting you on?"

"Pretty sure, yeah."

"Who all knows about this?"

"Well, Gina was kidnapped from her mother's house, so she and her husband know. And I brought in my cousin Teddy—"

"The cop?"

"Yeah, him. And now you know."

"Anyone else?"

"No...oh wait, and Melissa. She knows too."

"Melissa?"

"My, um...girlfriend..."

"You meet her at your SA meeting?"

"Yeah."

"She hot?"

"Smokin'."

"Cool."

"So, can you do this for me?" Bobby tried to keep the impatience out of his voice, but it was difficult, what with his daughter's life being on the line and all.

"How much does the kidnapper want?" Terry took another drink of his soda, the sound of the straw sucking in a mixture of air and carbonated beverage extremely loud through the receiver.

"$50,000."

Terry choked on his soda, unleashing a coughing fit that rendered him unable to speak. When at last he could, he sputtered, "$50,000? Are you kidding me? How the hell would anyone think you're good for that kind of dough?"

"I have no idea man," Bobby said. "It seemed like the guy just pulled that number out of his ass."

"To make that much money you'd have to put up at least $15,000. You got some cash on hand?"

"My cousin Teddy is good for seven G's. I was sort of hoping that you'd loan me the rest and I'd pay you back."

There was a long pause on the other end, so long that Bobby thought his bookie had hung up on him. "You there?" he asked, and he heard Terry sigh.

"Yeah…"

"So?"

"This is a big favor you're asking of me Bobby. I'll have to give it some thought."

"I understand."

"Do you? I mean, if I call you back and I say no, what are you going to do?"

Now it was Bobby's turn to be silent. "I have no idea Terry," he said after a lengthy pause. "Please man, you've got to help me. My daughter's life is at stake."

"I don't have that kind of cash just laying around you know."

"Sure, sure." Bobby felt a pang of anxiety course through him. If Terry couldn't help him, he didn't know where to turn. He only had one credit card, and it had a $2500 limit. Presently it was maxed and he was paying off the minimum balance each month. He might have to sell some things, but he didn't really have anything to sell, except for his truck and his house, but the truck wasn't worth squat (as Terry had recently pointed out), and he didn't want to sell the house, not if he could help it. It was the only thing he owned, and real estate didn't come cheap anymore in Southern California. The way he saw it, that house was his retirement fund. Also, there was no way to get money out of it fast enough. It would be a time-consuming process. No, for him to be able to get his daughter back, he was going to need a big chunk of cash that he could double or triple quickly.

"Let me make some calls," Terry said conclusively, and Bobby felt a small surge of relief.

"Sure man, sure. Get back to me when you can."

"If I do this for you I'm going to want a big return on my money."

"Of course."

"And you still owe me from last time."

"I know."

"The vig on this is gonna be huge, you hear me?"

"Yes."

Another pregnant pause, and once again Bobby thought Terry had hung up.

"Christ, Bobby," the other said at last. "What the hell do you get yourself into?"

"I don't know," Bobby answered honestly. "I really don't know."

Then Terry hung up.

◆ ◆ ◆

Bobby was working on his second to last pool of the day when Terry called.

"OK Bobby, I'll front you the eight grand and try to win you fifty large, but you better hope I'm damn lucky."

"Thanks Terry!" Bobby gushed, hope springing eternal like the proverbial pot of gold at the end of the rainbow. "Man, I'll never forget this—"

"I won't let you, trust me. Now, here's the deal: you meet me at our diner in an hour and bring me the money you got." He considered it a moment, then added, "And the title to your truck. I'm going to have to take it this time."

"OK," Bobby said, expecting this. "What are you going to do? Bet the horses?"

"There's no way that could work twice," Terry said brusquely. "That was a one-time deal."

"OK..."

"I got the inside scoop on a high stakes poker game, buncha guys who play for a thousand dollars a hand."

"Are you that good at poker?"

"You better hope I am."

"All right. Thanks, Terry, I really appreciate it man."

"Can it. Thank me when I have the money."

"OK."

"Oh, and Bobby?"

"Yeah?"

"Don't ever ask me to do something like this again."

◆ ◆ ◆

Bobby cut a few corners, finishing his last pool in record time. The owner had been home, loitering around, and Bobby was pretty certain she was drunk. She had a looseness to her gait that he recognized from his own imbibing, and every third or fourth word she slurred.

"So I told the son of bitch he could bang all the whores he wanted as long as he never came home."

What finally proved his supposition was when she came out of her house with a martini glass and gulped the whole thing down in a swallow. Her eyes teared briefly before she absently wiped them away.

"You want a drink?" she asked, and Bobby looked at her wistfully. Truthfully? Hell yes, a martini or two would be just what the doctor ordered, something to make the butterflies in his stomach take a brief hiatus, possibly disembark for sunny weather somewhere south of the Florida Keys. But to do that would be risking Gina's welfare, and if he couldn't stand tall in the face of adversity, what did that make him? A coward and a spineless jellyfish, that was what, and he'd be damned if he was going to be either of those.

"No thanks," he said sincerely. "But I appreciate the offer." He smiled at her, then added, "I have to drive."

"I understand," she said, looking at him somberly. "I don't drive much anymore, not with my arthritis."

"Sure," Bobby replied, scooping some leaves that were floating on the surface. He saw some debris at the bottom of the pool, something glittering in the weak afternoon sunshine, and after a quick glance at her ring finger and then back at the object in the pool, he thought he knew what it was. Should he fish it out or let the pool vacuum get it? It might be hard to wrangle it out without actually having to get wet, and judging by her demeanor, she'd probably tossed it in there herself. He never actually saw this woman swimming (not that he should, as whenever he was here he was cleaning it), but he didn't take her as a swimmer. Her husband was probably the one who used the pool, and he was never home when Bobby was around. He couldn't recall ever meeting him, but he must be a scoundrel indeed. Maybe he was one of the more transient members of his SA meetings, only showing up every blue moon out of abject guilt.

"Well, that's it," he announced. "I better get going."

"Do you have to go so soon?" she asked. "I could make us something to eat…"

"Sorry," Bobby lied easily (he had no trouble convincingly exaggerating the truth whenever booze and drugs were involved or, in this case, his daughter's wellbeing). "I have another house I have to take care of."

"I thought I was your last job of the day."

How did she know that? Had he told her? It must have been on a day he was high (from before he'd started going to the meetings), and he'd let it slip. He had to be very careful. When he was high or in a blackout, he never knew what he'd said to anyone, so it was possible to contradict himself at every turn.

"I added an extra house today because they had a pool emergency."

She waited, an eyebrow cocked, wanting to know what constituted a "pool emergency."

"Guests coming in from out of town," he said, packing up his gear. "Can't have a dirty pool when you're having company."

"No," she agreed, looking at her empty glass, most likely wishing it was still full, "I suppose you can't."

◆ ◆ ◆

Bobby got to the diner ten minutes before Terry told him to meet him, and while he waited he battled the urge to get a tap beer from the bar across the street. One tap beer wouldn't be a big deal, not after the day he'd had, but Bobby was smart enough to know where that one beer would lead: to six or seven more. Then, after he was good and buzzed, he'd be hankering for a bump and, once he had that, he'd need something to settle him down. The cycle was so obvious that it was a wonder he was helpless to repeat it over and over and over. You'd think he'd eventually learn.

Terry arrived a few minutes later, clutching a briefcase, and upon seeing it Bobby knew it was serious. This was it, make or break. Once Terry started betting, it was out there, into the stratosphere. With any luck, Terry was as shrewd at cards as he was with the horses.

"You better hope I get dealt some good cards," Terry told him, taking a seat across from him and setting the case on the table. Although he had a system for the horses, playing cards was another matter entirely. He knew how to bluff even the most steadfast professional, but the problem was so did they. Especially high stakes. "Maybe I can even make a few bucks for myself." He looked Bobby up and down. "You got the cash for me?"

"Oh yeah, right." At the truck stop Teddy had given him what appeared to be "mattress money." The bills were old and crumpled, held together with rubber bands. He took the bundles out of his coat pockets and held them out to Terry. Terry looked at them for a moment before begrudgingly accepting them, as if the bills were crawling with disease. If anything danced and cavorted over Franklin's displeased countenance, it was possibly just bedbugs.

"OK," Terry said, tucking the bills in the briefcase. "Did you sign the title over to me?"

"Yeah." Bobby removed it from his pocket and handed it over. This, too, went into the briefcase. Terry shut it with a flourish of clicking latches, spinning a combination dial.

"I'll call you tomorrow."

"Huh?"

"The game ain't until later tonight. These types of operations don't go down till after midnight."

"Of course," Bobby said. "You call me and tell me how it goes."

Terry nodded once and stood. "All right then. Talk to you tomorrow." He spun on one heel and left the diner without so much as ordering a cup of coffee.

Bobby watched him go, licking his lips. Man, he could really use a drink. When this whole thing was over, he'd treat himself nicely, even though it was the drinking that got him in this mess in the first place.

Here's to alcohol. The indisputable cause and solution to all of our problems.

Chapter Seventeen

When Terry called him the following morning, Bobby felt a weird, floating sensation envelop his brain. It was similar to how he felt when he got in too deep with the Xanax and suffered from mild withdrawals. It left his head feeling hollow, his gray matter seemingly scooped out and the cavernous space injected with helium.

Terry filled him in on what had happened the previous evening, and suddenly the once sunny day was now obscured by clouds. Bobby could practically hear the sound of popping bubbles as his brain cooked in a stew of its own rotten juices. He knew it was partly withdrawals from the pills, but it was more than that, much, much more.

"Those guys were a buncha sharks," Terry said. "For all I know, they were cheating."

"You lost?" The world slowly tilted, making him feel as if he was falling into an enormous chasm.

"As much as I hate to admit it, that's what I'm telling you. They took *me* to the cleaner's too." The truth was, Terry lost all of Bobby's money but only two grand of his own. When he sensed the ship was sinking, he was smart enough to put on a life preserver and get in one of the lifeboats.

"All of it?"

"All of it." Totally a fact. Bobby's money (borrowed from Teddy) had been redistributed among the other players, but mostly to a guy named Sal. He'd had a hell of a night, Sal did.

"Did they deal you bad cards?"

"No, they just dealt better cards to themselves. And that's why it's called gambling," he said, a hint of exasperation in his voice. "You don't know how things are going to turn out." He was quiet for a moment, and so was Bobby. He had no idea what to say. What Terry said next filled the gap in the conversation, but it wasn't exactly what Bobby wanted to hear: "The good news is I didn't gamble away your truck, but I own it now."

Somehow Bobby had known that from the moment Terry told him he'd lost and, all things considered, it was the least of his problems. What did it matter? He was already five grand in the hole; so what if he no longer owned his truck? He also owed Teddy seven grand, so he had markers out all over the place. And where was he going to get the money? He might have to put his house on the market after all. It was either that or the kidnappers may hurt Gina. Maybe they already had. Was it possible for him to sell a kidney on the black market? Whom could he call and ask?

"I'll get it to you today."

"No need," Terry said. "Keep the truck. I know you need it for work. Just don't crash it or anything." Again, the elongated pause. Bobby could hear his kitchen clock ticking over the sink. Sometimes at night, when he couldn't sleep, he wanted to rip the damn thing off the wall and sling it through the French windows over the kitchen sink.

"You know what?" Terry said at last, and just as Bobby was going to ask what, Terry answered his own question: "You *are* bad luck."

Bobby nodded silently. This was something he was well aware of.

"Yeah," he said. "I know."

◆ ◆ ◆

When Bobby got home from work that evening (skipping his NA meeting; what the hell, he was on a roll), the first thing he did was go to the fridge to get a beer, but as soon as his hand was on the handle he reminded himself that it was only Thursday and that he wasn't allowed a beer until Friday, and then he remembered that, until he found his daughter, he wasn't allowed a beer at all. This made him feel very unhappy indeed. After all, how could he be expected to be at his best when he was withdrawing from all the chemicals? Just like the damn Xanax, he was certain the alcohol cravings were only being held at bay by the fact that he allowed himself the pleasure of it twice (maybe three times) weekly.

He opened the fridge, looked inside, and saw that there were only two beers in there anyway. And why did he keep them around? They were the remaining two from a twelve pack he'd bought last week Friday. He knew they were going to tempt him for as long as they sat there, laughing at him.

"Hey, there's Bobby! How's it going dude; care for a cold one? What's that? You can't have one until Friday? Oh, you poor bastard! Wait! You can't have one until you find your missing daughter? Oh, that is a tough one brother, really, because with your luck you'll never find her. And the money? Good luck trying to raise that kind of dough! You might as well pound both of us right now and head straight to Hooligans! At least there you can actually achieve something. Tony's holding, you know. Fat eight balls for one sixty. And all the Xanax you can pop! Come on man, you know you want it..."

And he did, that much was true. But it was only Thursday, and he was supposed to be at his NA meeting, telling his fellow drug addicts what a fuckup he was. They were probably wondering where he was, most likely assuming he'd gone nutsack up in a massage parlor after a rousing meth-amphetamine induced rub & tug heart attack.

I wish I could go out like that...

But honestly, he had to think of a way to scrounge up a lot of money, fast, and the thought of wasting his time at the NA meeting depressed him even more; those battered hang-dog faces with desperation in their eyes, licking overly dry lips with discolored tongues, wanting just one more fix to take them out of their misery. What about Lily, sitting there and rubbing her terrifyingly damaged arms, track marks standing out in stark relief against all of that porcelain white skin? Her eyes pleading for someone to inject her with a hotshot, to slash her throat with a straight razor, maybe to fuck her until her uterus fell out like a gelatinous hunk of protoplasmic goo. Thinking about her made Bobby want to scream and cry at the same time.

The impossibility of his situation weighed on him heavily. Seriously, there was no way in hell he was going to get the kind of bread he needed to get his head above water. Whoever had his daughter must be one stupid son of a bitch, thinking he could come up with anything more than the scratch to buy some drugs and a few gallons of gas for a truck that was held together with Bondo and duct tape. If he had a motor-vehicle emergency, he was pretty much screwed, as he'd have to go without food for the month in exchange for getting it fixed. Not that it was really a concern anymore; Terry now owned the piece of crap. If it broke down, would he fix it? Good question, hopefully one he wouldn't need answered any time soon.

He continued to stare at the beer, his mouth watering. And then, without any will of his own, he saw his hand reaching forward, the fingers wriggling ever so slightly, the anticipation so strong he swallowed hard once, then twice, and his heart leapt into his throat.

Whatcha doin', Bobby? What the hell ya think you're doing?

His fingers moved closer and began to bend, ready to fold around the icy, refreshing bottle of tasty (well, maybe not tasty, it was, after all, Pabst) beer. Another couple of inches and his hand would touch the cold, glass surface, and from there it was merely a matter of twisting off the cap and lifting it to his lips. Once he dumped it down his throat it would do all the work and he could lie back and relax and forget about everything else for a while. Because after the first beer went down so smoothly, he'd surely enjoy the second. And then he'd be out, and he'd have to go get more, now wouldn't he? Damn straight he would. And drinking alone was boring; no, he'd be better off if he went some place where he could be among friends, a bar perhaps. An establishment that sold fine spirits. Why, Hooligans could be that spot, sure it could! It was the place where everyone knew his name. When he walked in the door, the little bell ding-a-linging over his head so pleasantly, announcing to everyone that Bobby Travis had made the time to come on in and be a part of their otherwise miserable lives. They'd all look up and say, "Hi, howya doin', Bobby? Glad ya made it!" And Tony would greet him with a smile, would wave him over and pour him a pint of something cheap (Milwaukee's Best, maybe, or Schlitz) and tell him that this one was on the house, and while Bobby was sipping it he'd look around to see if anyone was listening and when he saw the coast was clear he'd lean his head closer and ask if Bobby was looking for something to powder his nose with, and this was Bobby's chance to nod and say yes. And maybe a couple of those pills too, you know, to keep the old anxiety at bay. And Tony would know exactly what he meant, and he'd reach under the bar and he'd grab a hold of the afore-mentioned items, and Bobby would rustle around in his pocket until he came up with the cash, and they'd make the trade and then Bobby would be in the bathroom, opening the door to his favorite stall, the baggy in one hand, a bill he was about to roll up in the other, his heart beating in anticipation, his nostrils flaring with an eagerness that was otherworldly. And when the first blast of crystal hit his system, his cock would become rock hard, and all sane thoughts and reasoning would quickly flee, and the next thing he'd know he'd be snorting another line, then another, and then he'd be popping not one but two Xanax, and things would grow hazy after a while, and life wouldn't be so bad. Maybe he couldn't find the money to save his daughter, but in that moment he could certainly save himself, and that was worth something, right? That was something worth living for when you had absolutely nothing else.

A knock on his door broke his reverie, and to his surprise he saw that his hand was mere millimeters away from the bottle; another Nano second and it would have been in his hand. And once in his hand it would be all over. Just a small matter of twisting off the top.

"Coming!" he yelled instead, stepping away from the fridge and slamming the door, hard. Hard enough to rattle the handmade model of Leatherface that stood atop his Frigidaire, his booted foot resting on a decapitated head while he revved the chainsaw in expectation of his next victim. "Be right there!"

Bobby went to the door, knowing he'd narrowly missed what could have easily been next week's tale of debauchery at all of his meetings, his hands slightly shaking, a sheen of sweat glistening on his forehead.

◆ ◆ ◆

Carolyn called her coworker for two reasons: one was because she wanted to know what Bobby said when he asked him for the money. The other was to yell at him for being an idiot. Because while she was on her way to the Kwik-Stop to get a pack of smokes and some malt liquor (a beverage she could enjoy *before* work), she saw Gina walking with Ruby down the street in broad daylight, swinging her arms in that carefree manner that young girls do, looking like she didn't have a care in the world. The least of her concern was what her daughter was up to; her apprehension was triggered by the magnitude of the consequences if Bobby or someone who knew him saw her.

"What the hell are you doing?" she'd asked her daughter after pulling the rusty old station wagon up to the curb, the Chevy Malibu Classic that had seen better days back when she still had her original set of teeth, and not the dentures she wore because of a nasty meth habit in the early 2000s.

"Going to the store," her daughter had replied innocently enough. Beside her, the stupid dog looked up with an expression she always wore on her mug: a wide grin that seemed to prove there wasn't anything more than a brain the size of pea floating around in liquid gray matter. Christ, Carolyn really hated that freakin' dog. "That guy needs some cigarettes and told me I could get some chips and a candy bar with the change." She looked at her mother suspiciously. "Is there a problem with that?"

"No, no problem. But why don't you just get in the car and I'll give you a ride?"

"I'd rather walk." Then it occurred to her, of course. "Aren't you and Barry supposed to be on vacation?"

"Um..." Carolyn had momentarily forgotten that she was supposed to be out of town. This was all Greg's fault! If he hadn't let her out of the house, she wouldn't have stopped in the first place. She certainly had some choice words for him. His ear drums would be freakin' bleeding when she was done! "Our plans changed."

"Can I come home then?"

"We're...um, uh...having a staycation," she said quickly, the idea forming in her mind as the words left her mouth. Then another burst of inspiration. "We're having lots and lots of sex, mostly in the living room, and on the floor of the dining room."

"Gross!" Gina made a face that more than adequately expressed her shock and dismay. "I don't think I want to come back, like...*ever!*"

"Get in the damn car," Carolyn growled. "And don't let that dog slobber all over my windows."

When they'd arrived at Greg's house to drop off Gina, he wasn't in (another smooth move on his part), so Carolyn made a mental note to call him at her earliest convenience. Now was that time.

"What the Christ are you doing, letting the kid leave the house?"

"I needed some smokes—"

"She isn't supposed to leave the house! Bobby or somebody tied to him might see her and that would ruin the whole thing!"

"Whadya mean?"

Carolyn wanted to reach right through the receiver and strangle the stupid bastard. Of all the people she could have picked to kidnap the kid, she had to pick a guy who had as much intelligence as your average Labrador retriever. Or bulldog, take your pick.

"She's supposed to be kidnapped," she'd said in her serenest voice, the one reserved for when she wanted the other party to know both how angry she was, and how stupid they were. It worked wonders on Barry and Gina, but it sometimes failed to make an impact on Bobby. He wasn't as easily intimidated, but right now it was working its magic on Greg.

"How was I supposed to know?"

"You ever watch the movies, you numbskull? When someone is kidnapped, they don't get to just walk out of the house and go to the store! You been letting her use the phone too?"

"Of course not, I ain't stupid! And she doesn't even know she's kidnapped!" Greg snapped back, and this, it would seem, took some of the fire out of Carolyn. In the silence that ensued the two of them heard Gina singing along to an Adele song in the background. Her voice was peppy, upbeat, her innocence total, her belief that nothing was afoot evident in the way she hummed with the verses (where she didn't know the words) and sang along with the chorus where she did.

"I suppose," she'd said at last, her feathers ruffled but her demeanor not entirely shattered, "that we will just have to think of some reason for her to stay in, hmm?" She let this sink in before continuing. "When you asked Bobby for the money did you give him a time frame?"

"I told him he had thirty-six hours."

"Good man; I don't want this to take any longer than it has to. Light a fire under his ass by calling him and setting up a meet."

"You think he's got the money by now?" Greg sounded dubious. He did, after all, ask for $50,000. That wasn't walking around money for a guy who operated a one-man pool cleaning business. "It hasn't been thirty-six hours—"

"I told you: he gambles! He knows how to get that kind of money if he has to, and he's been cheating me out of extra child support payments for years. It's time to shake him down!"

"OK, OK, I'm just askin'." There was silence on his end of the line, except for Gina's voice in the background. Now she was singing to a Lady Gaga song. "So...what do you want me to do?"

"Call him and arrange to meet him somewhere! Do I have to spell this out for you? Jesus, you'd think you've never seen *The Big Lebowski*..."

"I seen it," Greg griped. "I didn't like it."

"Sorry to hear you have lousy taste in movies," Carolyn said, sounding anything *but* sorry. "Call him and tell him he either has the money... or else."

"Or else what?"

"What do you think? You're going to hurt the kid."

"That ain't very nice."

"Who said you were supposed to be nice? You're a kidnapper!"

"What if he wants to know what mob boss I'm connected to? What do I tell him?"

"Christ, don't you have any imagination?"

"Yeah…" In all honesty, he had no imagination—none. Everything he'd done so far had been scripted by Carolyn, except for the amount of money he'd asked for. That was the only bit of creativity he'd brought to the table.

"Do you?" she badgered him and he let out a loud sigh.

"Sure I do!" he said, not liking how she was riding him. If he knew what a bitch she was going to be about this, he wouldn't have gotten involved. But, then again, there was the money. He had some personal debts he had to take care of before his creditors decided to turn the heat up. "So what am I going to tell the kid, ya know, about why she can't leave?"

"Let me give that some thought and I'll get back to you. In the meantime, get Bobby on the horn and sweat him."

"I'll take care of it."

"You better," she said, and then hung up on him.

◆ ◆ ◆

Bobby let Melissa into the house, surprised to see her. They normally only hooked up after their SA meeting; he didn't even know she knew where he lived.

"Google holds the answers to all of life's mysteries, Bobby," she said, sprawling on his less-than-clean couch, and he nodded. He'd ask her if he could get her something to drink, but all he had was the Pabst Blue Ribbon and tap water. He asked her anyway.

"Do you have any coffee?"

He forgot he had coffee. "I got instant."

"Folgers?"

"No, the Safeway brand."

"Is it any good?"

"It tastes terrible," he said honestly. "I only drink it for the caffeine."

"I'll pass."

"So what brings you by this way?"

"I was in the neighborhood and I decided I wanted to have the grand tour of Casa de la Bobby."

"Really?"

"Hell no! I wanted to make sure you weren't drinking or using drugs." She scrutinized him carefully. "You don't look high."

"I'm not!" he said, a little too defensively, and she raised her eyebrows. "I'm glad you came over," he amended. "I might have been if you hadn't stopped by."

She smiled. "I thought you might've needed a little support."

"All I can get baby."

"Things getting a little rough?"

To this seemingly innocent question he answered with all that had recently occurred: borrowing money from Teddy, Terry losing all of it playing poker, and now he was less the money and the title to his truck, not to mention the $50,000 he needed for the kidnappers.

"And to make things worse, they haven't let me talk to her. I don't even know if she's safe."

Melissa commiserated. "Let me give you a back rub," she said. "Come over here."

She scooched forward on the couch and Bobby sat on the floor in front of her. "Take off your shirt," she commanded and he did. Her fingers began to knead his flesh, and it felt so good that for a moment he forgot about how close he'd come to drinking the two bottles of beer, and his dread over not being able to raise the money to get his daughter back. For a minute, he simply let the gentle motion of her fingers relax him, like listening to waves crashing along the shore.

"I have this recurring dream," he found himself telling her, why, he didn't honestly know. He'd never told anybody this, and not because it was embarrassing, but simply because he had no one to tell. "In it I live in a giant house."

"This house doesn't look too bad," she said, glancing around. "How much did you pay for it?"

"I inherited it from my Dad."

"Nice."

"Yeah, I'm lucky to have it. I'll probably have to sell it to get the money for the kidnappers, if they can wait while it goes through escrow."

"You won't have to sell your house Bobby," she said, working her fingers and palms into the small of his back. "Tell me about your dream."

"In the dream I discover I live in this giant house, and it always makes sense to me, like I deserve it somehow."

"What, you think you don't deserve it? Don't sell yourself short."

"That's nice of you to say. So anyway, I'm always discovering it for the first time, even though I know it's my house and I've lived there for a long time. The ground floor is beautiful, like a museum. Everything is ornate, complete with vaulted ceilings, candelabras, Ming vases, the whole deal. People appear, and I realize that they're my roommates, that I don't live in this house alone. Sometimes I recognize them as people I've known, sometimes they are total strangers yet I know them. Is that crazy or what?"

"Dreams don't have to make sense, Bobby." This said while she used an elbow to get out an especially hard knot along his spine.

"I know, but they always make sense while you're having them."

"That's what makes them fun. So, these people, do you talk to them?"

"Not really. They just sort of come and go. What the dream is really about is the house. I know that my room is on the fifth or sixth floor—"

"Wait, the house is *that* big?"

"It's freakin' huge. And it has all kinds of secret passageways and hidden staircases and rooms bigger than a gymnasium that appear from out of nowhere. And, like I said, it all makes sense."

"How long have you been having this dream?"

"As long as I can remember."

"That's not saying much."

"Touché," he said, leaning forward so she had more room to work with. "I don't know, since my mid-twenties. But that isn't the disturbing part of the dream."

"The dream doesn't sound disturbing at all."

"That's just it. It always begins harmlessly enough, but then it changes. The deeper I get into the house, the more stairs I climb as I get higher and higher to get to my room, the more dilapidated it gets."

"The more what?"

"Crappy, rundown. All of a sudden, the place is full of cobwebs, and large portions of the floor are missing, or the boards are so loose, you think they are going to give way under your feet. And when I get to the top floor, I see that parts of the roof are gone, and that I can see the sky beyond. And that's when it starts raining, and water is pouring in and soaking my bed."

"OK…"

"This beautiful place just turns into an enormous, cavernous mess, but it still is alluring, because there is so much space."

"So…you don't feel scared?"

"I never feel scared, yet I always know that the house is going to wind up in that condition, every time I'm in the dream. As I climb the stairs and get higher and higher, I know that everything is going to start crumbling, that everything is going to get worse and worse, yet I like it. It's still attractive to me."

"I think you just explained the meaning of your dream," Melissa said, cracking her knuckles, giving his back one last pat. "At least one aspect of it, maybe." She ruffled the hair on his head. "Get up and put your shirt on. You're going to give me a tour of your house."

"You figured out my dream?" He turned his head, looking at her expectantly.

She offered him a crooked smile. "Jesus, Bobby, haven't you? Now give me the grand tour or I'm taking my ball and going home."

"OK." He smiled, getting to his feet and slipping on his T-shirt. "Whatever the lady wants."

"You know what I want," she said seductively, shooting him a wink. "We'll end the tour in the master bedroom, and from there we'll discuss the Freudian themes of your dreams."

"I thought that sometimes a cigar was just a cigar," Bobby said, grinning.

"Not today it isn't. It's a throbbing penis. Now get a move on cowboy. I want to see the place my man calls home."

"Oh, so I'm your man now?"

"Don't make it weird Bobby," she said, pushing him forward. "Now get."

So he got.

◆ ◆ ◆

After he showed her the kitchen (which really could use the loving touch of a cleaning person, or at least some Comet, a scrub brush, and elbow grease), he segued into the family room where it was apparent the carpet needed to be replaced, like, decades ago. Stains of unknown origin (probably a good thing too, because to know what they came from would surely bring upon a visit by men in Hazmat suits looking for contaminants that may or may not contain trace elements of HN1 or the bubonic plague) covered it, and Bobby couldn't help but feel slightly embarrassed. There was also the matter of the chipped and faded paint, as well as windows showing spider webs of cracks.

"If you plan on selling this place you might want to list it as a fixer-upper."

"I was thinking of using the term 'rustic.'"

"That would apply."

He led her out the patio door and to the backyard beyond. When they stepped outside into the fading sunshine of the late July day, they were delighted to see three hummingbirds hovering over the nectar in a bird feeder, wings whirring so fast they were nothing but a blur of motion. Their colors were startlingly brilliant in the evening light, from a majestic cobalt to a dazzling magenta. Just as Melissa was about to remark upon the beauty of it all, her eyes scanned further and took in Bobby's swimming pool. Any compliments she was about to make were instantly cut short.

"Holy crap Bobby, for a pool cleaner you probably have the filthiest pool I've ever seen. Not much on keeping up the place I see."

Bobby opened his mouth, was about to tell her how he didn't have time, what with how busy he was, but, as with her, the words died in his throat before he could vocalize them because he realized what a damning lie it was. During the week? Yes, this was mostly true. But over the weekend he could surely run the vacuum or use any of his many tools and cleaners to remove the algae and pond scum and mold that had accumulated along the sides. Melissa was shocked to see plastic bottles, cigarette butts, beer cans, empty drug bindles, etc. clogging the pool as well. And on top of that was a patchy layer of dead leaves, the water beneath it a scummy-looking brown color. She looked at him and waited for his answer, but they both knew whatever he was going to say was bullshit. He had the time, but he was too busy pummeling his brain into goo over the weekends to tackle any domestic chores. His dream suddenly came to her mind, the literal connotations it denoted instead of the figurative ones, and she almost wanted to say something but chose not to.

"Wouldn't your daughter like to swim in the pool?" she asked instead, resisting the urge to observe how appropriate it would be if there was a body floating face down within it. "Wouldn't that be an incentive for you to stay sober one weekend a month?"

"I suppose it would," he agreed slowly. "If she was allowed to come here."

"Her mother won't let her visit you at home?"

"Not only her..."

Saying it made Bobby feel sick to his stomach. Even though Teddy had an in with a judge, ensuring a restraining order would never stick, the same judge wasn't crazy enough to allow the girl access to his home. God only knew what he was getting into in his spare time. In fact, if there was a God, he/she/it would be the only one that knew, for Bobby certainly didn't. He could piece things together by digging through his trash and reading his emails and texts, but that was about it. He'd once considered putting in security cameras so he could see what he was up to while blacked out, but how pathetic was that? Beyond pathetic and into the land of truly fucking sad, was what it was. It was his life and he was losing it one second at a time and counting.

Melissa put her arm around him. "That sucks Bobby, it really does." She wanted to console him, to tell him that if he got his shit together that maybe all that would change, but who was she to talk? She did, after all, meet him in a sex addicts group that gathered once a week in the basement of a YMCA in a less-than-favorable part of town where they usually had sex on a filthy mattress in the back of his (make that *Terry's*) truck. She wasn't exactly Mother Theresa.

"Yeah, it really does."

"Look," she said. "Everything is going to be OK." She didn't really think so, but she figured Bobby needed to hear something good right now. "You won't have to sell your house, and your daughter is going to be all right."

"I wish it was that simple," he said softly. "I really do. But things never seem to work out for me. I'm just a jinx..."

"You create your own problems because you make bad decisions Bobby."

He looked at her sharply, ready to hear the "speech" that everyone always felt compelled to give him, from his cousin, to the other cops on the force, as well as anybody Bobby ever had to talk to "professionally" (unfortunately Bobby was a case worker's wet dream), but he could see that wasn't the direction she was going in. She was genuinely concerned, that was all, and his expression softened. Hell, she could say whatever she wanted to him and he'd listen. She was, ultimately, the only person in the world who really cared about him, besides his daughter of course. Yet, unlike his child, this woman had real problems of her own, and was able to look at him more objectively. At least, he hoped so.

"You're right," he conceded, nodding, and she took his hand.

"Don't take it so hard Bobby, I'm not saying anything you don't already know."

"I know, I know. Maybe that's why it kinda sucks to hear it."

"Truth is always hard to hear, especially when it reveals who we really are. And, hey, Bobby? Do you really not understand your dream?" She gestured around at the trashed remnants of what had once probably been a really nice house. "I mean, this has to be a part of it, right?"

"I thought it was more, I don't know, psychological than that," he said, shrugging. "You know, something about the condition of my head, my dwindling sobriety and/or sanity."

"Oh, don't get me wrong, I think it has something to do with that too, but—"

"Are we back to the cigar?"

"Speaking of penises…I mean cigars…isn't it time we got to the part of the tour that includes the master bedroom?"

Bobby felt instant arousal, like a shot of heroin, course through him. He squeezed her hand within his own.

"Right this way ma'am, and I'll be glad to complete the tour of Casa de la Bobby—" he was saying when his phone rang in his pocket, the sound of an old-fashioned telephone. "Shit." That was his ringtone when it was one he didn't recognize. "Oh my God," he said breathlessly, "It could be the kidnapper."

"Don't just stand there," she advised him. "Answer it."

So Bobby pressed the button and put the phone to his ear.

"Hello?" he said, his erection starting to wane.

"I want the money," the voice on the other end snarled, and his hard-on disappeared completely.

Chapter Eighteen

"I don't have it," Bobby said. He could have lied, he supposed, if only to gain some leverage, but in all actuality that might make matters worse. Better to go with the truth on this one. "And I want to speak to my daughter."

Although he'd already been prepped to expect this demand, Greg hadn't given it further thought after Bobby's first request. *Goddamit!* Was what he thought at the moment. *I forgot about that!*

"Not unless I get the money," he said.

"That's not how this works," Bobby replied, more lucid than he'd normally be because he'd now been sober for six days, which was a personal best for him dating back to…Christ only knew. "I need to know that she's safe, and then I'll comply with your demands—"

"You don't get any say, you son of a bitch, not unless you got the money!"

"For all I know, you don't even have my daughter! How do I know I'm not just talking to some kook?"

"Anybody else aware that she's gone?" the kidnapper asked instead of answering the question, and Bobby had to admit he had him there, but he wasn't going to give in so easily.

"This isn't how it works," he repeated instead. "Seriously, I need to know she's safe."

Greg considered this for a moment. Gina was watching TV downstairs, some happy crappy garbage called I Carly or some such nonsense. He could hear her laughing every so often and talking to her…aha! That was it!

"I'll tell you what," Greg rasped. "I'll prove to you I have your daughter, and then you're going to get me the money. I do believe I put a time limit on our terms, correct?"

"I tried to get it," Bobby said wearily, "but it didn't work out and now I'm in debt with someone else. And who are you anyway? Who do I owe money to—?"

"Shut the hell up! I'll ask the damn questions. You just wait a minute; I'll be right back."

The phone made a clunking sound, and Bobby realized that the other had dropped it and left the room. He didn't recognize it for a moment, but then became aware that he was holding his breath.

"What the hell is going on?" Melissa stage whispered, loudly enough that if the man *had* still been on the line he would have easily heard her.

"I asked to speak with Gina, and he told me he was going to prove to me he had her."

"Jesus Bobby, of course we know he has her—"

"Do we? He hasn't let me speak to her. I, for one, think that's sorta suspicious."

Meanwhile, Greg had gone downstairs. Bobby had asked to speak to his daughter, but since this wasn't a "for real" kidnapping how was he going to pull that off? He couldn't get the girl to dupe her father by playing along that she'd been abducted, but he figured he had the next best thing. If this didn't prove it to Bobby, he didn't know what would.

"You want to what?" Gina asked, her attention momentarily diverted from the childish antics of the actors on the show she loved so dearly.

"She needs a bath," Greg said, hoping he sounded sincere. After all, he certainly didn't look like the kind of guy who even *liked* animals. "Let me take care of it. I'm sick of her wiping her ass on my couch."

"I clean up after her!" Gina protested, but then Carly said something really funny and her attention went back to the TV. "OK, but if she doesn't like it don't make her. She's kinda sensitive."

That's what I'm hoping, Greg thought, enticing the bulldog to follow him out of the room with a treat he'd already grabbed from the box in the kitchen. The pudgy little dog's eyes rolled when she saw the Snausage. She was beside herself with the promise of a snack. When he got her upstairs, he quickly ran the bathwater in the tub. At once Ruby's eyes looked panicked. She could endure almost anything for a treat, but a bath? That was asking a little too much, even for one of her beloved Snausage's.

"Come on, girl; hop in," Greg said, teasing her, and she let out a whine, which was exactly what he was hoping for. He quickly ran into the other room and grabbed his phone. When he returned to the bathroom, he closed the door and bent down on one knee. "OK, honey, into the tub you go," he whispered, wrapping an arm around her rotund middle and lifting her in. At once she began a litany of whining that he hoped Gina wouldn't hear but that Bobby would and be able to identify immediately—if only for the fact that he'd want to get Ruby out of the tub before he aroused the kid's suspicion. And it worked beautifully.

Over the other end of the phone, Bobby heard what sounded like Gina's dog, and she was definitely in distress. "What the hell are you doing?" Bobby cried. "Is that Ruby?"

"It sure is, Bobby, and it turns out she doesn't like getting burned with a cigarette lighter."

Ruby kicked and flailed in the tub, shaking herself and spraying water all over the place. Greg had to turn his back so his iPhone didn't get wet. Ruby was playing the part perfectly; good thing this dog really hated getting a bath. Her antics had Bobby practically shitting his pants on the other end.

"Don't you hurt her dog! Please! OK, I believe you! Just, please, don't hurt Ruby!"

Bobby couldn't believe it; the kidnapper was torturing Gina's dog! He'd recognize that whine anywhere, as he'd heard it countless times whenever Ruby wanted to get out of doing something she didn't like, and this time it was being ruthlessly burned by a sadistic bastard.

"I can do this all day, Bobby," Greg said, taking a towel from the cupboard and placing it on the floor in front of the tub. "If you don't get me the money, the next time I call it's gonna be Gina screaming, not the dog. You get me?"

"Yes, yes, I understand! I'll get you the money somehow, I promise! Just don't hurt anyone! Please!"

Worked like a charm.

Greg reached into the tub and scooped Ruby up, depositing her gently on the towel. When all was said and done, he didn't dislike dogs, nor animals in general, but it certainly got the job done, didn't it? And at the end of the day, that was all that mattered.

"You get me the money, Bobby Travis. I'll cut you some slack and give you twenty-four more hours."

"That's not a lot of time! How am I supposed to come up with that kind of cash?"

"Not my problem," Greg replied coldly. He was getting sick of being a babysitter, and the chubby dog genuinely *was* wiping her ass on his couch. Not that it was a great couch, mind you, but still, that wasn't the point. "You heard me, twenty-four hours."

And, as usual, the phone went dead in Bobby's ear.

◆ ◆ ◆

"That guy just tortured Ruby," Bobby said anxiously, his hands visibly shaking as he pocketed his phone. "That sick asshole!"

"Who's Ruby?"

"My daughter's dog."

"Oh, Bobby!"

He nodded, tears welling up in his eyes. Gina loved that dog dearly; they were practically inseparable. Whenever they got together, she always wanted to bring her along, and if she couldn't the kid felt bad. He tried to include Ruby in as many of their activities as possible, but not all of them were dog friendly. Like the movies, or the mall. But their visits incorporated a lot of walks in the park, and it was incredible how such a round dog with stubby legs could move when she wanted to. And could that bulldog chase a ball? Like nobody's damn business, that was for sure.

"I've got to get him the money," Bobby whispered, a tear running down his cheek and into his two-day stubble. "He said if I didn't that the next time it would be Gina screaming, not the dog." His lips twisted and writhed as he tried to keep himself together, but at last he lost the battle and he couldn't and he started sobbing and Melissa took him in her arms.

"Shh," she calmed him. "Shh, we'll think of something, Bobby. Don't worry."

But she truly wondered if they would, and she'd heard the last thing the kidnapper had said. He had twenty-four hours to come up with the money. How the hell were they going to do that without trying to take out a bank loan neither one of them could get if their lives depended on it?

Bobby snuffled back snot and took his head off her shoulder so he could look her in the eyes. "We?" he asked, and suddenly, as if she was run over by a bus that didn't so much as attempt to slow down, she realized she was in love with him. No bull, honest to goodness loved this pathetic goofball.

"Yes, Bobby, 'we.' *We* are going to get the money and get your daughter back. I promise."

"But how?" He wasn't kidding; he was totally at a loss. Unfortunately, so was she.

"I don't know, but we'll think of something, OK?"

"OK," he answered apathetically, and he rested his head back on her shoulder as another spasm of sorrow passed through him.

◆ ◆ ◆

"You did what?"

"Hey, I had to do something! It was either that, or he woulda got suspicious."

"Jesus, but the freakin' dog?"

Carolyn paced back and forth in the kitchen, lighting another cigarette off the stub of the one she was already smoking. This wasn't going as smoothly as she would have liked, and why the hell hadn't Bobby paid them yet? If he could get the money so quickly to get his own ass out of hock, why couldn't he do it for his daughter? Or maybe he just didn't care. No, he'd want to save her more than he'd want to save himself. Something wasn't right; that was for damn sure. Could she be wrong about his ability to procure funds via gambling when he needed to, or was he simply hitting a rough patch? Whatever the case, something had to give, and quick.

"Did you want me to put the kid on the phone? I'm sure she woulda played along, especially knowing she was lying to her old man." Greg puffed on a cigarette of his own, making the phone call in his bedroom while the kid continued to watch TV. It was all she seemed to want to do, was watch TV. Not to mention play with that stupid dog of hers, who actually wasn't all that stupid, seeing as she'd helped him in fooling Bobby that the kidnapping was for real.

"I suppose not," Carolyn relented, casting a jaundiced eye on Barry, who was lying on the couch, drinking a Silver Bullet while watching an infomercial about a hair loss product that *really worked*. Every so often he patted his growing bald spot wistfully, then tugged at the crotch of his jammy jams as if the two were somehow related.

"Look, he'll get the money," Greg continued. "He was practically crapping his pants when he heard the dog going apeshit. Trust me, it'll work."

"It better work," she said, and hung up. She glanced over at Barry again. He was studying the TV as if his life depended on it. "Is that all you've been doing all day?"

"Huh?" he said, glancing up at her and taking another slug of beer.

"I think the gutters could stand to be cleaned."

"The gutters?"

"It's time you earned your keep around here," she decided. "Instead of getting drunk all day, tomorrow morning you're going to get the ladder from the garage and a pair of those work gloves I keep in the cabinet with the gardening tools—"

"I ain't just been getting drunk!"

"Spare me, OK? I was born at night, but it wasn't last night."

He looked at her sullenly. "It ain't my fault Bobby can't get the money."

"No, it isn't. But I'm sick of looking at you sitting there doing nothing. I want you to get your butt off that couch and do something useful for a change."

"Fine!" he said, sitting up. "I'll clean the damn gutters tomorrow!" He chugged the last of his beer as dramatically as he could, slamming the can down on the coffee table. "But when we do get the money, I want to get something out of it."

"Like what?"

He pointed at the TV. "I want to get me some of that hair loss stuff." He patted the crown of his head. "I wanna mane like Fabio."

She rolled her eyes. "Fine. Consider it done. Happy?"

"Very." And he laid back down on the couch before realizing his beer was empty. "Honey?" he said.

"Yes?"

"Can you get me another beer?"

◆ ◆ ◆

Teddy sat behind his desk, scrolling through pages of criminal records on his computer. His shift had just started and since he presently had nothing better going on he figured he might as well do some sleuthing on Gina and Bobby's behalf while he could. He pulled up mugshot after mugshot, wondering as he stared into the eyes of some of Escondido's more infamous felons if any of them were the ones responsible for Gina's disappearance. This whole thing had him flummoxed; he knew what Bobby was capable of while on a bender, but for it to happen twice in the span of less than a week? That was ridiculous by anybody's standards. Even with Bobby's record-breaking blackouts, he pondered if that was truly possible. But, if it wasn't, then where was the kid? He thought about paying a visit to Carolyn and Barry, but abandoned the idea because he didn't want to draw attention to himself. Now, if they came to him, that would be a different story. His biggest problem, it seemed, was worrying how much or how little he should get involved, especially since Bobby hadn't been able to get the money, and had lost seven grand of Teddy's, not to mention the eight fronted by the bookie. Teddy wasn't so much worried about his lost dough but about Gina's welfare. When would the time come that he should start acting like a cop? And, besides, there was other business that may be a contributing factor.

"Hey, Teddy," one of his fellow officers said, poking his head around the partition of his cubicle, interrupting his thoughts.

"Hey, Daniels, how's it hangin'?" Christian Daniels always had a way of showing up at just the wrong time, like when Teddy was trying to do some actual work. He clicked on the X at the top of his monitor and closed the screen.

Prying eyes don't need to know.

"Pretty good," replied Daniels, as if he hadn't understood the question. "You working on something important?"

"Nothing that can't wait," he said, shutting down the computer.

"I don't want to interrupt," Daniels said.

"Nah, it's OK."

"You got a minute?"

Teddy looked at him for a moment before nodding quickly. "Of course."

Daniels stepped around the partition and stood before Teddy's desk, wringing his hands.

"You want to take a seat?"

"Sure, sure." Daniels slouched into the chair before him, but words were not immediately forthcoming. Teddy decided a prompt might be necessary.

"What can I do for you?"

"I got some information you might be interested in, and it's got to do with Bobby."

"What is it?" Teddy hoped (but knew it was unlikely) that what Daniels had to tell him was related to the kidnapping. Although improbable, stranger things had happened.

"What's going on?"

"Word is, and I didn't see this for myself mind you, it's secondhand, so don't go quotin' me verbatim on this—"

"Yeah?"

"It's OK to be candid with you, right?"

"You know it is," Teddy said impatiently. If this didn't have anything to do with Gina, he wanted to dismiss it and move on to something that did. He loved that girl with all his heart, and right now his cousin Bobby was realizing that more and more with every passing minute. Personally, Teddy was certain that Bobby had never loved the girl more than he did right now.

"It's about that dive bar, Hooligans."

"Yeah?" he said, his interest now piqued. He'd been secretly investigating the joint for several months, sometimes while on duty, but mostly on his days off. He hoped that the "contributing factor" he'd been considering a moment ago was nothing but a passing fancy on his part.

"This is some sensitive information."

"Then spill it."

Daniels leaned close and whispered loudly: "I think there's some heavy product being moved through that place."

"Heavy product?"

"Yeah, you know, cocaine, meth, maybe even heroin."

"Really?" Teddy had to play stupid; until he had ironclad proof, he wasn't going to make a move, not with Bobby involved. He didn't want to inadvertently take his cousin down at the same time. Also, he wasn't exactly convinced the two weren't somehow related.

"Yeah," Daniels said, looking around to see if anyone was paying attention. No one was.

"You plan on doing something about it?"

"Um, well, it isn't in my jurisdiction."

"Where did you come upon this information, if you don't mind me asking?"

"Not at all, Teddy." This said as agreeably as possible, because everyone knew it was where Teddy's cousin spent his weekends, *every* weekend, getting so loaded he generally needed either a cab or a police escort home, which was occasionally the county jail. "Kirk's been hanging out there on the weekends undercover—"

"On whose authority?"

"No ones. He's been there of his own volition."

"I see." Teddy mused at the others use of the word "volition" (*probably read it in "Boost Your Word Power" in* Reader's Digest *and made a point to fit it in a conversation*), but what was really on his mind was his rookie partner, Kirk, monitoring the activity at Hooligans, playing secret agent. If that asshole exposed himself, he could potentially blow everything Teddy had been working toward. He might have to intercede and have a word with him, but nothing forthright; he couldn't give his own investigation away.

"What kind of intel has Kirk come up with?"

"So far he's established that one of the bartenders is regularly dealing narcotics, as well as some schedule four pills. A Mexican American guy named Tony."

Nothing I don't know already.

"Such as?"

"Mostly Xanax, but Klonopin and Valium too. Sometimes he has legal drugs, ones you can buy from China or the UK over the internet."

"Research chemicals."

"Huh?"

"They're called 'research chemicals,' and they fall under the umbrella of gray area where the law is concerned. They're just as dangerous; they're simply not illegal. Yet."

"Oh."

Teddy tried to keep the anger out of his voice. He was more than a little peeved that Kirk was sticking his nose in where it didn't belong, and upon his own *volition* to boot. Why, if he dug a little deeper, he might really get to the heart of the matter, and Teddy didn't want that, not at this juncture. Not before all the pieces were in place. Then again, Kirk was probably just using it as an excuse to get wasted while pretending to work. For all Teddy knew, he was scoring drugs from the bartender, too. He supposed it wasn't something he should be too concerned about, at least for the time being. Right now, he had more important matters to attend to. And did he really think that somehow the two were intertwined—Bobby's missing daughter and the felonious activities going on at Hooligans? Was such an assumption merely jumping at shadows?

"Is that it?"

"Um, yeah, I guess that is."

"And why did you decide to share this little tidbit of information with me?"

Once again the man leaned forward, looking both ways before speaking, and Teddy almost couldn't stop himself from rolling his eyes. No one in the office gave a rat's ass what they were talking about.

"I wanted to give you a heads up so that you might tell your cousin to avoid the place for a while, you know, in case anything goes down."

"What's Kirk got planned?"

Daniel's face turned crimson. "Nothing I know of—"

"Then what's with the cloak and dagger business?"

"I just wanted to inform you, you know, in case Bobby is getting messed up with some business he shouldn't be."

Teddy was silent, brooding over this last statement. Bobby had got himself into some "business" all right, and none of it was good. What with his daughter's kidnapping, though, Teddy didn't have to worry about Bobby visiting that particular establishment, seeing as he was now on the wagon. But that was none of Daniel's business, of course.

"Thank you," Teddy said at last, nodding. "I appreciate you coming to me with this."

Daniels stood. "No problem, Teddy. Anything I can do for a friend."

"Sure." As Daniels left, Teddy wanted to tell him they weren't friends, but what would be the point? Instead he resumed his computer search, his mind reeling at all the possibilities before him. He worked on it until he got a call on the radio that there was a 1016 in progress at an address on East Washington. Unfortunately, he was nowhere closer to solving anything than he'd been when he started, but just the same he was glad he tried.

"Where are you Gina?" he muttered as he shut the computer down and put his hat on. "Where the hell are you?"

Chapter Nineteen

Gina held a wiggling Ruby between her legs as she swiped at her private parts with a Duoxo wipe. The poor dog was forever suffering from UTI's (urinary tract infections) because of her lousy bulldog build so, to try and avoid these, the veterinarian had advised her to clean Ruby's vagina after every urination. The problem was, besides being squirmy as all living get out, Ruby peed a lot.

"Come on girl," Gina begged, "hold still."

Ruby's hind quarters wagged back and forth in comic fashion, and it was all Gina could do not to giggle. Her bulldog was such a silly little girl. The second she had seen her in the cage at the pet store, she had fallen in love, and her daddy, despite his regular status of being "low on funds" had bought the dog for her, despite the $350 price tag. He'd put it on his credit card. Carolyn, however, had not been so keen on the whole idea, and had promised Gina that if the dog ever became a nuisance, it was off to the all-kill shelter for her. She emphasized that: *all-kill*. Not, "we'll have to find her a new home, dear," but "we'll have to put her down." Gina didn't realize it at the time, but that was a pivotal moment in her life. It was when she realized with no uncertainty that her mother was essentially a rotten person.

"Seriously, honey, we have to do this—"

The crash of splintering wood interrupted her; if she wasn't mistaken it sounded like the door had just been kicked in. Then came the shouting, Greg's voice first, followed by others she (obviously) didn't recognize.

"What the hell are you guys doing here?" Greg hollered, but he sounded more scared than angry. "I'm on probation! I told you not to come by the house during the day—"

The smacking sound of flesh on flesh, possibly a fist to the face, cut off whatever Greg was trying to say. He replied by issuing a pained

"Ooof," and then echoed it when he received either a knee to the groin or a fist to the belly. Whichever it was, it didn't equate to anything good.

"Ju ain't in no position to make no demands, hombre. Carlos is tired of waitin' for his money." The voice had a Mexican accent, but his English was clear enough. Apparently, Greg was in deep with some seriously shady characters.

"I'm working on that right now!" Greg said, when he was struck yet again, probably harder this time because at once there was a loud thump that was most likely his ass hitting the hardwood floor.

"We ain't got no time to wait around amigo. Ju don't make a man like Carlos wait."

"It isn't my fault," Greg gurgled, as if he was talking through a mouthful of water. But Gina knew what it really was; blood, it had to be blood. "I'm trying to get it."

"Consider joreself out of time," the other said curtly, and suddenly a gunshot rang out so loudly that both she and Ruby jumped. Not only did they jump, but Ruby barked and Gina screamed.

Silence from downstairs, then: "There's someone upstairs! Vamanos!"

Footfalls clambered over the wooden floor in the direction of the stairs, and knowing that she only had a brief amount of time, Gina ran to the table where the cordless phone was supposed to be, but as she'd known all along, wasn't. For some reason Greg claimed to have "misplaced it"; the entirety of her stay, the home phone had been unavailable to her, even though she'd seen or heard him use it several times. And because Carolyn was of the opinion that Gina was too young, and Bobby didn't have the funds, she didn't have so much as a TracFone. It wasn't simply the cost of the device, which was relatively low, but the cost of the monthly plan, and she couldn't afford it herself. Ruby had been the most expensive present her daddy had ever bought for her. She'd asked for a cell phone every Christmas plus her birthday since she was ten, but so far her request had been denied. She'd been told that she could have one when she turned sixteen, if her "lazy-ass father chipped in." Her friends echoed the sentiment that her folks were cheap. They'd all had cell phones since they were twelve.

The fact that there was no phone now made it impossible for her to call for help. She knew all she and Ruby could do was hide, and that would be of little good because eventually whoever was down there would find them. Having no other recourse, she scooped up the stubby yet stout little dog and carried her to the bedroom closet where she shut the door and cowered in the back, hoping Ruby could keep her whimpering to a minimum.

The footsteps reached the top of the stairs, and, one by one, the rooms were investigated. It didn't take long, and they were in her room.

"Find the kid and the dog," the man with the Mexican accent rasped, and it was less than a minute before the door was flung open.

"What we got here?" He was ugly, his rotten teeth capped in gold, wearing clothes befitting a Latino gangbanger. He pointed a gun at her. "Get outta there now!"

Clutching Ruby to her breast, she stood and walked out, her lips trembling, struggling but losing the battle to her imminent tears.

"Please," she muttered, "don't hurt us…"

"Who are ju? Ju Greg's kid?"

She shook her head violently back and forth. "N—n—no…"

"Who the fuck is this kid?" the man demanded of one of his cohorts, and the other shook his head. He too was holding a gun, but now he lowered it. Another man entered the room, and once he got a look at her he laughed.

"I know this kid!" he said cheerfully. "Ju in the wrong place at the wrong time, chica."

"Who is it?"

"She that fuckup's kid, Bobby Travis. He hang out at Hooligans all the time. He one of our best customers."

The leader lowered his piece as well, looked at her, considering.

"We can't jus let her go," he said at last. "She seen our faces."

"Ju want me to take her out?" one of the men offered, raising his weapon again, but the man in charge shook his head.

"No, she might come in handy."

"I could shoot the dog," the other said, and once more a shake of the head.

"No, she and the dog is coming with us." He grinned at the others. "They might offer us some leverage."

"With who?"

"Ju know who."

"Si," one of them conceded, tucking his weapon in his pants. "Ju co-min' with us, chica."

Gina wanted to say no, to struggle, but she could tell by the looks of these guys that insolence would seal her doom. Besides, she didn't want anything bad to happen to Ruby. So she nodded, although she had many questions, but knew it was pointless. These men weren't going to answer anything she asked. Her best bet was to keep her mouth shut and to do as she was told.

One of them stepped forward and took her by the arm.

"Vamanos," he said, and she went with them, out of the house, and into the waiting van outside.

◆ ◆ ◆

Carolyn had been trying to call Greg all morning, but his cell kept going to voicemail.

"Where the hell are you? I want to know what happened when you called Bobby. Call me!"

She waited most of the day, trying to be as patient as her tiny brain would allow, but to say it was difficult would be banal. She kept calling him, over and over, until Barry finally noticed.

"The hell ya doin'?"

"What does it look like? I'm trying to get in touch with Greg!"

"He ain't answerin' your calls?"

She stared hard at the other. "Of course he is, I just feel like calling him to listen to his voicemail."

"Huh?"

"Just watch your stupid show."

Barry had spent the better part of the morning working on the gutters, a project he wasn't enjoying in the least, but by lunchtime he'd abandoned the job so that he could imbibe some liquid libation. Three beers and a sandwich later he was sprawled on the couch again. Carolyn had wanted to send him back outside, but the fact that she couldn't get through to Greg was starting to unnerve her; why the hell wasn't he answering his phone? He was supposed to be watching Gina, and if he wasn't answering his phone then Christ only knew where the kid was. It didn't make any sense, and it could potentially screw up their plans. What she needed to do was go over there.

By three in the afternoon her mind was made up.

"Finish your beer, we got a job to do."

"What?" Barry had just slipped into what could best be described as a coma; the beer and the sandwich had rendered him as lazy and sleepy as any sedative would. "What's going on?"

"We're taking a ride over to Greg's house," she said. "He hasn't been answering my calls and I need to know that everything is OK."

"Why wouldn't it be?" He belched, tasted something that reminded him of his dinner last night, something deep fried and full of trans fat. "And ain't we supposed to be on vacation? The kid's gonna think something is up."

"Just put some pants on and get in the car," she said, wondering what it was she'd seen in him in the first place, when at once it came back to her: Bobby hated him. For Carolyn, that was good enough. Besides, his food stamp money and unemployment checks came in handy each month. If he hadn't been bringing anything to the table, he would have been out on his ass a long time ago.

She waited for him outside, and a few minutes later, he came out of the house clutching a beer in one knobby hand.

"So I suppose I'm driving?" This said while she was already behind the wheel, but she always liked to take a jab at him whenever she could. And he took it so graciously, the dumbass.

"Shotgun," was all he said in reply.

She fired up the old Chevy Malibu Classic and backed out of the driveway, almost hitting their elderly neighbor as he slowly walked by clinging to his walker, his unsteady legs barely keeping him vertical.

"Out of my way!" Carolyn shrieked at the senile old man, her voice like that of a witch's cackle, high pitched and warbly. By all reasonable accounts, it summed her up perfectly.

◆　◆　◆

When Teddy got the call, he didn't know if he should feign ignorance or admit to the fact that he'd known all along.

"Gina's missing!" was what Carolyn had first shouted over the phone. And she hadn't called 911; instead she'd called him on his cell phone. How she had the number was no mystery: because of her affiliation with Bobby she thought it was her civic right (an absolute entitlement) that she be hooked up with his connected cousin. She must have wrung it out of Bobby either when he was wasted or when she was threatening him with impending visitation rights. Either way, she was in possession of it. Thankfully she rarely used it.

"OK," he replied, wondering what else he should say, when her next comment took him entirely by surprise.

"They shot Greg!"

"Come again?" Teddy'd wondered why Carolyn hadn't made an attempt at contacting him, but had (logically) assumed it had to do with keeping a low profile. Since the kidnappers had said "no cops," calling him would have endangered Gina's life. No trouble understanding any of that. But he *had* been curious as to why she hadn't secretly sought him out after Bobby had failed to get the money for the kidnappers in the allotted time. In all honesty, he'd been expecting this call yesterday. But now this inclusion, well, it didn't appear to fit into the overall picture.

"Ain't I speakin' English? They shot Greg. In the head!"

"OK, OK, relax and start from the beginning. Where are you calling me from?" Teddy was presently off duty. He just left the grocery store and was en route to his car.

"Greg's house!"

"Who is Greg, and what does he have to do with Gina?"

This seemingly innocent question stopped her dead in tracks. She clammed up like, well, a clam.

"Hello?"

"Um, yeah, Teddy, uh…I guess I'm thinking…"

What the hell is there to think about? He wondered, when suddenly something occurred to him: this was why she hadn't made an attempt to contact him. He was no Sherlock Holmes, but neither was he a Barney Fife. Some pieces suddenly came together, and he didn't exactly like the way they fit.

"Who is Greg, Carolyn, and what does he have to do with Gina being missing?" he repeated, using his "police tone" this time. It usually worked very well on people who had lower IQs than pants sizes.

"They shot him, Teddy," she said instead of answering the question. "Somebody shot Greg…"

"Stay right where you are," he said, unlocking his car door and tossing the groceries in the back seat. "I'm coming over there right now. What's the address?"

She gave it to him and he memorized it. He knew that part of town, and it wasn't exactly on the nice side of the tracks. If this meant what he thought it meant, then Carolyn was a lot dumber than he'd ever given her credit for being. Turned out, he definitely hadn't given her enough credit.

◆ ◆ ◆

Standing over the body, many questions went through Teddy's head, none of which he could share with his present company, several of which he couldn't even share with the deputies once he called it in and they arrived on the scene. For starters, though, he needed to know all of the details before he brought the police in.

"Tell me what this man has to do with Gina's disappearance."

Carolyn looked at him and, even though her skull was as thick as a New York phone book, she knew this was the time to 'fess up.

"You know that Gina's been missing," she said flatly. "Bobby told you."

Teddy found there was no reason to deny this. "Of course I know. Why would Bobby keep that from me?"

"Because we...um...the kidnappers said no cops. He wasn't supposed to get the police involved."

Her use of the word "we" had not escaped him. "He didn't bring the cops into this," he told her. "He brought me in. We're related and he needed someone he could talk to about this."

"But you're the cops!"

"Yes, I am, but I'm involved as a friend." He eyed her levelly, his anger starting to mount. "What did you do with Gina, Carolyn?"

"Me?" she said in her best "why I've done nothing but my duty as an upstanding citizen Mr. Officer Sir" tone, but he wasn't buying it and she knew it. She hung her head. "I needed the money." She glanced over at Barry. "*We* needed the money."

"So you kidnapped your own daughter?"

"Bobby wasn't paying me and Barry enough child support—"

"Don't you mean Gina's child support?"

"You know what I mean! He makes more than he claims and can afford to pay us extra!"

"So let me get this straight: you hired this man Greg here to 'kidnap' Gina so that you could extort money out of Bobby because you didn't think he was paying you enough? That's pretty low Carolyn, even for you."

For a moment Carolyn was stunned that he'd put everything together so quickly, but then she realized it hadn't been much of a plan. Even Barry had said as much, and he was a freakin' retard.

"Well, when you say it like that you make it sound kinda, um, ya know…"

"Stupid? Is that what you were going to say? Because if you were, that is the exact word I was looking for."

"Barry thought it was a good idea," she said sullenly, but one look at Barry disproved this claim immediately. Teddy could tell by the expression on the man's face that he'd tried to talk her out of it, but to try and talk Carolyn out of anything she had her mind set on was practically impossible. Everyone knew that.

"Did he?" He looked at Barry. "You thought it was a good idea to fake a kidnapping to blackmail Bobby Travis for more money?"

Barry looked at Carolyn, knew what side of the line his allegiance lay, but went ahead and told the truth anyway: "No sir," he said. "I did not think it was a good idea."

"Did you know this guy?"

He shook his head. "No, I didn't."

"Who the hell is he?" The more Teddy stared at what was left of the man's face (and there wasn't much, not after what appeared to be a large caliber slug had torn the top of his head off), he thought he possibly recognized him. Could he be someone related to Hooligans and the narcotics operation that was going on there? He'd have to match the man's face to a mugshot later to be sure (along with his fingerprints that were most likely already in the system), but he wouldn't be surprised. This murder had "turf war" written all over it.

"I worked with him at Wal-Mart," Carolyn relented. "He's…he was a good guy. I knew I could trust him."

"So," Teddy mused, "who would want to kill such a nice guy and then take your daughter too? Whoever it was, *they* don't sound all that nice."

"I didn't know he was mixed up in anything illegal," Carolyn said, her eyes evading his as she did so, proving to Teddy for the moment that she was lying. Why did people think cops were stupid? Was it because they weren't required to have a four-year bachelor's degree? Or was it because they just thought the police were a bunch of dumbasses that couldn't get better jobs. One thing Teddy really, truly hated was being lied to.

"No? Then why would he go along with such an asinine plan as this one?"

"What did you call me?"

"He called you a 'ass-in-nine,'" Barry said. "I think it's a technical term for asshole."

"You shouldn't be callin' me names! My daughter's missing!"

"It's a little too late to play the bereaved mother, I think." Teddy stared down at the corpse, knowing that this whole thing had just become inexplicably more complicated. The plot, it would seem, had definitely thickened.

"You have to help me get my daughter back!"

Teddy stared back at her angrily, realizing with no genuine surprise that everything he and Bobby had done so far had all been for naught. Up to now this had all been a charade, perpetrated by a woman who was so stupid she was barely able to keep a job at one of the largest chain stores in North America, one whose exacting criteria for an employee was someone who could both show up on time and piss cleanly into a cup. She'd failed on both counts, but somehow kept her job. The fact that she'd wasted his and Bobby's time, not to mention all the stress and the worry this travesty had put on Teddy's wife, made him want to belt her across the chops as hard as he could until she couldn't see straight. Unfortunately, however, that was not within his rights as a peace officer. However, in regards to his rights as a man in good standing with the community…

He shook his head. The bitch would get hers; that much was true, but for now they had to spring into action because every moment they wasted was another moment that this case went cold. They had to find Gina as quickly as possible, because judging by the nature of Greg's death, they were dealing with some heavy hitters indeed.

"Is there anything more you want to tell me, on a personal level, before I call this in?"

Carolyn continued to play dumb. "What?" she said.

"You heard me: Is there anything else you want to tell me before this makes the six o'clock news? Spit it out, honey; we ain't got all day."

"You…you mean, you aren't going to arrest me?"

Teddy rolled his eyes. "I'm not going to waste my time dragging you into this…yet. First things first, we have a murder and a kidnapping to deal with. The guys that did this? They aren't playing around, that's for sure. These men are professionals and probably work for someone who can do this without blinking an eye and never lose a second of sleep. So"—his glare intensified—"is there anything else I need to know about this so I can better be of service?"

Carolyn had to think about it for a minute or so, her mouth working but nothing coming out. At last she had an answer, and when she said it, Barry, who had stepped forward and put an arm around her now that he knew his loyalty to her wasn't going to send him to the slammer, nodded as if she'd just said the most profound thing anyone can say.

"Her dog, Ruby, is with her."

"Well," Teddy said conclusively, "that solves everything."

Chapter Twenty

"Hi, my name is Bobby Travis, and I'm a drug addict."

"Hi, Bobby," the group said in unison.

Because he'd missed all of his other meetings this week, Bobby thought it was a good idea to make up this one. Besides, Teddy had told him to go about his regular routine until the kidnapper called again, and this was a part of the program. Hell, he needed it now more than ever.

"This might come as some surprise," he said, but no one save for the moderator so much as lifted an eyebrow to feign interest in what kind of nastiness Bobby had got himself into, seeing as nobody present knew him. Well, almost no one; Lily was in attendance, for reasons Bobby could only guess. She watched him from beneath hooded lids, looking as if she was going to nod off anytime. "I've been sober for one full week."

Silence, so loud it was almost like the hiss of static from a radio. A statement such as this one was boring. These people looked to each other for their entertainment needs to be satiated, but not only that, also for the barometer which they could pit themselves and their wretched lives against. They didn't want to hear good news, they wanted disastrous stories in which cars were totaled and women drowned their own children. Not only did this smug asshole look essentially healthy, but to listen to him claim he'd been *sober* too...what a prick!

"That's excellent Bobby," the moderator said, genuinely pleased. She, for one, really wanted him to make a full recovery. It was sadly apparent she was the only person in the room who was rooting for him.

Bobby saw the disappointment in the other addicts' eyes, and it should have been perplexing, but he knew where they were coming from. Good news was bad to them; it made them feel worse about themselves. "Also," he added (*in for a penny, in for a pound*), "I've only had sex with one person this week, and I remember her name." He smiled. This was the best thing he'd had to say in one of these meetings...ever.

Still, a long, protracted silence. Someone coughed; another blew their nose, making a loud honking sound.

"So..." the moderator ventured after a long lull. "Aren't we happy for Bobby?"

No one answered the question; instead they sat there looking at him, hoping he'd add, "OK, you got me. Actually, I got bombed and punched a priest in the face right after he blew me because he wouldn't swallow." Bobby knew there wasn't a single soul in the room (with the exception of the moderator) who had his best interests in mind, not even Lily, it seemed. She was firmly in the grip of a heroin nod, slouching over farther and farther in her chair, her dress hiking up to show her emaciated, bruised thighs. He was about to ask her if she was all right when his cell phone rang—well, vibrated—inside his cargo-shorts pocket. He pulled it out and looked at it (on vibrate he wasn't aware of the ringtone's assignment) and saw that it was his cousin. "I'm sorry," he said. "I have to take this." He pushed the button. "Hello?"

At first he wasn't sure if he understood what Teddy was saying, but after asking for an explanation and getting one, it quickly dawned on him, and from what he heard, his mood soured swiftly.

"She what?" he gasped, and at once he had an audience. Smiles of delight lit up around the room. *Aha!* Their smiles said. *There* is *drama in your life after all!* Unconsciously they all leaned forward on their chairs. "That stupid bitch!" Bobby listened some more before exclaiming, "Oh my God! I'll be right there!" He hung up his phone. "I have to go," he said. "Sorry everyone, but my daughter needs me."

And with that he was off.

♦ ♦ ♦

"She did what?" Melissa was driving because Bobby was so angry he was literally shaking. Not only his hands, but his whole body. "Jesus, what a freakin' psycho!"

He'd driven straight from the meeting to the Goodwill store where she worked, told her everything. After a brief but turbulent argument with her boss, she got the rest of the day off. It wasn't like he was going to fire her; she was the only employee he actually trusted. Besides, the customers loved her, well, the men anyway. Some of the women too, but mostly men.

"I was scared before," Bobby said, his teeth chattering, "but now I'm terrified." His eyes found hers, and the look in them was of a man lost at sea. "Man, I want a drink so bad..."

"Fight it, Bobby," she advised. "It's all you can do."

"I need something!" he moaned. "I've never needed chemicals so bad in my entire life!"

Melissa looked at him thoughtfully, knowing (as an addict herself) what it was like to repress an urge that was maniacal in its precision. It was like reaching inside yourself and ripping out your own beating heart. Then something occurred to her, and she pulled over to the side of the road.

"I think I can help," she said, putting the car in park.

"You don't have to enable me," Bobby said. "I really am better off if I don't drink."

"I'm not offering you a drink, stupid," she said, reaching for his zipper, and Bobby grinned. Well, he supposed, any port in a storm would certainly do...

And for about five minutes, he was able to let himself go, to calm down, to let nature do its work and ease his troubled mind. Well, maybe about four minutes and three point two seconds.

"Better?" she asked, wiping her mouth, and Bobby nodded sagely.

"Much."

"Now let's go meet your cousin."

◆ ◆ ◆

Now that it was a for real kidnapping (without the threats to "keep the cops out of it"), there was no need for a covert meeting. The three of them met at a diner in downtown Valley Center. Teddy was already there when they arrived, mowing his way through a platter of steak and eggs. One thing that could be said about Teddy: nothing ever caused him to lose his appetite.

"Have a seat," he said, and they sat down across from him. The waitress skulked over from where she was nurturing both a bruised eye and ego, respectively, and at the request of coffee simply nodded and sulked away. She returned quickly with cups that had last been clean sometime around the year they were manufactured in China, filled them, and went back to inspecting herself in a compact mirror.

"I can't believe it," Bobby repeated as he sipped the awful coffee. "I just can't believe it."

"It would make it a lot easier if you did," Teddy said, but his attempt at humor was lost on his cousin. Hell, he couldn't blame him. Things seemed hopeless before, but now it was even worse. It was one thing having your daughter kidnapped for the fact that you (theoretically) owed someone money. It made logical sense. But dealing with perps who could potentially be gangbangers? Downright scary, because little of what they did made sense. What they did, they did for other reasons, sometimes that being outright cruelty. Of course, unbeknownst to Bobby and Melissa, Teddy had to consider these were more than just gangbangers; these men could be more calculating and brutal than a bunch of street punks. Until he had some inkling as to what the truth was, however, he figured he'd omit that detail.

"What are we going to do?" Melissa asked, and Teddy shrugged.

"What we did before. We wait for someone to call."

"I can't believe Carolyn would do that to me," Bobby said, then reassessed his view. "Well, all things considered, I guess I can."

"What she did is unforgivable," Teddy said, "but now that her hoax has been exposed we have someone else to worry about."

"Who could have taken Gina? And why?"

Teddy wished he could assuage Bobby's fears by offering some nugget of information, but the truth was that everything he had was pure speculation. If it was what he thought it was, he'd know soon enough; that much was for sure. Hopefully soon enough to save Bobby's daughter. With that thought he took out his wallet and removed a wad of bills. He waved over the waitress and asked for the check. She begrudgingly scribbled on the paper and slapped it face down on the table top. Teddy picked it up, inspected it, then dropped the bills.

"I have something I have to look into," he said, standing. "You two might as well just let me do my job. Whoever did this, we don't know if they have your cell phone number Bobby. If they do, they'll probably call you so keep the ringer on."

"Gina knows my number. Whoever has her can get it from her."

"Right," Teddy agreed. "OK, I'll catch up with you two as soon as I have any leads." He gave Bobby a troubled glance. "Maybe it would be a good idea if you worked this weekend. It would keep you out of trouble."

"Way ahead of you. I canceled a bunch of jobs this week dealing with all of this so I have to make them up. Don't want to lose any business."

"I suppose I should go back to work too," Melissa said. "My boss would really like that."

Teddy nodded. "Good thinking. Just go about your lives, that's all I can recommend right now. Nothing will get solved by going off the deep end. And you, Bobby," he said as he placed a meaty paw on his cousin's shoulder, "It'd be best if you continued to stay sober. Think you can do that?"

Bobby looked at Melissa and the two exchanged a smile. Bobby returned Teddy's gaze.

"Yes," he said, and damned if he didn't sound as if he meant it. "I think I can."

◆ ◆ ◆

Teddy knew whom he had to see, although he wasn't sure if it would do any good. Also, he didn't want to lose all the ground he'd gained over the last several months. If he was going to do this, he had to do it carefully.

He got in his unmarked cruiser (the one he used for just such operations) and headed for Grand Avenue. It was one of the main drags catering to Escondido's illustrious night life. As darkness fell the respectable folks abandoned the area, replaced by the seamier elements that frequented such fine establishments as Pounders, Rowdy's, and Hooligans, to name only a few. Fistfights were the norm, as well as DUI's, robberies, dope peddling, and public intoxication. How did the old saying go? Just living the dream.

Teddy had been working on the force since he'd been twenty, straight out of the academy. He'd started as a cadet, doing mostly routine traffic stops, got bumped up to first response officer, then sergeant, and had wallowed there since, getting passed over yearly for what he considered to be his next step up the ladder: promotion to Lieutenant. All things considered the sergeant pay wasn't bad, but a lieutenant's pay was better, and he felt he could handle the extra responsibility. Maybe then he could get off of the night shift, too. Thus far, his superiors thought otherwise regarding an advancement. He worked hard, trying to prove them wrong, and this was why he took it upon himself to perform extracurricular investigations. It was, in fact, one of the reasons he chose to keep an eye on the shady dealings that may or may not be afoot at his cousin's favorite bar. The main reason, of course, was Bobby. Somebody had to look out for him, because Teddy knew damn well he couldn't look after himself.

During his time on the Escondido police force, he'd become accustomed to dealing with the scum that made up its criminal populace. This brought him face to face with thieves, rapists, murders, and, most importantly in this case, drug dealers. He'd long known that many of the bars and nightclubs on Grand Avenue and Valley Center Parkway were overrun with entrepreneurs plying the product of their trade, but what he didn't know was who was bringing it in. Well, he knew, he just didn't have any names. The dealers weren't entirely stupid; stupid gets you caught, and getting caught means that unless you give up your source you're looking at doing time. Since it certainly wasn't worthwhile to spend your days worrying whether or not you had a pretty mouth, silence was golden. Of course, it never hurt to grease a few palms on the way. Teddy didn't know for sure, but he supposed there were more than a couple of cops on the narcotics task force who were deliberately looking the other way.

Teddy had to be nonchalant about his research, of course, and so he tried never to show much interest. He did, however, know a guy who could never say no to a minor bribe. For twenty bucks, he'd rat out some other creep to save his own ass. He was a petty thief who worked the door at Hooligans, and every now and then he was good for a useful tidbit of information. Nothing serious, mind you, nothing that ever pointed in the direction of who was behind the supply side, but he came in handy whenever there was some smalltime dealer who needed to be taken down a peg after he shot up someone's house or raped a teenage girl.

What Teddy knew for sure about Hooligans was that they had the potential to move a lot of product, what with the mixed crowd that hung out there on any given night. One of the bartenders, Tony, dealt to the regulars; that was his part in it all, in that limited capacity as far as Teddy knew. If an employee at Hooligans was moving real weight, the large loads were most likely being distributed by someone other than Tony, dispersed around town to other drug dealers. Teddy thought it was possible that it could be the owner of the bar, a man named Ramon Pasquale, who by any other means probably never would have come into ownership of said establishment. He certainly seemed capable of such a deed. Teddy didn't know the extent of his criminal record in Mexico (that was beyond his jurisdiction, and he didn't want to alert anyone on the Escondido force to his clandestine operation), but ever since he'd been awarded citizenship through marriage, he quickly racked up several misdemeanors (mostly drug related, but one for vagrancy, and another for theft) before he had suddenly gone straight, found legal backing, and was able to purchase the building that not only housed the bar but three upstairs apartments. These were rented to various winos and junkies and other assorted lowlifes, but none of them made the crime reel on the evening news. They were obviously chosen for their discretion.

If it wasn't the owner then it could be his manager, Carlos Menendez, another upstanding individual who had come to the United States with a temporary green card and somehow established residency, be it real or counterfeit. He'd made his living fencing stolen property, and then worked his way up the ladder by ostensibly taking over Escondido's drug trade. So far, though, Teddy couldn't prove it, and he'd exhausted many leads trying to put him in place with the product on more than one occasion. Unfortunately, the dealers (local gangbangers) that got pinched never squealed, as previously mentioned. The biggest reason? They didn't know *who* was supplying it, they didn't have any names to give. Now, in Teddy's mind, that reeked of cartel activity. A Mexican drug cartel only told their American suppliers what they needed to know, which was very little. In fact, they kept every other aspect of their operation a secret. For the Mexicans they employed, it was different. If they snitched it not only meant death, but an especially painful one, and not merely for you, but for your family and friends and anybody else associated with you. Torture, kidnapping and murder were their calling cards.

Teddy's prior investigations into the drug activity on the Grand Avenue strip had turned up a local chapter of the Hell's Angels that were behind some of the lower quality methamphetamine that made its way through the local circuit and, as bad as they were, they were still no match for the cartel heavies. He'd made a few busts within their ranks, but never anyone high enough up the food chain to stop the barrage of drugs that cascaded like flowing water through the town's mostly working class population. Unlike the coastal towns twenty miles west, Escondido boasted affordable housing; you could actually make less than $60,000 a year and buy a house here.

Every now and then, the narcotics task force would make a big bust; they'd land some tip that would lead them to a dope house where cocaine, meth, and heroin were found by the kilo. It didn't happen often enough, and those who were arrested almost never gave up their source. If they did, they didn't last long in jail. Inevitably someone saw to it they'd never squeal again. But the names they gave up? Mostly dead ends. And if the name could be traced, the man matching the description was never more than a mere sentry in the organization, no one in a managerial position. Again, as much as Teddy didn't like to contemplate it, it had Mexican drug cartel written all over it.

That wasn't to say that the Escondido police force hadn't successfully arrested men associated with the cartels, but their operations were mainly run by local gangs; these were the hired hands who did the networking and distribution. The Del Norte gang had been one of the most recent to have been tied to a cartel from Baja, but like everyone before them, when they got caught they kept their mouths shut and simply did their time.

Teddy pulled over across the street from Hooligans and put the car in park. Danny, the door guy, was snoozing under the awning. Teddy beeped his horn once, a continuous blat, and this got the other to open his eyes and peer about him to see what the commotion was. Teddy waved at him through the window, and, begrudgingly, the other looked both ways to see if anyone was watching him before flat footing it across the street to the undercover squad car.

"Evening officer," Danny said, a touch on the dour side. "What can I do for you?"

"I'm looking for some information," Teddy said casually. "Maybe you can help me out."

Again, Danny looked around to make sure no one of any import was witnessing this little meet and greet. It would be bad for business if anyone saw him talking to the five-0.

"Whattaya want?"

Teddy held up a photo. "Ever see this guy before?"

The look in Danny's eyes said yes, but his (occasional) informant shook his head.

"Nope. Never seen him before."

"You sure?" He made a twenty appear in his other hand, but the doorman shook his head again. And what the hell, it looked like Danny was actually trying *not* to look at the picture.

"No man, seriously, I never seen him before."

"OK, OK, don't get your panties in a bunch." Teddy lowered the photo, considered stashing the twenty then changed his mind and kept it visible. The other just might have a change of heart. "You want to know why I'm looking for this guy?"

"No." This said as plaintively as possible. It was true; Danny didn't want to hear it, probably because he already knew.

"Someone shot him, in his house. One shot to the head. Looked like a gang hit to me." Teddy paused, gauging the other's reaction. He noticed that Danny did not look surprised to hear this. "Sure you don't know this guy?" He held up the photo again, pushing it closer to the other's face.

"Look, I never seen him before, OK? I mean, maybe he came in here, maybe he didn't, but a lot of dudes come in here. I can't keep track of all of 'em."

"So you didn't know him personally?"

"No man, I told you! Now get that photo out of my face." He looked Teddy in the eye briefly, a quick flash, then went back to shoe gazing. "And don't be waving that money around. You'll get me busted."

Teddy lowered the photo again, grinning. Criminals were so stupid. Danny might as well have just told him, "Yes, Sergeant Barnes, I definitely know that man. I'm not sorry he died, but I *do* know him."

"Hmm, that's very interesting," Teddy mused aloud, making the twenty disappear. It said a lot that his boy didn't want a little extra meth money. Maybe he needed some more persuading. He reached onto the seat next to him, grabbed some paperwork there. "Let's see what I have here...oh yeah, a photo of you breaking the terms of your parole by hanging out with known felons." He held up another photo, this one with Danny in the center of it. "These guys look familiar to you? The one in the middle must, since you see him in the mirror every day."

Danny's expression turned even more sour. It was obvious that Teddy had him by the short and curlies.

"All right, so what if I know him? I didn't kill him."

"Why didn't you just say so?"

"Because I didn't feel like it." This said as sullenly as a sulking teenager.

"Because you know who did?"

Silence, as profound as a confession. "I can sit here all night Danny." Teddy hoisted a paper bag. "I got a cold dinner and everything." He smiled. "Now why don't you just give me something I can use and you can go back to enjoying your nap, hmm? Sounds more than fair to me."

Once more Danny looked around, checking to see if anyone was watching him. Talking to the police always made him uneasy, especially when you never knew when you had eyes on you, eyes that might decide he'd look better without his head, or maybe his legs. So, he could toss him a bone, but nothing too serious.

"Tony could probably help you," Danny said at last. "He knows everyone who comes through the door personally."

"Tony the bartender?" This said as innocently as possible. Danny had no idea how long Teddy had been casing the place, and it was best to keep it that way. "He could help me?"

"Maybe."

Teddy couldn't say it, but Tony was the last person he wanted to know that there was police interest in Hooligans. Because if Tony found out, then whoever was behind the operation would find out, and that would make things a whole lot more difficult.

"He doesn't know you talk to me, does he?" Teddy didn't think so, but he had to ask.

"Are you fuckin' kiddin'? No one knows I talk to you. They did, and I'd be breathin' underwater."

"Good, let's keep it that way."

"So you ain't gonna talk to Tony?"

"Not today, but maybe later." Teddy scrutinized the man for a moment. "Who is Greg, Danny? What does he mean to this organization?"

Danny shuffled his feet and glanced about him yet again. "I'll tell you something if you'll leave me out of this, all right? I ain't doin' nothing more than the door here—"

"And obviously looking away at key moments too, huh?"

"What these guys choose to do with their time and money ain't none of my never mind."

"I'm sure it isn't," Teddy said, opening the sack and pulling out a sandwich. His wife had packed him tuna fish. He unwrapped foil and took a bite. Ah, just as he liked it. Lots of mayo and onions. "You were saying?"

"Jesus dude, you didn't hear this from me, but sometimes Greg held onto the product at his house, after it came across the border. That's all, he'd just hold it until the dealers came and picked it up."

"I assume it's safe to say that the product from across the border might be sponsored by members of a certain organization?"

"Not sayin' shit, bro."

"And I suppose I can also assume that the dealers are local gangbangers?"

"I don't know what ya mean."

Teddy scowled. "So they killed him because he held on to it too long?" He took another bite of his sandwich.

Danny rolled his eyes and Teddy knew he finally got to him. "No, some of the product started disappearing, was getting skimmed off." Danny's voice got real quiet, and he leaned closer. "You don't mess with these guys. If they give you something to hold, you don't touch it, you don't even look at it. You put it where they tell you, and when they show up to get it you stay the hell out of their way."

Teddy nodded. "So it's safe to say that the men who killed Greg Hanson did it because he was stealing from them, hmm? I suppose good old Greg was playing with fire." He took the last bite of his sandwich and asked nonchalantly, "Who do you think those guys might have been?"

Danny's face almost turned white with fear. "I can't say," he said hollowly, "but if I was a bettin' man I'd wager they weren't from around these parts." He swallowed hard. "I'd also recommend leaving well enough alone, unless you actually *want* trouble. These guys...it's best to stay off their radar if you can."

Teddy felt a coldness spread through his guts. It was what he expected, but he hadn't known for sure. Now, with Danny's confession, he knew that what he and Bobby were up against was a hell of a lot more dangerous than some random, local gangbanger. Because, when all was said and done, if what Danny was insinuating was true, it *was* a Mexican drug cartel behind Gina's kidnapping. And if that was so, she was almost as good as dead. The cartel men were as heartless as Somalian pirates, maybe even worse. Their lives and their trade depended on it. This was very, very bad news indeed. Bobby was not going to like this one bit, obviously. However, the biggest question that arose in Teddy's mind was the *why*. What could they possibly want from Bobby? He was as destitute as they come; he didn't even have the proverbial pot to piss in. What did he have to trade them?

"Thank you, Danny," Teddy said tonelessly, stuffing the crumpled tin-foil back into the brown paper bag. "You can go back to work now." He took the twenty-dollar bill from his pocket and held it out again. This time Danny took it.

"You didn't hear any of this from me, right?" he said, tucking the bill in his shirt pocket.

"Of course I didn't," Teddy reassured him. "But listen." He looked into the other's eyes with an intensity that enforced his request. "If you hear anything at all about a girl—a teenage girl who may be in their possession—you don't say anything to anyone about it except for me. You got that?"

Danny looked confused, and to Teddy that was a good sign. It meant his occasional informant wasn't holding out more information on him. Because if he was…

"Can I ask why?"

"You can, but I'm not telling you. I'm serious. You hear anything about a teenage girl you get in touch with me pronto."

Danny shrugged. "OK."

"Good enough." Teddy tipped his hat, started up the car. "Have a nice day."

Chapter Twenty-One

His right hand curled around a hacksaw, the man sat on a small wooden stool as he listened to someone on the other end of a phone tucked between his chin and right shoulder. Blood streaked his face, and his short, black hair was matted with the stuff. Smoke billowed around his head in a rank cloud from a cigarette clenched tightly between his teeth, and he nodded every now and then as he took another long, luxurious drag.

"Si," he muttered. "Um-hm, si."

His arm worked back and forth with machine-like precision, the ankle gripped in his hand very petite, indicating the gender was female. A few more strokes of the blade and the foot was free. He tossed it over his shoulder where it joined a pile of body parts.

He'd been working for the better part of the morning on a family of five—a mom, dad, a boy, a girl, and a small dog. He dismembered the dog first to get it out of the way. When he could help it, he avoided killing animals, but when it was necessary, well, he had to do what he had to do. It was part of the job. It didn't make him happy, but it was a necessary evil. This family had been hired by the Castillo cartel to live in a house in San Ysidro and simply maintain a smoke screen of normalcy. Seriously. All they had to do was go about their lives, meanwhile storing anywhere from fifty to two hundred and fifty kilos of coke, meth, or heroin in the house. They had to be quiet, respectful of the neighbors, and not cast any suspicion upon themselves in the community. For their discretion, they received a generous monthly stipend which they could spend any way they pleased. They just had to play the part of a normal, American family and everything was taken care of. The trouble with these fine folks, however, was that they couldn't keep their greedy fingers out of the stash. And not to sell, mind you. No, the entire family had become addicted to the nearly pure Columbian cocaine that was piled to the rafters in every available nook, cranny, and crawl space. Christ, even the two high school kids or, maybe, *especially* the high school kids, got in on the act. As soon as product started coming up short, well, it didn't take long to figure out where it was going, judging by the erratic behavior of the family. Unfortunately, due to their addiction, they were no longer blending in like they were supposed to. The kids were seen racing around town at all hours in their souped-up Mini Cooper, gritting their teeth like Hollywood tweakers, meanwhile the parents were often drunk and disorderly at the local Trader Joe's, doing bumps off of credit cards and laughing hysterically as they filled their shopping cart with cases of Three-Buck Chuck. Before long, the Castillo cartel knew they had to pull the plug before the law intervened.

Enter El Sádico. If there was someone who was causing the Castillo cartel trouble, he was the man they called. He was practically a ghost, with the ability to travel between Mexico and the United States virtually undetected. Most of the work he did for them, he did in the States, but every now and then he was needed in Tijuana or Baja. His expertise was removal. If someone needed to disappear, you called El Sádico. No one remembered his real name anymore; it simply didn't matter And he was not to be confused with a serial killer who boasted the same moniker. That asshole only killed four people (albeit extremely brutally, crimes perpetrated because of his hatred of homosexuals) and was serving a life sentence in a Mexican prison. As far as this El Sádico was concerned, he hadn't appropriated the name; he'd earned it. The other wasn't even worthy to lick the bloodstains off of his boots.

When he received the call regarding the family of five, he'd been watching free HBO at a La Quinta hotel in Carlsbad, off the Poinsettia Lane exit of Highway 5. He'd just taken care of one of the day mangers—a man who had been stupid enough to talk to two plainclothes cops about some activity that had been reported the previous weekend. He'd even gone so far as to give the two men a description of Mr. Sádico's car, and that, my friends, was not something you wanted to do if you expected to see your next birthday. The hitman had been pulled over by a CHP, had his driver's license run through the system and his plate checked. When it yielded nothing of any significance, he was let go, and Sádico's next stop was the La Quinta, where he remembered the man's face appearing in the office window shortly after he had used room 232 to dispatch of a snitch. As he watched the latest vampire show, eating a burger from In and Out, the manager hung from the shower curtain rod behind him, bug-eyed, tongue sticking out of his mouth, purple and grotesque looking. El Sádico had used the manager's own belt to do the honors.

"El Sádico," a soft voice had said on the other end of his untraceable, burner cell.

"Si?"

"We got a chob for ju."

"I listening."

"Family of five, San Ysidro. Can't keep their hands off the merchandise."

"Esta' bien." He hung up. He didn't need to know any more. A man like him needed very little information. Besides, he knew who the other was talking about. El Sádico had checked on them a couple of times, issuing their one and only warning not more than two weeks ago. It was now time for them to be replaced.

He'd caught them all at home at roughly three thirty on a Saturday morning, two of them sleeping, a couple of them awake, faces buried in a pile of cocaine that would have made Tony Montana green with envy. He'd killed all of them but one with his bare hands. The last one he'd had to cold-cock with a tea kettle before using a cheese knife to cut the kids throat. He'd almost made it out the door, the little brat, but really, where would he have gone? Sádico would have caught up with him eventually; he always did. Maybe it would be tomorrow, maybe the next day, but like the inevitability of the tides, El Sádico would eventually find him and the punishment would be swift and brutal.

He was presently receiving word of a new assignment, another one in which an animal was involved, apparently a bulldog. Now, as easy as it was for El Sádico to kill any human (woman, man, child), he truly did try and avoid violence toward his four-legged friends because he believed in their utmost incorruptibility. Whatever mischief they got up to, it was done purely out of innocence. For this reason, he was probably one of very few psychotic mass murderers who had a soft spot for *any* living creature. The majority of psychopaths had no empathy for anything. He supposed it was what made him unique. As he listened to the person on the other end of the phone, his mind whirled as to how he would keep the bulldog from coming to any harm, but he knew that if he was required to terminate it, he would do so without hesitation. That was why he was hired; it was why he made more money than the meth cooks, the drug mules, the runners and dealers. He could be counted on to make *anything* disappear at a moment's notice. He was like a magician that way.

"Ju want me to kill the girl and her dog?" he asked, slicing through thick neck tendons, at last reaching the spine. For that he had to switch from the hacksaw to the bone saw.

"Not jet," the voice on the other end replied. "We going to try and barter for her."

"Barter for what?"

"Her father's cousin been sniffing around one of our distribution centers, getting close. If he get any closer, we need him to take a vacation from law enforcement."

"Si." El Sádico deftly severed the spinal cord and soon the head was free from the body. He held it up into the light and looked into the wide, glassy eyes that were permanently blinded. "And what has the bulldog done to anyone?"

A groan from the other end. Everyone was well aware of his love of furry animals.

"She is to be used to manipulate either the girl or the girl's father."

"Si," El Sádico sighed. He threw the head over his shoulder and onto the pile. When he was finished with the dismemberment, he would dissolve the body parts in the tub with sodium hydroxide. Except for the feet. Those would be sent back to the house as a reminder to the new family about what would happen to them should they decide to sample (and continue sampling) the merchandise. It was, as they say, how they rolled. "Where and when?"

"We be in touch."

"Bueno." El Sádico put out his cigarette and hung up the phone. He stretched his arms, savoring the ache of his muscles. He glanced at the pile behind him, then the pile next to him, and got back to work.

◆ ◆ ◆

Bobby went to work on Saturday morning, servicing the pools he'd missed during the week, and schmoozing his clients who were home, doing his best to act as if everything was normal, which wasn't an easy task. The realization that the kidnapping had been a hoax up until this point burned within him like a raging wildfire, his hatred for Carolyn practically searing his insides. The nerve of that stupid bitch, using Gina's welfare to try and extort money out of him. The fact that he was now deeper in the hole was nothing compared to the reality that Gina was now in the custody of God-knew-who, but apparently, whoever it was they were a whole lot worse than your run-of-the-mill kidnappers; at least, that was what he gathered from Teddy's body language. He hadn't said it in so many words, but Bobby could tell when his cousin was unnerved. Over their brief meal at the diner, Bobby was well aware that there was something more than met the eye, but Teddy wasn't saying. He probably just didn't want Bobby to worry, but that made him worry more.

By lunch time his stomach was in knots, and it was hard to keep up the casual banter with some of his clients, but he managed. From house to house, pool to pool, his anxiety increased to the point where he desperately wanted a drink, or maybe a Xanax just to take the edge off, but he knew that one drink would lead to two, one Xanax would open the door to the possibility of meth or cocaine, and from there Christ only knew what would happen. The inevitable blackout, probably, and that wouldn't help to get Gina back.

A ripple of frustration erupted within him, well, more than a ripple actually—more like a tidal wave. His whole being was suddenly filled with a dreadful ache that seemingly nothing could fix. A pain so deep as to be almost real (real in the sense of an actual *physical* ache) nearly disabled him for a moment as he waited at an impossibly long light on El Camino Real and Aviary Parkway. His body went taut with a spasm, his hands locking onto the wheel, he clutched it so hard. And when the light eventually turned green, it took three blats from the horn of the car behind him to get Bobby moving again. As he drove along in the hazy midday sunshine, his unease turned to anger.

The hell I'm going to just take this lying down! he thought furiously. *I'll do whatever I have to do to get my daughter back!*

As he hit the corner of El Camino and La Costa, he suddenly decided there was someone he needed to have a few choice words with, and waiting wouldn't do. It had to be right now. Hitting his turn signal and cutting across three lanes of traffic, Bobby got into the left-hand turn lane while fumbling for his cell phone, dialing the number of his next client to tell him that he would be a little late.

◆ ◆ ◆

Carolyn had just returned from running some errands when she heard someone knock on the door. Thinking it might be something important, she dropped her purse and the plastic bag of cosmetics on the counter and strode toward the door, flinging it open.

"Yes?" she said, when Bobby stepped inside, pushing past her, and slammed the door behind him.

"You stupid bitch!" was all he got out before Barry appeared from the other room, clad only in a soiled pair of boxers, a can of Coors Light clutched in one hand, a cigarette burning in the other.

"Whatcha doin' here, Bobby?" he said, taking a drag from the cigarette as Carolyn collected herself from the fright he'd just given her. Not that Bobby ever rattled her cage (that was her job to do to him), but right now she was more than just a touch freaked out by what had transpired. And to think she'd believed Greg was a safe person.

"Hi, Barry," Bobby muttered, the sight of the wretched man somewhat defusing the situation. No matter what, Barry always injected a certain level of pathos into the status quo. But that was no reason to dissuade him from why he came here. He shifted his attention back to Carolyn. "Did you really think a plan like that had any way of working?"

"I don't know what you're talking about, Bobby—"

"Can the bull crap, sister. Teddy told me all about it."

Carolyn nodded. She had figured he would. Why she even tried to lie about it was beyond her. Just natural instinct, she supposed. She gestured toward the couch.

"Why don't you have a seat, Bobby?"

"I'm not sitting down," Bobby said, "because I'm not staying. I just want you to know how disappointed I am that you would stoop this low."

For a moment Carolyn was speechless; this was the first time that the shoe was on the other foot (Bobby chastising *her* for reckless behavior), and she wasn't sure how to respond. It simply didn't feel right. But she gathered herself quickly as she was, after all, a pro at things like this. Manipulation was her specialty, reproving her bread and butter. No one but no one came into her home and tried to make her feel like something the cat dragged in, even if she *was* guilty.

"I won't stand here in my own home and listen to you judge me, Bobby Travis!" she said with a vehemence that wasn't wholly contrived. "If you don't leave right this minute, I'm calling the police!"

"And telling them what, exactly? How you managed to get our daughter kidnapped by faking a kidnapping with someone connected to the mob?"

"We don't know that Greg was connected to the mob—"

"It doesn't matter who he was connected with! The point is that I'm right and you're not!"

"It's still our house, Bobby," Barry intervened, taking a tentative step forward. He took a swig of his beer for courage. "You best respect that."

"I'll respect that, all right," Bobby said, taking a step in his direction. "Right after the two of you apologize for duping me."

"For what?" This asked with genuine curiosity, but not regarding the why; once again Barry was proving just how limited his vocabulary was.

"You just get out of here, Bobby Travis! We ain't got nothing to say to you!"

"The hell you don't!" Bobby could feel the anger doubling within him, could sense his hands balling into fists whether he liked it or not. He wasn't a violent man, but these two had it coming. He took another step toward them, his body on autopilot, his brain no longer in control. He didn't think he could stop himself if he wanted to. It was like how he was compelled to drink and use drugs; it was an out-of-body experience. He merely watched on the sidelines as he did things he knew he best shouldn't but couldn't help it no matter how hard he tried. Yet possibly there was something more at work here. Maybe he was channeling his desire to drink and use drugs into violence. He figured it had every possibility of being true, and found he didn't mind. He raised his hands to chest level, the classic fighting stance.

"Just what the hell are you doing, Bobby—" Barry was saying when Bobby's right fist connected with his chops and dropped him like the proverbial sack of cow manure.

"Jesus, Bobby—" Carolyn peeped when his left fist caught her beneath the chin, lifted her off her feet and sent her sprawling into the coffee table behind her.

"I should kick both of your asses," Bobby seethed, "but I guess that ought to do. For now."

He turned around and stalked out the door, glancing at the time on his cell phone and seeing that if he really hauled ass, he could be on time for his two o'clock appointment. As he climbed into his (Terry's) truck and peeled out, two dumfounded dipshits were collecting their senses and picking themselves up from a floor that needed to be vacuumed a long time ago.

"What the hell got into him?" Barry wondered, noticing he hadn't spilled a drop of his swill. He took a drink, belched, took another.

"I don't know," Carolyn said, but it was only for show. She was well aware of what she'd done, and in all fairness figured she'd gotten off easy.

"Should I call the cops?"

She looked at the other for a long moment, and the look on her face would have given him his answer, if he was smart enough to pick up on it. Turned out, he was. Hell, even rats can be taught tricks, if given enough time.

"We deserved that, didn't we?" he said at last.

"Maybe we did, Barry," she replied after a moment. "Maybe we did."

Chapter Twenty-Two

A black van with tinted windows pulled up outside the rear of Hooligan's, and the driver put it in park, killed the engine, and stepped out. After locking it (to ensure his passengers couldn't escape) he quickly made his way up the service ramp and through the back door reserved for beer and booze deliveries, and once inside was immersed in the sound of aggressive heavy metal. He grimaced, having no taste for that kind of music. He'd take Tejano any day, hands down, but the bar catered to its patrons' tastes, which in this case were, in his opinion, downright awful. What did a song about pogo sticks have to do with the price of whores in Tijuana? He shrugged it off and walked down a long corridor until he was standing outside the door to the office. The door was closed. He reached out and knocked, two quick taps.

"Come in!"

He opened it and stepped into the dimly lit room. The boss was seated behind his desk, some sheets of paper spread out before him. As he got closer, he saw they were photographs.

"You have them?" Carlos asked in a crisp American accent. Although he was born in Mexico City, he deliberately disgraced his heritage by hiring a vocal coach to help him sound like a Southern Californian. He wanted to blend in. Armando knew that it helped to make him appear more like a United States citizen, but it irritated him just the same.

"In the van."

Carlos spun one of the photos around so Armando could see it.

"This man," Carlos said, pointing with a thick, hairy finger. "He's getting closer."

The other squinted at the picture, saw there were two men in it, but understood which one his boss meant. Sergeant Teddy Barnes had been photographed while talking to the doorman at Hooligans, the cop seated inside his undercover cruiser and eating a sandwich while the other apparently spilled his guts.

"Is it time?"

"Almost, yes. And we can get to him easier with the leverage we now have."

"The girl and the dog?"

"Exactly." Carlos reached into his desk and took out a bottle of Captain Morgan's spiced rum. He poured two fingers into a water glass and downed it in a breath. "El Sádico has been notified."

Armando couldn't help it; he shuddered involuntarily. Although he'd been in this business for two decades and counting, and was in fact second in command should Carlos be removed from duty, he couldn't help but fear the assassin who made their business possible through his vicious tactics. The man's methods, simply put, were atrocious. Of course, that was what the cartel needed to keep competitors from vying for their turf, but one couldn't help but be repulsed by the lengths El Sádico would go to prove a point. He was the one responsible for the piles of human body parts left in small villages in Baja, as a warning to the people who lived there. He hadn't originated the concept, but he performed it with amazing aplomb. And he did it because he wanted to, not to put on a farce of being dangerous. That was the scariest thing about him. Still, there was the matter of his weakness for dogs and cats. Armando and his peers would be inclined to show disrespect if they weren't so frightened of him.

"Will El Sádico take care of him?"

"No, I think in this case we shall handle this problem ourselves."

His response was not what Armando expected, and the startled expression on his face made Carlos laugh.

"You think we can't eliminate one meddler ourselves?"

"No, is just…isn't that the assassin's chob?"

"Maybe, maybe not." Carlos looked at the photo again, smiled, then returned his gaze to his second in command once more. "Let's just say I have a vested interest, and I'd feel a lot better doing it myself." He balled his fist and brought it down heavily on the photograph of Sergeant Barnes. "This local-yokel asshole thinks he can bring us down? Us? That'll be a cold day in hell!" Carlos' eyes looked feverish, maybe from the many memories of watching the surveillance footage from the cameras in the front of the bar, catching Sergeant Teddy Barnes talking with their door-man. "I want the pleasure of watching him die."

To this Armando did not know how to reply. Protocol dictated that they leave extermination to the professionals, and that they, upper tier management, stay on the business end of things. It was unorthodox for them to take on such a role in such a tightly run organization, however Carlos seldom did things by the book.

"You are going with me," Carlos continued, and Armando fairly bristled.

"Is not how it's done. Ju talk to Señor Castillo?"

"He doesn't need to know every last detail," Carlos said peevishly, his mood turning sour. "Do you think you know better than me?"

Armando shook his head. "No, jefe."

"Then you'll do as I say." He poured himself another shot of rum, drank it, and slammed the glass down. "You make the call and the ar-rangements. Our usual place, Monday morning at eight. And until then you'll see to it that the girl and her dog don't go anywhere."

"Ju want I should starve her?" Armando asked, resigned to his role as second in command to a lunatic.

Carlos shrugged, pouring himself more rum. "I don't think so. The girl hasn't done anyone any harm, and El Sádico will get upset if you mistreat the bulldog." He eyed the other over the rim of his glass. "You don't want to upset El Sádico, do you?"

"No, jefe."

"I didn't think so." He set the glass down, having drained its contents yet again, but refrained from filling it another time. "Be firm but don't be mean. We want this man to do what we want, and scaring the girl won't help. If he plays into our hands, then things will go much smoother."

Armando nodded, but personally he thought they should just ambush him. Two shots to the head, out of the picture. But Carlos didn't subscribe to the cartel's way of thinking; he'd been Americanized, like his accent, his haircut and his business practice. He thought things should be done with class, even in the world of narcotics trafficking. And that was dangerous, could wind up costing them dearly in the end.

"Do you have any questions?" Carlos asked while the other fidgeted before him.

"No," Armando said, realizing that it was time to go. He nodded again. "Buenos Dias."

"Yeah," Carlos said, picking up the photographs and placing them in his top drawer. "You too."

♦ ♦ ♦

Inside the van, Gina was doing her best not to cry. All eighty pounds of Ruby was in her lap, the dog's large mouth panting in her face. Like the traditional bulldog, her mouth was fixed in a sneer, lip stuck to the upper gums, with a quarter of her tongue hanging out at all times. Dog lovers found this endearing, while folks who didn't like canines thought of it as intimidating. Little did they know, Ruby was as passive as Gandhi, maybe even more so. She'd never for the life of her go on a hunger strike. Her favorite things to do in the world were eating, sniffing freshly mowed grass, and taking a nap in a pool of sunshine. She also loved taking walks with Gina, and she wondered why they hadn't taken one in a while. She was currently hungry, but that was pretty much a given, day or night.

"Good girl Ruby," Gina whispered. "Everything is going to be fine."

Ruby licked her face.

Suddenly the driver's side door opened and the man returned. Gina looked at him fearfully, but since his departure he didn't appear to be so surly. He got behind the wheel, started the engine, then looked back at her.

"If ju be a good girl and do as I say, everything be all right."

"O-o-OK..."

"We going to pick up one of my associates and then go someplace safe." The man scrutinized her unnervingly for a moment before asking: "Ju hungry?"

Gina nodded eagerly. "And my dog is too."

"We get ju something to eat when we get there."

"I...I hate to ask this..." Gina felt her chest tightening with fear. So far her dealings with this man had been just this side of terrifying. She didn't want to make any waves, but it was important he know this.

However, he smiled at her benevolently, nodding his head, encouraging her to speak. This sudden change in the man would have been frightening if it wasn't so welcome at this point. Something must have happened between the time he left the van until his return, because his attitude had done a complete 180.

"Si?"

"Um, Ruby is on a special hypoallergenic diet," Gina ventured. "She can't eat just anything."

"Is no problem," the driver said. "We make sure she get everything she need."

The relief on Gina's face must have been comical, for he laughed.

"Don worry," he said. "Is fine."

And he put the van in drive and they pulled away from the bar.

◆ ◆ ◆

Maggie knew something was bothering him because he couldn't keep up with small talk during dinner. Emily was staying overnight at a friend's house and Teddy had the night off, so he could enjoy a home-cooked meal and they could converse openly, although so far it hadn't been anything but small talk. He tried to nod and add subtle comments as she gossiped about the women in her book club, how none of them appreciated the new Nora Roberts novel, but after a few minutes his inertia brought out her curiosity.

"What's wrong," she asked, "besides the obvious? Is there some new twist in the case you haven't told me?"

"No," he lied, and not because he wanted to, but because he had to. He kept Maggie up to speed on everything that happened, except for his behind-the-scenes, clandestine research on some of the seedier dives on Grand Avenue and Valley Center Parkway. If she knew he was looking into possible narcotics distribution centers around the city in his free time (possibly supplied by Mexican drug cartels), she would slit his throat with a rusty razor just to have it over with. She'd excrete the proverbial chunk of masonry. He'd told her everything else about the kidnapping from day one, including the most recent wrinkle, that it had been faked by Carolyn and then made real by some unknown "someone else," but he'd left the details about the "someone else" vague because he didn't want her to worry. And the thing that was bothering him this evening? His sometimes snitch, Danny, was missing. Now, it hadn't even been more than twenty-four hours since he'd paid him a visit, and Teddy had no proof that any-thing had happened to the man, but when he drove by this afternoon after a trip to the grocery store to check on him, he wasn't there; another man was. Teddy wasn't stupid enough to go waltzing up to the new guy and ask any questions regarding Danny's whereabouts. Everyone knew who Teddy was, and it would call attention to his investigation. No, he just had to wait it out and see if Danny returned, which, the more he thought about it, was highly unlikely. Somebody must have seen their exchange and reported it to someone higher up. He desperately hoped that wasn't the case, but given the circumstances, it fit.

"You're lying," she said, getting up from the table and grabbing a bottle of inexpensive merlot. She refilled his glass before refilling her own and put it back on the counter. She sat down, but the expression on her face didn't change. "I always know when you're lying to me."

He sighed. "I don't want to lie to you, honey," he breathed softly. "I have to."

"Official police business?"

He nodded. "I guess."

"That sounds like a lie too."

"I love you dear, that's all that matters."

"Is it about Gina?"

"No, thank God."

"Do you have any leads?"

He hesitated before answering, and she knew she was wearing him down.

"One," he admitted.

"But you're not going to tell me." A statement, not a question.

He sighed and looked at her achingly. "I can't, honey. I just...can't."

She stared at him for a moment and then got up brusquely from the table, taking her wine glass with her.

"Honey—"

"It's OK," she said, but he knew it wasn't. A woman's declaration that everything was "OK" always meant the opposite of that.

"I'll tell you when it's all over, I promise."

She turned back to look at him. He expected wrath, the fury of demons, but instead there was a soft look on her face, one of desperate longing.

"God I love you Teddy."

"I love you too—"

"But right now I'm so frightened for you! You need to get someone else on the force involved with this whole kidnapping thing. Now that it's real, you don't have to play the hero and try to find her yourself! Get some young rookies to go rushing off into battle for you."

"It isn't that, honey. Christ, I wish it was—"

"Than what is it? Do you need the satisfaction?"

"Come on, Maggie; you know me better than that."

"Something's going on that you're not telling me."

"I think that's what I've been saying..."

"Fine!" She slammed her glass down on the counter by the sink. "Keep your secrets! I just wish you trusted me enough to let me in on what's going on!"

He exhaled sharply yet again, wishing he could tell her, wishing he could tell *someone*, but knowing that right now it wouldn't do any good. He was stuck with what he knew, and dragging anyone else in would be dragging them down. It was best to keep everyone else in the dark, for their own safety. Maggie should know that; she'd been a cop's wife for as long as he'd been a cop. But she was stubborn, and that was what had attracted him to her in the first place. Well, that and her red hair and freckles, as well as dimples that lit up the room when she smiled.

He silently watched her go. What could he say? He couldn't call her back unless he was willing to tell her what he was doing, and he loved her too much to do that. As he ate the last of his nearly cold supper, he heard her fetch a loud sigh and turn on the evening news, and he glanced at the clock. He wanted to swing by Hooligan's one more time, see if his boy had returned. He honestly didn't think Danny would, but he hoped like hell he did. He realized with no uncertainty that his life depended on it.

He got up from the table and took his glass to the sink, dumped it out, and rinsed it under cold tap water. He then placed it on the top rack of the dishwasher before picking up his hat from the counter and silently slipping out the front door.

Chapter Twenty-Three

Bobby got the call, the *real* call, from the kidnappers at 7:47 a.m. on Sunday morning. He'd been awake since six, lying in bed, tossing and turning, when he finally decided around 6:45 a.m. to get up and have some coffee. He'd just gotten out of the shower and was deciding whether or not he should shave when his cell phone vibrated on the counter next to him. He froze in front of the mirror, letting it vibrate three times before he sprang into action, snatching it deftly and breathlessly uttering "Hello?"

"Bobby Travis?"

"Yes?"

"We have jore daughter." Commotion from the other end of the line, another voice, and then "And her bulldog."

"Please," Bobby pleaded. "Don't hurt them."

"That all depend on ju."

"I'll give you whatever you want!" Bobby said before realizing how impossible that was. Didn't any of these people know he was busted as flat as an armadillo on a blistering Texas highway? How the Christ did they think he had anything more than the shirt on his back and a worn pair of shoes?

"How much is jore daughter and her dog worth to ju?"

Bobby felt a sense of déjà vu. *Didn't we already go through this?* He thought despairingly before answering: "Everything! She's worth everything I have!"

The person on the other end of the line chuckled. "Bueno, muy bueno, because what we want is very steep indeed."

"Look," Bobby said, not wanting to, but feeling that a full disclosure was probably necessary. "I don't have much in cash, but I have some assets. I have a pickup...oh, wait, no, I signed over the title to someone else..." Bobby scratched his head, thinking. "Um, let's see...I have a house! I can put my house up for sale. And there's always my business. Do you know that I have a successful pool cleaning business? It's all yours! Please, just let me have my daughter and her dog back!"

"We don want nothing of jores, Bobby. Is useless to us."

"I see..." he said, but he didn't. If they didn't want anything of his, what *did* they want? He supposed he was about to find out, but meanwhile there was something he wanted, something that had been denied him the first (the fake) time around. "Is...is my daughter all right?" he asked. "Can I talk to her please?"

Again, the ominous chuckle, but after a moment, the voice replied, "Si."

The phone was handed over, and then Gina was on the line. It was the first time he'd spoken to her in a week, since last Sunday when they'd gone out for ice cream.

"Hi, Daddy!" she gushed, and Bobby almost started sobbing. She hadn't called him "Daddy" since she was ten, give or take, and the fact that she was saying it now meant she was scared, badly scared, and he didn't blame her, not one bit.

"I'm here, honey; I'm here," he reassured her. "Are you OK? I've been worried sick about you!"

"I'm fine, Daddy. They've actually been pretty nice to me and Ruby. They've been feeding us and letting us watch TV. They won't let me take Ruby for a walk, though, and she hasn't liked that, but otherwise we're OK."

"Who are those people?" he asked, his voice hushed. He didn't have the nerve to ask them but supposed he'd try her. Maybe she was clued into something that could help Teddy figure it out.

She was silent, but then she whispered, "I think they're drug dealers, and they're standing right here, so, ya know, I probably shouldn't talk about them..."

"I understand," he said, and he did. It was best not to rock the boat. "I'm going to give them whatever they want to get you back, honey."

"I don't know what they could possibly want from *you,* Daddy."

"Me neither, but I want you and Ruby home safe." He paused a moment, swallowed hard. "As long as you're OK, I better talk to them again, all right, honey? I just want this whole thing to be over."

"Me too, Daddy," she said, sounding as if she was barely holding back from crying.

"Give them the phone back and be a good girl, OK? We'll work everything out and you'll be home safe before you know it."

"All right," she said, and then, "I love you, Daddy!"

"I love you too, honey; now give them back the phone. Give Ruby a hug for me."

"I will," she said, on the verge of tears, and he couldn't blame her. He was scared shitless. She said something to her captors and handed over the phone, and then the voice of the kidnapper was in Bobby's ear again.

"Ju satisfied?"

"I'll be satisfied when I get my little girl back," Bobby said, and damned if he didn't sound like he was trying to be a tough guy. The other saw right through it.

"Is no need for heroics, Mr. Travis. Ju give us what we want and everybody walk away happy."

This was it; the time was nigh. Speak now or forever hold your peace. "What is it you want?"

"Ju should know the answer to that Bobby," the other said, but Bobby had no idea. He had no money, he had no skills, no purpose, he was practically useless at everything he attempted in life. The only thing he'd ever been successful at was being a drunken, drugged-out sex addict. The gambling had only screwed him over time and again, as was obvious by now, and as for being a father, well, it was apparent no one was going to proudly recognize his shoddy efforts on that front either. Did they maybe want him to come over and black out for them? He could do that with amazing aplomb.

"I have no idea," he said breathlessly. "Please tell me."

"Jore cousin, the police officer."

"Teddy?" he gasped. *Why the hell would they want Teddy?*

"Is correct. We're offering Ju a trade: jore daughter for Sergeant Teddy Barnes."

"What do you want him for?" Bobby felt cold all over. He loved Gina with all of his heart, and nothing could stand in the way of that. But a trade for his cousin Teddy? Although he'd asked, he wasn't stupid. If these guys were drug dealers and they wanted Teddy, it was because he knew something and they didn't want it to get around. His silence was what they wanted, and how did you get that? The art of gentle persuasion? Hell no! What had happened to the fake kidnapper, Greg Hanson, spoke volumes in that department. He couldn't allow it, he wouldn't.

"Anything else," he found himself saying. "I'll give you anything else, please, but not Teddy."

"Is the only thing we want, Mr. Travis." The voice was calm, yet the cold certainty of his words was not lost on Bobby. "If ju don't trade him to us for jore daughter, ju never see her or the dog again. And then we kill him anyway. Is clear?"

"Yes," he whispered, his voice lost in despair. *Dear God, not Teddy...*

"Ju have twenty-four hours to make arrangements, and then jore going to meet us tomorrow at eight o'clock at the China Palace Buffet Restaurant on Mission Avenue in Oceanside. Ju bring Sergeant Teddy Barnes and we bring jore daughter and her dog. Ju understand?"

"Yes," Bobby whispered again, but he wasn't sure if he did. How would Teddy react to news like this? Would he willingly give his life to spare Gina's?

Yes, Bobby, a voice in his head spoke up. *Yes, he would. He loves you and your daughter, and he'd do anything to see her home safe. He's an officer of the law. He's bound by duty.*

"Please," he cried suddenly, "there must be something else I can give you!"

A pause, then: "Is nothing else we want, Mr. Travis. Ju heard me, to-morrow morning at eight. Don be late."

♦ ♦ ♦

On the television, an infomercial blared, a ridiculously buff dude in a tailor-made suit pitching the benefits of raising salmon in your own backyard.

"For pennies a day," he said, beaming into the camera with a smile that was just this side of imbecile, "you too can have your very own salmon farm!" He walked two short steps to an aquarium teeming with the aforementioned fish. "How many times have you said to yourself, 'Man, I really want some salmon right now,' but didn't feel like getting off the couch and going to the store? Fear not! Now all you have to do is grab your net (not included) and scoop one of these bad boys out! After you scale, gut, and slice it up (scaler and knives not included), you'll have yourself a meal fit for a sea captain. So don't delay; call today!"

Gina looked sidelong at one of her captors, a man covered in sketchy-looking tattoos who wore his pants practically around his knees, the whole outfit accompanied by a bandana worn so low over his eyes it was as if he was wearing a blindfold. He didn't say much, and when he did it was in short sentences punctuated with a lot of slang, some of which she didn't understand. But he wasn't all bad. He wasn't mean to her, for one thing. And he was very helpful when it came to Ruby's needs. One thing she hadn't been able to get her head around was how sympathetic they were when it came to her dog. They were so kind; it was almost as if their lives depended on it. She didn't understand it, but she was extremely grateful.

The man saw her looking at him, and he flashed gold teeth with a half smile.

"Ju need somethin', chica?"

"Um, no."

"Ju let me know if ju do."

"OK."

After he'd spoken with her dad, the man who had made the call left the house. He was dressed in a suit and acted as solemn as a businessman, quite the opposite of the guy he'd left to watch her. But so far the two of them had been civil with her, and she knew she was lucky for that. Presently, Ruby was snuggled up against her, snoring loudly as she snoozed. She assumed, but didn't know for sure, that these men were drug dealers. The reason for this assumption was because of her dad's proclivities during his free time, not simply because they were Mexican. OK, she sort of had to admit to herself that *because* they were Mexican, she suspected them of being drug dealers. She couldn't help it, what with all the things she saw on TV about the Mexican drug cartels. Besides, she had heard one of them make a reference to drugs. Nothing overt, but something regarding the care and handling of "product" and its intended distribution. It was a brief discussion between the man in the suit and the guy who looked like the poster child for gang warfare. She hadn't meant to eavesdrop; she simply couldn't help it. She was tuned into anything and everything that happened at this point.

The worst thing she'd heard, however, was what the man had said over the phone to her dad regarding her uncle Teddy. She'd only heard one side of the conversation, but she wasn't stupid. She knew what the drug dealer was talking about involving the ransom. She'd heard it quite plainly: they didn't want money, and then uncle Teddy was mentioned by name. And it wasn't as if they were going to sit him down and give him a talking to, maybe a time out in his room; no, they were going to kill him because that's what men like this did. They killed anyone who got in the way of their business. Just ask Greg Hanson, oh wait, you couldn't. He was dead, shot by one of these guys, which one she wasn't sure, and she wasn't about to ask.

Gina may have only been fifteen, but she understood the laws of supply and demand and basic socioeconomic functioning within a well-to-do society as pitted against one that barely struggled to keep its head above water. No offence to the Mexicans, but selling drugs was all they had to a certain extent. She'd only been to Mexico once; she'd visited Tijuana with her mom and Barry, and based on what she saw, she hardly thought the country could get by on selling trinkets like blankets, cheap guitars and other assorted crap. All the tequila in the world couldn't drag the country out of poverty as far as she could tell.

Thus far, to ensure her continued safety, Gina kept her mouth shut and didn't ask for anything but the most basic necessities for her and Ruby, and she tried to keep her anxiety to a minimum by telling herself that her dad wouldn't let anything bad happen to her. And she didn't really believe that uncle Teddy would just give himself to these people without a fight, without trying to do something, would he? It would be suicide.

She snuggled closer to Ruby, the dog's large mouth next to her ear, blowing tepid air accompanied by gentle snores. She wrapped her arm tightly around her and focused her attention on the TV. Hopefully this would all be over soon. Hopefully.

◆ ◆ ◆

"I knew it," Teddy said, taking off his hat and running a hand through his hair. And he did know it; he'd figured it was going to come to this. What with all of his poking around and the fact that his boy Danny hadn't returned, he knew he'd been made. And the poor bastard who'd been his snitch? If he was lucky all he got was a car ride out into the desert and two shots in the back of the head. If he wasn't lucky, well, in all honesty Teddy didn't want to think about that. He'd seen enough crime scenes to know in which direction his handling had probably headed, and none of it pointed to a peaceful passing.

"What are we going to do?" Bobby asked, sitting shotgun (next to the twelve-gauge shotgun) in Teddy's squad car. Teddy'd managed to switch shifts with Daniels after he got the call from Bobby, claiming it was a family emergency, which, all things considered, it was. He figured he might as well be on duty for what was going to come next, and this would give him the night at home with his family. What the hell, it might be his last evening with Maggie and Emily.

"Nothing we can do Bobby," he said wearily. "I turn myself in to them."

"But you can't do that! They'll kill you!"

"They made me Bobby, it's as simple as that."

"What the hell does that mean?"

"I've been investigating them for a long time, well, Hooligans anyway. I figured several of the dive bars along the strip had to be fronts for large-scale drug dealing enterprises, and I stumbled onto one of their distribution centers." He smiled wistfully. "Sucks that it couldn't have been an operation fronted by bikers and dope fiends, nope, had to be a Mexican drug cartel."

"If that's true then raid the damn place! Don't just walk into their trap."

"We're kind of caught with our pants down here, Bobby. If this had gone down any other way, I suppose we could do that. But they have Gina, and if they don't get what they want they'll kill her, end of story. Men like these don't negotiate."

"Shit..." It was all Bobby could think of to say. He didn't like this, any of it; in fact it had been the hardest thing he'd ever had to say to anyone. How do you tell someone that they have to walk into imminent disaster so that someone else can walk free? Only the stoutest of hearts would accept the terms of something like that, and here his cousin was doing just that, as Bobby had expected he would. Had the shoe been on the other foot, Bobby knew it wouldn't be an easy decision, but he was certain that if it came to Teddy and his daughter Emily, he would do the same in kind. Not that he'd ever know, and at present his heart was sick with the knowledge that Emily would potentially be without a father and Maggie without a husband, but he didn't know what else they were going to do.

"So...how are we, um, going to do this?"

Teddy turned and looked at his cousin, realizing with a certainty that bordered on psychosis that this may be one of the last times he'd ever see him. The reason behind his calm demeanor wasn't so much about him being bold as he was bowled over by shock. He was thinking, of course, about Maggie and Emily, and what they were going to do without him. A part of him wanted to be mad at Bobby, but then he realized that none of this was really his fault. Teddy had taken an interest in Hooligans in part because he knew Bobby was getting his drugs there, but that's where his participation ended. Bobby hadn't been the one behind the phony kidnapping; no, Teddy had Carolyn to thank for that act of stupidity. She'd been irresponsible enough to hire someone she didn't know had ties to drug dealing activities, someone who inevitably linked them to a Mexican drug cartel. He couldn't hate her for her ignorance, but found he did just the same. What a dumb bitch. He'd gripe that Bobby really knew how to pick them, but that wasn't true either. The poor schlub didn't even remember screwing her.

"We're going to do it exactly as they asked, Bobby." He shrugged, his eyes dry nonetheless there was a profound sorrow in his voice. "We're going to meet them and do the exchange. Once you have Gina and Ruby, you get them someplace safe, and then I want you to call nine one one and tell them what's going on. Can you do that?"

"We can't do this, Teddy—"

"We can and will, Bobby. We have no choice!"

Bobby sat there mutely for a moment, his mouth hanging open like the village idiot. And what the hell, maybe he *was* the village idiot; he did, after all, screw everything up on such a regular basis that his status had to be recognized. Maybe he should be awarded the dunce cap just to make his title more official.

"I don't want to lose you, Teddy..." Bobby said at last, and on the last word his voice broke as sorrow overtook him.

"Oh Christ, Bobby, don't do this," Teddy said harshly, yet grief wasn't far off, and not for himself, but for the people he would leave behind. It wasn't that he didn't care about his own welfare; in fact, he was terrified. The cartel people would want to know whom he'd shared the information with, and they certainly weren't going to be satisfied with the truth. In all honesty, he'd told no one except for Bobby. They would probably torture him until they at last believed he hadn't told anyone else on the force about his discovery, and it would be a painful process until their belief had been belied. Unless, that is, he could convince them that he had told someone else; it was possibly his only bargaining chip to ensure his continued existence.

"I love you, man," Bobby said, leaning in for a hug, and Teddy leaned forward as well, the two of them awkwardly bypassing the twelve-gauge to "man-hug," which is to say a one-armed back patting affair replete with affirmations of each other's affection by repeating "I love you, man" like a mantra to live by. When the moment eventually passed, the two men parted, but a silence hung uneasy between them. Bobby couldn't help but feel guilty, as if this was all his fault, when in reality it wasn't. Teddy couldn't help but accept the fact that his life was flashing before his eyes, and he knew that tonight, at home, he needed to reassure his daughter that he loved her, and he needed to make love to his wife one more time.

"What time are we meeting them tomorrow?" Teddy asked at length.

"Eight o'clock in the morning."

"Where?"

"The Chinese Buffet Palace in Oceanside, on Mission."

"Since when is a Chinese restaurant open at eight in the morning?"

"I think that's why they picked the place."

"I suppose." He shrugged. "Probably another one of their distribution centers."

Again, they lapsed into silence, the two of them thinking their thoughts. As bad as Bobby wanted his daughter back, the thought of losing his cousin was enormously disconcerting. He wished there could be some other way, he really did, but no ideas were forthcoming.

"You're not just going to turn yourself in to them, are you?" he instead asked again, and the look Teddy gave him was all the answer he needed.

"Go home, Bobby," he said. "I think I'll knock off work a bit early, you know, so I can spend some time with my family."

"OK," Bobby said, not knowing what else to say. It turned out it didn't matter anyway.

"Get out of the car, Bobby," Teddy said. "I'll see you in the morning."

Bobby got out of the car, watching for the last time as his cousin pulled away.

Chapter Twenty-Four

El Sádico had the windows rolled down, trying to rid the car of the scent of excrement. He also smoked a particularly stinky Mexican cigarette to aid his efforts, but the smell lingered. It was an unavoidable byproduct of his occupation, but it never failed to irritate his olfactory senses. He hit his blinker to make a lane change, and when he did so he looked down and saw how filthy his nails were. He shuddered. He hated having dirty nails, it made his whole being feel soiled.

The man he'd left buried in the desert had been a textbook case; he'd done what they all did, said what they all said. He offered nothing new to the context in which El Sádico based his living, and to a certain extent that was just fine by him. Yet on another, a deeper level, he was slightly disappointed. These random, low IQ jerk-offs offered no real sport, and for a man with his intelligence it gave no satisfaction. Sometimes it made him hurt them more than he had to, in spite. It wasn't a deliberate attempt at cruelty; it was necessitated by boredom, followed by the all-consuming desire to alleviate it. He hadn't meant to disfigure the man after making him dig his own grave, it had simply happened. In fact, he'd known he was going to do something horrible the second the man defecated in his pants. It was at that exact moment when El Sádico knew that torture was no longer an option but an obligation.

If he could script his life, it would easily go something like this: the phone rings, he answers. Someone gives him a name, sometimes a location. He gets in his car; he drives to the site. Using a photo or a physical description, he finds his target. He then engages said target in conversation, makes some jokes until they are comfortable, offers some ruse to single them out from a crowd, if necessary. Then he strikes, incapacitates them, gets them in his car. Once they are his prisoner, he tells them why they are in his custody, and what he intends to do. These people, they never like what he tells them because it never varies. His intentions are as portentous as a coming storm, as inevitable as the setting sun. They have no options, zero, and this never fails to frighten them badly. In this case (as in many cases) they lose control of their bladder or bowels. The fear of death has a tendency to do that to you.

As soon as he transported his latest prisoner to the desert, El Sádico ordered him to dig his grave. It didn't have to be deep, about three feet was sufficient. It wasn't as if he was trying to hide the body so much as stash it for a while until animals came sniffing around, dug it up, and ate it. He'd asked the man some questions, all of which were answered promptly in between pleadings for his life. They all did that: begged for their lives. They should know that once they were under his wing, all bargaining was off the table. The outcome was written in stone.

After he'd received his answers, he tortured the man for a while, burning him with his lighter, cutting him with a knife, removing one of his ears as a trophy. The man had continued begging through his screaming, and it gave El Sádico a hard-on. He couldn't help it; torture and killing were sometimes sexual to him, even though he seldom defiled the corpse when he was done. Not to say it never happened, but it wasn't often. When he finished his job and the body was growing cold, he'd take care of his own needs quickly, almost furtively, removing the ejaculate from his hand with a handkerchief and disposing of it. It was the closest thing he'd had to sex since he could remember, and he wasn't the kind of man who dwelled in the past.

He drove along, the scent of shit slowly fading, along with his memory of the man's face. He was a keen stickler for details, but once a job was done, it was done. He moved swiftly onto the next thing.

This man, for all of El Sádico's efforts, had only coughed up two names, and both of them were already on the cartel's radar. In point of fact, he was never hired for interrogation purposes. Once he was called into action, the person's fate had already been sealed; the cartel had all the information it needed. He was only called upon to make people disappear. In this case, however, he'd felt like doing a little investigating of his own, just to see what else he could (no pun intended) dig up. If the ex-doorman of Hooligans hadn't been lying, it was apparently just the cop and his cousin who knew what was going on (as well as anyone close to them), and Bobby never would have known had the other not been snooping around where he shouldn't have. Likewise with anybody *he* may have told. Like an angry swarm of bees whose nest had been disturbed, the cartel's retribution would be immediate and ruthless. The cop should have known that. In all probability, it had most likely been a mistake. Had Sergeant Barnes known he was messing with the Castillo drug cartel, he certainly wouldn't have dived in headfirst by himself; he'd have let the rest of his department know.

And now he was going to die at the hands of the Castillo cartel; he was slated for termination tomorrow. Sádico had been surprised when Carlos informed him he was going to handle the situation himself, but it didn't bother him. There were always other things he could be doing, like heading over the border to take care of some business in Tijuana. While he settled other matters he'd wait for the call from the cartel, giving him the green light, and then he'd return and clean up the rest of their mess, starting with the girl's mother and stepfather, then moving on to the cop's family. After that he'd take care of Bobby, his girlfriend, then the girl. It was going to be one hell of a bloodbath, yet he was always up to the task. Tonight he'd visit a few of his contacts in Tijuana, see what was up. There was always someone who needed killing, somewhere, and Sádico was an equal opportunity assassin for hire.

Have gun, will travel, he thought with a slight smile.

As he turned off the highway and flicked his butt out the window, he noticed that the smell was at last beginning to dissipate, and this made him feel a little better. But maybe he'd get one of those air fresheners shaped like a maple leaf when he stopped and filled up the tank of his Lexus with premium, just to make sure the odor didn't linger. Yes, that might be a very a good idea indeed, and a part of him wondered why he hadn't thought of it before.

Turning on the radio and tuning it to an AM talk radio station, he whistled a little tune as he took a left on Valley Center Parkway, prepared to pull into the next gas station he came upon.

And that's just what he did.

◆　◆　◆

"There has to be some other way," Bobby said, his arm around Melissa's waist as they lay in bed together. "I can't let him do it."

Melissa sat up, leaned over the nightstand so she could take a cigarette from the pack and light it with her Bic. "There *is* no other way," she said, and for a moment this made Bobby angry. How did she know? What made her the resident expert on how to handle a kidnapping at the hands of a gang of vicious drug dealers? But the anger faded quickly because, when all was said and done, he truly was relieved that Teddy would make the ultimate sacrifice for a child that wasn't his own. He'd half (OK, totally) expected it, but once he'd heard it from the other's mouth, he'd felt his anxiety slip away. He'd been so worried about the fate of his one and only daughter, and to know that his cousin, the one man he trusted above all others, was going to end his life by saving hers, it drained all the tension right out of him to know she'd soon be safe.

However, the thought of losing him was not boding well. The outcome was what he wanted, but the means to the end were much less than desired. He didn't want it to be like that, and hated himself for the relief it gave him.

"There has to be something we can do," he said again, and she took a long drag on her smoke before turning to him, catching his gaze and holding it powerfully within her own. At times like these, Bobby doubted his own beliefs that she had low self-esteem. When she looked at him like that, he honestly believed she had the strength to do anything.

"He told you why this happened, Bobby. To a large degree this is his own fault." Her eyes softened. "Not that he probably knew who he was messing with, but he did seek it out."

"It's his job to seek it out—"

"Not by himself it's not." She stubbed out her half-smoked butt. "If he had done it by the book they wouldn't have singled him out, and you know it."

"Yes," he relented.

"It sucks that Carolyn would put all of you in this situation, but even she didn't know what she was up against."

"Stupid bitch," Bobby muttered, and this made Melissa smile.

"There is no denying she's a stupid bitch," she said, kissing him softly on the lips. The taste of tobacco was strong on her tongue, but from her it didn't taste bad. It didn't taste good, mind you, but it didn't repel him either.

"I can't believe this is happening," he said, ignorant of the fact that it was his drug-fueled actions that made Teddy curious about Hooligans in the first place. He could blame the mother of his child all he wanted, but his cousin's curiosity was partially precipitated by his own wanton desires. Had Bobby known that, his guilt would certainly have been compounded. Perhaps it was good that he was oblivious to it; it would make everything that much easier believing it was something his cousin brought totally upon himself, coupled by Carolyn's unequivocal stupidity.

"It would help if you did believe it," she said, cupping his face in both of her hands, and he couldn't help but feel as if he'd heard those words before, where, he wasn't sure. "Just be glad that after tomorrow this will all be over."

The finality of her statement made him cold all over (*oh Teddy...*), yet he had to admit she was right. He couldn't wait to get Gina and Ruby back safely, and once he did he'd try to scrape up the dough to hire the best lawyer he could find so he could challenge the previous judge's ruling on who should be her primary caretaker. Carolyn had proved inexorably that she wasn't fit to be her guardian; that was for damn sure. Anyone who'd fake their own daughter's kidnapping should be charged with something, like criminal mischief, or a crime of that nature. Surely what she did couldn't be misconstrued as "legal."

"I can't wait to see her again." He exhaled heavily, and she patted his face lightly with an open palm.

"That's the spirit," she said, then reached down and patted something else on him. "Care to make it a double header?" she said, and this made him smile.

"Bartender," he quipped, "make that a double."

"Coming right up sir," she replied, and their conversation, for the moment, was over.

◆ ◆ ◆

In another household two people lay in bed, but they were not engaged in passionate lovemaking. These two were arguing.

"Why can't you ever admit you're wrong?"

"I'll admit I'm wrong when you admit you're a dumbass!"

"I ain't never admittin' that!"

"Then I'm not wrong!"

"Fine!"

Silence between the two of them for a moment, then: "Can you go get me a beer?"

"Get your own goddamn beer!"

"I guess I will!"

Barry got up, his skinny ass sweating in the early evening heat. To save on bills, they rarely turned on the air conditioner, and the house was so poorly insulated that the temperature outside was the same as within, if not hotter. He was half-tempted to turn on the air, but he knew Carolyn would gripe about it.

"While you're up get me a beer too."

Barry wanted to turn the tables, to tell her to get her own damn beer, but like the subservient little puke he was, he merely nodded. He walked to the kitchen gingerly on bare feet that bore no calluses from overuse, nor work of any kind. In another lifetime, it seemed, he'd been a telemarketer, selling food processors or school supplies or some such crap. He actually hadn't minded it; he was one of the rare few who totally didn't care that he was calling people at home and interrupting them during a meal or watching TV to pitch them something they could have easily lived without, or basically have gone to the store (or Amazon.com) to purchase should they so choose. He spoke over their protests, making him a good salesman indeed because he never listened to anything they had to say. He barreled ahead until they hung up or bought something. Believe it or not, this tactic worked like a charm. The only reason he wasn't still employing his trade was because of something imprudent his ex-manager had said to the unemployment board when asked why she fired him. She'd foolishly told a whopper of a lie. The real reason? Mary Beth Johannsen simply didn't like him; he rubbed her the wrong way. Maybe it was his greasy hair, or the way he talked, or his coffee/cigarette breath. She simply couldn't stand the sight of him. But she couldn't tell the unemployment board that, so she made up a story about him running over her dear puss-puss and not offering to pay to replace him, nor saying sorry. How, the labor board had asked, did Barry run over her *house cat* at work? Since she wasn't much smarter than Barry, she had no answer for that, hence the board decided to award him unemployment for wrongful termination. Unless, of course, she wanted to hire him back. She didn't.

And so Barry got to drink beer every day and watch NASCAR or football, or baseball or mud wrestling or whatever it was that unemployed alcoholics liked to watch. He'd been enjoying this status for almost a year now with seemingly no end in sight. All he had to do was "look" for work, and if he couldn't find it, the checks kept rolling in. It was peculiar that the unemployment board did not consider it odd that he claimed he couldn't find another telemarketing gig, because those places were practically giving jobs away to anyone with a hand to dial and mouth to talk, but who was he to question why?

He grabbed a couple of silver bullets, standing for a moment in the cold mist of the refrigerator to contemplate their missing daughter. She wasn't really his daughter, but he felt he'd done a good job of helping raise her. Even when she didn't ask for advice, he offered it anyway, and when she tried to leave the house wearing something he didn't approve of, he made her change into something else. She'd thank him for that later. He sighed. He'd been the best damn stepdaddy a man could be. And he'd never once tried to rape her. That had to count for something.

"Where the hell is my beer?" Carolyn shrieked from the bedroom.

"Coming!" he blatted in return, closing the refrigerator door on all the leftovers that were lying in wait to give them gastronomic distress at some later point, like when they were hungry next.

"What are you doing, playing with yourself?" It was one of Carolyn's standard lines, and it worked every time.

"I ain't playin' with myself!" he declared, returning with her beer. He popped open the tab and handed her the can. She snatched it from him greedily and took a sip.

"Took you long enough," she muttered, and he shrugged and crawled back into bed beside her. "I have something for you," she said, and lifted the covers. A smell worse than the local slaughterhouse took his nose hostage and beat it into submission. She cackled delightedly as he struggled not to lose his gorge. Watching Barry try not to puke always made her day, but when he didn't stop, she started feeling stupid.

"Come on," she said, "it isn't that bad."

His face looking a pale shade of green, he managed a wan smile.

"Course it ain't, honey," he said, then gagged inadvertently. "Course it ain't."

Chapter Twenty-Five

In the early light before dawn, Teddy got out of bed. He'd made love to Maggie the night before, after the two of them had shared a bottle of good wine. It was something he'd picked up from the fancy liquor store on Washington Road, something better than the Three-buck Chuck they normally bought from Trader Joe's. She'd remarked on it, asked what the celebration was, and he told her it was because he didn't have to lie to her anymore; he'd solved the case. This made her happy, and over the bottle of wine he made up a story about a clandestine operation he'd undertaken, and how, in the end, he got his man.

"That was why I had to keep it a secret," he'd said, and she covered his face with kisses.

Before that, at dinner, he'd listened to his daughter tell him all about her day, laughing at the appropriate times, and commiserating with her when required. It was later, after Emily had gone to bed, that he and Maggie slipped up to their room as silently as possible and did the horizontal bop once, then twice. In the afterglow, they talked for almost an hour, and Maggie seemed so happy knowing that her nagging had finally coerced her husband into fessing up. They'd kissed passionately once before the light was extinguished, and over the course of a long, tortuous night, Teddy thought about how much he loved them both, and was saddened by how much they would miss him.

He quietly gathered his clothes from the closet and the dresser, and went into the living room to dress. He then dumped coffee into a filter and turned on the coffee maker, and while waiting for it to brew, he sat at the kitchen table with a pen and paper and wrote his goodbye note. In his heart, he desperately hoped he'd see them again, but he knew the odds were greatly stacked against it. He felt within him a sense of betrayal at not telling his wife of over twenty years to her face that she was about to become a widow, but he was powerless to do it any other way. He loved her tremendously, and within that love was a man who knew his wife very well. She'd stop at nothing to save him, even if it meant sacrificing Gina. Not that she would do it deliberately, but she'd feel that the law had to intervene, that they could, and *would* save the day. She wasn't aware that the Mexican drug cartels played by no rules except those that they dictated, and theirs were fast and hard, unbreakable by any mortal. When a situation called for death, they offered dismemberment to boot. Like America's stance on terrorists, they too did not negotiate. When he finished, ending the letter on a high note, insinuating he'd return, he placed it by the coffee pot, and strode silently toward the door, exited, and got in his vehicle. There was one more stop he had to make before he met with Bobby and they drove off to his imminent demise, but he was going to keep that errand to himself, if only for Bobby's safety. The less he knew, the better.

Backing the car out of the garage, he hoped the sound of the electric door opener wouldn't awaken either his wife or child, and as he pulled out of the driveway and onto the barren street, he acknowledged that he got his wish.

"I love you both," he whispered as he drove away. "Please know I didn't want it to come to this…"

◆ ◆ ◆

Bobby stood next to his truck, shivering in just a t-shirt and shorts. Melissa had just left to go home and get ready for work, and he'd called his first four clients and told them he had to take a day off because of a family emergency. Only one of his clients had asked what it was, and he'd drawn a blank, clutching the phone in one hand while his other gave his sack a good rummage. Some people scratched their head while they were thinking; Bobby liked to tug on his pecker. To each their own.

"My daughter needs me," was what he eventually came up with, and this satisfied Ms. Albright.

"OK, dear. When can you clean the pool?"

"Can I make it up on Saturday?" he'd asked, and she said that was fine.

He stood there waiting for some time, and just when he was going to go back in the house to get a jacket, he saw Teddy's cruiser turn onto his street. He felt a flash of fear streak through him, a gut-wrenching uneasiness that made him shiver all over, this time not from the early morning desert cold. He felt as if he was watching a ghost drive toward him and wondered how he'd go through life without Teddy. It didn't seem possible, now that he really thought about it. Teddy was his oldest and dearest friend. He was his *only* friend, not counting his chemical-imbibing counterparts. His breathing suddenly hitched, and without him realizing it, a sob escaped him, sounding more like the moan of the aforementioned ghost. As his cousin pulled the car over to the side of the road, he felt a hollow feeling in the pit of his stomach, an aching melancholy that couldn't be quelled. The passenger window rolled down, and Teddy's face appeared. Bobby looked in at him, vaguely noticed that something about his uniform was different. It looked like he was wearing a larger coat than usual.

"You going to stand there all day, or are we going to go and get your daughter?"

Bobby stood there dumbly for a moment, not knowing what to do or say, when Teddy leaned over and opened the door for him.

"Get your ass in here. It's chilly outside."

So Bobby got in, and in the hush of the predawn morning they drove away.

◆　◆　◆

They didn't have to wait long once they arrived at the Chinese Buffet Palace, a fancy name for a crap shack that offered nothing but deep-fried artery-clogging fare. A black Mercedes pulled up about five minutes after they'd parked, and when a man got out of the car by himself, Bobby did the same.

"I'm glad to see you did as we asked, Mr. Travis," the man said, and Bobby realized he recognized him from Hooligans. He was the manager, Carlos. Bobby had only met him in passing (most times wasted), but he remembered his face.

"Yeah," Bobby said quietly, wishing someone else would pull into the lot, maybe a family of six-foot-six famished sasquatches, but it was too early for egg rolls and chop suey. Besides, they were in the back of the place, away from the street, just as Carlos had ordered. "What are you going to do to him?" he asked, although he didn't want to hear the answer. The other looked back grimly in return.

"You know what we are going to do."

Bobby glanced back at the Mercedes. Because of the tinted windows, he couldn't see if anyone else was inside.

"Where's Gina and Ruby?" He nodded toward the car. "Are they in there?"

Carlos shook his head. "No, but they are safe."

"They're not here?" A frown creased Bobby's face, the idea of treachery amplifying his disquiet. "I thought we had a deal!"

"You'll get your daughter, Mr. Travis, as soon as we have Sergeant Teddy Barnes in our custody."

"That isn't fair."

"I never said this was going to be fair," Carlos said coldly. "You should know that until our interests are taken care of, we'll do anything to protect ourselves. Do you understand?"

"Oh yeah," Bobby said, a feeling of vertigo overtaking him. For a moment, he felt as if he was going to faint. "When do I get my daughter?"

"After we get your cousin." Carlos regarded him blandly, not even attempting congeniality. He hated repeating himself. "We'll call you."

Bobby looked down for a moment, squinting his eyes against tears that wanted to form and trying to keep his breathing even. He should have known they'd try to trick him. They weren't exactly what you'd call gentlemen.

"So...I'm supposed to hand over my cousin and then...just wait for you to call me? Pardon me for saying, but I think that sucks." He choked back another sob, almost certain he'd never see his daughter again. "I think you're setting me up."

Carlos shook his head. "No, Mr. Travis, that is not what we are do-ing." He smiled, but it was devoid of anything remotely humorous. "Now go."

"Go?"

"Yes, Mr. Travis, go. We'll call you."

"But I, um, I drove here with, um...Teddy."

"The bus that stops on Mission and Regal will take you back to Valley Center, but you have to make sure to get a transfer pass. You'll be switch-ing buses." He pressed a five-dollar bill into Bobby's palm. "Now get out of here and wait for us to call."

Bobby turned and took a last look at Teddy, sitting behind the wheel of his cruiser. His cousin's face was seamed with wrinkles that seemingly sprouted up overnight, his bleak expression betraying his apprehension, but his steel gray eyes showing a fortitude most men could not sum-mon even if they had a gun to their head, which soon enough he would. Bobby's mouth opened wordlessly, and, as if he'd heard everything they just said, Teddy nodded. He mouthed one word: "Go."

Bobby didn't know what else to do, so he did what was requested of him: he turned around and walked away, taking one last look over his shoulder and nodding slowly at the man he'd grown up with, a man who'd helped him through his entire adult life as he found nothing but trouble. He sometimes thought that Teddy had become a cop just so Bobby had someone to bail him out every time he got arrested. It was a standard joke he'd made every year at Thanksgiving, if he was sober enough to attend. To walk away from him like this, the other condemned to die, made him feel very low indeed. There was also the matter of his daughter still being in their clutches. Someone was getting fucked here, and it didn't take a rocket scientist with a wall full of degrees to figure out who it was. Christ, he could practically feel the balls slapping against his taint. As he shuffled away, he wondered who was going to help him now, whom he could trust once Teddy was gone.

When no answer came to him, he realized, without any uncertainty, that there was no one. He was all alone. A moan escaped him yet again, followed quickly by another. This was how he made his way to the bus stop, one choked sob at a time.

◆ ◆ ◆

After Bobby disappeared around the corner of the building, Teddy took a deep breath and opened the door of the squad car, stepping into the bright, early morning sunshine. He was about to close the door when the man in the suit called out to him.

"Stop right where you are, Sergeant Barnes, and remove your duty belt."

"I'll need both hands to take it off."

"Do it, but slowly."

Teddy's duty belt had a three-way buckle system called a "Coplock", which required him to depress a third release catch to unbuckle it. This extra security was so that no one but the wearer could remove the belt, and required two hands. His nervous fingers fumbled with it a moment, and when it was open he gently placed it on the ground and kicked it toward the other.

"Shoulder holster?"

Teddy unzipped his jacket down to his sternum and showed the other he did not have one.

"Ankle holster?" Carlos wasn't taking any chances. If he did it was his ass, and that wasn't how this was going to go down. The Castillo family would lop off his balls and mail one to his first wife, and one to his second, just to make a point, especially since he was eschewing standard procedure and doing this without assistance from the assassin.

"Why don't we just go inside and you can search me there," Teddy said, glancing around. The neighborhood was starting to wake up, people slowly trickling by in ones and twos. Nobody of any importance, mostly old ladies on their way to Big Lots, and winos passing through en route to their favorite liquor store, but Carlos got the point. It might be best if they had some privacy.

"Don't try anything stupid," he advised Teddy, and the other grimaced.

"That's original," Teddy said, slowly walking toward him. "You come up with that yourself?"

Two men got out of the Mercedes, two very large men, and suddenly Teddy didn't feel like joking anymore. His mouth went dry just looking at them. They both had blank expressions on their otherwise unpleasant faces. It was apparent that they were the welcome committee.

"These two gentlemen will escort you inside," Carlos said, a smile flitting upon his lips, and at once everything stood out in stark contrast against the brilliant blue sky. As they walked forward, time seemed to slow down, and instinctively Teddy catalogued the various sounds that swirled around him, from the blaring of a car horn on Mission to the squawk of a seagull fighting with another over some prize in a nearby dumpster. The sun stopped at its point in the sky, and Teddy's shadow froze in a position of supplication as the two men approached, one on each side. Taking him by his arms, they helped him along to the rear delivery door, where Carlos was busy with a key, opening it and the screen door beyond, ushering them into the darkness inside, then following close behind. They marched through a hallway that bypassed the kitchen, the stench of stale grease and teriyaki floating in the air like a noxious cloud, leading them into the dining area. Carlos flipped a switch and a bank of lights flickered on along the far wall. The rest of the room lay draped in shadow.

The two men stood on each side of him, and following a nod from their boss, they reluctantly let go of his arms. He knew they'd search him soon, so he spoke quickly, trying to distract them from the inevitable.

"Where's the girl and her dog?" he asked as casually as he could. Nonetheless, his stomach was twisting and roiling. He could feel sweat trickle down his sides, and he hoped there wasn't a visible sheen of perspiration on his forehead. He wanted to appear calm, strong, and sweat would disprove that in a heartbeat.

"You don't have to worry about that," Carlos guffawed, grinning a truly awful smile. "In a few minutes you won't have to worry about anything anymore."

"Humor me, huh? It couldn't hurt."

Carlos looked at him for a moment, mentally deciding something, then he shrugged. "I suppose it couldn't. You won't be walking away from this."

"So...I'm right?"

"Right about what, Sergeant Barnes?"

"You guys work for a drug cartel, and you're moving narcotics through Hooligans."

Carlos laughed again, this time with genuine sincerity. "Of course we are. That's why you're here." He looked at Teddy contemptuously. "Is that really all you wanted to ask me?"

"No," Teddy said, "I just wanted to get that out of the way." He licked his lips, knowing that the answer to the next question was not going to make him happy. In fact, he knew it was going to be downright depressing, but he wanted to know, *needed* to know. "So Bobby and Gina, and the dog...you're not going to let them live either, are you?"

The smile left Carlos's face, replaced by a look so sinister that Teddy was afraid it would be the last question he'd be allowed to ask. But instead the man shook his head, his eyes burning fiercely in his sockets, virtually radiating venom.

"If it were up to me, maybe *I* would," Carlos said, taking out a pack of cigarettes and tapping one out. With his other hand, he removed a gold lighter from his pants pocket. He lit the cigarette, and smoke swirled and eddied around his head. "But it isn't up to me; it is up to the Castillo family, and they don't want any loose ends."

"So you let Bobby walk away so you could what, kill him later?" At once something occurred to him. "Is Gina still alive?" He couldn't help the note of fear that entered his voice, and he couldn't believe he hadn't thought of that sooner. It wasn't as if he'd walked into this without a plan, but on another level (most likely wishful thinking), he actually thought that these men would have brought the girl. Of course, when he considered the fact that he was dealing with men who worked for a Mexican drug cartel, all bets were off, way off.

Carlos chuckled once more, and it sounded so smug that Teddy wished he could punch the smile right off the bastard's face. He nearly raised his hands, ready to ball them into fists, when he thought of the bigger picture, took a deep breath, and left them hanging by his sides.

Wait for it.

"Is she?" Suddenly it was very important that Teddy know this, for it was imperative to his scheme.

"She's with somebody safe," Carlos said, and Teddy's blood ran cold. He thought of his snitch, how the man had disappeared from work mere hours after Teddy had spoken with him, never to show up again.

"For how long?"

Carlos shook his head. "You certainly do have a lot of questions for a man who isn't in any position to do anything about it." He dropped the half-smoked cigarette onto the floor and crushed it with an expensive looking Italian loafer. Then he looked at his men, gave them a nod. "Search him, make sure he's clean, then get rid of him."

As the words were leaving the other's mouth Teddy realized this was it, time to make or break. His plan was shit; he was well aware of the fact, and it still may leave his wife a widow and his daughter fatherless, but it was all he'd had time to prepare for. As it stood he didn't even know if it would work. He just had to have faith that his half-assed preparation was going to save (more like possibly *salvage*) the day.

He took three long steps back, away from the two guards, and unzipped his jacket completely, revealing the block of C-4 strapped around his stomach with his belt. Duct taped to the top was a small detonator with a single toggle switch. From it two wires were attached to blasting caps embedded in the side of the block. It was of shoddy construction, but he knew it would do what he intended, should it come to that.

"Take one step toward me and I'll blow us all sky high," he warned, his hand on the switch, and this stopped the men cold.

Carlos blinked once, then twice. His face didn't so much as twitch as he quickly assessed the situation. It only took him three seconds to realize that they should do as he asked.

"I tole ju we should have let the assassin take care of this!" one of his men said, and Carlos glared at him.

"Shut up, Armando, and stay where you are," he said, and the other scowled at him in return but held his tongue and his ground. Carlos lowered his voice, attempted amiability. "So, a standoff is it, hmm?"

Teddy smiled. "I guess so."

"We can't let you leave," Carlos said, and his words were so sincere that Teddy had no reason to doubt him. The triumph he'd felt for a brief moment was swiftly washed away. "We'll die either way, you see? If you don't kill us, the Castillo family will for letting you get away." Carlos regarded Teddy with a forbidding "we're all in this together" look. "Go ahead and detonate it. At least we'll have done our job."

Again, Teddy should have realized this, and he cursed his own thoughtlessness. Did he really think he'd show them the bomb and they'd just let him walk away? For the love of freakin' Jesus he actually *had* thought that, and if not *thought* it at least hoped it could happen. But these weren't run-of-the mill criminals; not to beat a dead horse, but they were *cartel* men. They didn't do anything by the book. They died when they had to, simply to save the organization. They went to prison instead of snitching because to snitch was to undergo a slow, painful death. And letting someone go who could blow the whistle on their operation? They'd rather watch half of their men get killed than have the whole business crumble. And Teddy had foolishly failed to make this connection, and now it was too late. He could kill these men (and unfortunately himself as well), but it would not save Gina, Ruby or Bobby.

"Have you thought about your own family?" Carlos asked, and suddenly he had Teddy's attention in a big way. He flinched as if struck, but his hand never left the toggle switch.

"You keep my family out of this!"

"You are an imprudent man if you didn't think we'd planned every little detail," Carlos said, taking a confident step forward. At once he no longer seemed afraid. "We can't take the chance that your family knows something, now can we?"

"They don't know anything!" Teddy cried, taking a step forward to match the others, although his was wrought of fear. How could that detail have eluded him? "You leave them out of this!"

"If you kill us, you leave the others no choice. Their orders are to terminate your family, should something happen to us." Carlos shook his head. "It would be a terrible thing if something bad happened to them."

With these words Teddy immediately understood something: no matter what he did these men (or others in the cartel) would go after his family. Carlos was probably lying to try and save his life (that Teddy's wife and daughter had a chance of survival), and the truth was that everyone connected to this breach of information was slated for termination. If he killed them, others who worked for the organization would go after Maggie and Emily, yet if he let them live, that would undoubtedly be their next stop before heading over to Bobby's house. No matter what he did, all roads led to one great big massacre until everyone who may know anything about these men were dead and buried, more likely picked apart by coyotes. Teddy steeled himself against the inexorable, becoming aware that this was no longer a bluff, if it ever had been. Probably not.

"Go ahead," he said, the thumb and forefinger of his left hand firmly clamped to the toggle switch that would effectively detonate the C-4. Meanwhile his right hand slipped stealthily to the clasp on his belt. Even though he'd misjudged Carlos and the cartel, he'd had the foresight to use one of his tactical belts to hold the bomb in place. Unlike a regular belt (and his duty belt), these were easily opened by squeezing the top and bottom of the plastic fastener. "Do whatever you want to my family, but none of us is walking out of here."

Yet again a look of fear crossed Carlos's otherwise calm features, but this time it passed quickly. In his business (as in Teddy's) death could come any day to claim you. He'd obviously made peace with that fact a long time ago, although Teddy was still at odds with such an outcome. So, this was when he decided a lie was in order, maybe something that could perhaps save his family.

"I sent a letter to my attorney's office. There are instructions in there he should follow, in the event of my untimely demise."

"You don't say." Carlos didn't believe him for a second, but he indulged the other his fantasy.

"That's right," Teddy said hastily, licking his lips. "I have all of your names in a file, and photographs to prove it, in a safety deposit box. I told him where the key was..."

Carlos shook his head. "I'm disappointed in you Sergeant Barnes," he said. "Surely you can come up with something more convincing than that."

"It's true."

"I'm certain that you believe it is."

Teddy hung his head, wished he was a better liar. "So, that's it then, huh?" he said, and the other nodded.

"I guess so."

"Now what?"

"You know, Sergeant," the trim, neat Mexican man said. "Either let us do our job, or go ahead and blow us up."

Teddy's hand trembled on the switch, his muscles tensed, sweat now cascading down his brow like the Niagara Falls. He knew his eyes were wide, crazy looking, and whose wouldn't be, right? Not when you're staring at your own death in the face, and you haven't done everything you wanted to do yet in this lifetime.

I wanted to see Emily grow up, to graduate from high school, then college. I was supposed to walk her down the aisle when she got married, was supposed to be the one to throw her and her husband a surprise party on their ten-year anniversary. Maggie and I were going to grow old together, live well into the twilight of our lives, spending it on some beach in Hawaii while Emily and her husband gave us grandchildren we could come back to California and visit. I wasn't supposed to die here in this derelict Chinese restaurant with a bunch of men who were willing to die for an organization that wouldn't let them live if they didn't do their jobs properly. A bunch of goddamn lowlife criminals nobody gives a crap about. It wasn't supposed to end like this, not...like...this...

"What are you waiting for, Sergeant?" Carlos said again, and something in Teddy's mind snapped.

"This," Teddy said, and in one deft movement he released the clasp on the belt then flipped the toggle. The last thing he saw was the look of terror on Carlos's face before the world turned to fire.

◆ ◆ ◆

Three blocks away, Bobby first heard the explosion, then a moment later actually felt the concussive wind of the blast. A warm breeze hit him and with it the smell of gun powder and burned plastic. The obstreperous sound of shattering glass and pulverized cement soon followed. He swiveled his head around on a neck that felt like it was attached with rubber bands and saw thick black smoke rising up into the sky from the direction of the Chinese restaurant. His mouth fell open; if it had been on a hinge, it would have made a screech like a rusty door. Instinct sent him running toward the billowing clouds of noxious flames, and from somewhere unknown he heard someone screaming. It didn't take him very long to cross the distance from the bus stop back to the Chinese Buffet Palace, but by the time he got there the entire place was engulfed in flames.

"Oh my God!" he gasped, his eyes wide, his heart beating wildly in his chest, almost as fast as it did when he was snorting meth or cocaine. For the second time in the space of an hour, he thought he was going to pass out. Traffic stopped on Mission Avenue as drivers rubbernecked, and pieces of wreckage rained down intermittently from the sky, scorched and burning embers of plastic, wood, and other indeterminate material. "Teddy!"

He ran around to the back and saw that the Mercedes was ablaze, covered in seared rubble. Teddy's squad car sat deserted, the driver side door open. No one emerged from the building, and there were no bodies lying in the immediate vicinity. Everyone was dead, burned alive. But how did it happen? Bobby wondered. Who detonated a bomb?

Like the slap of an open palm against his face, Bobby suddenly knew.

Teddy did. Those guys were going to shoot him, so he came prepared, like a good cop would do. Only he couldn't get out on time, and the captain had to go down with the ship.

A strangled cry escaped him, this time with the dread certainty that his cousin was now, once and forever more, dead. The sob was followed by another, and soon tears were running down his face. He fell to his knees, buried his head in his hands, and that's when he heard the sirens, quickly approaching. Without another thought he stood, took one step, then two.

They still have Gina and Ruby. He backed away, watching as the flames licked hungrily at the remains of the building. *I have to get out of here; there is nothing the police can do for me.*

So he bolted, not knowing exactly where he was going, but certain that he couldn't be associated with this, not now. If he talked to the police, then it was over for his daughter. He was sure about that. The men who had her, they wouldn't think twice about killing her if Bobby spilled the beans about their operation.

On legs that felt as if they would collapse anytime, he hastily fled the area, taking a roundabout course back to the bus stop, hoping he could find his way home.

Chapter Twenty-Six

Carlos had arrived at the house around seven thirty in the morning, shortly after Gina had gotten up, and the gangbanger escorted her and Ruby outside so she could take care of her business. Her guard smoked a cigarette while he waited, but Ruby was like a well-oiled machine; she always urinated and defecated promptly because she knew there was going to be a meal that soon followed. She was no dummy. While she did her thing, Gina watched as Carlos leaned over the seat to tell the driver something, then primly exited the Mercedes and proceeded slowly up the sidewalk, his eyes on hers. She'd tried to hold his gaze but couldn't. She quickly looked away.

"Good morning young lady," he'd said, and she muttered something unintelligible in return. Although they'd met only once, and briefly at that, she didn't like him. Gina could see right through his phony civility. She knew that inside him beat the heart of a scoundrel, a man who would stop at nothing to get what he wanted. It practically oozed from his pores like sweat.

Fortunately, Carlos's visit had been short. He'd spoken briefly with her sentry and then made a quick departure with Armando in tow, and as far as Gina knew today was no different than any other day. She did wonder, however, when she was going to be set free, but she knew better than to ask. These men had been almost kind to her (in that they hadn't hurt or frightened her), and the last thing she wanted to do was ruffle any feathers. And their respect for Ruby had been almost unheralded. They truly must be dog lovers.

So, after Ruby had enjoyed a bowl of her hypoallergenic dry food topped with a tablespoon of canned, Gina took her place on the couch in front of the TV, and the gangbanger (his name was Sid) took his usual

240

seat in the recliner. Their morning ritual had evolved over several days, but it was now mutually understood and agreed upon that they started with Good Morning America, and then segued into Dr. Phil, then the Jerry Springer show. It was over Springer that they really bonded, the two of them agreeing that the people who appeared on the program were righteously messed up indeed. They laughed together, sometimes even high-fived. Gina hated to admit it, but she was starting to like the guy. In his seamy, tattooed way he was kind of cute.

If Sid was asked what he thought of Gina, (he wouldn't, but what the heck, for the sake of the conversation), he'd most likely say she was pretty hip for a fifteen-year-old girl and (if it was one of his buddies asking) that her budding breasts and glossed lips were a precursor to the sexy woman she would become. She was pretty damn smart too; she caught on to things faster than most girls he knew her age.

"Ju want some Fruit Loops?" Sid asked after he turned on the television.

"Yes, please," Gina replied, smiling a pretty smile, and he got up from his chair to prepare their breakfast. When he returned, he handed her a jumbo-sized plastic dish she could have easily used a soup ladle with, overfilled with milk and the sugary cereal.

"Thank you," she said, and he smiled, flashing a gold-plated grin.

"Jore welcome."

So they got on well, the three of them, and it was only later when they caught wind that an extremely dangerous man would soon be crashing their party that they realized they had become friends of sorts, but by then it was too late to really do much about it.

◆ ◆ ◆

The bus dropped him off on Valley Center Parkway, about two hours after his journey began. He hadn't had to use public transportation in a long time, and he'd forgotten how inefficient it was out in this neck of the woods. You could get where you were going, but it took a while. He'd had to switch buses three times, once while still in Oceanside, then in Vista, and once more in San Marcos. It was just before eleven when he stepped off the bus into the dazzling sunshine. His first thought was that he should go home, get his (Terry's) truck and go to work, but when he thought about Teddy he felt nothing but apathy. The last thing he wanted to do was clean swimming pools. It was hopeless, everything was lost. With Teddy gone he didn't have a shot in hell of getting his daughter back, and the thought of losing her, too, made him so depressed he was nearly despondent. He stopped, looking in the direction of Bear Valley Road, and then turned and went the other way. Since he didn't want to work, he figured he might as well backslide the whole damn way down the hill. He didn't have any cash, but he did have his credit card, and if he was correct, it still had a little bit of credit on it.

When he walked through the front door and the familiar scent hit his nose, two feelings occurred to him simultaneously: the first was a sensation of pleasure, but it was quickly followed by a sickening lurch in the pit of his stomach when he thought about how one thing always led to another, and that what may seem right to him at the moment would later be *so* wrong when he was waking up on the floor of a flophouse with his pants around his ankles and gerbil stuck in his ass...or something of that nature. It was always a crap shoot, but the end results were continuously the same. Christ, and how long had he been clean? Almost two weeks? Man, did he really want to throw it all away?

"Bobby!" someone called, and he looked down the bar and saw that it was Tony. He nodded and smiled, not knowing what else to do, and because he'd been acknowledged, he now felt obligated to buy a drink. "Long time no see, man!"

"I didn't know you worked during the day," Bobby said, pulling up a stool and taking a load off.

"That's because you're never in here during the day, and if you are, you don't remember it," Tony said, smiling casually, opening a freezer and taking out a chilled mug. He poured a draft beer, and after laying down a coaster, set it on top. "This one is on the house."

Bobby looked at it, at the thousands of tiny bubbles as they danced from the bottom to the top of the glass, at the condensation that formed on the outside, little beads of water that popped up then slid down the side once they got too heavy. It was...perfection, beauty, a thing of joy, and he was so parched, wasn't he? So thirsty he could hardly produce any spit. He reached for it, gripped the handle loosely.

"I heard you were on the wagon," Tony said, removing a towel that was draped over his shoulder and wiping a glass with it.

"I am," Bobby replied, letting go of the handle, retracting his hand. If he was on the wagon, this was not the place he should be, that was for damn sure. He fumbled for his wallet, almost falling off the stool, he was so desperate to get it out.

"I told you Bobby, this one is on the house."

Bobby shook his head. He wasn't looking for money, he was looking for his sponsor's card, someone he could call who would talk some sense into him. He'd never used it before; hell, he'd never needed (wanted) to. In all actuality, he'd forgotten who his sponsor *was*, but right now he needed that person more than he'd ever needed anyone in his life. He dug through bank receipts, unused gift cards for long-closed stores, a library card he seldom used, business cards of people he was never going to call until, at last, he found it. It had the AA logo on it, a number, and a name.

Oh, shit.

The name was Ricky Bukowski, and he sure as shootin' couldn't help Bobby, not anymore. Hell, even if the poor bastard was alive, the last thing Ricky would ever do is try and talk someone *out* of having a drink. Dead or alive, the card was useless. Why had he been his sponsor anyway?

Because you didn't want to quit drinking.

Right. That made sense. That's why he couldn't remember whose name was on the damn thing; he'd never had occasion to use it.

Good choice, man. Good fucking choice.

Bobby looked up and saw the expectant look on Tony's face. Here he'd gone and given Bobby a free beer, and Bobby was trying to think of a way not to drink it. Now, that wasn't very neighborly of him, was it? It sure seemed like a crappy thing to do. I mean, someone had to pay for that beer, and even if it was only a Pabst Blue Ribbon, one of the all-time crappiest of American-made swills, it was free, and that wasn't a price you argued with, not if you were a decent human being. How could he be so rude?

Bobby reached out and grasped the handle again. He could swear there was an evil glint in Tony's eyes, but as he hefted the glass he told himself it was just a trick of the light. He lifted it high, brought it to his lips. A flood of faces came to him: Teddy's, Gina's, Ruby's (with her big grin and her tongue flopping out), Carolyn's, and then, at last, Melissa's. Oh, man, was she going to be disappointed in him if he screwed everything up.

But that's how he rolled. Undoubtedly, it was what was expected of him. When the going got rough, the tough got wasted. It was the American way, or something of that nature. And who cared anyway? Everyone he knew and loved would be dead soon anyhow, maybe even himself, so he might as well loosen up a little and have a drink. Christ, one couldn't hurt him.

With his first sip an explosion of delight detonated within him, and he chugged the beer in a breath. Tony watched him with a look of amusement on his face, continuing to clean beer mugs. The place wasn't exactly hopping, not like on a Friday night; he had time to tool around. The beer hit his empty stomach, got dumped into his bloodstream, and then bounced right up into his head, giving him a pleasant glow he hadn't experienced in what felt like so, very, very long. He almost wept with pleasure, and before he could think he was holding out the mug.

"Refill, please," he said, and Tony took it and gently set it into a sink of sudsy water.

"Sure, tiger, sure. But you better not drink 'em all like that, or you'll blow chunks all over the place." He got a fresh glass and poured him another Pabst. "You gotta pace yourself."

Bobby ignored him and chugged the second as well, then the third. And when the three beers collectively hit him, he felt another need arise, one that certainly spelled trouble for Bobby, and anyone whom he would later deal with.

"Hey man," he said, looking around furtively to make sure no one was listening, "you holding?"

"Always," came the reply, and shortly thereafter (following a trip to the ATM and a handshake hand-off) Bobby was in his favorite stall with a rolled-up dollar bill to his nose, insufflating poorly ground crystal that burned as if he'd inserted a flame thrower in his nostril. And when his heart started beating in time to a Five Finger Death Punch song (one that was playing in his head over and over at 180 beats per minute), he popped one and then two Xanax. After that he had another beer, and then another line, and then another Xanax.

And then he didn't remember anything at all.

♦ ♦ ♦

The phone on the wall rang once, twice, three times, was about to go to voicemail when Maggie scrambled to pick it up.

"Hello?" she said breathlessly. She'd read Teddy's note no less than five times when she'd awoke this morning and found him gone. She'd paced and fretted, but she'd kept a brave face in front of her daughter when she came downstairs for breakfast, in fact had allowed her to go over to her best friend's house when she was finished, to do whatever it was teenage girls liked to do during the summer. Listen to music, maybe, probably talk about boys. It was better she was out of the house anyway; she didn't want Emily to see her this upset while she figured everything out. After she'd left, Maggie called the police station, desperate for an answer. The officer she talked to hadn't known anything about Teddy meeting drug dealers who may be responsible for kidnapping Bobby Travis' daughter, but he assured her that he would look into the matter and get back to her as soon as he could. He'd sounded curt at first, maybe thought she was putting him on, but by the end of the call she was certain she had his attention. "This is Maggie."

There was a brief pause, yet it was long enough to fill her with dread. As she sat there in limbo, she hoped against hope that it *was* the officer she'd talked to, that he was calling her back to let her know that everything would be all right. She urgently needed for it to be so because if something happened to Teddy, she had no idea what she and Emily would do.

"Hello?" she said again, the earnestness in her tone undisguised.

The person on the other end spoke, issuing instructions, but initially what they said made no sense.

"Who is this, and what are you *talking* about?"

The other spoke again, slower this time, carefully outlining what she had to do, and when they stopped speaking she understood entirely. Being a policeman's wife, she was used to being given serious warnings and was intelligent enough to know when she should act upon them immediately. Having said their piece, the phone went dead in her ear. She placed it back on the cradle, much calmer now, and went upstairs and packed a bag. She then packed one for Emily. When she was finished, she called her daughter's best friend's mother, asked her politely how she was doing, then informed her that she would be coming to get Emily. There had been a death in the family, and she was going to take her to be with relatives. The woman expressed shock, asked if there was anything she could do and if she should tell the girl.

"Thank you for offering, but no. There's nothing you can do. And I'll tell her myself," Maggie said. "Please just make sure she's ready to go in about fifteen minutes. I'm leaving now."

"I will," the woman said. "I'm very sorry for your loss."

"Me too," Maggie said, and hung up the phone.

◆ ◆ ◆

Bits and pieces of memory were scattered here and there; like body parts strewn along a highway after a gruesome car wreck, Bobby found there were a few things that stuck with him after the proverbial lights went out. Like a tall, red-headed stripper at The Wolves Den taking the sunglasses off his head, inserting them someplace the sun didn't shine, putting them back on his head, and he and some random strangers taking turns sniffing them. Quick cut to: standing five deep in a stall in the decrepit bathroom of the place, everyone waiting their turn to take a bump of crystal, and once they did, going around the circle one more time. One of the guys lingered after everyone had gone, and he offered Bobby a blowjob if he'd hook him up with a little dope to take home. The memory was as warped as a wooden porch railing after twenty years of steady rain, but Bobby recalled telling him no.

There were a few more scattered recollections, like riding shotgun in a rundown pickup truck, destination unknown, the bed filled with hooting and hollering Mexicans who didn't know any English and smoked weed like it was going to be declared obsolete at the stroke of midnight, and later proposing to some mystery woman while he was holding on to a life preserver, trying desperately not to drown in what appeared to be a pool filled with Jell-O.

But that was about it, and maybe that was for the best after all.

◆ ◆ ◆

"Bobby, earth to Bobby! Come in, come in!"

He felt a palm smack him across the face, but the pain was remote, distant.

"Bobby, wake the hell up!"

This time a flurry of blows struck him, and he could feel cold wetness trickling down upon him. As if he were struggling to rise from the depths of an immense ocean, he arose within his mind swimming faster, feeling as if his life depended on it. Up and up he went, and finally, consciousness returned to him, and he opened his eyes. The first thing he saw was that he was in a bathtub. The second thing he saw was Melissa kneeling beside him. Guilt blossomed within him as the realization of what he'd done came to him, accompanied by a wave of nausea that shot through him like bolt of lightning.

"You don't look so hot—"

He suddenly erupted in a hot, slimy gush, and Melissa back pedaled, trying to get out of the way.

"Jesus, Bobby!"

He hung his head over the side of the tub, retching pathetically.

"I'm sorry," he babbled, puke dribbling off his chin. "I'm so sorry…"

Instead of yelling at him and getting mad, she waited for his barfing to subside, then cradled his head in her hands, whispering "shh" as she did so. When he stopped shaking and his stomach settled, he raised a hand to his lips, wiped his mouth, then lifted his eyes to meet hers.

"I know I shouldn't have done it," he said sheepishly, "and I know it didn't help anything, but I just couldn't stop myself."

"We all fall down sometimes, Bobby," she told him softly, and at once he realized he loved her. Any other woman probably would have hollered at him and called him a worthless drunk, but not Melissa. This chick, she was all right.

"Is it Tuesday morning?"

"Last time I checked."

"I skipped work yesterday, and it looks like I'm skipping it again today."

"I think there are worse things, don't you?"

"Teddy's dead," he said, and she nodded gravely.

"I know, Bobby."

"You do?"

"You told me last night."

"I did?"

"Yes, right before you proposed to me."

"I did what?"

"You asked me to marry you," she said, and again a surge of emotion raced through him.

"What did you say?" All of a sudden the answer was very important to him. Even though his head was aching fit to beat the band, his vision making everything appear as if he was swimming in molasses, and his sinuses felt as if they had been scraped raw with sandpaper, he desperately needed to know her answer to his question. How his life went forward from this moment counted on it.

She looked at him primly and shook her head. "As a card-carrying sex addict, I don't know where it can go from here. I adore you Bobby, but that's one hell of a commitment."

"But...but, all the time we've spent together...doesn't that mean something?"

"Of course it does, Bobby, you know that."

"So what are you saying?"

"Are you sure you can live with the fact that I might get the urge to fool around?"

"That depends; the football team or the cheerleading squad?"

"I'm trying to be serious, Bobby."

"I am too, and you know I have the same kind of problems—"

"Not like I do, Bobby," she said. "Think about it. Can you deal with it?"

He opened his mouth to answer, but she put a finger on his lips. "Shut up. Think."

He closed his yap and considered it. Meanwhile the world spun around him in a foggy miasma of swirling colors, the light undulating through the ripped and soiled curtains that had been hanging there since he was a boy. He blinked his eyes once or twice to try and clear his vision, but inside his head a siren was blatting, a motor was belching smoke, and his brain pan was dripping extract of fart vapor, but none of that mattered, not now.

"I don't care if you blow Mickey the Mouse while Minnie watches! I love you!"

She smiled, a wide, bright smile that lit up the whole room. "That's all I needed to hear, Bobby." She batted her eyes seductively. "The answer is yes."

His heart did a flip-flop in his chest. "Really? That's great!" He reached out for her, gave her a half-assed hug. "But can you deal with me?"

"You'll get your shit together," she said, winking. "I'm sure of it. As long as sobriety doesn't make you weird." She inspected him closely. "You're not going to start fondling little kids, are you?"

"Not my style," he said, trying to get up. "I prefer animals and inanimate objects."

"Wow, settle my beating heart! Sex is going to be very interesting, I think."

"You ain't seen nothing yet," he said, returning her wink.

"Are you ready to get out of the tub? You're more prune than man."

"How long have I been in here?"

"Long enough."

"Give me a hand?"

She took him by one arm and helped to hoist him out. When he stood, he realized he was naked.

"Holy cow," she remarked, "you give the term 'shrinkage' a whole new meaning."

He looked down at himself, then had to squint. "Someone must have lopped it off last night."

"Don't tell me it was the stripper who stuck your sunglasses up her ass."

"Huh?" He looked at her self-consciously again. "I told you that?"

"Don't worry about it. I threw them away."

"Crap! Um, I mean…good?"

"That's better. Now get dressed and come into the living room. I have some medicine for you that will make you feel better."

"OK."

And she left him alone to TCB.

◆ ◆ ◆

"Weed?" he said, taken by surprise. "The medicine you're talking about is weed?"

"Yes, Bobby, marijuana. My advice is that you take two hits and sit back on the couch for a few minutes. It'll get rid of your headache and allow you to think things through."

"The last thing I need is drugs."

"No, the last thing you need is booze and methamphetamine. This will actually help you."

"It will?"

"Trust me."

She handed him a large glass pipe and a Bic lighter, and he looked at it uncertainly for a moment before shrugging and toking up. He'd smoked weed plenty of times in his life, but he'd graduated to the harder stuff pretty quickly, shortly after becoming an alcoholic. He took a big hit, held it, and then blew it out.

"That tastes pretty good," he said, licking his lips.

"Take another one."

"OK." He lit it again, taking a bigger hit, and this time he held it until he absolutely couldn't anymore. When he blew out the smoke, he felt the familiar feeling of the drug settle over him like a calming blanket, and he wondered why he'd eschewed it so long ago in favor of other, more dangerous drugs. "That feels pretty good," he said, handing the pipe back to her. She took it and the lighter, sparking up a massive plume of smoke before inhaling for all she was worth. She smiled as she held it, then blew it out.

"I figured you'd think so," she said.

"How long have you been a smoker?"

"Since I was a kid."

"How come you've never smoked in front of me?"

"Because I didn't know how badly you needed it."

"What's that supposed to mean?"

"Your impulse control is out of hand. This stuff right here will put it all in perspective."

"What?"

"Quiet, we're not going to talk right now. We're going to just relax and think our own thoughts for a bit, all right?"

"OK..."

For twenty minutes they sat there, and Bobby could not believe how right she was. His thoughts decelerated, and he found he was easily able to catalogue and evaluate all the things he had done in the last twenty-four hours. As he looked back on everything, he realized what an idiot he'd been. It all came to him so clearly; he was surprised that it hadn't before. He reflected on all the events that transpired to bring him to this exact point in time, every last thing, and as he finally caught up with the present he was in awe of how silly (and downright dangerous and reckless) some of the things he'd done were. Not just over the last day, but over the last twenty years.

"I'm a total retard," he said at last, and Melissa looked at him with a crooked grin.

"Not totally, but let's just say you are sometimes 'judgement impaired.'"

"I don't know what the hell you see in me," he said honestly. "I'm surprised I'm not in prison."

"Luck probably has a lot to do with that."

"And Teddy..." Sorrow swept through him. "Oh man, Teddy..."

"Not your fault, Bobby. You did nothing to put his life in danger. Everything he did for you he did to help, and I'm sure he didn't know who he was getting involved with when he was doing his investigating."

"Hooligans must be a front for a Mexican drug cartel."

"Must be."

"They might even come after me."

"Honey," she said softly, "they undoubtedly will."

He lapsed into silence, the impact of her words making his heart skip a beat. Another thought hit him hard, figuratively between the eyes, and it was so staggering he almost fell off the couch with the weight of it.

"Holy shit!" He looked at her with large, fearful eyes. "If they come after me, they're going to come after everybody I know, too." He swallowed hard, not liking his train of thoughts but knowing he had to voice them. "That means—"

"It means they're going to come after me too, Bobby," she said, reaching out and massaging his shoulder. "That's why I needed you to smoke. I needed you to think." She shook her head. "We're both dead if we don't do something, you know that, right?"

"I do now," he said, and he did, he really did. "I was so stupid to waste my time getting fucked-up. For all I know, Gina could be dead by now!"

"We don't know that," she said soothingly, "but we have to find out. You can't beat yourself up for what you did; you have to move on from that. What we need is a plan. We can't just sit here and do nothing. We have to come up with a way to help her."

He nodded, knowing that stagnation would be the death of him and everyone he loved, but in a way, it felt hopeless. For the life of him he couldn't honestly think of what to do.

"Do you have any ideas?" he asked her. "Because I, for one, am tapped out."

She nodded. "I have a few thoughts on the matter." She looked at him earnestly. "Would you like to hear them?"

"I'm all ears."

So she told him her plan, and the more she said, the more excited he got.

"You think it might work?" he asked when she finished.

"I don't know, Bobby, but we have to do something."

"OK," he agreed, "then we'll do it." He stood. "No better time than the present, huh?"

She looked at her watch and nodded. "No better time." She appraised him briefly, making a decision. "But give me your keys," she said at last. "I better drive."

Chapter Twenty-Seven

Pacing nervously, Carolyn chain-smoked one cigarette after another as she stalked from one end of the living room to the other. Barry sat on the couch in his usual place, engaged in his usual activity, which was akin to doing nothing. Silver Bullet in one hand, cigarette in the other, infomercial for a hair loss remedy on the tube. Did life get any better than this? If it did, he didn't want to know about it. But after a while, Carolyn's restlessness got to him.

"Why don't you sit down? You'll wear a hole in the rug."

"We haven't heard anything about Gina in over a day," she said, taking a deep drag from her cigarette, stubbing it out in an overfull ashtray, and immediately lighting another. "Teddy should have called us by now." She frowned, well, frowned deeper. "Or Bobby." She took a jittery drag. "Somebody should be telling us what's going on."

"Don't you worry babe," Barry said, his eyes never leaving the screen. "I'm sure Teddy has everything all taken care of."

As if in proof of his statement, irrefutable as the day is long, someone knocked on the door.

"I'll bet that's Teddy now," he said, but made no move to get up. She looked at him expectantly until he shrugged. "You're standing," he said, and she rolled her eyes and walked to the door. She didn't bother looking through the peephole; she just threw the door open with an air of expectation, so what she saw took her slightly by surprise.

"Yeah?" she said.

A tall Mexican man dressed in a dark suit stood on the stoop. There appeared to be a raspberry jelly stain on the collar of his white shirt, but otherwise he was neat as a button. His hands were clasped behind his back. He nodded courteously.

"Buenos dias, señora. May I come in?"

"Who are you?" she asked suspiciously, and not because she was racist. OK, totally because she was racist. If he was a white guy, she probably would have opened the door wide and offered him a drink.

"I am an associate of Sergeant Teddy Barnes. He send me here to relay some news."

"Oh thank God!" she gushed, opening the door wider. "Come in, come in." She ushered him through the door and slammed it behind him. "Please, have a seat."

He entered the room, eyeing Barry carefully as he moved slowly toward the battered recliner, and after inspecting it briefly and deciding he had no other choice, sat down.

"Can I get you something to drink?" she asked him. "We got beer."

He glanced at his watch, noting that it was ten in the morning, and shook his head.

"Gracias, no, I prefer to get down to business."

"OK," Carolyn said, taking a seat on the couch next to Barry. "Why don't you turn that thing off, huh? This guy has news about Gina."

"What? You want me to turn off the TV?" Barry gawped, as if he'd just been asked to strip naked and shimmy up and down a fireman's pole for their entertainment. Carolyn snatched the remote from him and hit the "power off" button.

"There. You were saying?"

"Si, I am here bearing news about your situation."

"Is my little girl OK?" Carolyn asked anxiously. "Please tell me she's OK!"

"The girl and her dog is fine. They are in a safe place."

"Can she come home? Did Teddy track down who took her?"

The man eyed her judiciously before shaking his head. He spoke slowly, enunciating his words carefully. "I do apologize, but this is where I have to impart upon you some news that is, how you say? Much malo, um…bad, very bad."

As he talked, Carolyn mentally noted how well he spoke the English language. He had an accent that he wasn't trying to disguise; nonetheless, his words were clipped and curt. And he only used a few Mexican words here and there, ones she basically understood. She thought that was mighty good for a wetback.

"What's the bad news?"

"I'm afraid is in regards to Sergeant Barnes."

"What about him?"

"Tragically, he die in the line of duty."

"He's dead?" Carolyn couldn't believe what she was hearing and thought maybe there was something getting lost in translation. "You mean dead as in *dead*?"

"Si, señora, he es muerto. He is no more."

"What happened?" She was aghast, but also she couldn't help but think that maybe, possibly, she might have something to do with it, in some remote way.

"He was attempting to retrieve jore daughter, Mrs. Travis—"

"It's Mrs. Mantello."

"Pardon, Mrs. Mantello." He reached out and smoothed an invisible wrinkle on his pants. "As I saying, he was trying to rescue jore daughter from the men who have her, but his attempts were in vain."

"The men who *have* her?" Barry asked, getting in on the conversation for the first time. "I thought you said she was safe."

The man nodded. "She safe."

"So, where is she?"

"She is with an associate of mine."

Both Barry and Carolyn stared at the Hispanic man, their brains whirring as fast as they could process the information. If what he was saying was correct, Gina wasn't safe at all. She was still in the custody of the kidnappers. So, that would make this guy...

"Holy shit!" Carolyn exclaimed. "You're with them!"

He smiled for the first time, a forbidding, truly horrific smile, one that made both Barry and Carolyn's blood run cold. "That is correct, muy bien." He crossed his legs with exaggerated slowness, the smile turning rabid upon his robust lips. "I here to tie up loose ends."

"To what?" Barry said, taking a slug of his beer and looking at Carolyn. "To tie up what?"

Carolyn got to her feet quickly, was maybe three feet from the front door when the man sprang into action like a cat, moving so fast it was like watching smoke blow in a strong breeze. He grabbed her by the hair, yanked her back and put her in a headlock. She tried to scream, but his thick forearm cut off her air, and her attempts to fight him off were swiftly curtailed with a quick, sharp twist of her neck. A loud snapping sound issued forth, and she went limp in his arms. He let her drop to the tattered carpet. Meanwhile, Barry sat there, eyes wide, stunned. He looked down at Carolyn's lifeless body, then back up at the man who was casually running a hand through his short, black hair, smoothing it back.

"Did you," Barry gulped, "just kill her?"

The man smiled again, but this time there was some benevolence in it. He found it very amusing that this man was so stupid that he didn't know he should get up and run. Oh well, he mused. It certainly made his job easier.

"Let's say," El Sádico ventured, "I send her to better place."

"Aw crap!" Barry cried, getting it at last, staggering to his feet, but by that time it was too late. Sádico picked up a lamp from an end table, a piece of junk that would have better been at home in a landfill than actually decorating someone's home and, yanking the cord from the wall, stepped forward and wrapped it around the other's throat. Barry tried to batter the intruder with his fists, but he was too drunk and slow, and two and a half minutes later he was lying dead on the floor next to his wife. Jesus, but that had been easy. There were some days when his job did itself with little help from him at all. He was merely the conduit from which the action sprang forth. It was amazing how people trusted strangers if they were dressed nicely, or had a good-looking haircut. He thought of Ted Bundy, of John Wayne Gacy, of himself. Hide in plain sight was his motto, now and forever.

So, what to do with the bodies? Did he need to remove them now, or should he complete his mop-up after the others were dead? He stood there for a moment and thought about it, mentally making a list of the others he needed to visit by the day's end—everyone who knew something about the Castillo family who could possibly make trouble for them. Fortunately for him and his business partners, Teddy had acted alone. He'd brought in no one in from the Escondido Police Department, at least no one who they had immediately detected. He supposed in the next few days they would know for certain on that count. In the meantime, he only had to contend with the cop's family, the girl, her father, and the woman he was seeing. Maybe even the bartender at Hooligans, Tony, he believed his name was. Even though the man had proved himself to the Castillo organization, he wasn't a Mexican citizen nor was he a close friend or family. If his absence was necessary, Sádico would gladly silence him. All in all, it was a pretty short list, and if everything went as smoothly as it had gone here, he should in all probability wrap it up today, tomorrow at the latest.

Presently, however, there was always the off chance that someone might drop by, so the bodies shouldn't be lying around in plain sight, drawing flies. He didn't have to dismember them and dissolve them in sodium hydroxide until later, but it would be a good idea to stash them somewhere in the time being.

As he dragged them into the back of the house, he put his plan of action together in his head in the most logical order he saw fit. He liked to do the easy tasks first, and move on to the harder ones later. It made things more of a challenge.

Once the bodies were stowed inside a closet in one of the bedrooms, he decided where his next stop would be, and the one after that. The first one didn't bother him at all, but the second one filled him with dread for what he'd have to do. As an animal lover, he never liked to hurt them, so maybe he could come up with a way to keep the bulldog out of harm's way. Still, he was working on a timeline. If he couldn't do it quickly, he'd have to simply do what was necessary. It was unfortunate, but those were the rules.

He went into the kitchen, found some antibacterial soap, and thoroughly washed his hands. He didn't mind the killing (in fact he delighted in it), but he didn't like the germs. Keeping clean was as important to him as never getting caught, and as coldblooded as he was, he didn't even remotely consider that a possibility. It was a waste of time, like the two dead people in the back bedroom were a waste of life.

As he exited the house, sensibly locking the door behind him, he was certain there was no one who would care that these two people were no longer drawing breath.

Turned out, he was right.

Chapter Twenty-Eight

"Hi, my name is Bobby Travis, and I'm an alcoholic."

"Hi, Bobby," the group said in unison.

"Now, I don't usually attend this meeting so some of you might not know me," Bobby said, looking around, actually recognizing a few of the faces. Not a lot, but some. When he'd first started coming to the AA meetings, he'd attended them every day, he *needed* to. To do the program properly, he'd been informed by the moderator, it was in his best interest to go to as many meetings as he could. After he'd gotten a good hold on his problem, he cut back to three times weekly, then two, then one. He hadn't been to a Tuesday meeting in almost a year. He was surprised to see who was still regularly attending. Weren't they making any progress? He guessed he wasn't one to talk, seeing as he was high right now, but *seriously*. "Um, but even though you don't know me, I'm here today because I need help—"

"Glad you made the extra effort, Bobby!" Tommy said, waving at him.

Bobby nodded, wondering what catastrophic event had to transpire to motivate Tommy to take in a second meeting this week but figured the answer could wait. "Thanks," he said, then looked at the others gathered. "Uh, this might come as some surprise, but my daughter's been kidnapped by drug dealers and I need help getting her back."

The group sat there silently, waiting for the punchline. For all intents and purposes, it was as if he'd just spoken Mandarin Chinese to a group of Eskimos. When nobody said anything and someone near the back simply cleared their throat, he decided to continue.

"I'm not here today to tell you a story about blacking out—"

"But I was with you at the titty bar last night!" Tommy said, then realized he'd just given himself away. The reason for him attending another meeting suddenly revealed itself to Bobby. "Uh, I wasn't drinking though," he added quickly. "I was just there to see some boobs." He nodded at the curious onlookers and the scowling moderator. "Some mighty nice shaved beeve too, I gotta say."

"Anyway," Bobby continued, "my cousin died trying to save my daughter's life, and now it's up to me to rescue her." He looked around the room. "I can't do this alone. Is there anyone here who is willing to help me?"

Silence so profound everyone could hear Stacy's stomach rumble. "Sorry," she said. "I didn't eat breakfast."

"Please!" he implored. "Melissa and I can't do this by ourselves!"

"Who is Melissa?" the moderator interjected, and Bobby realized introductions were in order. "Everyone, this is Melissa, and I met her at my Sex Addicts Anonymous meetings."

"And she's with you why?"

"Um, because we've been having sex...look, that isn't the point. The point is that we came here today to see if we could recruit some of you to help us." Bobby looked around the room, his eyes burning with a sincerity that was otherworldly. "I've been coming to these meetings for over a year and a half now, and those of you who know me listened to me tell tales that should have found me dead, or in jail...well, I did wind up in jail quite a few times...but the fact is I've been here not only for myself but so that other people could feel better knowing there is someone out there worse than *all* of you combined. Someone who can't stop himself from screwing up over and over and over." He stopped, considered. "Well, except for you Jerry. I think sometimes you might have me beat."

A man near the front nodded, cracked open a can of Schlitz and took a long drink. After emitting a belch that lasted in duration and volume for roughly thirty-four seconds, he nodded again. "That's mighty nice of you to say, Bobby."

"Will you help us then?"

"Can't," Jerry said. "I'm too drunk."

"Fair enough. Anyone else?"

Bobby looked at them intently, trying to catch anybody's eyes who had the nerve to look at him. For the most part, they were all downcast, except for Tommy's. Bobby regarded him expectantly, raising his eyebrows.

"Is there a reward involved?" Tommy asked.

Bobby looked at Melissa, and she shrugged, then nodded.

"Yes," Bobby said. "There's a reward."

"Great!" Tommy said. "Then I'm in."

"Thank you, Tommy, you won't regret this."

"You don't know that," Melissa said, and he silenced her with a quick glance. She smiled weakly.

"Uh-huh, no problem" she said, back-pedaling. "Piece of cake."

"OK, then. Anyone else?"

The group sustained its collective silence, all eyes on their shoes. When all was said and done, Bobby guessed that he couldn't blame them. They'd come here for the free coffee, to smoke cigarettes, and to listen to and tell stories about their ridiculous exploits while they were inebriated. Sometimes some of them cried, from time to time they yelled, and occasionally some broke down and claimed they'd be better off dead. But when Bobby took center stage, it was like the whole room lit up and the show was on.

Still, that didn't mean those who knew him were willing to burden themselves on his behalf, and Bobby could honestly understand that. He was, after all, asking quite a bit. He shrugged and nodded at Melissa.

"OK, well, we gotta get going. If we make it back alive I'll tell you all about it." Bobby looked over at Tommy, who was still sitting. "Tommy? You coming?"

"Huh? Oh, yeah, sure." He got up and the three of them headed out the door. When they were gone, the moderator looked around the room.

"How many of you think that was a ruse so that they could get drunk and have a three-way?"

Every hand in the place went up.

"Me too," the moderator agreed. "Man, the things Bobby will come up with just so he can get wasted and brag about it later." He shook his head sadly, thinking, *it must be nice...*

"Would anybody like to share with the group?" he asked, and Jerry raised his hand. "Yes, Jerry?"

"I'm drunk right now," Jerry said, then eructed another long, loud and slightly noxious belch before putting the beer can back to his mouth.

"And how does that make you feel?" the moderator asked, and the meeting continued on as usual.

◆ ◆ ◆

"Hi, my name is Bobby, and I'm a gambling addict."

"Hi, Bobby," the group said in unison.

"Now, I know that none of you here knows me..."

Since they didn't have any time to spare and Bobby's and Melissa's Sex Addicts Anonymous meeting wasn't until that evening, they decided to hit a Gambling Anonymous meeting instead. It went without saying that they couldn't wait until the next day to go to Bobby's usual GA meeting, so they did the next best thing and simply went to one that was already in progress.

"I know you, Bobby," Terry said, waving at him from the back of the room. "How's it going? You ever get your daughter back?" And then, when it suddenly occurred to him he said, "You're being easy on the truck, right? You remember that I own it?"

"Hey Terry," Bobby said. "Yeah, the truck is fine, and I'm gonna pay you back, but I'm here to ask everyone a favor."

Blank stares regarded him. These folks, after all, didn't know him from Adam. The moderator knew him well, of course, but he was slightly annoyed because he wasn't expecting to see Bobby today, and he hadn't smoked weed before starting the meeting. He liked getting stoned to better enjoy Bobby's stories, since they were such a hoot. And judging by the glassy appearance of Bobby's eyes, he was evidently torched on some wacky tobacky himself, the bastard.

"What are you doing at this meeting, Terry?" Bobby asked, and the other gave him a "shut the hell up" look.

"Why, whatever do you mean Bobby?" Terry asked innocently, and Bobby guiltily ceased and desisted his line of questioning.

Terry, of course, trolled all the gambling anonymous meetings, as he was always looking for fresh blood. In a week's time, he hit them all. Bobby wasn't the only client he'd gotten from the meetings. It was a secret between him and the moderator, because he, too, was one of Terry's clients. As was previously mentioned, he had an unusual fixation with Mexican wrestling and had lost thousands over the years.

"Um, nothing," Bobby quickly corrected. "My mistake."

"What can we do for you and your friends today, Bobby?" the moderator asked, glancing uneasily at Tommy, then suggestively at Melissa.

"I came here to try and recruit some people to help me. It's a long story, but my daughter has been kidnapped by drug dealers and I need to get her back."

Just like the last meeting they visited, there was silence all around. No one here, with the exception of Terry and the moderator, knew him, so obviously, no one felt obliged to offer him any assistance. Hell, the people who *did* know him hadn't felt obligated. He couldn't say he blamed them. He looked at Melissa.

"I think this is a dead end," he told her, when Terry stood up.

"If I help you, will it get me my money back quicker?"

Bobby looked at Melissa, and she nodded enthusiastically.

"Oh yeah," Bobby said. "We take care of this and I'll pay you back in cash."

"Sweet," Terry said, buttoning his coat. "I'm in." He looked around the room. "If anyone needs anything, you have my number."

And the four of them exited the room. When they were gone, the moderator glanced around at the rest assembled.

"How many of you think that was a ruse so they could get drunk, go to the horse track, and then have a four-way at a seedy motel?"

Every hand in the room went up.

"Me too," the moderator said. "Now, Jocelyn, you were saying?"

"I gambled away the grocery money again this week on lottery scratch offs."

"And how does that make you feel?"

"Hungry."

And the meeting continued on.

◆ ◆ ◆

"I guess that's everyone," Bobby said once they were outside, and Melissa looked around at the group, an expression of consternation on her face.

"We need someone else."

"We can't wait until tonight for our SA meeting," Bobby countered. "This'll have to do."

"I know someone who might help."

"Who?"

When Melissa offered her suggestion, Bobby did a double take.

"Really?" The idea would never have occurred to him for many reasons, but the biggest was because of the tryst they'd had during one of his many blackouts. The thought of being in close proximity with the other, depending on him to help save his daughter...what kind of toll would he have to pay for a favor of that magnitude? He wasn't sure if he wanted to find out.

"Yes Bobby, really," she said, fishing her phone from her purse.

"How come you have Lance's number?"

"Because he wanted to try straight sex to see if he liked it."

"Did he?"

"Hard to say," she admitted. "He couldn't get an erection, and he was too grossed out by my vagina to get anywhere near it."

Bobby was relieved. "So you didn't have sex then."

"I guess," she said slowly, "if you don't count me strapping on a dildo and riding him from behind—"

"I'll take that as a no!" Bobby said, putting his hands over his ears. "But if you really think he'll do it, then call him."

"OK." She scrolled through her contacts, found his number, dialed, waited for a moment, and then said, "Hey, Lance, what's up?" She made a face. "TMI, Lance. Look, when he gets off on you, you think you can meet Bobby and me and some other people downtown? We sort of need a favor." She nodded. "Of course he'll let you blow him." She tipped Bobby a wink. "Why now after turning you down all those other times? Let's just say he really needs a favor and he'll do anything to get it." She shook her head. "I'm not sure if he'll do that...or that...no, I can't vouch for that either...Look, will you meet us or what? We really need your help. What do you mean you can't talk with your mouth full? Oh, it's a joke! I get it. Sex addict humor! We'll be at that diner across from the Rialto. Just look for us in a booth in the back, say in about thirty minutes...or whenever he finishes in your face. Yep, no problem, see you then." She hung up the phone. "He's in," she announced.

"But do you really think he can help us?"

"Bobby, we need everyone we can get right now. With him that's five people, and that still isn't enough, but we don't have anywhere left to turn."

"What about my narcotics anonymous meeting?"

"You told me yourself: Ricky's dead and he's the only one who would have even considered it."

"But we don't know that for sure—"

"We don't have time for this Bobby! We have to get going before it's too late." She took his face in her hands and forced him to look her in the eyes. "Your daughter's life is at stake."

"I know," he said miserably. "I know, and I'm so damn scared..." His buzz was wearing off, and the reality of what they were about to embark on began to worry him. Butterflies fluttered in his stomach like hornets on steroids.

Melissa looked around at the others. "Give us a minute please," she said, leading Bobby a few feet away. "Being scared isn't going to help her," she whispered tersely.

"But how do we know this plan is going to work?" he whispered back.

"We don't, but there is nothing else we can do. If we go to the cops, they kill your daughter. Are we on the same page or what?"

Bobby shook his head, his eyes radiating malaise. Man, he'd do anything to have his daughter back, but this was suicide. If any of the others assembled knew they were walking into a gunfight armed with butter knives, he doubted any of them would accompany him. As it stood, they were completely in the dark as to what they were being asked to do. Seriously, they didn't have a clue what Bobby wanted of them.

"We have to tell them," Bobby said at last, and she nodded.

"We'll tell them what we have planned when we get to the diner." She frowned. "Hopefully they'll still be onboard."

"Shoot," Bobby said, "Maybe we *should* lie…"

"They have to know what they are facing, and if they decide not to go with us then I guess it's just you and me."

"Christ, I love you," Bobby blurted, and this made her smile.

"You know what? I love you too Bobby Travis." She looped her arm through his. "Now let's go and try to save your daughter."

◆　◆　◆

"You slept with my brother, sister, mom and my dad?" the severely over-weight, acne-ridden, English-mangling, trailer-park-trash girl gasped at the dangerously underweight, acne-ridden, English-mangling trailer-park-trash guy, and he nodded boastfully, grabbing his crotch for added effect.

"I done (bleeped) 'em all!" he announced cheerfully, his words dread-fully garbled because of the fifteen rings in his lips. The ones that were making it especially hard for him to be understood were the ones that were attached to both the top and bottom lip.

"I'll (bleepin') kill you!" she screamed, diving from her chair and tack-ling the guy before the Springer security guards could "stop" her. They let the fight carry on for a few minutes before Jerry gave them the nod and they peeled the giant woman off of the skinny, wife-beater-wearing nob-gobbler. In the fracas, she pulled a couple of his lip rings out. He tossed a string of profanity at her, but none of it could be understood because it was all bleeped out.

Gina and Sid high-fived.

"Best episode ever!" she declared, and Sid agreed with her.

Armando had been gone for over a day now, and besides a phone call he received from another hired hand, instructing him to hold down the fort and keep the kid safe, Sid had received no word as to what exactly was going on, not from Armando or Carlos. He honestly didn't care, he was having so much fun with this kid and her dog. Ruby the bulldog was hilarious, with her tongue sticking out of her mouth all the time, and the way she could move her rotund self around with amazing agility. And the girl, well, if she was only a little older (or the US laws were laxer like they were in Mexico), he'd totally ask her to go out with him. In fact, the two of them had hardly moved from where they were sitting, had actually been watching TV practically around the clock since Carlos had left with Armando. As long as the girl and the dog didn't leave his sight, Sid figured he was doing his job.

So, when his phone rang halfway through the program, he couldn't help but feel a twinge of irritation. That was, until he answered and found out whom he was speaking to. The conversation didn't last long, as El Sádico wasn't a man to mince words, but the message came through loud and clear: he was coming for the girl and the dog. And when El Sádico came for you, no one ever saw you again. Sid was as afraid of the man as he was of any of the top tier men in the Castillo cartel, but Sádico was surely the worst, for he had no remorse for anything he did. He could kill you while eating a breakfast burrito and be more concerned that there was not enough hot sauce to suit his taste.

His weakness, however, was animals, but it sounded as if El Sádico had made his peace with the fact that Ruby had to go. When Sid hung up the phone, his brown face was pale.

"What?" Gina asked him. "What's going on?"

"Good question," Sid said, mulling it over. What *was* going on? What *was* he thinking exactly? If he was thinking what he thought he was thinking, he was a goner for sure. But how could he simply let a man like El Sádico come and take Gina and Ruby? Sid would feel as if he were in on it himself, which in truth, he was. It was his job.

"Answer me!"

"We got to leave," Sid said, getting up from the recliner. "Get jores and Ruby's things, quickly. We don have much time."

"What do you mean?"

"What ju think I mean?" he said cruelly, more so than he meant to, but he had to make her understand. "I'm a idiot, and I going to die for this, but we got to try."

"Try what?"

"A very bad hombre named El Sádico is coming to kill ju and take jore dog. He be here anytime."

Apparently telling Gina the truth was the right thing to do. She was on her feet in a shot, her bag packed, Ruby's things tucked inside a paper bag from Trader Joe's.

"Let's go," she said and, without bothering to shut off the TV, they exited out the back, where Sid's El Camino was parked.

◆ ◆ ◆

Somehow (no one would ever really know how) Lance was already at the diner when the four others arrived. He came out of the men's restroom, wiping his mouth, and sat down next to them in the booth. He casually plucked a menu from the metal rack, announcing he was "*so* famished!" He cast a jaundiced eye upon Bobby, leered at him like a stalker in a flasher coat standing stark bollocks naked in a school yard full of children.

"Hey Bobby, how's it going?"

"Good, Lance," Bobby replied. "Thanks for coming."

"That's what he said," Lance quipped, but no one laughed.

"Anyway," Bobby continued, "I think it is only fair that Melissa and I tell you what we have in mind, in case any of you want to back out."

"Don't you mean 'blackout'?" Tommy said, and he, too, was ignored.

"You said we were going to try and save your daughter from drug dealers?" Terry said, lighting a smoke before realizing he couldn't smoke inside, and then put it out on the table top. "What's the big deal?"

"Yeah," said Tommy, wishing he could have a smoke too. "And how about some beers while we plan this whole thing? A guy can get pretty thirsty concocting a plan."

Bobby glanced at Melissa and she nodded, so when the waitress arrived he ordered a round for anybody who wanted one. He and Melissa were the only two to decline. When everyone was comfortable, and he had their undivided attention, he told them what he had in mind. The group was quiet while he talked, no one asking any questions, and when he was finished and their silence went unbroken, it began to unnerve him.

"So?" he asked abruptly. "What do you think?"

"What do we think?" Terry said, about to light another cigarette when he again realized he couldn't. "I know what I'm thinking!"

Here it comes, thought Bobby, but what the other said took him completely by surprise.

"We need some freakin' guns!"

"Yeah!" Tommy agreed, and Lance nodded in turn.

"Do you own any guns?" Bobby asked Terry hopefully, but the other shook his head. He looked at Tommy, and he frowned and shook his head as well. "I guess we're screwed."

"I wouldn't be so quick to say that," Lance said, and all eyes turned to him inquisitively. "What? Can't a gay man also be a member of the NRA? Is there something in the constitution that bans my right to bear arms?" He looked at them with no small amount of derision. "I mean, in most states we can't get married, we can't be openly Republican, and we certainly can't hold hands at Disney Land, but we sure as shit can pack some heat!"

"Wait, are you talking about *real* guns?" Tommy said, confused, and Melissa shushed him.

"How many guns are we talking here?" she asked, amused, and he swallowed the last of his beer and stood. "Let's take a walk," he said, and after they split up the check (taking time to calculate the exact division of the 20 percent tip), they left the diner, Lance leading the way.

Chapter Twenty-Nine

Driving along, El Sádico's mind was awhirl with misgivings. Someone had tipped off the cop's family; when he'd arrived and searched the house, there was no one home. He noted that clothing was missing from the master bedroom and from the kid's room (he judged this to be the case by the empty clothes hangers and open dresser drawers), so he knew it would be useless to check with the closest neighbors, unless he thought they knew something, which was highly unlikely. You didn't casually mention to Sally Housedress that an armed killer was coming for you, not with the stakes as high as they were. The cop's wife couldn't be that stupid. So they had fled, to where, who knew? He'd have to deal with that later if he wanted to stay on schedule. Right now he'd deal with everyone who was present and accounted for. Before leaving, though, he checked the mail, grabbing everything in the box for later scrutiny. There might be something there that could point him in the right direction.

It was obvious to him who'd told them; it didn't take any amount of imagination to know that Bobby Travis had made the call. Well, it would be one of the last things he'd do, but right now he could wait as well. His next obligation was to take care of the kid and her dog, which led to yet another qualm he had. What was he going to do with the bulldog? He surely didn't want to kill it, but he couldn't take her with him. In his line of work, having a dog was an extravagance he could ill afford. Maybe if there was time he could find a local shelter and drop the dog off there. That way she'd have a better chance of living, more so than him simply depositing her by the side of the road and leaving her to fend for herself, hoping someone would be kind enough to pick her up. With this thought he felt much better about the whole thing. He'd relieve the guard of his duty (he'd gotten too close to the girl, his position compromised, so it was

Sádico's orders to kill him, too), then he'd get rid of the girl, and finally he'd take care of the arrangements for the dog. If he was quick about it, it should only take about forty minutes, maybe an hour tops. And most of that time would be spent relocating the dog. But he could make it work; he was, after all, a professional.

After that he'd take care of Bobby and the slut he was screwing, which should leave him enough time to track down the cop's family and lay them to rest. It might take a little longer than he planned—possibly the next day, maybe by mid-afternoon—but that was OK. These things happened from time to time. And after that he could take a much-needed rest. He'd certainly earned it.

When he arrived at the safe house, he noted how barren the place looked, and was actually thinking pleasantly of how well the kid's guard was doing his job until he entered and found it actually *was* abandoned. No one home, the TV still on. He dashed to the back door, saw the tire tracks in the gravel driveway where el guardia had parked his car (his name was Sid, El Sádico remembered), and he went to inspect them. Judging by the look of the gravel, something had crawled up Sid's ass in a big way, and it didn't take a genius to realize what that could have been. He'd been cool on the phone, but he must have suspected that his job was in danger of termination, as well as his life. Either that, or he had a hard-on for the girl. Maybe a little bit of both. He'd really been hauling ass too; once his tires hit the pavement he'd fishtailed, leaving a trail of rubber that showed he took a left at the end of the alley. Sádico frowned, momentarily at odds with this impromptu escape when something dawned on him. If memory served him right, Sid was a Chicano through and through. That meant he drove either a Chevy Impala, a Bel-Air or a low-rider El Camino. Sádico would bet money on that. No Chicano worthy of his status would be caught dead in anything less. By the look of the skid marks, the car appeared to be rear wheel drive, which unfortunately could be either of the three, but it also made a good case for his point. Still, that was three distinctly different possibilities. The good news, though, was once word got out that Sid had the kid and was on the run, there would be no safe place for him to go. The Castillo cartel was in cahoots with every major Mexican gang between Escondido and Tijuana, stretching down into Baja. He would stand out like a sore thumb. If, that was, he was dumb enough to stay in that car. Within the hour he might have a new set of wheels.

"Shit," Sádico cursed, mostly because his job continued to grow more complex, but also because he'd wanted to see the bulldog Ruby. He was really fond of bulldogs.

Now the question was: did he want to expedite the process by bringing in others for a job he was supposed to take care of himself (making him look foolish in the process) or did he want to spend the extra time to track them down alone? He'd never asked for help before, but the more intricate this became, the better their chance at getting away. No one had ever gotten away from him before, *no one*, and he wasn't about to let that happen now, yet this was taking twists and turns that were further complicating matters. Did he want to put the Castillo family at risk if any of them escaped?

"Shit," he said again, kicking gravel with his toe. But what the hell, he was sure of himself and his skills. He knew that since the time he'd made the phone call they couldn't have gotten far. He also figured that Sid would think along the same lines as Sádico; all of the safe places that he once knew were now off limits.

With this last consideration in mind, El Sádico decided he would track them single-handedly. He still had plenty of time. It was, after all, just before noon. If Sid was making an all-out run for it, he'd most likely head down to San Diego, maybe hole up for the night in a motel in San Ysidro, a town a mere three miles from the Tijuana border. He and the girl might try to sneak into Mexico on foot. If that was their plan, he had to stop them before they left the States. If that indeed *was* their plan. All things considered, that would be idiotic; he'd be safer in the States where the cartel had to remain inconspicuous. So maybe they intended to remain nearby. It was very possible that they might not even leave Escondido, if Sid had someone he could trust right here in town. But who could that be, and what would compel him to stay this close when he knew the dangers that he (El Sádico) presented? He'd have to have cojones of steel to bank on getting past one of the most ruthless killers ever employed by any Mexican drug cartel. Either that or he had to be stupid. Really, really stupid.

Time would prove he was a little of both.

◆ ◆ ◆

Standing in Lance's garage, with the door closed to keep the neighbors' inquisitive eyes from seeing anything they shouldn't, Tommy let out a low whistle.

"Holy crap, dude. What the hell are you armin' yourself against? The zombie apocalypse?"

"Nothing that trite, I assure you," Lance said, taking an Armalite AR-15 semi-automatic rifle from the wall and cradling it lovingly. "And since most religions don't condone homosexuality, I'm not planning on Armageddon either. According to the Catholics, all of us cocksucking rump rangers are going to burn in hell."

"You said it, not us," Tommy mumbled, and Melissa shot him a dirty look. "Sorry," he said.

"I suppose I started collecting them and I got sort of carried away." He set the Armalite down and picked up an M-16. "This gem was responsible for killing children in Vietnam."

"Neato," Terry said.

"Where did you get all of these?" Bobby asked, and Lance smiled lasciviously.

"Why, do you want to hold my gun, Bobby?"

When Bobby didn't reply, Lance decided to answer the question.

"Gun shows mostly. Sometimes through the paper. At gun shows, the sellers know what they have, and you pay at or above market value. But when people sell them through the want ads, it's mostly widows of men who've gone to the final shooting range in the sky."

"Old age?"

"No, mostly dead from gunshot wounds." Lance put down the M-16 and took what appeared to be a bazooka from the wall. "I got this bazooka from a little old lady in Pasadena. She had no idea what she was holding on to. I got it for a steal."

"Great, so you're fleecing old ladies out of their guns," Melissa said. "Real nice."

"Hardly my fault if they don't take the time to learn what they have. I just offer a price and if they go for it, yay me!"

"Spoken like a true capitalist," Terry said approvingly, about to light a cigarette when Lance stopped him.

"You want to blow us up?" he said and Terry begrudgingly put the pack away and pocketed his lighter.

"Sorry."

"Look," said Bobby, "we don't have time to go into the individual history of this arsenal of yours. Right now we have to outfit ourselves and get moving."

Lance eyeballed Bobby. "I'd take you for a twelve-gauge man any day." He removed one from the wall. "How about a Remington? Heft this sucker once and tell me how you feel."

Bobby took it and tucked it into his armpit. He had to admit, it felt pretty good.

"Feel tough?"

"I feel like I can walk into a room and take charge."

"Instant enlightenment," Lance said. "All right, let's get everyone hooked up with something they can handle, and then we can get into some of the other hardware."

"Like what?" Tommy asked. He'd done some shooting before, and personally he was barley restraining a boner that was threatening to spilt open his skin-tight jeans.

"I got smoke bombs, grenades, a rocket launcher (used only a couple of times during operation Desert Storm), flak jackets, zip strips, flash bombs, chain mail—"

"Chain mail?" Bobby said, and Lance smiled.

"I was just checking to see if you were listening."

"OK," Melissa said, reaching out and taking a gun from the wall. She had no idea what it was, but she figured, judging by the size, that it would make do. "Let's get going, huh? We don't know what's going on with Bobby's daughter, but we have to assume that time is of essence."

So with Lance directing them, eventually everyone was paired with a firearm that appeared to suit their individual need. And after that, the extras were passed around as promised, everyone taking advantage of Lance's proffered military clothing to stow bombs and other assorted tools of mayhem in the many deep pockets.

"Ya know," Terry said, "for a fag you ain't half bad."

"That's what the last guy who blew me said," Lance replied, and when Terry looked back at him uncertainly, and an awkward silence spread itself out over the ensuing several seconds, Melissa stepped in quickly, diffusing the situation with a hearty (yet wholly affected) laugh.

"Good one," she said jovially. "Good one indeed." She glanced around at the men, everyone now armed to the teeth, decked out in camouflage pants and vests. "Let's get going, huh?"

"Yeah," agreed Lance. "Let's blow this ice cream man, um…popsicle stand."

Everyone laughed except for Terry.

♦ ♦ ♦

"What are we going to do?" Gina asked anxiously as Sid took a corner two times as fast as he should have and the car almost went up on two wheels. "A guy was coming to kill me and Ruby?"

"Not jus any guy," Sid said. "El Sádico is the most vicious, ruthless mercenary ever employed by any cartel…ever."

"What makes him worse than everybody else?"

"Ju don wan to know, trust me." Sid took another turn much too fast, and both Gina and Ruby almost ended up in his lap. "For what I jus did, I dead too."

"Where are we going?"

"I tryin' to think a that, chica, and I ain't so sure jet."

Just as El Sádico had speculated, Sid knew that almost everyone he used to trust would now be his enemy. It was all for one and one for all when it came to the drug cartel, except when you crossed them. Then it was all for them, and your life wasn't worth a hill of refried pinto beans. Seriously. In layman's terms, you were totally fucked.

It did cross his mind to go down to San Ysidro, but going into Mexico would be worse. Down there, the cartel was law. At least in the United States, they had to hide. In Tijuana, they could walk the streets with automatic weapons (just like in those *Desperado* movies) and blow shit up, and nobody would care. Well, they would care, but there was nothing they could do about it. Everyone would simply get the hell out of their way. And why wouldn't they? The drug cartels may be slaughtering whole villages and using piles of their severed limbs as examples for their enemies, but they were also giving a little back to the community, and how was that for good Samaritanism? *Lo que el Cristo*, they were practically saints!

No, they were much safer in the United States, possibly even Escondido, because Sid knew it better than any other town in either North or San Diego County. He was, after all, born and raised here; his parents were illegal immigrants who had been able to obtain legal status for him and his siblings because of their foresight to have their children enrolled in the US school system. With that status, he could have taken advantage of many opportunities, yet he'd thrown them away for a lucrative career first as a drug dealer, then as a guard in the Castillo organization. He'd been very lucky to be assigned such a position; Mexican cartels rarely (if ever) employed anyone from the United States. That had been one loophole he'd been fortunate enough to get around, because of his friendship with Armando, whom Sid had met when he was in his teens. Armando had taken him under his wing, persuaded his higher ups of the young man's value and brought him into the fold, treated him like a brother. Unfortunately, though, the two weren't bonded by blood, and that decision could ultimately come back to haunt him, if he were alive to witness it. You see, for the organization to maintain confidence in a properly functioning workforce, they needed something they could hold over their head, like relatives in Mexico who would be tortured and killed if an employee ever broke their trust. Sid did not have anyone in Mexico they could hurt if he went rogue. In fact, his parents were dead. For that reason alone he could be considered a loose end, one they wouldn't hesitate to get rid of should the right reason ever come up, something other than deciding impetuously that he liked a white girl named Gina more than he liked his job. His decision to help the girl was a *guaranteed* death sentence, and he figured he'd come to regret it, but he simply couldn't help it. Her smile was infectious, her laughter the tinkling of angelic bells. He couldn't stand by and let her be murdered simply because the cartel didn't want her around. It just wasn't right. And something must have happened to his friend; the fact that Armando hadn't called meant something must have gone wrong, and he was no longer around to protect him. His life may have been on the line anyway if Armando's had been threatened.

But where could they go? There were eyes everywhere. What the Americans didn't know was that Mexican drug cartels were spread far and wide; they just did a very good job of laying low. That guy mowing your lawn and trimming your trees? He was eyes for a cartel. The man bagging your groceries at the local Von's? Cartel man. Not to beat a point to death, but they blended in and were more numerous than *anyone* realized. The general public thought they were only affiliated with the Mexican and Puerto Rican gangs. Wrong. They did business with anyone who had cash. They supplied the Crips and the Bloods, even though the two gangs were constantly at war with the Mexican gangs. They were equal-opportunity employers. And the Castillo cartel was enormous, stretching from Tijuana all the way down to the tip of Baja. They had more operators than even Sid knew of. They had to get off the street and stash his car as quickly as they could.

Somebody suddenly came to him, someone whom he might be able to trust. He was family, which was good, but in a case like this, it also did not matter. What was most important was how he presented his case. He had to have a compelling reason for taking this girl and her dog on the run from the Castillo cartel, and not a lot of people in the greater vicinity would think *anything* was compelling enough of a reason. Yet he had nowhere else to go, and someone would spot him eventually in his garish, bright yellow El Camino. As soon as El Sádico put the word out on the wire, everyone with a firearm would be taking shots at them.

"Any ideas yet?" Gina asked as he took another hairpin turn.

"Si," he said, spinning the wheel *Dukes of Hazzard* style and executing a perfect one eighty that would throw off any would-be pursuers. "I do. We jus better hope he home, and that he unnerstands why I done what I done."

"Why did you do what you done?" Gina asked, and when he looked into those blue eyes and saw the curiosity burning there, he couldn't help but feel heat spread throughout his chest.

"Because, little chica," he said softly, "the man would have kilt ju."

"And Ruby?"

Sid shook his head. "Maybe not the dog. El Sádico, he has a soft spot for the animals."

Gina digested this bit of news, then asked, "Would he have killed you?"

"Maybe." He nodded. "And that is what we tell him: that Sádico was going to kill us both, and that's why I ran."

"This person, where we're going...they wouldn't care that you saved just *me* from getting killed?"

Sid shook his head. "Is not how it works. No one is immune from the cartel. When they say is time for ju to die, is time to die. No questions, ju might as well pick out jore tombstone."

"So," Gina ventured further, "even though you trust this guy to take us in, he's going to wonder why you didn't just let me get shot?"

"That will be the biggest question on his mind."

"Who the heck is this guy?" she asked, unable to fathom how they could all be so single-minded when it came to their purpose.

Sid sighed. "He is mi hermano...my brother," he answered simply. "And if I could think of anyone else, I go there instead. Unfortunately, I cannot. Is our only choice."

"OK," Gina said, hugging Ruby tight to her chest and getting a good face licking in return. "At least he's family."

"Ju say that now," Sid said, grinning sadly. "But it might be the biggest mistake I make jet."

And like the scriptures, the prophecy was foretold.

Chapter Thirty

Palm trees swayed in a gentle breeze as beautiful women sunned themselves on the veranda surrounding an enormous Olympic-sized swimming pool. A squat, burly Mexican man with a hairy chest covered in gold chains used his pudgy, ring-clad fingers to clutch a burner cell, which he held to his overly large head. Behind him on a glass table was a huge pile of cocaine, but it wasn't for him. He seldom, if ever, used the stuff. It was for the beautiful women, and they indulged like the shit was going out of style, which was good, because it kept his dick from having to suck itself.

He listened to what the person on the other end was saying, and although he was pleased that the cop was out of the picture, he didn't like the fact that his trusted management had suffered a hit as well.

"Carlos es muerto?" he asked, and waited as the other gave a lengthy explanation as to how his inside man in Escondido could have succumbed to a local law enforcement officer. "Why ju not tell me 'til now?" Inside, he seethed. He was supposed to be apprised of everything that happened, *when* it happened, and this breach of protocol had him itching to start shooting until every last member of his organization was dead. While he listened to the explanation, he cooled down a little (not a lot, but a little). Apparently, the chain of command had suffered a serious meltdown. With Carlos out of the picture, as well as his successor, Armando, the man on the phone (the next in line for their job) hadn't known what to do, and he panicked. They'd never prepped him for something of this magnitude, and he was shitting the proverbial brick. As the old saying goes, the messenger is the one who normally gets shot when bad news is imparted. Apparently, Carlos and Armando's replacement had not wanted to get shot. Still, to withhold information from him was reason enough to shoot him anyway, which he most likely would in due time. But an even bigger question took front and center. "Why did Carlos try to take out the cop hisself? That's the assassin's chob."

"He insist, Señor Castillo."

"That stupid bastardo! And he take Armando with him? Idiota!" With this kind of incompetence, it was a wonder they could keep afloat with all the other cartels in operation. As it stood, they had only a tenuous grip at best on Baja and Southern California; other cartels were moving in with a speed that wasn't the least surprising, given the nature of their enterprise. It was beginning to look like it was time to put their back-up plan in motion, the one reserved for when only the very worst was expected. And this might require he make a trip to Escondido to ensure that it was done right. He sighed. He hated to travel if he didn't have to. "What about Ramon? Where is he, and what does he know?"

The owner of Hooligans, Ramon Pasquales, was set up to be their patsy, in case the crap ever hit the fan. He was not in on their operation, although he appeared to be, based on all of his shady dealings in the past. In truth, the cartel had purchased the establishment and put him in "charge". They had an agreement: he could live the life of a wealthy American business owner, enjoying all the perks to his heart's content, but if there was ever any trouble and the cartel's operation was jeopardized, he was their fall guy. Now, the obvious question was: why would Ramon agree to something that could possibly end so poorly for him? Socioeconomics 101. He'd been a peasant, a poor man living in Mexico. Taking the job was worth the risk to him and his wife, just so that they could live luxuriously, for however long it lasted.

"Ramon is in town, and he knows nothing, except that his manager has not showed up for work," the other said, and the burly man (Martino Estabon Rodriquez Estevan Castillo) nodded.

"Bueno," he said, lighting a cigar. "Keep it that way." He puffed grandiosely. "What about El Sádico? Where was he when this happen?"

"He was in Tijuana when Carlos and Armando get killed."

"Why?"

"Carlos say he didn't need him."

"Estúpido son of bitch...Ju call him?"

"Si. He come back this morning. He cleaning up."

"Is the kid dead jet?"

"No se. He will call when he finished and we will arrange the other half of his payment."

"Si." He took another large puff of his cigar. "And the others?"

"Sádico will take care of la chica, and then he will kill her father and anyone else who knows about our operation in Escondido."

"Muy bueno," he said, and he hung up the phone. However, it was anything but muy bueno. Mistakes like this could cost him dearly, and Christ knew they'd made plenty of them. Like employing anyone who wasn't a friend or a relative; trust came at a premium, and one could never trust anyone they didn't know. It was too risky. Carlos had been like a son to him, but he wasn't actually a blood relative. Armando had questioned this time and again yet he'd dismissed his fears, told him to mind his own business. Well, it turned out Armando was right, but there was nothing he could do about that now. Little did Martino Estabon know that a man Armando had vouched for had also fucked them, indicating that the dominos were falling, fast and hard.

Pocketing the phone and trying to put his doubts to rest, he noticed one of the women was at the pile of cocaine, and once she had a taste of *that* it was time for her to have a taste of something else. He gave her a crooked smile, fingering his zipper with his pudgy fingers, and, trying not to gag, the woman silently accepted that she had to earn her keep. Oh well, it kept her in cocaine.

Martino Estabon Rodriquez Estevan Castillo waddled toward her, unzipping as he did so.

◆ ◆ ◆

Sid gave Gina a hang-dog look, his large, liquid brown eyes moist and shiny.

"Ju and Ruby wait here 'til I come back." He paused, wanted to tell her that if he didn't come back that she and her dog should run for it, but he didn't want to frighten her. Besides, she was a smart kid. She'd probably figure it out.

"Is this gonna be cool?" she asked, and he shrugged.

"No se. I guess we find out."

He got out of the car and crossed the littered street in a neighborhood that looked like it belonged in an active warzone and walked up to a house that, like all of its neighbors, had bars on the windows and a barking pit-bull behind a chain-link fence. He looked back at her once after he rang the bell, and following an interminable stretch of time, someone opened the door. Gina saw that it was a man who looked to be the same age as Sid, but much bigger. He had a giant tattoo on his face, of what she couldn't tell, and as Sid talked the man looked over his shoulder at Gina. His eyes blazed furiously, but at last he nodded, gave Sid some instructions, then closed the door. Sid turned around and returned to the car, got in and started it up.

"He won't help us?"

"No, he will," Sid said, pulling away from the curb. "We must hide the car in back, in garage."

Sid pulled into an alley and drove down three houses, where he stopped, got out, and opened a rather dilapidated door that led into the dusty confines of a garage that had seen worse days than the house before it.

"Get ju things and get out," he told her, and after she did he parked the car inside and closed the door. "We go," he said, and she followed him to the back door of the house.

He rapped once on the flimsy wooden screen and Sid's brother opened it, ushering them in and quickly closing it behind them.

"Hola, güey," his brother said. "Ju a dead man."

"I was a dead man anyways if I wait for El Sádico," Sid said, escorting Gina and Ruby into the living room, where he bade them to have a seat on the couch.

"How ju know for sure?"

"Armando disappear," Sid said, choosing his words carefully. "Without him, I nothing to them."

His brother made a noise that sounded neither like acceptance or denial, and this was when Sid decided it was as good a time as any to introduce them all around.

"Gina, this is mi hermano Enrique. Enrique, this is Gina and her dog Ruby."

"Better not let her out back by Slaughter. He tear her a new asshole."

"Who's Slaughter?" Gina asked, and Enrique glared at her.

"Only champeen of the neighborhood. Ju look at him; he has the scars to prove it."

"I'll take your word for it," Gina said, not wanting to stay at this house any longer than they had to. She'd felt a lot safer when they were at the other place. At least at that location there wasn't a bloodthirsty dog that might attack her poor Ruby. Ruby wasn't a fighter, she was just one big lump of love. She decided that if they had to stay too long, and Ruby had to go outside, they'd go out the front. And Sid's brother looked as scary as he was mean. The tattoo on his face was of a demon, and it stretched down his neck like tendrils of smoke. He also had teardrops under each eye, and since she was no stranger to *Raw Lock-up*, she knew that meant he had probably killed somebody, most likely in jail. She was glad that Sid didn't have any teardrop tattoos.

"So El Sádico has jore number, huh, Sid?" Enrique said, and to Gina it sounded as if there was lighthearted joy in his voice. "Ju and her, hmm? Is this jore new chica?"

"I watchin' her. Her uncle was investigatin' Hooligans."

"What does she know?"

This was where Sid thought it would be best if they spoke in private.

"Can we talk in jore room?" he asked his brother. "Por favor."

Enrique cast an angry glare at Gina and Ruby yet again, then nodded compliantly.

"The remote for the TV is on the coffee table," he told Gina, then looked at Sid. "Vamanos."

And the two left the room, leaving Gina and Ruby alone with their fear.

◆ ◆ ◆

"Look, amigo, she don know nothin'," Sid said while his brother took apart a .9 millimeter Beretta and put it back together. "Her uncle din't neither. Was a lucky guess."

"So who else knows?"

"Her old man does, but she don know shit." Sid shook his head vehemently. "This kid don deserve to die Enrique, and neither do I!"

"Maybe ju don't, but ju can't escape the Castillo cartel, Sid. Ju know that."

"I can if I get out of California, maybe I go to Denver, or Chicago... some place where they don find me."

"They everywhere, hombre." Enrique shot him a twisted grin. "Ju think ju can outsmart them?"

"I ain't tryin' to outsmart nobody, amigo; I jus gotta get outta sight." He shrugged. "Maybe after a while they forget about me."

"They never forget," Enrique said grimly, and Sid felt the hair on his arms stand up.

"Look," Sid said, the desperation in his voice as apparent as his unalloyed fear. "Will ju help me or what?"

"What ju expec me to do?"

"Get me a car. I can't use mine no more."

"Jus a car?"

"And ju know, dinero, for the road."

"So ju gonna take off with this girl jus like that, eh? If I get ju car? Ju must have cojones a steel, mi manito."

"It's either that or we die, Enrique. It ain't like I gotta choice."

"Ju should have thought a that when ju started workin' for 'em." He stood, looked at his brother for a moment before shrugging his massive shoulders. "OK," he said at last. "I get ju car."

"Ju help me?" Sid asked gratefully, unable to keep the note of relief out of his voice.

"Jore mi manito," Enrique said. "Why wouldn't I help? Besides, what would our madre think if she knew I left ju out in the cold?"

"She beat ju instead of a piñata," Sid said, smiling, and the two shared a laugh. When they sobered, Enrique said,

"Let me make some calls, and I find ju a car."

"Ju won't fuck me, right?"

"I no gonna fuck you, Sid, relax. How else I gonna find ju a car?" He moved toward the door. "Now ju go out there and sit with jore little chica and let me handle this. As soon as I find one, I go get it, and ju can get outta here. Comprende?"

"Si," Sid said, walking to the door. "Gracias, Enrique. I pay you back, I swear."

"Si, you will pay me back. But we talk about that another time." He smiled, but it didn't reach his eyes. "Now get out and let me get to work. Go bang that little chica before I do."

"Gracias," Sid said again, then showed himself out, shutting the door behind him.

◆　◆　◆

"He's going to help us get a car?" Gina asked, and Sid nodded.

"Si, but it means we must leave town as soon as he return."

"But what about my dad?"

"He will have to deal with El Sádico."

"Who *is* this guy?" Gina hugged Ruby close to her, possibly a bit too tightly because the dog whimpered slightly.

"I tole ju; he is a mucho malo hombre—a very bad man—and like the rain, he is an eventuality that will always come to pass unless ju can escape the reach of his grasp."

"How far do we have to go?"

"Colorado probably, maybe even further."

To this Gina gave no reply; she honestly didn't know what to say. Leaving Escondido to go on the road with a man she'd just met, a guy who worked for a Mexican drug cartel…her head was fairly swimming. And the knowledge of what her daddy had to deal with, this man who sounded like a stalker from a horror movie…could this really be happening? It seemed so surreal.

"I can't leave my dad," she moaned hoarsely, and Sid reached out tentatively and took hold of her hand.

"We have to," he said. "This man, El Sádico, he will find us if we stay here, trust me. He won't stop, not until we dead. We have to make chure he don find us."

"I can't believe this is happening," she muttered, giving voice to her thoughts, and he pulled her closer, gave her a hug.

"I sorry ju got mixed up in this, chica, I am, and I want to do everythin' I can to help."

"Do…do you really think this man would have come after you too?" she whispered, not wanting Sid's brother to hear. "Or are you doing this for me?"

*A little bit of both…*he thought, but that was not what he wanted her to hear.

"Si. And I like ju, little chica," he said, smiling. "I like jore dog too." He nodded his head dolefully. "I don wanna see nothin' bad happen to ju."

"Thank you," she whispered, a tear sliding down her face. "Thanks for helping us…"

"Is my pleasure."

"Get a room!" Enrique said, startling them both. He walked toward them wearing a different shirt from the sleeveless T-shirt that had barely concealed his muscled pecs. He now wore something a little more ethnic. "I found ju a car," he said. "I go and get it. Ju sit tight, and I be back."

"And dinero?" Sid asked, and Enrique nodded.

"I get ju couple hunnerd dollars, maybe even a stolen credit card. I see what I can do."

Sid stood, held out his hand to his brother. "Gracias, mi hermano," he said, taking his brother's hand, and the two shook.

"No problemo, mi manito," Enrique replied, giving his brother's hand three dry pumps before letting go and turning toward the door. "I return soon." He looked back in their direction, his hand on the handle of the door. "Oh, one more thing."

"Si?" Sid asked.

"If someone knock on the door," Enrique said, "don answer it."

Chapter Thirty-One

Everyone in the car was silent, all hands (except for the driver's) clutching firearms. The radio played softly, songs from the '70s that sang of long summer days in the sun, of beach-time hijinks, and rollicking sex in a Chevy van. The song about the van a-rockin' was presently playing.

"I love this song," Tommy muttered, and everyone (except Lance) nodded in agreement.

"Give me the Village People any day," Lance said, and no one disagreed with him because he had, after all, supplied them with the guns.

Terry sat behind the wheel of his car, chain-smoking like a man condemned to die. Well, for all they knew, they quite possibly were.

"Do you think this will work?" Tommy asked, and when no one said anything Melissa shrugged, looking at him dourly.

"We can't be certain of anything, except that if we don't do something, Bobby's little girl is going to die."

Apparently that was a good enough answer for everyone, because no one asked anymore questions. For the rest of the ride they drove in silence, listening to the radio, everyone fingering their new toys. Lance, of course, had been smart enough to give them a crash course in their chosen weapon before they'd left his house, one of the most important points being to keep the safety on until they needed to use it. Only one firearm had been accidentally discharged in the garage of his home before they departed, and fortunately for all parties involved, no one got hurt, so Lance didn't have to retaliate and "bust a cap in some fool's ass," which he may or may not have done, given the situation was rife with amateurs.

When they arrived at their destination, Terry pulled the car over to the curb and put it in park, but he didn't immediately kill the engine. During the day, the street was full of shoppers and commuters and regular folks; they were out in droves, going about their everyday business. The bookie didn't know about the rest of them, but he felt mighty conspicuous. And the dump they were planning on shooting up? To him it looked like the place was ready to fall in on itself, the ramshackle building one strong gust of wind away from becoming a pile of bricks and rotting lumber, yet this was ground zero for their operation today.

"What's the plan?" he asked, and everyone turned expectantly to Melissa.

She looked around at all the faces, felt a flush of pride that for once she was in charge of something more important than arranging an impromptu orgy on a come-stained mattress in a seedy motel on the outskirts of town. She actually had a chance to do something significant; this was truly her moment to shine.

"We're taking the place by force—" she was saying when suddenly a large black van drove up to the front of the building and five large men carrying automatic rifles got out and went inside. They all watched, opened mouthed, and only after they registered this unexpected interference did she continue. "After those guys leave."

◆ ◆ ◆

As El Sádico drove slowly down Valley Center Parkway, looking in the parking lot of every fast food joint/cheap motel/gas station he passed and anything in between, his cell abruptly rang.

"Sádico," he said. He listened for a moment, and then a grin split his face from ear to ear. "This information is correct?" he asked, and when the person on the other end of the line validated its authenticity, he replied, "Bueno" and hung up. He tossed the phone back on the passenger seat and swung the car around in an illegal U-turn and headed back the way he'd come.

◆ ◆ ◆

"How long has it been?" Gina asked, and Sid looked at the time on his phone.

"About an hour."

"Ruby has to go potty."

Sid got up and looked out one of the back windows. "Slaughter is out back. Take her out the front, but do it quickly because we don want no one to see ju."

"OK."

She got up from the couch and the bulldog jumped down with her. Always thinking with safety in mind, she reached into the paper grocery sack and retrieved her leash. After clicking it in place, she took her to the front door, peeked out the window first, then quickly went outside. Sid got up and went to the front window, parted the grimy drapes and watched as they took care of business. It looked like the dog was just wrapping things up (potty done yet continuing to squat so she could pertly drop a deuce) when the back door crashed open behind him, and the sound of footsteps entering the foyer made him jerk his head around so quickly he almost gave himself whiplash.

"Who's there?" he called, trying to sound tough, but he knew there was an edge of fear in his voice. Before he could get an answer, he saw a flash of fire and then an explosion went off in his head and everything went dark.

◆ ◆ ◆

El Sádico was just passing the house when the little girl and the dog came out on the porch and walked down to the front lawn, upon which the dog immediately squatted.

Good-looking dog, he thought.

He quickly turned around the block, pulled into the alley, and parked the car behind the garage, effectively blocking an escape, should el guardia's car be parked inside.

It turned out he'd caught them unprepared, and he quickly dispatched of the girl's bodyguard, smiling as the back of Sid's head splattered a Rorschach design on the wall behind him. Sádico used a silenced .357 Smith and Wesson because he didn't want to waste a single minute. Close up kills were always good fun, but sometimes time was of essence; he needed Sid out of the way promptly because, after he collected the girl and relocated her dog, he had to add another chore to his list: making one Enrique Puente Vasquez disappear. It had been very convenient of him to commit the cowardly act of betraying his own brother (hence looking after his own interests when it came to the cartel), but it also meant that he, also, knew too much. Like a loose thread on a sweater, you had to cut the whole thing off if you wanted the entire garment to keep from coming apart. El Sádico's "to kill" list inexorably grew longer and longer as this insanely protracted day unspooled itself before him. Therefore, the .357 with a silencer. He planned to get the girl in the car, drive her someplace isolated to shoot and then dump her, bring the bulldog to a shelter and turn her in (if time allowed; it was already well past lunch and he still had quite a few things on his plate, so to speak), then return to this house, eliminate Enrique, then locate Bobby Travis and his slut and wipe them off the map. There was also the cop's wife and daughter, couldn't forget them. For anybody else this may have been a daunting task, but for Sádico it was all in a day's work. He'd been lucky that Sid's brother was a traitor. He might not get that lucky when it came to finding Bobby. And then it hit him: he realized *exactly* how he was going to find Bobby, and he smiled an insidious smile. It would be a whole lot easier than he thought.

He walked further into the house, picked up Sid under his armpits and quickly dragged him down the hall and dumped him in a closet. Dashing back to the front, he saw Gina walking up the steps with Ruby in tow, and as soon as she reached for the door he removed the gun from his waistband and aimed it at them.

"Don scream, or I kill jore dog," he said, pointing the gun at Ruby, but the girl couldn't help it; she let out a loud, piercing shriek. Ruby in turn began barking, and Sádico knew he must do something, but for the life of him he simply couldn't shoot the dog. It wasn't the right thing to do. While he was considering this, the girl turned around and bolted, practically dragging the poor, round dog behind her.

"Fuck," he muttered, taking off after her. He was at the bottom step of the porch when he realized his error, so he turned around and went back through the house, exiting out the rear.

Getting in his car, he fired it up, then peeled out of the alley backward, just missing a bearded man pushing a shopping cart full of empty soda cans.

"Watch where yer goin'!'" the man yelled, and El Sádico lifted his gun, casually stuck it out the window, and turned the man's head into jelly. He did a back flop into the dirt, one of his shoes flying off a filthy, sockless foot. Sádico wasn't typically so reckless, but had no time for this nonsense. When he got to the street, he spun the car around, then headed in the direction he'd seen the little girl and the dog go. About two blocks away they came into view, so he slowed the car, looking around to see if there was anyone around who would make trouble for him. Some kids were loitering in a front yard that was more mud than grass, and an old lady sat on her porch gently rocking in a chair that could have been (probably was) salvaged from a local landfill, but he decided they were unimportant. It wasn't as if this was a good neighborhood; these folks were used to the sound of gunshots, of seeing drug dealers peddle their wares in city parks to kids hardly old enough to wipe their own asses. In other words, it just didn't matter. Besides, the plate on his car wasn't registered in his name. The man who'd owned the car had died a painful death as ants slowly ate his head while the rest of him was buried deep within their hill. Sádico doubted he was in any position to complain about a moving violation, much less abduction and multiple murders.

He pulled alongside the girl, pressed a button to roll down the passenger window.

"Hey!" he called, showing her the gun but keeping his voice and his facial expression friendly. "I need ju to get in the car. I no going to hurt ju."

Gina looked at him, her heart beating so fast she doubted she could count the beats if she wanted to. She'd never been this scared in her life, and the last several days had been harrowing indeed. She didn't stop, nor did she slow down. She figured this man couldn't just take her and put her in the car, not in broad daylight with people around.

Sádico saw she wasn't going to give up easily, and yet again irritation filled him. Everyone wanted to fuck with his time.

He swung the wheel sharply, and the car hopped the curb, cutting her off. He put it in park, opened his door and jumped out in one fluid motion, taking her by the hair and placing the gun to her left temple. At her feet, the dog yipped.

"Get in the car," he said calmly, and just as she was about to cry out, to try and kick him in the shins, a man exited a small Mexican restaurant, a napkin tucked into the collar of his shirt. He had a look of recognition on his face, and Gina was about to weep in relief when he said, "Ju need help corralling jore chica, mister?"

"Si," Sádico said, and this stranger, some guy who didn't even trust himself not to spill refried beans on his guayabera, wrapped his arms around Gina's waist, and when El Sádico opened the door, dumped her and Ruby inside. "Gracias," Sádico said, keeping his gun trained on the girl until he got behind the wheel.

"Buenos Dias," he told the man before putting a slug in his head, blood spattering the pane of glass behind him. "Buckle up," he told Gina, then floored it out of there.

◆ ◆ ◆

"Is that Ramon Pasquales?" Terry asked, and Bobby squinted into the bright daylight. He'd only met the man a couple of times, and it seemed like, for the owner of the joint, he sure didn't spend much time there. Carlos had always been the one around when someone in charge was needed. But those two times had seared the man's image in his brain, because, if anything, Pasquales just didn't seem to be the owner type. Bobby wondered how many of the decisions he actually made.

"Yeah," Bobby said. "That's him. How do you know him?"

"He likes to gamble."

They all watched as the burly men carrying automatic rifles escorted him out to the van. Ramon didn't look very happy about it, that was for damn sure. In fact, he looked undeniably distressed. It was anybody's best guess as to what was going on, yet it was Lance who voiced the opinion. "Change of guard." To everyone in the car this made sense.

When the van drove away, everyone was silent for a moment until Melissa said, "I think this is our cue."

"What's the plan?" Tommy asked.

"Yeah," Terry agreed. "What are we doing?"

Melissa laid it out for them, and after asking a few questions, receiving their answers and digesting the info, they all nodded in turn.

"OK."

Guns and ammo were checked, grim expressions set on their faces as they readied themselves for battle. Then they got out of the car, crossed the street, and went into the bar.

◆ ◆ ◆

"Please mister," Gina whimpered, clutching Ruby tightly to her breast. "Don't hurt me and my dog."

"This is jore lucky day," El Sádico said, keeping one eye on the road, and the other and the .357 on the girl. "Jore dog will be fine."

Gina was simultaneously relieved/dismayed by this information. In all honesty she didn't know what to say. What she did know was that she wished Sid was still with her, and she really wanted to see her daddy. Also, she was angered that her mother and her stepdad concocted a dumbass plan that wound up backfiring on them and actually got her kidnapped. She hated them more than she hated anybody right now, and if her dad knew what was going on he'd do everything in his power to get custody of her when this was over.

If this ever is over, she thought distressingly. *It might be "over" for me anytime...*

The thought made her cold, as it was a heady one for a fifteen-year-old girl with her entire life in front of her. Facing one's impending death might be easier for someone a bit older, but for a kid who'd never had anything more serious then strep throat, this was terrifying. But to know that Ruby would be safe...at least she had that.

Sádico placed the gun momentarily on the dash, then retrieved his phone from his jacket. He held it out to her. Time to put his plan into action and get this over with.

"Call jore father and tell him ju will be shot if he does not meet us."

Looking at the phone as if it was a venomous snake, Gina gulped air and swallowed thickly. This man must think she was an idiot. He'd just told her he was going to kill her, so why would she call her daddy and allow him to get killed too? It felt so, so...traitorous. He may have missed a few of her birthdays and was far from being the perfect father, but there was no way she was going to march him to his death. This man, this crazy, scary man, apparently was going to kill her either way, so she might as well not make it easy for him to find her daddy. Let him do his own homework.

"I don't know his number," she lied easily, "it's in my phone."

"Where is phone?"

"Greg took it from me when I was staying at his house. He didn't want me to call my daddy."

Like a chip off the old block, she found within herself the ability to lie when she had to, just like her old man whenever he was in hot water from blacking out. On this occasion, it was a very good thing indeed. Besides, it almost was the truth; Greg *had* hidden the house phone from her, to keep her from knowing that she'd been "kidnapped." Again, another surge of anger made her bristle just picturing her treacherous mother's face and her dipshit sidekick.

El Sádico nodded his head as if he'd expected this, and returned the phone to his pocket.

So much for that plan…no one knows anyone's number anymore because of these damn phones.

He picked up the gun again, resumed aiming it at her.

"She is good-looking dog," he said, and this took Gina slightly off guard.

"Her name is Ruby."

"I find good home for her, I promise," he said, and Gina recognized the sincerity in his voice.

"You…you like dogs?"

"Animals are the only thing in the world that make sense to me," Sádico said, making a turn that took them further from civilization. Now that he knew the girl couldn't (or wouldn't) lead him to Bobby Travis, he might as well shoot her and get it over with. There was no sense wasting any more time. However, he felt like imparting his wisdom upon her before he took her life, and if he dumped her in the desert, he wouldn't have to dissolve her body later.

Gina realized he was taking her out by the wild animal park, a popular tourist attraction known for its wide variety of wildlife from all over the world, especially those that hailed from the African savannah. She'd known all along he wasn't bluffing, but this certainly proved it. He was taking her farther away from town with each turn.

"Humans," he continued, wanting a cigarette but resigning himself to having one once the girl was dead, "are evil, full of flaws. Everything an animal do, they do because is natural, honest. There are scavengers that steal, but they do it simply because they must eat. Everything the animals do has a higher purpose that isn't intended to deliberately swindle another. Humans are jus the opposite; they are mostly liars and cheaters." He looked her in the eyes, eyes that were as cold as the frozen tundra polar bears called home. "Humans are a disease. It is easy to kill them because they are so full of lies they don even know what the truth is."

"Isn't killing bad?" she said, trying to hold his gaze. She knew he was trying to draw the truth out of her, but she was damned if she'd tell.

"Not if it is done with the best of intentions," he replied, looking back at the road.

"Well, I never lied to you mister," Gina fibbed bravely, and at this he smiled bitterly.

"Maybe ju have, maybe ju haven't; it is unimportant to me now." He glanced at her again with a look that appeared to see right through her, eyes as penetrating as laser beams. The coldness she perceived now seemed like fire. "I have nothing agains ju, little chica. I jus doing my chob, and for that I am well paid. I will not delight in chooting ju, of that I assure ju."

"Do you have to?" she asked, and at this he laughed.

"I have chob to do," he replied curtly, and that, seemingly, was the end of the conversation.

They passed the entrance to the wild animal park. After that there was nothing but cactus, rock outcroppings and ostrich farms. He could practically pull over anywhere, shoot her, and ditch her body. Gina felt, and not for the first time in recent weeks, that she truly wasn't in control, that nothing in this world mattered. She was going to be shot in cold blood and dumped in the desert. Maybe, if she was lucky, the shot would kill her right away and she wouldn't be aware of being eaten by insects or wild animals. She shuddered. You really *were* screwed when that was your view of optimism.

Sádico was just turning onto an unpaved ranch road when his cell phone rang. He looked at it, letting it ring several times before he sighed and picked it up.

"Si?"

The look on his face changed considerably; it went from somber boredom to one of relief, or was that essentially joy? For the first time, the man seemed happy.

"Si, si, the girl and I be there in," he said, consulting his watch, "fifteen minutes."

He swung the car around without hardly slowing down, and Gina had to hold on tight so she and Ruby didn't tumble to the floor.

"Ju are a very, very lucky girl," he said. "Ju get a brief reprieve."

"You're not going to kill me?"

"No," he shook his head. "I still going to kill ju, but ju may have the honor of dying with jore father, and I think ju will agree that, under the circumstances, that is very generous of me indeed."

He sure didn't know her all that well if he thought she would consider *that* generosity, but the idea of seeing her daddy again certainly appealed to her.

"We're going to see my daddy?"

"Si, little chica, we are."

And from there they drove in silence.

Chapter Thirty-Two

"Everyone get on the floor now!" Melissa yelled, and the barflies looked up from the drinks they were drowning in and regarded her with bored curiosity. No one made a move to do as she'd asked. "Didn't you hear me?" She pointed her weapon at the ceiling and pulled the trigger, but it made a dry clicking sound.

"Safety's on," Lance said, and it took her a moment to locate the little lever, flip it the other way, then pull the trigger once more. This time a loud explosion broke the relative silence in the room, and the drunks hit the deck, hiding under their bar stools.

"Jesus, Bobby," Tony said, coming out from the back room carrying a case of beer. "What are you guys doing?"

"Hey, Tony," Bobby said, grinning at the other a touch foolishly. "We're, um, taking the place over."

"What the hell for?" He set the beer down on the counter, knotting his eyebrows.

"The men who are moving drugs through this dump have Bobby's little girl," Melissa announced loudly. "And we're here to get her back."

"I don't know what you're talking about."

"Cut the crap," Melissa said. "You know damn well what's going on." She looked pointedly at Bobby before she continued. "Where do you think your manager Carlos went, on an extended vacation?"

"What he chooses to do with his free time is none of my business—"

"Why did those goons just take Ramon Pasquales out of here at gun-point?" Lance interrupted. "It didn't look like he was going willingly."

"Business meeting," Tony said, but his voice got lower and his eyes shiftier. "They're some of our beverage suppliers..."

"That's some booze I gotta try!" Tommy said, and Melissa shot him a dirty look.

"Tony," Bobby said softly, "the jig is up. My cousin Teddy died because of those guys, and they have my daughter." He didn't want to do it, but he felt he had no choice; he pointed the shotgun at him. "You know what's going on and you're going to help us or I'm going to shoot you. Is that clear?"

Tony grinned. "Come on Bobby, you're not a killer. I know you, you're a drunk. Say, I know what we can do: drinks on the house, for you and all of your friends. What do you say? Put down the guns and have a seat and I'll hook you up. We can forget all about this nonsense."

"Sounds good to me," Tommy agreed, putting his weapon down, when Bobby activated the pump lever on his twelve-gauge, depositing a shell into the chamber.

"I don't think so, Tony," Bobby said. "And get your hands where I can see them. I don't want to have to hurt you man, I really don't."

The pained expression on the other's face almost made Bobby feel bad, but he reminded himself of why he was here, and damn straight Tony knew what was going on. He'd be an idiot not to since he was the one who pushed so much of the product to the patrons.

"You're making a big mistake Bobby," Tony said, raising his hands. "these aren't guys you want to be messing with."

"Well we're here to, just the same."

Terry stepped forward. "We know you know what's going on dickhead, so get on the phone and call whoever it is that has Bobby's little girl and tell them to bring her here now, or we're going to torch this place. But not until after we call the cops and every DEA agent in the state."

"Terry," Tony said, "you know me too."

"Yeah, and you owe me two hundred and fifty bucks!"

"I'll get you the money, I swear!"

"This isn't about the money; this is about Bobby's little girl." He glared at the other. "I *do* want my money though."

A look passed over Tony's face, one of regret, maybe remorse, but intermingled was fear.

"The guy that has Gina...you really don't want to tangle with him," Tony said quietly, and for the first time he actually sounded sincere.

"You know who has her?" Bobby said, and Tony nodded.

"He's probably shot her already."

"What?"

"Those are his orders: to kill her and then kill you." He looked at Melissa. "And you." He glanced around at the others. "And if the rest of you don't want your names added to the list, I'd suggest you get the hell out of here right now. This guy isn't human; he's like a force of nature. His orders are to tie up all the loose ends, and that means you guys."

"I don't give a flying fuck who this guy is," Bobby said. "Call him right now and tell him to bring me my little girl. He can have me in trade."

"You don't understand...he doesn't want to trade. Both your necks are on the chopping block, see? The Castillo family can't have anyone else know about this!"

"And what about your clientele here?" Lance asked, gesturing around at the barflies who were listening in.

"They're all dead too," Tony whispered, and a couple of them looked up listlessly from their drinks. "Hell, I might even get a slug in the head." He looked forlorn, worn out. "Turn around, just get out of here while you can. Leaving town is your best option at this point."

"Not without my little girl," Bobby said, stepping closer, training the gun on Tony's head. "You call this guy right now and tell him I'm here waiting for him. You can do that for me, can't you?"

Tony nodded slowly. "I can."

"Do it then!" Bobby hollered, and Tony lowered one hand, dipped it into his pocket, his fingertips just grazing the phone when Lance pointed his pistol at him.

"Slowly!" he warned, and Tony froze.

"It's just my phone," he said.

"Bring your hand up real slow so we don't shoot you thinking you're pulling a piece on us."

"Sure..."

Tony lifted his hand, and sure enough his iPhone with cracked glass was in his hand.

"Now make the call," Bobby said, and Tony dialed.

◆ ◆ ◆

Ramon Pasquales had no idea where it was these men were taking him, but of one thing he was certain: he was no longer in charge of Hooligans. He'd never made any real decisions regarding the bar; in fact, all he and his wife did was take vacations. Carlos had handled everything. That had been a part of the deal he'd made with the Castillo cartel when they bought the bar and put him charge.

"Can ju take the hood off me?" he'd asked his captors, and received no reply. These men, they were trained not to think; therefore, answering questions was *way* above their paygrade. All they provided was muscle, and in turn they received a very generous salary indeed.

He could tell when the van left regular pavement and went off-road. The going suddenly got very bumpy. His heart thudded sickly in his chest. This was not good, not good at all.

After what felt like an eternity, the van slowed to a stop, hands grabbed him under his armpits and dragged him to his feet. They took him out of the van, and with no ceremony, the hood was removed. He blinked several times in the bright sunlight, tears forming in his eyes.

"Do ju know why ju are here, Ramon?" a familiar voice asked, and when he turned his head, he saw it was the benefactor of all his success.

"Hola, Señor Castillo," Ramon said bravely. "No se. Why ju honor me with jore presence?"

Martino Estabon Rodriquez Estevan Castillo regarded the other with a look of disgust on his face. "Ju fat, lazy piece of shit," he said, and

Ramon bowed his head. Surely this was it for him. "Is time for ju to honor jore promise."

Ramon felt his stomach roil dangerously, his lunch perilously close to coming back up. When he was given the piece of property that would serve him so well for many, many years, he was told that it would come at a price. It wasn't guaranteed that Ramon would have to pay this price, but in the event that he had to, he would have to accept it for what it was. It was either that or continue working as a gardener, enduring backbreaking labor in the hot, unforgiving sun.

"Si," Ramon replied.

"The Castillo cartel will never suffer the indignity of dealing with the US DEA, comprende?"

"Si, Señor Castillo."

"By honoring jore promise, ju and jore wife will be allowed to live, and ju can rest assured that we always take care of those who have served us well. Ju will receive the finest treatment."

"Si, Señor Castillo," Ramon repeated, but this "fine treatment," he knew, was merely an expression. What he was going to endure would be much, much worse than the hard labor that had threatened to be his way of life until they had come along, of that he was certain.

"We will return ju, and when the time comes, ju will do as agreed." Castillo stepped closer, lifted Ramon's chin so that he was staring the other in the eyes. "If ju don't, jore life will be very, very miserable indeed. Ju will wish for death, but ju will receive only pain. Ju will watch as we rape and dismember jore wife. Then we will torture ju for as long as jore body holds out. Ju will beg for death but will not get it. Comprende?"

"Si."

"Bueno." He let go of Ramon, wiping his hand on his pants. "Bring him back into town. If this does not go as planned, mi amigo is ready to sacrifice himself." He turned away, but was compelled to turn back. "Ramon," he said, and the other looked at him hopefully. "There is always the chance of salvation."

Ramon raised his eyebrows questioningly.

"If things work out, we go back to the way it was before...until something comes up in the future."

"Gracias!" Ramon gushed, grateful that this had merely been a threat, not a promise made in stone.

"Ju better hope everything work out."

"I will pray to Chesus that everything is fine," Ramon said and Castillo shook his head.

"Ju better pray to someone with more clout than that." He looked at his men. "Get him out of here."

And Ramon was once again hooded and dragged back into the hot confines of the van.

◆ ◆ ◆

"I hope you're happy," Tony said, pocketing his phone. "The most ruthless murderer in Southern California is now heading this way."

"With my little girl?" Bobby said, and Tony nodded.

"Yes, with your daughter."

"What are we going to do when he gets here?" Tommy asked, and by anybody's standards, it was a damn good question. Yet again, all heads turned to Melissa, but this time she wasn't as quick with an answer. She was momentarily at a loss.

"There must be something he wants," Bobby said. "Something we can trade him."

"This guy doesn't want anything but to see us all dead," Tony said. "Thanks for making my day, Bobby. I wanted to watch the Angels on TV tonight."

"You ain't a Padres fan?" Terry said, then gave it some thought. "You wanna bet on the game?"

"Quiet everyone!" Lance interrupted. "Here's what we're going to do."

And he gave out orders, directing them all like a choreographer does his dance students. Everyone listened raptly, nodding their heads. Since none of them had ever been in a situation like this before, and it could get really ugly before it got anywhere close to pretty, they hung on his every word. When he was done, they fanned out.

"And I want you to stay right where you are," he instructed Tony, who hadn't moved an inch from where he was standing.

"Great, so I'm a sitting duck."

"That's what you get for being involved," Lance said.

"You too," Tony shot back.

"Touché." He glanced around at all assembled. "Are you ready?" he asked, and after several Adam's apples bobbed up and down from gulping fearfully, all heads nodded. "Great. So when he arrives, you follow my lead."

It turned out they didn't have to wait that long.

Chapter Thirty-Three

He pulled the car alongside the curb outside of the bar, looked around at the passersby on the street, noticing nothing but the usual pedestrians and shoppers. No one who looked as if they were concealing a gun. Be that as it may, discretion was at a premium.

"Ju stay right there," El Sádico commanded the girl, and she nodded somberly. He stepped out of the car, moving quickly around the front. He arrived at her door, opened it, and ushered her and her dog out at gunpoint. Placing her directly in front of him, he walked slowly from the car to the front door of Hooligans. Surely entering from the front was bold indeed, but there was no more time to waste. No one would do anything, not even the little girl's father, not with the girl as his personal body armor.

With one arm around her neck, the dog straggling miserably beside her, he placed a hand on the door and cracked it open. Yes, as he'd thought, he was walking into what was intended to be an ambush. He'd see about that, yes indeed he would. Sádico opened the door and strode in, nearly lifting the girl off of her feet.

"Gina!" Bobby exclaimed at the sight of his daughter, and the smile she cast back was rife with apprehension. He wanted to rush to her side, to assuage her fears, but Lance cleared his throat loudly.

"Stay in position, Bobby," he warned.

"Hi, Daddy," Gina replied, her voice warbly with fear. Ruby echoed the sentiment with a throaty whimper.

"I see ju have assembled a posse, Bobby Travis," Sádico said, smiling a smile that reeked of the gallows. "Do ju truly think ju can stop me from my appointed task?"

Bobby had no answer, he simply looked at the man in awe. His appearance did indeed live up to the introduction Tony had made. There were dark circles around his eyes that made him look like a vampire. If he smiled and showed fangs, Bobby wouldn't be surprised. His attire was fastidious, from his short black hair to his manicured hands, but an air of violence enveloped him like a cloak.

"I...I want my daughter back," Bobby said, almost forgetting that he was clutching a Remington twelve-gauge in his hands.

"No one," El Sádico said, his words echoing off the cheap stucco walls, "is going to get out of this room alive. Comprende?"

"I don't think so, dude," Lance said, stepping forward, double fisting a pair of .44 Magnums. "You recognize this gun? This is a .44 Magnum, the most powerful handgun in the world and would blow your head clean off, so you've gotta ask yourself one question: 'Do you feel lucky? Well, do ya, punk?'"

"Spare me the *Dirty Harry* cliché," Sádico said, keeping the gun pressed against Gina's temple as he advanced upon them. She squirmed slightly in his grasp, a lone tear running down one pale cheek. "As long as this little chica is in my arms, I doubt ju are going to do anything so much as finger the trigger. Isn't that right, Bobby? Ju want me to shoot jore daughter?"

"Look," Bobby said, lowering the shotgun. "You can have me instead, OK? Just leave her out of this and you can do whatever you want to me. Just let her go."

"I'm afraid is out of the question." Sádico shook his head, an expression of feigned unhappiness on his face. "I say again: no one is leaving this room." He looked at the barflies as they glanced at him curiously from under their barstools. "No one."

"Jesus mister," one drunk said, rising from a crouch and taking a dubious step forward. "I don't know who you are, or what you're talking about. I got nothing to do with this."

In a moment quicker than a flash of lightening, Sádico removed the gun from Gina's head and shot the man in the neck. With the silencer still attached it made no sound; there was a muzzle flash and then an explosion of gore sprayed forth like a geyser. The drunk fell to his knees, clutching his torn throat, gurgling on the blood that would drown him. And just like that, Sádico had the gun against Gina's temple again. She strained against him, but his muscled arms were like steel bands.

"Consider me the angel of death," he proclaimed. "And it has come to my attention that all of ju have sins that need atoning for. I be swift, ruthless jet kind. Embrace jore death, accept jore fate."

Terry stood open mouthed, unable to believe that a man who owed him five Gs was dying on the floor near his Redwing boots. He'd never get his money now. He stepped aside quickly before blood got on his soles. It was really hard to get that stuff out of the treads.

Tommy wished he was anywhere but here right now. Hell, he'd gladly be sitting at his mother-in-law's house, watching Opera with her and drinking Sanka. Why the hell had he decided to join these guys on what was surely a fool's errand? Damn, he needed a drink.

Melissa was motionless, watching the killer carefully. El Sádico had just shot a man swifter than her eyes could even register, true, but they had him outgunned. If they played their cards right, maybe they could end it right here, right now, before anyone else got hurt. It didn't help that he had Gina as a shield and the speed of the devil, though.

"Let the girl go and fight us like a man," she said, as courageously as she could, even though she was swallowing compulsively, a fear response to a situation that was rapidly spiraling out of control.

"Like a man, eh? That's something I expec from a woman: some emasculating bit of tripe. Is supposed to be intimidating?"

"Um…yes?"

"Help me, Daddy, please!" Gina implored, and again Ruby seconded the motion with a pitiful moan.

"I grow bored with this," El Sádico said. "I think is time ju all drop your guns and accept jore death."

"You don't need to hurt her," Bobby said, his heart aching watching his daughter squirm in the man's wiry arms. This was awful, truly, truly awful; there had to be a solution, some method they could employ to get her out of his grasp and safely away from the line of fire. Maybe if they reasoned with him he'd let Gina and Ruby go. There had to be some shred of humanity in the guy. He couldn't be as atrocious as Tony had claimed, could he? "Please," Bobby said, his voice earnest, his eyes searching the others beseechingly. "She has nothing to do with any of this. Just let her go and you can...I don't know...torture me...or whatever the hell else it is you need to do."

"Are ju deaf or jus stupid?" Sádico retorted. "What about 'no one gets out of here alive' do ju not get?"

Obviously, reasoning was not a judicious tactic. If you were dealing with a killer, apparently you had to act like a killer. Bobby hoisted the gun to his shoulder once more, glanced around at the others to see that theirs were raised as well. "OK," he said. "If you want a gun fight, you'll get one." He struggled yet succeeded at looking the other in the eyes again, this time with an attempt at menace. "But how about a little wager first, huh? You a gambling man?"

Sádico lifted an eyebrow. "Que?"

"I'll take that action!" Terry blurted. "What are the odds?" He thought about it, considered. "What's the bet?"

"I bet he can't kill all of us before we kill him," Bobby said, trying to sound strong, confident, and Terry in turn looked pale.

"Um, I don't know if I want to back that horse..."

"Surely ju can't be serious," El Sádico said with a wry smile. "Ju saw how quickly I kill the drunk."

"Hey man," Tommy said. "We're all drunks here. You'd best watch your tone."

"Let's see you try then," Bobby goaded. "Let my daughter and her dog step outside and you can show us what you got." He paused, taking a page from Melissa. "If you're man enough, that is."

Sádico chortled, a full-throated, unaffected laugh that unabashedly proved he was sincerely tickled.

"Man enough?" he said, his mirth nearly overtaking him. "Man enough? Vete a la chingada!"

Yet again, with an otherworldly speed that was terrifying, he fired his gun, and another drunk's head exploded in a shower of blood and brains as the poor bastard collapsed amidst a pile of peanut shells, going through rigorous death throes on a floor that hadn't been cleaned with disinfectant since the last soldiers came back from Vietnam.

"Is that 'man enough'?" he asked dryly, and Bobby had to admit the killer truly had them by the ass hairs. He swallowed again, wondering what they were going to do next.

Die, most likely. We're screwed...this dude ain't playing around.

"I growing tired of all this talk," El Sádico declared, and indeed he honestly did appear weary. "Everyone line up agains the wall and I make it quick—"

"I don't think so," someone said, and when everyone looked around for the source they were amazed to see it was Tony. He was now in possession of an automatic rifle, and the look on his face was something that Bobby had never witnessed before. Laughing, smiling Tony, the jovial barkeep who kept him nose-deep in cocaine and methamphetamine—and right now he looked like he just did three tours of duty in Afghanistan and wanted to do another three before getting shipped off to Iraq. "Let the girl go."

"*Ju* dare to challenge me?" Sádico said, amused. "The bartender who keep all his patrons high on drugs? Who died and made Ju Chohn Wayne?"

"I mean it." He frowned sternly down the barrel of the rifle. "Step down or I'm going to fill you with so much lead you'll sink swimming back across the Rio Grande."

The irony of a Mexican American saying that to a Mexican was not lost on the others. Sádico, however, ignored it.

"Ju would take this little girl's life in jore hands to be a hero? What if ju miss and hit her?"

"I got my sight right on your forehead." He retracted the lever on the side, depositing a round in the chamber. "I'm not going to ask again. Let go of the kid or your head is gonna look like a watermelon after Gallagher took a sledgehammer to it."

There was a moment of silence, one long enough for everyone to hear the dripping of water from a shoddy pipe overhead. Outside, an ambulance went by. In the sky above, a plane flew over. Tommy licked his lips with a tongue so dry he could cut it on a postage stamp. Bobby shuffled from one foot to the next like a little boy who had to pee, one who had been holding it so long that he could barely contain it anymore. Melissa cleared her throat with an arid, raspy sound. Terry rubbed his mouth with one hand, his gun clenched in the other. Man, but he needed a smoke.

And the hush carried on, all eyes trained on the killer with the girl clutched in his long, bony fingers, fingers, by the way, that were not trembling in the least. While the others were clutching guns that shook and wobbled in their collective grasp, he looked as cool as they come, not an ounce of concern in his demeanor. And why should there be? He was, after all, a stone-cold murderer. They were tourists in his world, and he knew it.

Sádico's muscles tensed; the gesture was almost imperceptible but Bobby noticed just the same. The fiend was readying himself for an onslaught that would kill them all, was preparing himself like Bruce Lee before kicking the crap out of fourteen bad guys who were imprudent enough to think they could take him. Were they all *that* stupid? Apparently so, but Bobby knew he had to do whatever he could to try and save his daughter. He looked at Melissa, cast her a glance that aptly conveyed "nice to know you," and she nodded in return. "I love you," she mouthed, ready for all of them to be blown to hell and beyond, when suddenly the sound of screeching tires came from just outside the door, followed by the coarse sound of men's voices.

The front door flew open, and five huge goons carrying automatic rifles came sauntering in.

And that, my friends, was when everything was jump started into roaring, kicking life.

◆ ◆ ◆

Ramon Pasquales thought furiously as the van drove him back from the desert, returning him, presumably, to Hooligans. That would be good, as his car was parked in the back by the dumpster, the Mercedes he'd bought when he thought he had the world in the palm of his hand. Presently he was thinking about how much he did not want to go to prison, did not want to get raped by big, muscled men whenever he was alone in his cell or caught somewhere that the guards weren't watching. He considered the possibility of fleeing the state, of taking his wife and going somewhere that the Castillo family could not find him. He was grateful to them for the position of power they'd given him, but he did not necessarily want to be their scapegoat should it come to that. Could he run, could he hide? These were thoughts that preoccupied him until he sensed they must be getting close to Escondido. It was very warm within the confines of the hood, and as he was mentally bemoaning his fate, one of the men snatched it off of his head. He took a deep breath and glanced around and saw the driver of the van turning onto Valley Center Parkway while the goons appeared to snooze in the seats surrounding him, weapons clutched in hands as big as dinner plates.

Ramon wasn't completely stupid. During the course of his "owner-ship" he'd known it couldn't last forever, but he'd been desperately hoping that they would be the ones to get arrested so as not to be required to live up to his end of the bargain. Why couldn't a rival cartel cut them down? Shouldn't they be involved in some sort of turf war? Wasn't that the way these things tended to go? He had no idea, though, because all along he hadn't been paying attention. He and his wife just took the money they gave him and spent it on lavish things that made them feel upwardly mobile, that helped them to pretend they weren't really labor-ers, when indeed that was the world they'd come from, he in Mexico, she working crappy jobs in the States. Maybe if he'd prepared for this day, he'd be better equipped to deal with the consequences. Of course, how do you prepare for spending the rest of your life in prison, binge watch *OZ*? He shuddered at the prospect. He really hated that show.

When they pulled up in front of Hooligans, one of the men opened the sliding door, about to toss him out, when he saw a car parked outside that he recognized. He decided to call it in to the boss.

"Que?" Castillo asked.

"El Sádico is at the bar."

"What's he doing?"

"No se. We parked outside. I looking at his car right now."

"Ju stupid pendejo! Go in and see if he has finished the chob!"

"Si," the guard said, and hung up his phone. "We go inside," he told the others. He looked at Ramon. "You stay here." He eyed him prudently. "We need ju for other things."

Ramon couldn't help it; he blurted, "I know what ju need me for."

The guard ignored him. "Vamanos," he said to the men and they stood, making no effort to conceal the weapons they carried. And who was going to stop them? He couldn't think of a sane person who would approach five large men armed with automatic weapons and make a stink about it. Not if they wanted to walk away in one piece, that is.

They exited and headed for the front door, and Ramon got lost in thought again, wondering how he could escape. Surely there must be a logical approach, and if pressured he was certain he could think of a way out. So, he considered every angle, every nuance. Take a plane out of the country, maybe to Canada? No, too cold. Maybe to Europe and disappear in France? No, he thought sadly. He wouldn't be able to understand a thing they were saying. What about Spain then? He and his wife would be able to understand *their* language. He smiled to himself. That was it! They would get plane tickets to Spain and simply vanish, leave the Castillo family to clean up their own mess. Surely the cartel couldn't find them there.

Abruptly the sound of gunfire came from inside the bar, startling him. He sat up and looked out the passenger side window. Bullets shattered one of the front plate glass windows, and then shells began to pelt the truck, rocking it back and forth.

"¡Hijo de puta!" he gasped, deciding that the van probably wasn't the safest place to be. He got out, and without another glance, flat footed it down the block, around the corner, and away from the ensuing chaos.

◆ ◆ ◆

The door opened and five large men carrying automatic rifles entered. They assessed the situation and saw Bobby and his group of friends with their guns drawn, aimed at El Sádico, who held the girl in his arms, a gun to her head. He turned to glance at them briefly, a look of annoyance on his face.

"Boss wants to know if ju get the chob done," one of them muttered, and Sádico rolled his eyes.

"Does it look done?"

"No?"

"Is your answer then."

"Ju want help?"

"No, I have this under control!"

But the men remained, looking from him to the others, and back.

"Vamanos!" Sádico commanded, yet they stood their ground.

Tony saw this as an opportunity; he could now take a clean shot while El Sádico was occupied. He squeezed the trigger, holding his breath as he did so, but his aim was off and it struck the man in his shoulder instead of the head.

"Bastard!" Sádico exclaimed, absorbing the gunshot like a pro, yet taking this as an exit cue, scooping up the bulldog and backing away with the girl. "Clean this up!" he ordered the guards, and they began firing into the bar. Bedlam instantly followed with the splintering of wood and the shattering of glass. Using the distraction, he stealthily positioned himself behind the goons, then slipped silently out the door with his bounty in tow.

"Gina, no!" Bobby screamed, watching in horror as the killer stole away with his daughter, her cries dampened by the noise of the automatic weapons. He dropped to one knee, raising the twelve-gauge and unloading both barrels into the nearest man. For an amateur, he was extremely lucky; he hit one of the attackers in the chest, knocking him off his feet and sending him crashing into the wall behind him where he left a gruesome stain reminiscent of modern art. Bobby stared at the dead man, amazed that he'd just shot someone. He didn't know he had it in him. Bullets flew all around him, some of them close enough for him to feel the wind from their passing, yet he crouched there unflinchingly, dumbfounded. Once again Gina was gone, and unless he and the others could get past this army of killers, she was a goner for sure.

Jesus Christ, not again.

Melissa dove behind a booth, popping her head up and firing randomly, her shots flying wildly. "Keep shooting Bobby!" she screamed over the din, but he couldn't hear her, he was lost in a daze.

Lance sprung forward as he fired both weapons, squeezing the triggers with crazy abandon. He hit one of the men in the leg, knocking him down, and plugged another in the stomach. Tummy-wound dropped his weapon and tried to staunch the flow of blood with both hands, although it was too late for that. Lance could see a loop of intestine hanging out, promising a painful, bacteria-ridden death.

"Eat that ya cock knocker!" he laughed gleefully as he jammed another clip into place.

Across the room, Terry was doing his best imitation of the Human Statue. An alarm was sounding in his brain, screaming that he should be shooting, but he was like a rabbit caught in the headlights of a truck. His gun he clutched loosely in hands that were frozen into claws, an expression on his face akin to that of a man watching a bad storm blowing in and knowing he isn't going to get inside in time to stay dry. Because of his inertia, a slug finally planted itself in his arm, then another in his forehead. A hot blast of blood spurted from the head wound, and he collapsed first to his knees, then face down onto the floor. One of his legs twitched and kicked as a pool of crimson fanned out around him.

"Jesus H Joseph and Harry!" Tommy cried and sprinted to the bar, joining Tony on the other side. Bullets rained above them and bottles exploded in a mist of crushed glass and sour booze. The sound was overpowering, deafening. The smell of gunpowder comingled with whisky hung heavy in the air.

"What are we going to do?" he rasped, out of breath.

"Shoot at them!" Tony bellowed, peeking his head up and firing off a couple of rounds. A spray of bullets filled the air, and he ducked just in time to avoid getting his hair parted Yosemite Sam style.

It took a ricocheting bullet to finally bring Bobby around, the shot screaming off the battered wooden floor and just missing his shnoz by a pubic hair. He could practically feel the heat from the round and, enraged, he squeezed the trigger again, only to realize that he had to pump the gun to reload it. He did so, firing off a shot before ducking behind an overturned table. There were three goons left, and two of them were bleeding. They continued their vigilant defense nonetheless, firing seemingly endless rounds into the drunks, their stools, the walls, anything they could shoot at. The drunks flailed like out-of-control marionettes, doing a gruesome Texas Two-Step that left the floor awash in viscous fluid. Bobby shivered as he watched them die, knowing they didn't deserve the fate they'd been bestowed with. He also knew that the longer it took to waste these bastards, the further away the killer got. And with enough time on his hands, he'd finally complete his task. He hastily broke the gun open and shoved in more shells, closed it and pumped it. He was now ready to send these assholes to hell.

Lance emptied both clips and reached into his pocket for more. As he groped, his hand came across a grenade. He retrieved it, then shouted to Bobby and Melissa, "Grenade!" and lobbed it at the three remaining men. Two of them dove out of the way, but it landed at the feet of the third, who looked down at it with an expression of horror before it detonated, sending him and large chunks of wood and masonry through one of the front windows. He landed on the sidewalk outside, his clothing on fire, an enormous hole where his torso used to be.

"We got 'em on the run!" Lance hollered, jamming another clip into one of his .44s and getting to his feet, firing furiously at the remaining men. Unfortunately, his aim suffered from his jubilation, and when he fired his last round high over the largest goon's head, the other smiled with savage pleasure. He advanced upon Lance, his weapon doing the talking, peppering the other with machine gun fire. Blood spurted from the many wounds as the slugs penetrated him. It would turn out to be the last time Lance was ever penetrated again. He did an eerie jig in the dim bar lighting before sagging to the floor in a heap, his eyes wide but unseeing, his mouth open and slack as blood poured forth.

Tony popped up from behind the bar again, firing at one of the men and finally finding his mark. A small hole presented itself in the goon's forehead, while simultaneously the back of his skull exploded in a torrential rain of blasted brains. That left only one man, and he was smart enough to know when he'd been licked. He dashed toward the front door, evading the volley of bullets, and escaping into the broiling air beyond.

At once it was still in the bar, the silence lingering like the last traces of gun smoke.

"Holy freakin' Toledo!" Tommy said, looking at Tony in awe. "Where did you learn to shoot like that?"

Tony smiled, but the gesture was brief because Melissa broke the quiet by announcing what nobody but Bobby had noticed while the gunfight was in full swing:

"Gina's gone!"

Bobby came out from under the table, dropping the twelve-gauge and scrubbing his mouth with the back of one hand. He looked about the bar, surveying the damage, seeing the regulars lying in states of repose from which they'd never get up, then ran to the front door and opened it. He looked both ways down the street, seeing nothing but gathering pedestrians, rubberneckers, people who wanted to know exactly what the hell was going on in Hooligans at two thirty on a Tuesday afternoon. In the distance, sirens were getting closer.

Then Tony was behind him, taking him by the arm and attempting to lead him back inside the bar.

"We need to talk," he said, but Bobby could barely hear him. Again he looked left, then right, wondering where the murderous son of a bitch had gone with his daughter before allowing himself be led inside, disorientation taking from him the last of his energy. Tony walked him to a barstool, told him to sit. He went behind the bar, poured a shot of Jack Daniels, downed it in a breath then poured and drank another. He raised an eyebrow at Bobby, and the other shook his head. After his third shot, he replaced the bottle, then looked at Bobby gravely.

"This might be a little hard to believe," Tony began, and Bobby felt like he was experiencing déjà vu. "But I work for the DEA, undercover division."

"What, you? How?" Melissa said, looking at him disbelievingly.

"It wasn't easy. It took me years to worm my way into their organization."

"But you're a drug dealer!"

"I had to sell my role by doing whatever it was they asked of me. If I had to peddle narcotics, so be it." Tony shook his head, then rubbed the back of his neck. "I've done worse things I'm not proud of..."

Tommy lit a cigarette, looking at the bodies of Lance and Terry briefly before turning to the bar. "I need a drink," he said, and Tony poured him a shot, which Tommy swallowed quickly, nodding his head to indicate he needed another. Tony poured again.

"DEA?" Bobby said weakly, unable to comprehend what had just gone down. The killer escaped with his daughter and Terry and Lance were dead—two men who had nothing at all to do with anything, yet they had given their lives to help him. He felt a surge of incredulity, and he looked at Tony through hooded eyelids. "You work for the DEA and you let us get into a gun fight with a bunch of cartel heavies? Are you nuts?"

"Bobby," Tony countered, "I tried to talk you out of it. I asked you all to leave the bar before things got out of control, but you didn't listen."

Bobby considered this and realized the other was right. He had no way of knowing that a bunch of thugs were going to engage them in battle, but hadn't they come here looking for that? He supposed they got what they'd asked for.

Outside, sirens were getting louder, closer. Soon several police cars pulled up outside of the bar, and then the cops burst in, guns drawn.

"Freeze!" one of them hollered, and everybody froze.

"The guys you gentlemen are looking for are dead," Tony said, holding up a badge he pulled from under his shirt. "Except for one who got away."

"Who the hell are you?" one of the cops demanded.

"Officer Eugenio DePasco, DEA undercover."

"What happened here?"

"Cartel hit," Tony (Eugenio) replied.

"We're going to need more information than that."

"You'll have to get it from my superior," Tony said. "Sorry guys, but that's the best I can do for you."

"No reason to be sorry," the policeman said, removing his handcuffs. "Everybody's going downtown while we sort this out." He turned to another officer. "Call in the CSI team, and tell 'em to bring a lot of body bags. Jesus, what a mess."

A few minutes later, the remaining living souls in Hooligans were summarily cuffed and stuffed and taken to the police station for questioning.

Chapter Thirty-Four

When Tony fired the shot that caught him in the shoulder and the gunfire commenced, El Sádico knew his position had been compromised and he had to evacuate immediately. The way he saw it, the Castillo hired guns would take care of everyone in the bar while he was free to eliminate the girl and find a suitable home for her dog. He was of the opinion that there was no way a bunch of amateurs could get past such battle-hardened crooks as the Castillo gang. Besides, he wanted to get the dog out of the line of fire. She'd done nothing to hurt anyone.

Once he got Gina and Ruby outside and safely in his car, he sped quickly away. Safely for him and the bulldog, that was. He certainly couldn't say the same for the kid.

"We shouldn't have left my daddy in there," Gina sobbed. "He's going to get shot."

"I don wan to rain on jore parade, chica, but so are ju," Sádico said, gunning it through a yellow light while pressing his handkerchief against the bullet wound to staunch the flow of blood. He could feel the bullet lodged in his shoulder and knew he'd have to remove it as soon as time allowed, but for now the pain wasn't a problem. He'd been shot before; it was a necessary evil that went with the job. "Rest assure I find good home for the dog."

"Thanks?" Gina said, and hugged Ruby, receiving yet another sloppy kiss from a tongue that was dry on the tip from always hanging out of her mouth.

El Sádico left Valley Center Parkway, then turned left onto Bear Valley Road. Gina was all too familiar with the area. Her daddy's house was nearby, tucked away in a far corner on five acres of land. It was a shame the court wouldn't allow her to visit him there because the place had so much potential. If he could abstain from drinking and cleaned the pool once in a while, it would be a great weekend getaway for her and Ruby, someplace her mother and Sir Dicks Alot couldn't find her. But he was too big of a screw-up, and the court wouldn't allow it. Yet he had looked good in the bar, his clothing clean, his face shaved. If she didn't know better, she'd say he looked sober, and that was saying an awful lot for Bobby Travis, daddy or no daddy, loved one or not. And maybe, she supposed, he was sober on account that he was looking for her, was trying to keep it together so that he could get her back. Wouldn't that be something? She had seen the sincerity in his eyes; he really, truly loved her. A sob escaped her, then fat tears spilled from her eyes and down her cheeks.

"Don mourn for jore death. Is simply a transition to another reality."

"I'm not crying for me," she said, her words garbled because it was hard to form them when her lips were contorted with sorrow. "I'm crying for my daddy."

El Sádico nodded somberly. He knew what it was like to love a parent. Although he was a merciless killer, he'd always had love in his heart for his family.

"That," he said, "is understandable. Ju go ahead an mourn him. He probably dead by now."

Gina thought that it was the most callous thing he could say to her, yet she figured she'd take it as a compliment.

"So you're taking me somewhere to shoot me," she said, not a question, a statement. "Why don't you just do it and get it over with?"

"I no want to do it in front of the dog." He eyed her levelly. "I take you and do it where she can't see. One shot, you feel no pain, is over."

"Thanks?" she said again.

He passed Bobby's house, took a turn, then another, found a dirt road, turned on it and began what he hoped to be the last leg of this part of his journey. He was getting tired. After this was finished, and he found and executed the cop's wife and daughter (and anyone who was harboring them), and Sid's traitorous brother, he wanted to take a nice break, maybe indulge in a little night life to celebrate a job well done. There was also the matter of his bullet wound, but that was something he could take care of himself. He'd done it before. He smiled faintly, wondering how the Castillo family was going to explain a shoot-out at Hooligans (what they'd instruct Ramon Pasquales to say), but he was sure it would include a desperate group of alcoholics who tried to rob the place, the attempted theft quelled by brave citizens, friends of the owner. And if that didn't work, Ramon took the heat, the Castillo family disappeared like smoke, and the Escondido police were none the wiser. The cartel would bide their time and then reappear somewhere else in a few months. Maybe Vista, maybe San Marcos; they could reopen the operation anywhere, as where there was demand, there would always be supply. That was the way business operated. If there wasn't such a huge call for the product, the cartels would be out of business. It was as simple as that. Thanks to the war on drugs, the cartels easily had the market cornered with cocaine, heroin, and methamphetamine. They could spend their tax free money however they liked: on submarines, tunnels into the United States with electric trains, cryptocurrency they could easily launder and convert into cash, modified airplanes specifically designed for smuggling, whatever they required. It helped that the Americans were greedy and strung-out. They wanted their drugs by the shipload and would have it no other way. They had no idea how hard the many people behind the scenes worked to get them their precious narcotics—from the overworked drudges in the industrial-sized meth labs in Mexico, to the farmers in South America who grew the coca leaves and received a pittance for their labor. Not to mention the men who processed the leaves into cocaine and the mules who transported it at great personal risk through the jungles of Peru to Guatemala, where pilots loaded it onto planes and flew it to Mexico, all the while trying to evade military aircraft that stealthily stalked them via radar at night through clear skies and cloud-studded superstorms. And once the cocaine made it to Mexico, then and only then was it distributed to the cartels, who at that juncture had a whole new set of problems to deal with, mainly concerning the guaranteed transportation of their product to its intended destination. Getting the meth and cocaine over the

American border was the part of the job where they had to get extremely creative. When the stupid Americans were tooting up, they had no idea how many lives had been ruined or lost simply to get them their drug of choice. They were clueless to the human toll that was paid by people who merely wanted to survive.

Sádico reached the end of the dirt road and saw a small, abandoned-looking shack that was weathered and neglected. This was it, the end of the line. He'd take her around back and shoot her and then be on his way. If someone actually lived in the dilapidated hovel and saw him, he'd shoot them too, shoot as many people as he had to so that he could get on to his next piece of business. He pulled up in front and put the car in park.

"Ju get out and come with me." He looked at Ruby. "The dog stay here."

Fresh tears formed in the girl's eyes. "Let me," she sobbed, "say goodbye to my dog…"

"Of course," El Sádico said, nodding his approval. The love of a human and their dog was a very special bond indeed, one that transitioned beyond one world and into the next, one that superseded death.

Gina hugged Ruby close to her and could smell the damp doggy odor of her fur, the slightly stinky scent of her breath. She clung to her tightly, her eyes closed, and when she opened them briefly she saw Ruby looking back at her, her large brown doe eyes full of confusion. Ruby was familiar with tears; however, she couldn't for the life of her understand why they were coming from Gina now. The scent she got off the man wasn't bad. She could tell he liked her, so to her that bespoke a person with a kind heart. Of course, poor Ruby had no idea what the man had in mind for her owner, even though it had been apparent he hadn't been very nice to Gina's dad.

He reached for his door handle and opened it, when his cell phone rang. He sighed. Another goddamn distraction. He picked it up, saw that he didn't recognize the number (briefly wondering how that could be), then put it to his ear.

"Si?"

"I know who you really are," the voice on the other end said. The timbre was deep, American.

"Que?"

"Pablo Diego José Francisco Maldonado, born in Mexico City in nineteen sixty-nine, a fugitive from justice since nineteen eighty-three when you committed your first murder in Ensenada, Mexico. A case that has gone unsolved…until now."

The man's words struck a chord in El Sádico, and he drew in a sharp breath. "Who is this, and where ju get this information?"

"It doesn't matter," the other said. "What does is that I'm prepared to use that evidence if you don't let Gina go."

"I cannot do that—"

"One phone call and I'll have half the cops in the greater Southern California area looking for you, ready to bust your ass and extradite you to Mexico, where you'll face multiple death sentences for all the homicides you've committed." The person speaking paused, letting the weight of his words sink in. "If only you had more than one life to give," he expounded, "then the United States could extradite you from Mexico and execute you again for all the murders you've committed on our soil."

"How ju get this number?"

"Let's just say we have a mutual friend."

"This is nothing but a hoax," El Sádico seethed. "I have the girl and I plan to dispose of her. Is nothing ju can do about it."

"Really Pablo? Let me check my information again." A rustling of pages, then: "Your mother's name, her *maiden* name, is Maria Anna Garcia, and she lives in Puerto Nuevo, Baja, the lobster village if I am correct. She works at a seafood restaurant on the main drag, right off Highway 1. I have the exact address right here. She is still alive…at least, she will be alive if you cooperate with me."

"Ju leave mi Madre out of this!" El Sádico was as cold and heartless as his name implied, but there was one thing in this world he loved besides dogs, and that was his sainted mother, whom he still visited whenever he could, when the job allowed.

"I see your pop has gone to the great taco stand in the sky, but I know where your mother is, and I'm not afraid to send someone after her, maybe rearrange her dental work, if you know what I mean."

A feeling of helplessness surged through Sádico, an infinite swelling of anger and fear and sorrow. This person on the other end of the phone, he knew what he was talking about, but how? Sádico had lost his name and his humanity so long ago that it was if they had never existed. For someone to find out who he really was, they must have gone to great lengths indeed.

"It wasn't that hard," the other told him casually, correctly predicting the train of the assassin's thoughts. "You just have to know where to look." He chuckled. "You think you're untraceable, but you've left a few tracks behind. Not many, but enough for me. I was lucky your arrogance caused you to get sloppy. I looked into unsolved homicides in the past month where unregistered fingerprints were left behind, and you know what I found? No? I'll tell you: an index fingerprint and partial thumb print at the La Quinta Hotel in Carlsbad, where the day manager was hung with his own belt. The prints were on his penis, Pablo. What, did you remove your glove to fondle him, maybe jerk him off before he died?"

"Ju el pendejo! Is lies...all lies!"

"Then I did some digging," the other continued calmly, "and after I ran it through a data bank of fingerprints, I was able to match those prints with a set on file in San Diego County, where I got a photo and a name. I found out you spent three months in the San Diego County cooler in '86 on an aggravated assault and battery charge. You don't like being called a spic, do you? I can't blame you for that. Those frat boys probably had it coming. And you damn near killed them, but that was the idea, right? I have to hand it to you though; it was the last time you, Pablo, got caught, for anything."

"Is bullshit! You lie!"

"Really, Pablo? Those prints you left are pure gold. You'll probably be sentenced to death by firing squad, or whatever it is the Mexicans do to murderers. *Multiple* murderers, I might add." He laughed again. "You wouldn't believe how willing the Mexican government was to cooperate with my investigation. Turns out, they really want to fry your ass too."

Sádico sighed. So this was it, finishing this job was gradually slipping away from him, unless he wanted to call the other's bluff. Except it wasn't a bluff, not at all. This man had done some digging and he'd uncovered information that no one ever had, which was why Sádico was a ghost and could move about at will with no ramifications. When you had no identity, you were invincible. Once someone recovered your name, you became vulnerable. Why had he removed his glove to fondle the day manager? What had he been thinking?

"OK," he said at last, while the other breathed into his ear through the phone, "I meet ju, but ju come alone, comprende? If I sense ju bring anyone else, I forget about mi Madre and I kill la chica without a second thought. Ju unnerstand? Jus you or the girl es muerto."

A pause on the other end, the man thinking about it. At last: "OK, I promise I'll be alone."

"Ju don't, she die."

"I get it."

"Bueno. So where ju want to meet?"

◆ ◆ ◆

The drunk tank was familiar to Bobby, a home away from home. The only thing that was missing was the presence of his cousin Teddy, and the realization made him sad. When he'd been questioned, he was surprised that the subject of Teddy never once came up, and he'd been certain that it would. However, all they wanted to know was what he knew about the man who had his daughter (nothing) and why he thought he should arm himself and go after the guy like a crazed vigilante. His answer to that had been simple. "I wanted to get my daughter back." The police did not argue that, and their interrogation didn't last long.

"Where did you carve your name the last time you were here?" Tommy asked him, and Bobby smiled.

"I never did," he said, shrugging. "Maybe now is a good time."

"You got a shiv?"

Bobby shook his head. "Nope. I guess that means I'll have to pass."

They whiled away the time talking to some of the other detainees, listening to their tales of woe, and soon after their arrival Tony (Eugenio) was escorted to the cell by a guard so he could fill them in on what was going on.

"Since no one but Lance had a permit to carry a gun, you're all going to be charged with illegal possession of a loaded firearm, which under California law is punishable by a $1000 fine and up to a year in jail." When neither Bobby nor Tommy replied, he continued, "You guys are lucky I have some clout. You'll get off with just paying the fine."

"Sweet!" Tommy said. "Can I borrow a thousand bucks?" Tony (Eugenio) ignored him.

"How's Melissa doing?" Bobby asked.

"She's fine. I just talked to her."

"OK," Bobby said, but he sounded doubtful

"You boys will be processed shortly, and then you'll be free to go."

"What about my daughter? The killer has her...we don't even know if she's still alive!"

"I gave the police a description of him and his car. They're looking for that bastard now. He can't get too far."

"He could already be in Mexico for all we know."

Eugenio nodded. "He could be, but he isn't. I got a good feeling about it."

"How?"

"I don't know. Call it cop's intuition."

Bobby swung his arm in a shooing gesture and turned away. He went to a bench in the back and sat down.

"So," Tommy said, "what happens now?"

"I just told you."

"I mean about the bar, about the drug cartel."

"I told the police everything that I was allowed to, and the DEA are in position at Hooligans."

"They shutting down their operation?"

"I can't talk about any of this with you, sorry. That information is classified."

Tommy laughed. "Of course it is."

"You boys sit tight and one of these officers will be back to process you. Until then, get comfy."

"Thanks," Tommy said, but behind him Bobby said nothing, didn't even look in their direction. In his opinion, Tony (Eugenio) was a traitor for pretending to be someone he wasn't. Bobby had bought drugs from him for so many years, blacking out and driving and doing God knows what. He should hate him for almost killing him, but inside whom he really hated was himself. It was because he was such a fucked-up loser that this was happening in the first place. If he wasn't such an idiot, he wouldn't have to worry about his daughter. Of course, if he wasn't such an idiot, he wouldn't *have* a daughter. He supposed he'd have to give that some more thought. In the meantime, somewhere out there was a madman in possession of Gina, and Bobby had no idea if she was still alive. And now he was locked in the county jail simply because he had taken matters into his own hands to try and get her back safely without getting the police involved, as he'd been instructed by men who dismembered people for disobeying them. Surely they could understand that, couldn't they? Two of his friends were dead for crying out loud, killed by thugs who probably had so many notches on their collective belts they were whittled threadbare. No one would miss those scumbags, except maybe their employer. And even then it was simply because he had to go to the trouble of hiring new help.

So Bobby sat there and waited it out, his brain turning over and over, hoping against hope that someone on the Escondido police force would find the killer's car before it was too late for Gina. Because if something bad happened to her, he knew he couldn't live with himself, and he certainly would have nothing more to do with Carolyn and Barry. Those two were dead to him.

Little did he know that they already were dead to him, as the police were just finding out. He wouldn't know until a bit later, and when he found out he'd be hard pressed to say that it made him sad, very hard pressed indeed.

♦ ♦ ♦

When he got to his house, the first thing Ramon did was call his wife. He would have called her sooner, but he'd left his cell phone in the office at Hooligans. He had another at the house, one he used for his personal calls, which was the better of the two to use anyway. He'd always felt that the one he used for "business" was tapped by the Castillo family. It was safer this way.

"Mi Amor," he said breathlessly, "come home at once!"

She protested until he whispered the words that silenced her: "We finished."

"OK," she said quietly. "I be home soon."

He hung up and went to his closet in the master bedroom and grabbed their suitcases. He'd pack and then he'd get online and book two flights to Spain, leaving as soon as possible. If they couldn't get anything leaving San Diego today, he would book their flights at LAX and they would depart as soon as she arrived. He'd make sure he had everything ready.

He dug through their clothes maniacally, throwing random items over his shoulder helter-skelter as he picked out what he thought they would need. It didn't really matter; they could buy all new things when they got there. And with that thought, he paused in those duties to do something of even greater importance: he went to the wall safe, hidden behind a mirror, the mirror he trimmed his nose hairs in, the one where he styled a comb-over that would make Donald Trump proud. He spun the combination dial to the appropriate numbers and opened it, revealing the piles of cash within. Ramon was no dummy; he'd been saving up for the proverbial rainy day. And now, mi amigos, it was definitely pouring perros y gatos. He grabbed stacks of cash and stuffed them in the bag he intended to carry on, but not too much. He'd read the story about the American rapper (Snooze Dog, he believed his name was) who had tried to bring large amounts of cash through LAX. It had not gone over well, to say the least. Between them he was certain they could have ten grand apiece (this was just a guess) so he figured they would have to start anew once they were settled. This was, however, a lot better than going to prison for the rest of his life. You had to count your blessings while you had them.

He ran around in a flurry of motion, things flying every which way, when he heard the front door open downstairs. Ah, his wife was home, and before he could even book the flights. She could finish packing their bags while he hammered out the finer details.

There were footsteps on the stairs, and as he went to greet her, he suddenly realized that he was hearing more than one set. In fact, it sounded like several. It was them, the Castillo Cartel, coming for him! What should he do? He looked about the room frantically, remembering the .38 he kept in the drawer of the nightstand by the bed. He dove for it, extracting it just in time for the door to open.

"Ramon Pasquales, you are under arrest!" a voice declared. "Freeze where you are!"

He'd be lying if he didn't admit that he felt a momentary surge of relief, knowing it wasn't the cartel, but it was quickly dispelled because it appeared, in light of who was giving him orders, that this was the cartel's strategy coming to fruition. He wasn't going to get shot, he was just going to get arrested, as they'd planned all along.

"I am innocent!" he avowed, but the police were having none of it. One stripped him of his weapon while another put his arms behind his back and cuffed him. "What are the charges?" he asked meekly as he was being led out of the room.

A cop gave him a dirty as-if-you-don't-already-know look. "You are under arrest for the storage, sale, and distribution of dangerous narcotics.

You have the right to remain silent, anything you say can and will be held against you. You have the right to an attorney. If you can't afford one, one will be provided for you..."

Ramon hung his head. Somehow, throughout all the chaos, he'd still become the patsy, as Señor Castillo had planned all along. He must have some very important friends indeed, people in high places who saw to it that he and his operation wouldn't be exposed, yet there would be someone who would go down for narcotics trafficking so the police and the community could have closure. It was not a good day for Ramon and his wife. Speaking of...

"Where is my wife?" he asked as they were crossing the threshold of the front door, when he saw her in the back of a squad car. Apparently, she'd shown up at the same time they did. "Mi Amor..." he muttered desolately as he was placed in a separate cruiser, presumably so they couldn't collude on a story. It was a sad day for the two of them, undeniably a very sad day.

Chapter Thirty-Five

Sádico knew he had nothing to fear from the man who'd given him his instructions; however, he deliberated his countermove cautiously as he drove along in the waning afternoon sunshine. If the other betrayed his trust and brought anyone else with him, the consequences would be deadly. He meant what he'd said, and even at great risk to his dear Madre he would honor his word. He had to prove he wasn't a man to be trifled with.

Beside him, the girl looked excited for the first time since he'd abducted her. The promise of her freedom was all she needed to regain her spirits. He couldn't say he blamed her, for all living creatures clung to life as desperately as they could, from the smallest, single-celled amebae to the largest monstrosities that dwelled within the ocean's depths. This was to be expected. He was, of course, angered that he had another interruption, something keeping him from completing his prearranged duty, so her joy brought him some annoyance. It would be short lived though, ultimately unrequited. Because whoever this man was with the evidence against him, Sádico wasn't concerned, for he was not going to let him escape with his life. Nor the girl. His criminal exposure was certainly not the design he had in mind, nor was losing sight of his mission. Since the man had irrefutable personal information about him and his family, it was best to take care of the matter at once, so as to keep his Madre out of harm's way. But he would be grossly misjudged if it was thought that the threats made by this stranger caused him the least bit of anxiety. Oh no. Not by a long shot. This was simply another fork in the road, another person added to his need-to-kill list. This man didn't know it yet, but he was already dead. Sádico would see to that.

He took the next turn, only minutes away from Ryan Park, one of Escondido's larger nature preserves known for its youth soccer fields, hiking trails and natural wonders. He marveled at the cojones on the man who demanded to meet him there, alone no less. Because, all things considered, it was a good choice of venue for what he intended to do. Besides the soccer fields, the place was fairly isolated and there was enough acreage for them to conduct their business without observation. Unless a random hiker came along, or a family intent on a picnic. If there were more casualties, so be it.

He pulled into a large parking lot, occupied by only a few cars. A large sign announced that the soccer fields were temporarily closed to only scheduled events due to field repairs, and Sádico realized that this was why the man on the phone had picked this place. When the games weren't being played, the park was fairly deserted. He disengaged the transmission and turned off the car.

"Ju do what I say, and I promise a painless death," he told the kid. "Ju do something stupid, and I not be held responsible for my actions."

"OK…" she agreed, although he could sense the disingenuousness in her tone. He knew, because he heard it all the time. She was going to do whatever it took to get out of this intact. She would tell him what he wanted to hear and then do the opposite. Oh well. Just for the record, he really did intend to torture her if she tried to get away, as much as time allowed. He had to teach her a lesson, even if it was her last one.

"All right then, we go."

They got out of the car and headed deeper into the park, walking toward the destination the man on the phone had instructed them to go to.

◆ ◆ ◆

For the first time since this ordeal began, Gina experienced a surge of optimism. She'd seen the frustration and anger in the killer's eyes and heard the irritation in his voice. Someone had something on him, that was obvious, yet it remained to be seen if they would be able to capitalize on it. She certainly hoped they did. Maybe she could escape him after all, the death that he'd been promising her possibly postponed until she was a little older, say in her eighties or nineties.

She thought about her daddy as they pulled into the park, wondered if he'd gotten out of Hooligans alive. It seemed impossible that he had, but she could always hope. The only way she'd know was if she made it out of this in one piece, so it could very well be a moot point.

As much as the thought of dying scared her, the thought of living without her dad scared her even more. If he had been killed, maybe she didn't want to deal with it, maybe death would be better after all.

She shook her head angrily and gave Ruby a squeeze.

The hell with that! Living is still living. If you're dead, you have nothing.

This thought toughened her up. Made her focus. She needed to be in tune to everything that was going on in order to get free, so when he parked the car and asked her to die peacefully, she told him what he wanted to hear. If she was caught, or if he overtook the other man and she did anything to try and help him, she knew he'd live up to his word. She had no doubt about that. For one thing she gathered very quickly about Sádico was when he told you he was going to do something, he did it. Not like other people who said this and that, just meaningless babble, harmless chit chat. This guy didn't mince words, and he didn't mess around. If he said he was going to make her pay if she turned on him, then he was. She truly believed that. For cripes sake, he was shot and bleeding and he didn't even care! The man clearly wasn't human.

Nevertheless, she knew she had to do whatever it took to get away from him, she and Ruby. Whatever. It. Took. Period. No wasted words, no wasted movements. The person who was meeting them had some leverage; with any luck he was also packing a gun, because that would really help too. It appeared he was armed with knowledge, but a firearm would take them a lot further at this point.

"OK…" she'd agreed, but she'd do no such thing. She and Ruby were going to fight their way out of this. Fight their way out or die trying.

She really wished it wouldn't come to that though. She really didn't.

♦ ♦ ♦

They stood on the sidewalk outside the county jail after they were released, none of them knowing where to go. Apparently Tony's (Eugenio's) status was such that he'd bumped them to the top of the list. They'd been processed and released in record time. An officer approached them and offered Melissa a set of keys attached to a fob shaped like a pair of dice.

"What are these?"

"Ballet tickets," he said, grinning. "What the hell do they look like?"

"Those are Terry's keys," Bobby said, reaching for them, and the officer handed them over.

"The car's in that parking lot." He pointed to a lot surrounded by a chain-link fence topped with razor wire. "Tell the guard at the gate Officer Cruz sent you."

"Thanks."

The three walked to the lot, gave the guard the info, and he in turn let them have the car after he processed the paperwork.

"She's a beauty," he said appreciatively, and when no one agreed with him he shrugged and went back into the kiosk.

Bobby looked at the others. "Where should we go?"

"We could go to a bar," Tommy proposed, lighting a smoke, and Bobby shook his head adamantly.

"I have to find my daughter."

"Cops are on it."

"Maybe, maybe not. But getting drunk isn't going to help."

"That's the smartest thing I've ever heard you say, Bobby," Melissa said, and he smiled.

"What about 'I love you'?"

"Probably the dumbest."

"All right…"

"But I'm with you Bobby. We have to do something."

He nodded, yet he didn't know what they *could* do. What was left to them, what were their options? Did they even have any? He honestly didn't think so. They had no leads, no clues, nothing. Going to a bar was pointless; going anywhere was pointless unless it led them to her, and if the cops couldn't find her, what chance did they stand?

"I'm open to suggestions," he said, and Melissa opened her mouth to speak but words were not forthcoming. She shrugged. She had no idea either. It seemed their only choice was sitting back and seeing if the police could find him, the car, whatever. Either that or her body, giving Bobby a conclusion to this whole sordid affair. That clearly wasn't what anybody wanted, but sometimes closure was all you had.

Little did Melissa and Tommy know, but despite the face Bobby put on, he wanted a drink worse than life itself right now, wanted to snort meth or cocaine until the capillaries in his nose burst and he sneezed blood like Mt. Vesuvius. He wanted to get so high on Xanax that he wouldn't remember anything, ever again. Nothing. Just put himself into a drug-induced coma and forget the world ever existed, that he was a father, that he'd had a daughter, but she was murdered because her mother was a rotten, greedy whore.

His mind churned like an overworked, under-oiled truck engine as he thought this, so it was Melissa who had to nudge him, actually shake his shoulder to bring him out of his reverie.

"What?" he asked, the aggravation in his voice perceptible, the anxiety in his eyes radiating like neon.

"Your phone is ringing."

It was true. His cell was both ringing and vibrating in his pocket, and he recognized the ringtone. It couldn't be, yet it was. Somehow it spelled foreboding, and he felt helplessness course through him again. He let it ring another time before he rummaged into his pocket to retrieve it. Then he let it ring again before he answered. His fate was calling; did he want to accept the charges?

No, but he figured he had to anyway.

"Hello?" he said, and then the person on the other end of the line spoke.

◆ ◆ ◆

"Stop right where you are," someone said, and El Sádico halted in mid-stride. He held onto Gina as he had at the bar, in front of him as a shield, his gun drawn, the muzzle pressed flat against her right temple. She was wide-eyed, sweaty, but there was a fierce determination in her gaze. She looked like she was full of spunk, and El Sádico didn't like that; it spoke volumes about what she wanted to do.

A policeman emerged from the tree line before them, someone whom Gina and Ruby recognized. Sádico was familiar with him as well, but only from a photograph. They had never met in person. He had to admit he was surprised to see him, but that didn't change matters in any way. Soon he would be dead, as he was supposed to be.

Gina's heart beat excitedly in her chest. She couldn't believe it. Suddenly things didn't seem so bad. Surely this was a very good omen for her and her dog.

"Ju come alone?"

"I did."

"If ju are lying, I shoot la chica."

"I'm not lying," the other said gravely, and Sádico heard the truth in his voice.

"No sniper in the trees?" he asked anyway, and the man shook his head. "OK," he conceded.

"I'm glad we trust each other," the policeman said, taking a step closer. "Now you do what I tell you and you can walk away."

Sádico knew *this* was a lie. "Ju must think I very stupid," he said, watching the .9 MM that was pointed at him with a wary eye. The cop behind it looked very capable of using it, and accurately too. Bobby and his cohorts had been a bunch of amateurs; in contrast this fellow was a seasoned pro. This looked as if it presented a challenge, yet one thing he thrived on were challenges. "Ju shouldn't tell such lies while I still have the girl in my arms."

"Let her go," the cop said. "Let her go and just get out of here."

"Ju say that, but jore eyes reveal is not true." He shook his head. "I do no such thing without a better offer...or a fight, so which is it?"

In all honesty, there was most likely no better offer, only the promise of a shootout, but Sádico wanted to test the other's cleverness, to see if he truly had a proposition. He didn't think so, nothing more than the "I'll let you go" business, but he figured it would buy him some time while he thought things through. He could just shoot the girl, evade the other's counter shot and then kill him while he was recovering. That was a viable option, one he felt very good about. But what if the officer sensed this and took a shot at him? Or what if El Sádico shot the girl and el tamarindo shot him before he could fire back? If he had questions, then he had doubts. And where there was doubt there was hesitancy. He had to consider his choices thoroughly, had to make no mistakes, not only for himself, but for his Madre. For what would become of her if he was shot, here in this lousy park in Escondido, California, over some kid who was nothing more than a job to him? This man or others like him might decide to hurt her, and he couldn't have that. She needed his protection.

"I can read your eyes too," the policeman said, "and I can see your indecision to just blast me and get it over with. I'll choose to take that as a good sign."

"I not going to let her go," Sádico announced. "So what now ju propose?"

The other was silent. He too was pondering the matter carefully. And what were his thoughts, what act was he visualizing? It was a mystery to El Sádico as alas he could not read minds. If he could then he would always have the edge, but that wasn't going to happen, not now, not ever. He simply needed to be smart, to act before the other could so he had the advantage. And he could do that, obviously, it was how he made his living. The question was: could he shoot the cop and get away? Just when he thought he could, there was something, some gleam in the other's eyes that made him falter. This fucking cop, certainly he wasn't his match, but until that guy came along, he seemed close, real close, and it was beginning to bother him.

♦ ♦ ♦

He watched the killer, saw unwavering grit coupled with contrasting uncertainty in his eyes. He seemed to bounce back and forth like a ping-pong ball. Maybe the assassin was tired, maybe he'd been at this too long and just wanted the whole thing to be over, or perhaps he was in pain from what looked to be a bullet wound in his left shoulder. All he could do was guess. And guesses weren't good enough. He needed to take charge of the situation in any manner possible, so he decided to talk, if only to give him the time to get the edge on the other.

"What you want to ask yourself Pablo," he said, speaking with no hint of urgency, although he felt prickles of unease inside him that made him wish he could trust himself to just take a shot and hit this sucker between the eyes and end it, "is what will happen to your mother should something happen to you. Do you really want something bad to happen to her?"

The killer's eyes flickered an expression of disgust, distaste, fear and undeniable anger. The cop saw his hand clench the gun tighter, and that was a good thing. Anger made a man do rash things, made his decisions and reactions more impetuous than they otherwise might be. And, hopefully, it would throw his aim off.

"I know where she lives, and what I know, others know."

Sádico laughed. "No one knows anything ju know. Ju a dead man."

He laughed as well, although there was very little humor in it. "Maybe, maybe not. But you'd be surprised what a dead man can accomplish, seeing as that gives him so much time on his hands."

The killer's expression was one of unnerving calm as he processed this information. Then he spoke again.

"So what if ju tole others, then what? If ju try to kill me and fail, then I carry out my mission. If ju succeed, I know nothing of what comes next because I dead."

"Don't you believe in the afterlife?"

"Religion is nonsense," he scoffed.

"I'm sorry you feel that way, but I guess it makes sense, coming from you. If you died and had to atone for your sins, you'd probably burn in hell."

This made the killer bristle, and the cop sensed he touched a nerve. Good. He had to figure out a way to keep doing it, to burrow under his skin until he was inside out and his guts were exposed like raw pig gristle on a slaughterhouse floor.

Just keep him off-kilter, keep getting him more upset, that's what I need to do—

Out of the blue a shot rang out, no warning, no preamble. The officer clutched himself and fell backward, the sunlight suddenly bright and painful in his eyes, agony dappling his world like a stone on a pond's surface, clarifying yet muddying everything, and then he heard the other make a noise he didn't like; no, he didn't like it at all. The killer, El Sádico, his throat made a sawing sound, garbled and throaty.

The bastard is laughing…the lousy bastard is laughing at me…

♦ ♦ ♦

When he took the shot, he wasn't sure if it would hit his mark, but when the policeman collapsed, he was glad to see his aim was true. He smiled, a truly sinister smile that lit up his face like a Halloween jack–o'–lantern. The girl, who had been taut the whole time, her muscles flexed like she was made of steel cords, suddenly relaxed in his grip. She sagged against him as she put everything together: her would-be savior's failed attempt to rescue her, and the fact that it was now her turn, at last, to die. Nothing was going to save her from that fate now.

"Ju kept your word," he told her, letting her and the dog go. She could run, he was aware of that, but it didn't bother him. Where would she go? She wouldn't make it more than ten steps, and he'd shoot her in the back to stop her, then the head to silence her forever. "Ju saved joreself a lot of pain. Ju should be glad for that."

"Just get it over with," she said, the resignation in her tone the obvious conclusion to all this foreplay. She'd come full circle like most did when confronted with death: fear, anger, denial, bargaining and, eventually, acceptance. She was now fully onboard, ready for her passing to play itself out. She was tired of this game.

"Spoken like a true warrior," he told her approvingly. "Ju've grown up, little girl," he said. "Ju've become a woman."

This had little effect on her. Apparently it was barely a token satisfaction, and hardly that even. She shrugged, then leaned down and unclipped Ruby's leash, holding it loosely in one hand.

"Take her," she said, looking down at her dog with fierce, aching melancholy, figuring it would be the last time. A tear streaked down her face, then another. "Good-bye, honey," she said, leaning down again and planting a kiss on her forehead. "Now go on." She gently pushed Ruby in the direction of the other before straightening up. "Thanks for not killing her too," she muttered. "Find her a good home…"

Ruby looked up at her master sadly, wondering what was going on. Was she relinquishing her to another? Did she have the right to do that? Ruby looked back and forth between the two, from the girl who had been her owner since she was a puppy, to the tall man who seemed to have pleasant feelings toward her, but not toward her owner. She felt mystified about this unusual situation.

It was then that Gina broke down, her whole body shuddering with the force of her outburst, dropping to her knees. Ruby furrowed her brow and began to whimper, echoing her owner, and clearly this upset the man with the gun. He squatted on one knee and reached out to her, feeling fresh blood from his wound trickle down his shoulder.

"Come here, girl," he said, and when she backed away and ran to Gina, a look of puzzlement crossed his face. Despite his love for animals, he was decidedly lacking in empathy, a truly important sentiment that generally explained a lot of things others were feeling. Therefore, he couldn't understand why she wouldn't come to him. "I say," he repeated in a stern voice, "come here, *now!*"

But Ruby didn't listen. She stayed with Gina as she continued to weep, whimpering along in a throaty voice that sounded almost human.

She jumped up, placing her large paws on the girl's shoulders and licking her tears. Sádico got to his feet, raised his gun and aimed it at her.

"Come here now!" He didn't want to shoot the girl in front of the dog of he didn't have to, but the dog wouldn't budge. If this went on for too long, it very well might be that he'd have to shoot them both. Time was slipping away. He needed to move if he was going to see to the safety of his madre.

Gina perceived this, and she pushed Ruby off of her. "Go on, girl," she said between sobs. "Go to him."

But Ruby wouldn't listen. She jumped up again, her butt wagging her non-existent tail, and Gina stroked her head lovingly before gently shoving her down once more. "Go on, girl," she said, and this time Ruby eyed her questioningly, then turned to look at El Sádico.

"Is right," he said, holding his arms open. "Come here." He watched her as she tried to make a decision, her head swinging one way, and then another.

At that moment, the policeman stirred from behind them, getting up from where he was lying, holding his gun before him while his eyes glimmered wetly. There was blood smeared across his face, but he looked happy, exultant.

"Drop the gun asshole!" he yelled, his voice hoarse but confident, and Sádico turned toward him, the surprise on his face almost comical before it turned to a snarl of rage. He swung the pistol toward the cop, when Gina realized she was still holding the leash. Not thinking, simply reacting to circumstances that were above and beyond anything she was used to, she stood and twirled the leash in her hand until it was a blur of motion and then released it in the killer's direction.

"Come here Gina, quickly!" the policeman cried, and the girl recognized her cue and ran toward him. Sádico fired at her but missed; an inch to the left and he would have shot her in the back of the head. An instant later the metal end of the leash struck him in his wounded shoulder and he howled in pain, toppling to the ground and dropping his gun in the process.

The cop sheltered the girl with his body, exhaling a shaky breath. What he'd just done was impetuous, a calculated risk fraught with peril, but seeing that it worked, he didn't dwell on it. And the kid, wow, talk about stepping up in the face of adversity. He wondered how many teenage girls would have thought of that. Her aim was dead on.

"Good shot," he told her, watching the killer where he lay, writhing in pain. He felt good, better than good actually. He felt *great*. The shot was a through-and-through, nothing to worry about, really, besides the bleeding. Sádico had shot him in the fleshy fold of his right armpit just above his Kevlar vest. It hadn't hit anything vital. And Gina was with him and safe. That was the important part.

"Ruby!" the policeman called. "Come here girl!"

The bulldog issued a short, choppy bark and then ran to him and Gina, a smile on her face, her large tongue hanging ten in the breeze like a giant banner, dripping saliva all the way.

◆ ◆ ◆

Sádico thought he'd had the situation under control when an explosion of agony erupted from his shoulder, and he felt himself tipping over backward. Somehow his opponent had gotten up from where he'd been lying, gun in hand, and the kid managed a counter move that left him stunned.

The fucking bitch! She'll know what real pain is before this is all over.

Things were starting to go downhill, spiraling out of Sádico's control. This was not the way it was supposed to happen. He was meant to be the winner, was truly the one who should be emerging victorious with his many scalps in tow.

He fell onto his back, gasping at the sharp pain as it spread through his entire arm, and the gun sprang from his hand as if ejected, tumbling away and well out of his grasp. He glanced at it longingly, then looked up at the other, at the gun that was pointed at his head. So, this was it then.

"Go ahead," Sádico said in an eerily detached voice. "Shoot me."

"I'm not letting you go that easy," the cop replied. "You're under arrest. I'm going to make sure you pay for all the people you've killed."

"I rather die."

"I'm sure you would, Pablo, but this isn't about what you want, not anymore." Keeping the gun steady, he reached into his pocket and retrieved his phone. He handed it to Gina. "Call your dad and let him know you're safe. Then tell him to call nine one one and send the cops to Ryan Park. Tell 'em we're out by Potato Chip Rock."

"OK." She took the phone, did as she was instructed.

"Think of all the paperwork," Sádico continued. "It fill up jore whole afternoon. Surely a waste of time."

"Nope, I'm good. I've got nothing better to do."

Sádico's eyes flickered back and forth, as swiftly as a snake's tongue. He was looking for a way out, something he could use to take back control. This was not how it was going to end, him losing the girl to some stupid meddling cop who didn't know when he should take his nose out of other people's business.

And then he saw it before him, how to end this and get away. It was all too simple. Everything was lined up perfectly in his mind; all he had to do was execute (*heh-heh*) it.

So that's what he did, and the other never saw it coming until it was too late.

Chapter Thirty-Six

Bobby couldn't believe it. When he answered his phone, the last person in the world he expected was his daughter Gina, yet it was true. Her voice in his ear was like the singing of an angelic choir.

"Hi, Daddy!" she said exuberantly, and he almost wept in relief.

"Hey, baby," he croaked, "where are you?"

"I'm at Ryan Park, out by Potato Chip Rock, and you'll never believe who's with me!"

Before she could confirm his belief based on the ringtone, there was the sound of growling, increasingly louder, and then Gina screamed, a long, desolate utterance that sent a chill down his spine.

"Gina?" he cried hoarsely into the phone. "Gina! What's going on?"

He heard what sounded like a struggle, and then the phone made a noise as if it was dropped. He could make out Gina's voice, pleading, crying, and behind it there was the continuing din of a scuffle. He could discern grunts of exertion, and the hard, flat, smacking of fists connecting with soft tissue.

"Gina!" he wailed, and then the phone went dead, the call dropped. Melissa and Tommy were watching him closely, eyes wide.

"What happened to her?" Melissa asked. "Is she OK?"

"She was at first..."

"Did she tell you anything?" Tommy said, and Bobby had to think on it hard, as the disturbance that interrupted her initial salutation was all he could focus on.

"She said," he sputtered, trying to remember. "She said I'd never believe who was with her." He looked first at Melissa, then Tommy, his eyes wide. "I...I honestly can't believe it..."

"Where is she?"

"Oh man, poor Gina…"

"Where is she, Bobby? Think! If she's in trouble, we have to get there now!"

Bobby thought about it, trying to concentrate, but for the moment all he could hear in his head were her screams, so pitiful, so full of anguish. She'd initially sounded as if she was out of harm's way, but then it changed in a heartbeat.

"A park," he muttered. "She said she was at a park."

"There's lots of parks in Escondido," Tommy said. "You gotta be way more specific than that."

Something was coming to him, something about a tortilla, or a corn chip, or…a potato chip…that was it! Potato Chip Rock!

"Ryan Park!" he exclaimed. "She said she was at Ryan Park!"

Melissa then took charge. "OK, you two have to get there right now." She reached out and twirled Bobby in the direction of the car. "You two get your asses to Ryan park stat. You know where it is?"

"I do," Bobby said. He'd been there before, had taken Gina and Ruby there for a picnic once.

"I'll tell the cops, now go!"

So they went, Bobby fishtailing away from the curb in a squeal of rubber that would have made Terry cringe had he been there to see it. Fortunately, (or unfortunately, as it may be) he was not. And like it or not, Bobby now owned his truck again, for better or worse.

◆ ◆ ◆

When he saw his chance, he took it. While the girl was on the phone, the cop took his eyes off Sádico for just a moment, and that was all he needed. Ruby was the only one who noticed the killer rousing, and she began to growl. Ignoring her, he rose to his haunches then sprung himself forward like a lion at its prey. Sádico tackled the other around the knees, bringing him to the ground.

"No!" Gina screamed, dropping the phone and issuing a shriek that easily competed with Ruby's barking and growling. "Help! Help! No! Get off of him!" She jumped back to get out of their way and she stepped on the phone, cracking the glass and ending the call.

"Ooof!" her would-be savior grunted, the wind knocked out of him, and then El Sádico was upon him, dishing out vicious blows that rendered the other momentarily helpless. Blood began to pour forth copiously from the wound in his armpit; Gina's protector was taken by surprise, hardly able to fight back. She had to do something to help, but what? She looked around her for something she could use as a weapon, then saw a piece of wood the size of a Billy club and dashed to it and snatched it up. Holding it firmly in both hands, she approached the men from behind, lifting it over her shoulder like a baseball bat. Ruby barked frantically while cavorting and dancing around her feet, getting in the way, and Gina nearly tripped over her several times.

"Get back girl!" she told the bulldog, but Ruby wasn't listening. Obviously, she didn't know she was impeding her owner's progress.

Sidestepping around the dog as if she were performing a pirouetting musical number, Gina got into position, the back of the killer's head before her like a shining beacon of hope (*in case of psychotic killer, bash repeatedly until incapacitated*), and once she figured she had it firmly in her sights, she swung with all she was worth. As she did, the policeman was able to get an edge on his attacker, and they rolled over just in time for Gina's swing to go over their heads.

"Shit!" she swore, trying to get closer, and once again Ruby got in front of her, and this time Gina didn't see her and she tripped over the dog's plump body, landing on the ground near the two men.

Sádico sensed movement nearby, turned his head slightly, and saw that the girl was on the ground beside him, near enough to grab. He reached out quickly and snatched a tangle of her long hair, entwining it in his fist until he had a good grasp, then got to his knees, swiveling so that he could elevate to a crouch, then hopped to his feet with just enough time to kick the other man under his chin, sending him sprawling flat on his ass. Even though the policeman was bigger, El Sádico was lithe and moved with the agility of an acrobat. Yet again he had the girl around the neck in a half nelson. Now all he needed was his gun and he could finish this business once and for all. And, sadly, the bulldog would have to witness her owner perish.

The cop, surprisingly, got to his feet a lot quicker than Sádico would have imagined. The blow he dealt should have left him stunned, yet the other had brushed it off as if it hadn't been a big deal, and regrettably for the cartel hitman, el bastardo was still in possession of his firearm.

"Let go of her or I'll shoot," he threatened, but El Sádico had come too far and was so close to eliminating his target that nothing could hold him back. Scrapping plan A, he decided to switch to plan B, which involved twisting her neck until it snapped, and then avoiding the expected gunshot and taking the other out before he could fire again. This made the most sense to him, his brain whirring with the speed and precision of a finely tuned German automobile.

The cop recognized his ill intentions and fired a shot, just missing Sádico by mere inches. This gave the killer pause.

"Seriously," the policeman said. "You let the girl go or the next shot is going to take the back of your head off. No more BS, I'm through playing around."

The words sounded sincere, but El Sádico was beyond that now. Failure wasn't an option. He'd adopted a self-preservation mode when he was younger, walking away when he knew he had to so he could live to fight another day, but this time he was in too deep. There was no other option; he had to stop the cop and kill the girl, and now possibly the bulldog too because there was no more time left. He was sorry for that, as she had done nothing wrong, but those were the breaks. The time for caring about her life had passed.

Following these thoughts, another observation struck him: where *was* the bulldog? He glanced around but he didn't see her.

And that's when Ruby decided to join in on the action. Seeing her owner in peril at the hands of the man who had already mishandled her, she dove at El Sádico, and as she did, Gina was able to twist her body so as to get out of the way. The running start accompanied by a good leap found the pudgy dog airborne, with jaws open wide, a feast of tube steak smothered in underwear in her immediate line of sight. And that is just where she landed: mouth-first on Sádico's crotch.

"Ahhhh!" he bellowed, the pain instantaneous, like a fire ablaze in his pants. Sádico lost his grip on Gina and the girl scrambled away while he squirmed desperately, trying to shake Ruby off, but the fat bulldog was attached to him with a grip like a vice. She shredded his pants, tearing away the zipper to reveal a pair of purple bikini underpants beneath. This made Gina and the cop laugh, and the laughter seemed to trivialize Sádico's pain. Oh how he wanted to hurt them, to not just kill them but to tie them up and pour battery acid down their throats while he tasered them repeatedly until they were crying and it was he who was laughing. No one laughed at El Sádico, no one!

He batted at the dog, pummeling her head and, finally, one of his punches hurt her, and when she cried out her hold on his crotch loosened, and he batted her effortlessly to the ground where she rolled away, whining. He then turned to the cop and the girl, seeing the laughter die on their lips, and with a roar of pure fury he launched himself at them.

The policeman did the only thing that was left for him to do: he fired his weapon, discharging it until the clip was spent. El Sádico took every one of the slugs, blood jetting wildly as he continued to lunge forward. The cop's final shot (just as he'd promised) took the top of the killer's head off, and he landed in a crumpled heap at their feet, his bullet-riddled body convulsing as the last of the life ran out of him. When the echo from the last shot subsided, Ruby got up from where she was cowering and ran to Gina.

"Good job, honey," Gina told Ruby, leaning down to give her a kiss. The rotund bulldog smiled and licked her face.

"Crap," the cop said. "I really wanted to arrest that guy."

As this remark was leaving his lips, two men came out from a break in the trees, running toward them. One of them stopped when he was within ten feet and just stood and stared. Gina ran to him, and the policeman smiled.

"Took you long enough to get here," he said, watching Bobby embrace his daughter, hugging her tightly, then kissing her on the cheeks and the forehead until he at last looked up, the shocked expression on his face only marred by the smile lighting up his eyes. He clasped Gina's hand in his own and walked slowly toward him.

"Aren't you supposed to be dead?"

"Supposed to be, yeah. But what do you know? Here I am." Teddy grinned, enjoying the moment.

"But...the whole restaurant blew up!" Bobby looked confused, but he was elated to see the man he'd grown up with, the relative/friend who'd gotten his ass out of hot water so many times the two of them had lost count.

"I got out through the back," Teddy said, walking toward El Sádico while extracting his handkerchief from his back pocket. He placed it over the dead man's head so Gina didn't have to look at it. The expression on the hitman's face wasn't one you wanted to stare at too long. It was the stuff of nightmares. "All things considered, I got very, very lucky."

"Did *you* detonate a bomb?"

"Not one of my better ideas, but, yeah."

"Why didn't you tell me?"

"Captain's orders. I had to tell him what happened, what I discovered, and we decided it was best if I pretended to be dead so that I could investigate further without alerting the cartel that the police had become involved. Your bartender was in on it with me."

"Tony?"

"If you mean Eugenio, then yeah, that's the guy."

"I don't believe it..."

"It'll take some time, but you'll come around." Teddy looked over at Tommy, who was standing several feet away, smoking a cigarette. "Who's your friend?"

Bobby looked over at Tommy. "Hey man, come over here," he said, then turned back to his cousin. "This is Tommy, and he risked his life to help me try and save Gina."

The two men shook hands. "Nice ta meet ya," Tommy said.

Bobby glanced again at the body on the ground. "Is he dead?"

"As many times as I shot him, he better be," Teddy said, and this made them all laugh. When at last the laughter subsided, Teddy took his walkie-talkie from his holster and called it in. When he finished, he replaced it and apprised the others. "I'm going to have to write this up and make a statement. An ambulance is on its way to tag and bag this SOB. Why don't the three of you get out of here before this place is crawling with uniforms and we'll talk to you down at the station tomorrow. I got it from here."

Tommy didn't have to be asked twice. He backtracked to the path faster than you could say "drinks on the house." Bobby, Gina, and Ruby however, lingered.

"You confronted this guy all by yourself?" Bobby asked incredulously, and Teddy's grin beamed.

"I had to. He would have killed her otherwise."

"Jesus Loueesus...um, hey man, you're bleeding."

"The prick shot me."

"You OK?"

"Nothing a couple of stitches and some naproxen can't handle."

"I really can't believe it's you," Bobby said, and stumbled forward and hugged his cousin in a clumsy bear hug that made the other laugh.

"Not so hard, Bobby," he said, chastising him mildly. "I might have a couple broken ribs too."

"You should have seen him fight the bad guy, Daddy! He saved my life!"

"I owe you man," Bobby said, his voice choked with emotion. "I really owe you for this one."

"You don't owe me anything, but there is one thing you can do for me."

"Anything, just name it."

Teddy looked Bobby in the eyes, really looked at him, deep down into his soul. His penetrating gaze wiped the smile off of Bobby's face, and he knew he truly had his attention. "Stay sober, huh? You have a daughter you need to take care of."

Bobby hugged Gina tight to his chest, stroking her light blond hair with a hand whose nails were bitten down to the cuticles.

"I think I can do that, Teddy," Bobby said, trying to force back his tears. "I really think I can…"

The sound of a siren arose in the distance, and Teddy looked over their shoulder in its direction.

"Get out of here," he said. "We'll talk about this later."

"OK," Bobby agreed, and he led Gina and Ruby to the path where Tommy waited anxiously for them. He, for one, had had enough of the police for one day. Bobby turned back. "I'll see you soon, Teddy."

"Yes, you will," his cousin replied, smiling. "Yes, you will."

Epilogue

Laughter cascaded from the backyard of the ranch-style home on the far side of Bear Valley Road. Splashing could be heard from the swimming pool. The pool, once an algae-ridden, coke/speed bindle–littered, swamp-like mess, was now a sparkling blue. The owner of the house was standing on a newly erected diving board, taunting his wife and daughter with the threat of a cannon ball.

"You can't get us wet from here," Gina said, sticking her tongue out at him, and her stepmom concurred.

"Yeah Bobby," Melissa said dryly. "You'd have to gain a couple hundred pounds for your splash to even register on the Richter scale of splashes."

"I'm about to show you two how wrong you are," he said, taking a big breath, holding it, and running the length of the diving board until he reached the end, bouncing upward, tucking and landing in the exact manner as they expected. A weak splash followed, hardly the tsunami he had prophesied. More laughter ensued. This was Bobby's new life, and it would only get better as time went on.

Shortly after Gina had been recovered from the cartel hitman known as El Sádico, Bobby discovered that her legal guardians, Carolyn and Barry Mantello, had met their unfortunate demise at the same killer's hands. With them gone, Gina had been lucky enough to be sent to live with her second cousin Teddy, while Bobby attended AA, SA, GA, and NA meetings every day for a year until the court would finally allow him to petition his case before them, asking for custody rights. During this time, he hired Melissa to help him with his pool cleaning business (which he'd almost lost during the turbulent weeks when he was trying to rescue Gina from her kidnappers because he was either late or didn't show up for many of his accounts), and with her help had doubled, then tripled the business. Learning that his friend needed a job, he hired Tommy on as well. Tommy liked the job a lot better than most of his other jobs because he could smoke as much as he wanted. He had to limit himself to only three beers at lunch, but he didn't mind.

During the time they were battling it out in court for Gina, Melissa and Bobby had decided to get married in Vegas. That had been a very rough weekend for the both of them, in light of their many addictions, but in the end they didn't succumb to their wanton desires, and a Wayne Newton impersonator (in favor of Elvis) confirmed they were man and wife shortly after two o'clock in the morning on Tuesday, August 27. At the airport after the "ceremony," it was all they could do to get past the thousands of blinking and flashing lights, and for old times' sake, they decided to bet twenty dollars in a slot machine on a single pull of the handle. They lost the twenty bucks in about two seconds flat when three lemons popped up on the screen, effectively ending Bobby's gambling addiction.

After their marriage, while still awaiting the court's decision, they fixed up casa de la Bobby and turned it into a home that was not only livable, but downright cozy indeed. The pool was cleaned up and restored, and the backyard was redone with a dozen rose bushes, avocado trees, orange and pear trees and enough succulents to supply a small jungle. The inside of the house was remodeled from its 1970s wood panel, wallpaper and stucco walls into a modern home that now actually had resale value, should they ever decide they wanted to move up in the world.

And all the while Bobby stayed sober, he stayed out of trouble, and was no longer hounded by the demons that used to dwell in his head like unwanted party guests who refused to go home. He channeled his energy into the business, pleasing his wife, raising his daughter, and his new hobby, golfing. He was lousy at it, but chasing the little white ball was better than chasing a meth or coke high any day.

Near the end of the custody hearings, an additional surprise lay in wait for Bobby, when another man came forward (no one knew why, unless he thought there might be money involved) and claimed to be Gina's real dad. Since he seemed sincere Bobby and Melissa played along and allowed a paternity test, and it turned out (much to everybody's surprise) that he *was* her real dad. Evidently, Carolyn had conned Bobby all along, allowing him to believe that he was the father because Gina's actual dad disappeared after he heard the news she was expecting a child. Because of Bobby's impaired memory, Carolyn knew he'd believe it without question and simply do what he was asked without requiring an inkling of proof.

Gina was crestfallen, this sudden twist taking her for a loop. She didn't want to be sent to live with some guy she'd never met. Providentially, it turned out he was an even bigger screw-up than Bobby...well, the old Bobby that is. Her real father didn't have a dime to his name and was unemployed, and the court wouldn't grant him custody because it was eventually determined he only came out of hiding to try and get free government money, as they'd all suspected. Request denied.

The Castillo cartel disappeared like smoke from Escondido, and the couple set up to be their patsies, Ramon Pasquales and his wife, Lupe, were saved from going down as the masterminds behind the organization thanks to the testimony of DEA agent Tony (Eugenio). They still went to prison, receiving hefty fifteen year sentences (with time off for good behavior) for their involvement in the importation, storage, sale, and distribution of dangerous narcotics. They could have received lighter sentences, had they been willing to give up information that led to the arrest and conviction of Martino Estabon Rodriquez Estevan Castillo, but both Ramon and Lupe had family in Mexico who would be placed at risk—a fact Ramon tried to impart on the judge and jury but received no leniency. In an attempt to keep his butthole out of harm's way, Ramon became a prison snitch after his first year and had to be quarantined from the general populace after word got around so he wouldn't become the unwanted recipient of many a late-night pillow party. Lupe, on the other hand, fared very well and started her own women's book club, in which she was the acting president. They weren't exclusive; anyone of any race could join. It just went to show how different men's and women's prisons were. She took a wife two years into her sentence and is still happily married to this day to an African American woman named Cerise Bloomington.

And the years passed, Melissa and Gina making fun of Bobby and his ineffectual cannon balls, or the occasional failed jackknife. Life was just fine for the four of them as the succulents grew larger, the avocado tree produced delicious avocados, and the roses bloomed year after year.

Teddy and Bobby stayed as close as brothers, actually became even closer as time went by. Eventually, Teddy rose in the ranks in the Escondido police department, moving up from Sergeant to Lieutenant, and then Captain before retiring at the very young age of fifty-five with a full benefits package and a pension. He bought an RV, and he, Maggie, and Emily went on cross-country trips every year to the Grand Canyon, New York City, British Columbia, and Maine, to name a few destinations. Sometimes Bobby, Melissa, Gina, and Ruby joined them, when they could get away from the business.

As life has a tendency to do, it continued to move forward with the rapidity of an approaching train. Ruby went to the great dog park in the sky at the old age (for bulldogs) of eleven, and Gina mourned her miserably until Bobby got her another puppy, this time a tan male who had a similar scowl. Ruby would have been pleased. Gina named him Teddy.

Gina grew up to be a very pretty woman, and she went to college at USC (Teddy the bulldog stayed with Bobby and Melissa), majored in economics with a minor in film, got a job at Universal Studios as a gopher after she graduated, then later as a budget director. She got to work with some of the biggest names in Hollywood, and whenever she could, she invited her mom and dad and bulldog to come and see her on location or at Universal Studios. She eventually fell in love with a director of war movies, and they got married in a large ceremony where Bobby had the pleasure of giving his daughter away, then dancing with her at the reception. His new son-in-law was quite a drinker, and he challenged Bobby to a drinking contest if "the old guy was up to it," but Bobby declined, sipping his Sprite and smiling from the corner where he sat quietly, holding hands with Melissa.

Tommy became the manager of Pool's Gold (the name Bobby and Melissa had given their pool cleaning company) and was awarded the honor of hiring new workers and overseeing the entirety of their territory, which they'd expanded into San Diego and East County. He cut down on his drinking eventually, about a day before he went to his eternal reward in 2025. The cause of death? Lung cancer.

In memory of Lance, several members of his SA group hosted weekly orgies at one of their condos in Encinitas, where men, young and old, could come and come again without repercussion, although everyone needed to prove they were STD free at the front door, complete with written documentation from their doctor.

Terry would always be remembered for what a generous guy he was (just kidding), and a year after he was cremated Tommy, Melissa, and Bobby scattered his ashes where his will specified, at the Del Mar horse track during opening week of the season. The will also stipulated that they place a bet in his honor, which they did, a two-dollar "win, place, or show" wager on a horse named "Beetlejuice." The horse came in last and the two dollars was lost. It seemed fitting, somehow.

Hooligans closed down for a while after the tumultuous discovery of it being a drug den supplied by cartel heavies, but it eventually reopened and is currently doing great business. There is no bartender named Tony working there, nor do their records show that a man of that name ever did. Cocaine is no longer supplied over the bar at this establishment; if one needs coke, heroin, meth or benzo's, they are instructed to go down the road to Pounder's, where a guy name Brian will gladly hook you up, for a price, of course. Don't tell him I sent you.

The End